Women's Writing 1945–

Women's Writing 1945–60

After the Deluge

Edited by

Jane Dowson
De Montfort University

palgrave
macmillan

Softcover reprint of the hardcover 1st edition 2003 978-1-4039-1309-8

First published 2003 by
PALGRAVE MACMILLAN
Houndmills, Basingstoke, Hampshire RG21 6XS and
175 Fifth Avenue, New York, N. Y. 10010
Companies and representatives throughout the world

PALGRAVE MACMILLAN is the global academic imprint of the Palgrave Macmillan division of St. Martin's Press, LLC and of Palgrave Macmillan Ltd. Macmillan® is a registered trademark in the United States, United Kingdom and other countries. Palgrave is a registered trademark in the European Union and other countries.

ISBN 978-1-349-72440-6 ISBN 978-1-137-07430-0 (eBook)
DOI 10.1007/978-1-137-07430-0

This book is printed on paper suitable for recycling and made from fully managed and sustained forest sources.

A catalogue record for this book is available from the British Library.

Library of Congress Cataloging-in-Publication Data
Women's writing, 1945–60 : after the deluge / edited by Jane Dowson.
p. cm.
Includes bibliographical references and index.
1. English literature—20th century—History and criticism. 2. Feminism and literature—Great Britain—History—20th century. 3. Women and literature—Great Britain—History—20th century. 4. English literature–-Women authors—History and criticism. 5. World War, 1939–1945–Great Britain—Influence. I. Dowson, Jane

PR478.F45W66 2003
820.9'9287'09045—dc22

2003058086

10 9 8 7 6 5 4 3 2 1
12 11 10 09 08 07 06 05 04 03

For my parents

Contents

Acknowledgements

Permission to cite from Elizabeth Jennings, *Collected Poems* (Manchester: Carcanet, 1987) has been granted by David Higham Associates. Bloodaxe Press granted the right to use lines from Denise Levertov, *Selected Poems*. Time Warner Books have given permission to use extracts from *Me Again: Uncollected Writings of Stevie Smith*, eds Jack Barbara, and William McBrien (London: Virago, 1981). Random House have agreed the quotations from Iris Murdoch's *The Bell* and *The Sandcastle*.

I am grateful to the expert Pat FitzGerald for preparing the CRC text. It has been a joy to work with all the contributors and I have appreciated their efficient and encouraging co-operation. I have learned a lot from their scholarship and been inspired to read new works. Thanks to the team who prepared the *After the Deluge* conference with me: Julia Briggs, Clare Hanson, Imelda Whelehan and Kathy Bell with invaluable assistance from Andrea Peterson, Melanie Aldridge, Angela Marriott and Andy Mousley (De Montfort University, 1 July 2000). Thank you to all who attended and made it such a warm and stimulating occasion.

It is a great sadness to learn from Kate Fullbrook that her chapter here will be her last published piece, written while terminally ill with cancer. At the same time, her characteristically stimulating insights on Doris Lessing honour this book; may it stand as a tribute to her inspiring model of feminist scholarship.

I have dedicated this book to my parents who have always talked about 'the war' and its aftermath with mixed feelings of nostalgia and relief. I am ever grateful to their lifelong support in the face of my own workings out of intellectual femininity.

Loving gratitude, as always, to Mark.

Preface

These essays review the perception that the 1940s and 1950s were a dull or reactionary period for feminism and in women's writing. The significance of some novelists, Elizabeth Bowen, Iris Murdoch, Doris Lessing and Muriel Spark, is increasingly acknowledged. As widely read were Nancy Mitford, Elizabeth Taylor, Barbara Pym, Vera Brittain, Agatha Christie and Rosemary Sutcliff whose novels reveal the pleasures and repressions of woman as consumer in this period. The works investigated here are characterised by resistance to and retreat from postwar ideologies of femininity. They include historical and crime fiction, poetry, drama, adaptations of women's novels for screen and non-fiction. The writers' negotiations between 'literary' and 'popular' boundaries participate in the democratic ideologies of postwar Britain; they also add to an emerging history of twentieth-century women's literature which allows the writer and reader to both indulge and scrutinise women's desires.

The book is divided into four sections: 'The Legacy of War'; 'Home: Retreat and Restraint'; 'Gender, Love and Marriage'; and 'Across the Threshold: Spirituality, Colonisation and Subjectivity'. However, the ghost of war, contesting and containing the domestic, gender transformations, romance and spirituality are intersecting impulses and themes in all genres. We also see women's interest in racial injustices and global politics, notably anti-semitism, apartheid and declining colonial power.

I have not been able to include all the contributors, nor all writers, such as Daphne Du Maurier and Antonia White, who should be here – and there should be more Muriel Spark, but I envisage that the debates recorded and stimulated by these contributors will carry on.

Chronology

1945

Events

VE Day
Landslide Labour government led by Clement Attlee
USA drops atomic bomb on Hiroshima and Nagasaki, Japan
Introduction of Family Allowance, state payment to mothers
BBC radio extends with Home Service and Light programmes

Poetry

Sylvia Lynd, *Collected Poems*
Ruth Pitter, *The Bridge: Poems 1939–1944*
Kathleen Raine, *Ecce Homo*
Edith Sitwell, *The Song of the Cold*

Fiction

Elizabeth Bowen, *The Demon Lover*
Vera Brittain, *Account Rendered*
Betty Miller, *On the Side of the Angels*
Nancy Mitford, *The Pursuit of Love*
Mary Renault, *The Middle Mist*
Anya Seton, *My Theodosia*
Elizabeth Taylor, *At Mrs Lippincote's*

1946

Events

Republics of Italy, Hungary, Albania
Civil War in Indo-China
Report by the Royal Commission on Equality: recommends equal pay for women teachers, local government officers, civil servants
Reith Committee report recommends New Towns
Postwar baby boom starts

First commercially available washing powder
First Film Festival in Cannes, France

Non-fiction

Dorothy Sayers, *Unpopular Opinions*

Poetry

Frances Bellerby, *Plash Mill and Other Poems*
Lilian Bowes Lyon, *A Rough Walk Home and Other Poems*
Denise Levertov, *The Double Image*
Ruth Pitter, *Pitter On Cats*
Kathleen Raine, *Living in Time*
Anne Ridler, *The Shadow Factory: A Nativity Play*
Vita Sackville-West, *The Garden*
E.J. Scovell, *The Midsummer Meadow*
Dorothy Wellesley, *Desert Wells: New Poems*

Drama

Agatha Christie, *Ten Little Indians* (repr. of *Ten Little Niggers, 1944*); *Murder on the Nile*
Phyllis Bottome, *The Lifeline*

Fiction

Daphne DuMaurier, *The King's General*
Storm Jameson, *The Other Side*
Mary Renault, *Return to Night*
Elizabeth Taylor, *Palladian*

1947

Events

School leaving age raised to 15
'Cold War' with Europe
India and Pakistan granted independence from 1948

Poetry

Edith Sitwell, *The Shadow of Cain*

Fiction

Elizabeth Taylor, *A View of the Harbour*
Barbara Comyns, *Sisters by a River*

Storm Jameson, *The Black Laurel*
Naomi Mitchison, *The Bull Calves*

1948

Events

National Health Service established
Apartheid in South Africa
SS Empire Windrush brought 492 West Indian immigrants to Tilbury Docks
Olympic Games in London
Institute of Homeworkers
Beveridge report
John Newsom, 'The Education of Girls'

Poetry

Frances Cornford, *Travelling Home and Other Poems*
Lilian Bowes Lyon, *Collected Poems*, introduced by C. Day Lewis
Elizabeth Daryush, *Selected Poems*, ed. Yvor Winters
Dorothy Wellesley, *Selections from the Poems of Dorothy Wellesley*

Fiction

Margaret Irwin, *Elizabeth, Captive Princess*
Hope Muntz, *The Golden Warrior*
Sylvia Townsend Warner, *The Corner That Held Them*

1949

Events

Independence of the Republic of Ireland
Communist China under Mao
Clothes rationing ends

Non-fiction

Simone De Beauvoir, *The Second Sex* in France
Naomi Mitchison, *Women in a Man's World*

Poetry

Frances Bellerby, *The Brightening Cloud and Other Poems*
Nancy Cunard, ed. *Poèmes à la France*
Kathleen Raine, *The Pythoness and Other Poems*

Edith Sitwell, *The Canticle of the Rose: Selected Poems 1920–1947*

Fiction

Enid Blyton, *Noddy* books start
Elizabeth Bowen, *The Heat of the Day*
Nancy Mitford, *Love in a Cold Climate*
Elizabeth Taylor, *A Wreath of Roses*
Stevie Smith, *The Holiday*

1950

Events

The Archers starts on BBC radio
Watch with Mother starts on BBC television

Non-fiction

Storm Jameson, *The Writer's Situation and Other Essays*

Poetry

Anne Ridler, *Henry Bly and other Plays*
Edith Sitwell, *Façade and Other Poems 1920–1935*
Stevie Smith, *Harold's Leap*

Fiction

Phyllis Bottome, *Under the Skin*
Doris Lessing, *The Grass is Singing*
Rose Macaulay, *The World my Wilderness*
Barbara Pym, *Some Tame Gazelle*
Elizabeth Taylor, *A Game of Hide and Seek*
Antonia White, *The Lost Traveller*

1951

Events

Conservatives win General Election
Festival of Britain in London 3 May–30 September
Eirene White, Labour MP, introduces bill to make possible divorce by consent. Forced to withdraw it

Poetry

Ruth Pitter, *Urania*
Anne Ridler, *The Golden Bird and Other Poems*

Fiction

Daphne DuMaurier, *My Cousin Rachel*
Nancy Mitford, *The Blessing*
Antonia White, *The Sugar House*

1952

Events

Death of George VI and accession of Elizabeth II

Poetry

Kathleen Raine, *The Year One and Other Poems*
Edith Sitwell, *Selected Poems*

Drama

Agatha Christie, *The Mousetrap*

Fiction

Elizabeth Taylor, *A Game of Hide and Seek*
Ann Mary Fielding, *Ashanti Blood*
Storm Jameson, *The Green Man*
Doris Lessing, *Martha Quest*
Naomi Mitchison, *Travel Light*
Barbara Pym, *Excellent Women*

1953

Events

Coronation of Queen Elizabeth II
Over 300,000 new homes built

Non-fiction

Kinsey Report: 'Sexual Behaviour in the Human Female'
Simone De Beauvoir, *The Second Sex* in Britain

Poetry

Elizabeth Jennings, *Poems*

Elizabeth Jennings, *A Way of Looking*
Ruth Pitter, *The Ermine: Poems 1942–1952*
Edith Sitwell, *Gardens and Astronomers: New Poems*

Drama

Agatha Christie, *Witness for the Prosecution*
Jane Welch, *Not Like This*

Fiction

Rosamund Lehmann, *The Echoing Grove*
Barbara Pym, *Jane and Prudence*
Mary Renault, *The Charioteer*
Sylvia Townsend Warner, *The Flint Anchor*
Cecil Woodham-Smith, *The Reason Why: the Story of the Fatal Charge of the Light Brigade*

1954

Events

End of rationing

Poetry

Frances Cornford, *Collected Poems*
Dorothy Wellesley, *Rhymes for Middle Years*

Drama

Enid Bagnold, *The Chalk Garden*
Jane Bowles, *In the Summer House*

Fiction

Barbara Comyns, *Who Was Changed and Who Was Dead*
Daphne DuMaurier, *Mary Anne*
Rosamund Lehmann, *The Ballad and the Source*
Doris Lessing, *A Proper Marriage*
Iris Murdoch, *Under the Net*
Rosemary Sutcliff, *The Eagle of the Ninth*
Antonia White, *Beyond the Glass*

1955

Events

National Council of Women, conference on single women

Poetry

Elizabeth Jennings, *A Way of Looking*
Dorothy Wellesley, *Early Light: The Collected Poems of Dorothy Wellesley*

Fiction

Elizabeth Bowen, *A World of Love*
Storm Jameson, *The Hidden River*
Barbara Pym, *Less Than Angels*

1956

Events

Report on Marriage and Divorce, the Morton Commission

Non-fiction

Beryl Conway Cross, *Living Alone*
Lella Florence, *Progress Report on Birth Control*

Poetry

E.J. Scovell, *The River Steamer*
Kathleen Raine, *Collected Poems*
Anne Ridler, *The Trial of Thomas Cranmer: A Play*

Fiction

Mary Borden, *The Hungry Leopard*
Bryher, *Beowulf*
Doris Lessing, *Retreat to Innocence*
Rose Macaulay, *The Towers of Trebizond*
Iris Murdoch, *The Flight from the Enchanter*
Mary Renault, *The Last of the Wine*

1957

Events

Report by the Royal Commission on Mental Illness and Mental Deficiency

Non-fiction

The Sexual Responsibility of Marriage
Mary Macaulay, *The Art of Marriage*

Poetry

Valentine Ackland, *Twenty Eight Poems*
Frances Bellerby, *The Stone Angel and the Stone Man*
Denise Levertov, *Here and Now*
Edith Sitwell, *Collected Poems*
Stevie Smith, *Not Waving but Drowning*

Fiction

Doris Lessing, *Going Home*
Mary McCarthy, *Memories of a Catholic Girlhood*
Muriel Spark, *The Comforters*
Elizabeth Taylor, *Angel*
Rebecca West, *The Fountain Overflows*

1958

Events

Notting Hill race riots
National Council of Women, conference on working mothers

Poetry

Nancy Cunard, *Sonnets on Spain*
Elizabeth Jennings, *A Sense of the World*
Denise Levertov, *Overland to the Islands*
Stevie Smith, *Some are More Human than Others: A Sketch-book*

Fiction

Doris Lessing, *A Ripple from the Storm*
Barbara Pym, *A Glass of Blessings*
Mary Renault, *The King Must Die*
Muriel Spark, *Robinson*
Rebecca West, *The Court and the Castle: a Study of the Interactions of Political and Religious Ideas in Imaginative Literature*

1959

Events

The Enforcement of Morals Act, Lord Devlin
Mental Health Act
Obscene Publications Act

Poetry

Anne Ridler, *A Matter of Life and Death*

Drama

Shelagh Delaney, *A Taste of Honey*

Fiction

Christine Brooke-Rose, *The Sycamore Tree*
Anaïs Nin, *Cities of the Interior*
Muriel Spark, *Memento Mori*

1960

Events

The Pill introduced in USA
Coronation Street starts on ITV television

Non-fiction

Marie Robinson, *The Power of Sexual Surrender*

Poetry

Frances Cornford, *On a Calm Shore.*
Jenny Joseph, *The Unlooked-for-Season*
Denise Levertov, *With Eyes at the Back of our Heads*
Sylvia Townsend Warner, *Boxwood*

Fiction

Christine Brooke-Rose, *The Dear Deceit*
Jennifer Dawson, *The Ha-ha*
Doris Lessing, *In Pursuit of the English*
Nancy Mitford, *Don't Tell Alfred*
Edna O'Brien, *The Country Girls*
Muriel Spark, *The Bachelors*

Notes on Contributors

Kathleen Bell is a Senior Lecturer in English at De Montfort University. In addition to women's writing, her research is on twentieth-century poetry and working class writing. She is currently editing a volume of prose and poetry by Ethel Carnie Holdsworth.

John Brannigan is College Lecturer in English at University College Dublin, where he teaches modern and contemporary British and Irish writing. His publications include *New Historicism and Cultural Materialism* (1998), *Literature, Culture and Society in Postwar England, 1945–1965* (2002), *Brendan Behan: Cultural Nationalism and the Revisionist Writer* (2002) and *Orwell to the Present: Literature in England, 1945–2000* (2002). He is currently working on a book on Pat Barker.

Julia Briggs is Professor of English Literature at De Montfort University, Leicester and an emeritus fellow of Hertford College, Oxford. She is the author of a history of the ghost story, *Night Visitors* (1977), a study of renaissance literature in its historical context, *This Stage-Play World* (1983, revised 1997), and a biography of the children's writer *E. Nesbit: A Woman of Passion* (1987). She acted as general editor for thirteen volumes of Virginia Woolf reprinted in Penguin Classics, and is currently at work on a major new study of Woolf that focuses upon the process of her writing (Penguin 2003/4). She is also preparing an edition of Hope Mirrlees's poem 'Paris' for the second volume of Bonnie Kime Scott's *The Gender of Modernism.*

Jane Dowson is Senior Lecturer in English at De Montfort University. Her work on twentieth-century women poets includes *Women's Poetry of the 1930s: a critical anthology* (Routledge, 1996), *Selected Poems of Frances Cornford* (ed., Enitharmon Press, 1996) and *Women, Modernism and British Poetry 1910–39: Resisting Femininity* (Ashgate, 2002). She is currently working on *A History of Twentieth-Century British Women's Poetry*, co-authored with Alice Entwistle (Cambridge University Press, 2004).

Alice Entwistle is a lecturer at the University of the West of England, Bristol. She has published various articles on twentieth-century Anglo-American poetry and is currently working on *A History of Twentieth-Century British Women's Poetry* which she is co-authoring with Jane Dowson for Cambridge University Press.

Kate Fullbrook is Professor of Literary Studies and Associate Dean in the Faculty of Humanities at the University of the West of England. She is the author of *Katherine Mansfield* (1986), *Free Women: Ethics and Aesthetics in Twentieth-Century Women's Fiction* (1990) and, with Edward Fullbrook, *Simone De Beauvoir and Jean-Paul Sartre: The Remaking of a Twentieth-Century Legend* (1993) and *Simone De Beauvoir: A Critical Introduction* (1998). In addition, she has edited a number of books and published many articles in reviews. Her major interests are in twentieth-century fiction, American literature and literature and ethics.

Tammy Grimshaw is in her final year of doctoral studies at the University of Leeds, School of English. She is a recipient of the Overseas Research Scholarship, awarded by the Committee of Vice-Chancellors and Principals, and the University of Leeds Tetley and Lupton Scholarship. She is writing her thesis on gender and sexuality in Iris Murdoch's fiction.

Clare Hanson is Professor of English at Loughborough University. She has published books and articles on a wide range of women's writing from the late nineteenth century to the present day. She is currently completing *A Cultural History of Pregnancy*, to be published by Palgrave in 2004.

Mary Joannou is Senior Lecturer in English and Women's Studies at Anglia Polytechnic University's Cambridge campus. She is the author of *Contemporary Women's Writing* and *'Ladies, Please Don't Smash These Windows': Women's Writing 1918–1938*, and editor of *Women's Writing, Gender, Politics, History*.

Elizabeth Maslen is a Senior Research Fellow at the Institute of English Studies, University of London. Her most recent work is *Political and Social Issues in British Women's fiction 1928–1968* (Palgrave 2001). She is now working on a literary biography of Storm Jameson.

Linden Peach is Professor of Modern Literature and Head of the School of Humanities at the University of Gloucestershire. His published work includes studies of Virginia Woolf, Angela Carter and Toni Morrison, and he has also published extensively on Welsh writing. He is currently researching the representation of the criminal in nineteenth- and twentieth-century literature and culture.

Sarah Sceats is a Senior Lecturer at Kingston University, London. She specialises in twentieth-century fiction, especially women's writing. She has published on Angela Carter, Doris Lessing, Margaret Atwood and Michele Roberts, among others. *Food, Consumption and the Body in Contemporary Women's Fiction* was published in 2000 by Cambridge University Press and *Image and Power: Women in fiction in the Twentieth Century* (co-edited with Gail Cunningham) by Longman in 1996. She is currently working on several projects including the idea of home, the aging body and the fiction of Betty Miller.

Claire Tylee is Senior Lecturer at Brunel University, West London, where she teaches courses in war and literature and in gender studies. She has spoken and published widely in the field of women and war, writing articles for journals such as *Tulsa Studies, Women* and *Shakespeare Survey*. She has edited *War Plays by Women* and *Women, the First World War and Dramatic Imagination*. Her monograph *The Great War and Women's Consciousness* (1990) was widely received as groundbreaking. She is at present carryng out research into writing by Jewish women in Britain.

Diana Wallace is Lecturer in English at the University of Glamorgan. Her publications include *Sisters and Rivals in British Women's Fiction, 1914–39* (Macmillan, 2000). She is currently working on a book on women's historical fiction in the twentieth century.

Susan Watkins is a senior lecturer in English Literature in the School of Cultural Studies at Leeds Metropolitan University. Her research interests are mainly in twentieth-century women's fiction and feminist theory. She is the author of *Twentieth-Century Women Novelists: Feminist Theory into Practice* (Palgrave, 2001) and co-editor of *Studying Literature: A Practical Introduction* (Harvester Wheatsheaf, 1995).

Introduction

Jane Dowson

Women's fiction, poetry, drama and non-fiction represent the complex nexus of continuity and change in the British consciousness following the Second World War. They revise residual myths that the 1940s spawned an homogeneously egalitarian culture which evolved into a classless Britain in the 1950s, that feminism was an anachronism and that literature was exhausted. These essays extend histories of postwar literary trends which tend to concentrate on the novel, to the exclusion of other genres. They restore the cultural and literary significance of women as readers and writers, examining their various transmutations of international, national and domestic politics. The woman-centred writing illuminated in this collection also enhances the tradition-in-process of women's literature which often shifts between conventional categories. In this period, women's artistic practice negotiates between the realism and fantasy variously associated with high modernist, popular 'middlebrow' and prewar liberal realist writing.

The promise of Clement Atlee's 1945 Labour government to remove inequality and deprivation with the miracle cure of a welfare state was partially successful. There were much trumpeted changes in dole, income, health and education but they were allegedly thwarted by the realities of austerity, notably rationing did not end until 1954. However, cultural revisionists question the reliability of the narratives which constructed egalitarianism as a genuine article in the first place.[1] For a start, Richard Hoggart's seminal *The Uses of Literacy* (1958) registers the perpetuity of the 'us' and 'them' oppositions encoded in literature, the media and institutionalised education. Other records of the period also unsettle the image of 'one society' achieved during and after the Second World War and suggest that nationalism, as much as the economy, trampled the democratic dream. The gradual devolution of colonial rule, the fear of communism and the large immigration from the West Indies, starting with the *Windrush* in 1948, combined to challenge the notion of Englishness which had been integral to the sense of the war's success. Furthermore, nostalgic notions of English identity advertised in conservative public rhetoric collided with the increasingly popular and available Americanised entertainment industry. As Harry Hopkins remembered it:

> The peculiar psychological condition of the British at the end of the forties, suspended between the old England that was dying and the new England that was yet to be born, had endowed the American article with a quite peculiar potency.[2]

In 1939, 19 million attended the cinema weekly and in 1945 this number had risen to 30 million. In 1954 there were 28,000 cinemas and 40,000 in 1965, although cinema going decreased between 1954 and 1959 due to the surge of television – TV ownership increased from 4 per cent of the population in 1950 to 80 per cent in 1960.

Film and television which threatened British literary tradition and authority inevitably also forced literary innovation. There were new sproutings from the cross-fertilisation between Britain and America and between traditional genres and popular media Although work has been done to rescue the British novel from blanketing depictions of an exhausted formally low-key literary activity, the particular vibrancy of women's writing has been less celebrated.[3] There is a growing body of criticism on the cultural and literary significance of established novelists such as Elizabeth Bowen, Iris Murdoch, Doris Lessing and Muriel Spark. As widely read were Nancy Mitford, Elizabeth Taylor, Barbara Pym, Vera Brittain, Agatha Christie and Rosemary Sutcliff whose novels reveal the desires and power of women as consumers in this period. Poets and playwrights, meddling with oppositional prescriptions of gender, class and nation, conjunctively confuse conventional literary distinctions. As Gill Plain states, this process was happening in women's fiction before and during the Second World War:

> The blending of detective fiction with historical sagas and the later flowerings of the modernist aesthetic will also, I hope, serve to continue the process, begun by Alison Light (1991) of breaking down the boundaries between high and low cultures that function only to limit and constrain our analysis of the period.[4]

The interchange between literary and popular referentiality is particularly exploited by women writing in this period; arguably, they were liberated by the vocabularies of postwar democracy and the appetite for fantasy.

In postwar Britain, many women writers were alienated from the patriotic feminine ideal sentimentalised by popular ideology and disparaged by male-dominated literary enclaves. They tended to a complicated relationship with national pride when they were disenchanted by Britain's imperialistic discourses but had enjoyed the emancipation of wartime activity. However, they also tended to avoid explicit gender politics because any championing of women's rights contradicted the assumptions of government and media machinery. Their roles were clearly prescribed and officially, at least, given high value. Women had been hailed as heroines during the war and afterwards, their prime functions, as wives and mothers, became elevated through social provisions, notably the family allowance in 1945. Domestic work was professionalised and the home glamorised as the centre of social stability. Women married younger and were adorned with labour-saving devices to free their energy for bearing the nation's future and for attending to their husbands. Anecdotally, the first production of Daz washing powder was accompanied by a free daffodil; a household chore was typically packaged in feelgood terms which a woman would be churlish to contradict.

The welfare state enhanced the dominant ideology of family as the microcosm of national health. As Harry Hopkins recorded soon after the 1950s:

> In the old battle of 'Women's Rights' little remained but mopping-up operations. For thirty years Governments had saluted the principle of equal pay for equal work while protesting that, unfortunately, the financial position made this quite, quite impossible. Then, suddenly, in 1955, in the civil service and in teaching the thing was done. The long-standing civil service rule barring the employment of women after marriage had been dropped a little earlier. Almost without a fight, the last male strongholds were falling. In 1946 even the foreign office had opened its doors to women. In the Fifties, Oxford (and later Cambridge) overcame its traditional monasticism at least to the point of removing the historic quota limitation on women undergraduates, which the Warden of Wadham now boldly declared to have been 'most foolish, out-of-date, finicky'. Women's 'societies' were at last

> admitted to be 'colleges' with full status opening up – theoretically – the possibility of a woman Vice-Chancellor and women proctors. And if the Oxford Union still wavered, the House of Lords in January 1959 grasped the nettle and resolved on a motion of Lord Reading to do what it had hitherto repeatedly refused to do – admit hereditary peeresses in their own right. A powder room was installed – the first women life peers had been introduced the previous October. By the end of the Fifties, only the church, the London Stock exchange, the Jockey Club and a few Pall Mall clubs continued to hold out.
>
> Yet to the veterans of the Cause, the victory seemed somehow hollow.[5]

The underside to pervasive ideologies of domestic fulfilment hinted at here has not been obvious since it was difficult for women to express disaffection with the public cause when eroding English colonial strongholds, communist upheavals and increasing nuclear power engendered shared human concerns for peace and justice; additionally, the uncertainties of population decline and housing shortages stifled any murmuring about inequality for women in employment; men needed rehabilitation into an employment market which was different from the one which they had left and women were in demand as a labour force. In 1951, 20 per cent of women were working and this figure rose to 32 per cent in 1961. Research by the British Federation of University Women found that only 10 per cent desired more career opportunities for married women and 40 per cent were engaged in some employment after marriage, often part-time.

New developments in BBC radio and the spreading ownership of television disseminated family values with programmes such as *Watch with Mother* (1950). The increasing number of women's magazines in the immediate postwar years idealised happy families and trained women in home economics, such as making do with ration books. By the mid-1950s, 12 million women were reading women's magazines twice a week from a field of 50 and new ones were still being launched.[6] These magazines concentrated on mothering, domestic knowledge and, famously, instructions for the good wife.[7] As prosperity developed in the 1950s, women's role as consumers was heightened and they became prime targets of the fashion industry. Perfect models of women who combined moral wisdom, utility and glamour were exaggerated by the influx of American films and musicals, such as *Gentlemen Prefer Blondes* (1953) and *West Side Story* (1957). Thus, in the 1950s, men and women were presented with images of woman as fulfilled wife and mother who was still a domestic genius, but also now a sexually appealing one – Marilyn Monroe was, of course, the 1950s icon of sexual femininity. Following the war, there was a flourishing black market in nylons, chocolate, perfume and other scarce pleasures.

Feminist history acknowledges and interprets the unwelcome fact that universalising ideologies of gender were seductive to many women. At the same time, it contests the myth of corporate feminist inertia. In 1950, the *Manchester Guardian* published the research of Eva Hubback which stated that 40 per cent of women did not want a job and 20 per cent had help in the house by their husbands at weekends. However, 50 per cent were unduly bored:

> The cause of reasonable feminism has been virtually won. These developments have had the effect of glossing over the differences between the sexes. For biological reasons there is sexual division of labour, but culturally women have the same needs and desires as men. The new advance must be in the direction of so organising home life and the education of girls that women are competent to bring up families without so much sacrifice of health and personality that they are unable to return to a broader life in middle age when they will not only contribute to the community through their work but find life worth living outside the immediate family.[8]

From 1947 to 1952 a conference ran on the Feminine Point of View. It was attended by a number of key women and culminated in a report published in 1952.[9] Gertrude Williams' paper *Women and Work* (1945), part of The New Democracy Series, elevated consciousness about the new possibilities for women.[10] Some Mills and Boon books presented positive images of women in jobs.[11] The 'Special Number on Women' of the journal *The Twentieth Century* illuminates the debate between and within women about their emancipation.[12] There were still women's organisations, although the Women's Freedom League was the only one with any militancy. The Six Point Group waged war against financial inequalities and support for women's need for childcare and pensions. Other groups were Women in Westminster, the Status of Women Group, Open Door Council and the National Council of Women. The wave of divorce and illegitimacy also undermines conservative nostalgia about postwar traditional family values. In 1945 there were 25,000 divorce cases and 50,000 by 1947. According to the Marriage Guidance Council, 40 per cent of girls under 20 were pregnant on their wedding day and one quarter of all births were illegitimate. This Council and other organisations were set up to stem the rising tide of divorce. The large number of cases was, of course, partially accounted for by service men and women who had struck up wartime alliances.

The Women's Liberation Movement of the 1960s, which was germinating underground during the 1950s, was undoubtedly nourished by the English publication of Simone De Beauvoir's *The Second Sex* in 1953. De Beauvoir contested the claims of social equality and pointed to women's psychological repression:

> The privileged place held by men in economic life, their social usefulness, the prestige of marriage, the value of masculine biology, all this makes women wish ardently to please men. Women are still, for the most part, in a state of subjection. It follows that woman sees herself and makes her choices not in accordance with her true nature in itself, but as man defines her.[13]

Ten years on, in *The Feminine Mystique* (1963), Betty Friedan's seminal survey of women in America over the years 1942 to 1959 unwrapped the deadly 'dailyness' of prescribed femininity which had suffocated women. Friedan diagnosed 'Housewives fatigue' which the professionals had concealed:

> The suburban doctors, gynaecologists, obstetricians, child guidance, clinicians, paediatricians, marriage counsellors and ministers who treat women's problems have all seen it, without putting a name to it, or even reporting it as a phenomenon. What they have seen confirms that for woman, as for man, the need for self-fulfilment – autonomy, self-realisation, independence, individuality, self-actualisation – is as important as the sexual need.[14]

The 'problem that has no name', which drove women in America to tranquillisers, alcohol and psychiatrists, was a sense of failure to live up to unattainable ideals. Both single women, discarded as awkward abnormalities, or married women who had the lot – husband, home, children and the opportunity to work – suffered an unpresentable void. In Britain, the same climate of suppressed desires is evident in British records including women's novels of psychic breakdown such as Veronica Hull's *The Monkey Puzzle* (1958), Edna O'Brien's *The Country Girls* (1961), Jennifer Dawson's *The Ha-Ha* (1961) and Doris Lessing's early 1960s novels. Women's fiction thus records their cultural restrictions but also has the potency to imaginatively transcend them

– albeit temporarily. The activity of writing manufactured an alternative subjectivity and subculture for both writer and reader. Many authors appropriated, developed or subverted the formulaic conventions of popular fantasies while pressing upon the boundaries of traditional 'realist' representations.

The diversionary appeal of many women's texts both enhances and occludes their subversions of idealistic constructions of social propriety. Stevie Smith's essay 'A London Suburb' (1949) characteristically cracks the protective shell of British decency:

> It would be wrong to suppose that everything always goes well in the suburbs. At number 71, the wife does not speak to her husband, he is a gentle creature, retired now for many years from the Merchant Navy. He paces the upstairs rooms. His wife sits downstairs; she is a vegetarian and believes in earth currents; she keeps a middle-aged daughter in subjection. At Number 5, the children were taught to steal the milk from the doorsteps. They were clever at this, the hungry dirty children. Their father was a mild man, but the mother loved the violent lodger. When they were sent to prison for neglecting the children, the lodger bailed the mother out but let the father lie.
>
> Life in the suburb is richer at the lower levels. At these levels the people are not self-conscious at all, they are at liberty to be as eccentric as they please, they do not know that they are eccentric. At the more expensive levels the people have bridge parties and say of their neighbours, 'they are rather suburban'.
>
> ... And behind the fishnet curtains in the windows of the houses is the family life – father's chair, uproar, dogs, babies and radio.[15]

Stevie Smith offers both a pastiche and parody of the 'ordinariness' and understatement typical of writing in this period. Her measured assertion of social order draws attention to the sanitised or prejudiced versions of respectable English routine which studiously veil class differences and domestic strife. The works in this book penetrate the worlds behind and beyond 'the fishnet curtains'.

'The quarrel will go on as long as men and women fail to recognise each other as equals; that is to say, as long as femininity is perpetuated as such', concludes De Beauvoir in *The Second Sex*. To what extent do the woman-centred texts of this period draw the curtains on the literary feminine? Nicola Beauman's features of twentieth-century women's novels before this period still prevail: War, Surplus Women, Feminism, Domesticity, Sex, Psychoanalysis, Romance and Love.[16] Writers in this collection indicate women's complex relationship with the raised status of home and domestic labour since it was both politically progressive and regressive. They draw attention to women's nature and roles but rarely debate them explicitly. However, self-sacrifice, a wartime virtue for men and women but returned to women afterwards, becomes more scrutinised in the available currency of psychoanalytical concepts of repression. Marriage and motherhood are represented as secure but often as stunting mental and spiritual growth while divorce and adultery feature more openly. Literary spinsters, like Stevie Smith's parodic 'middle-aged daughter', warrant attention for their psychological mutations of the stereotyped single woman. Women's sensuality and sexuality are exposed, although 'the body' was still a vexed site of representation.

The central question of what constitutes masculinity and femininity and the line between them vibrates in many works. These essays suggest that women writers prioritised women's economic and political equality over validating female distinctness. One strong thread is the cross-gendering of sexual identity in 'masculine femininity' or 'female masculinity'. Domesticity was advocated by some but a social conscience and global issues also feature in many women's consciousness; interestingly, the wife in Stevie Smith's suburb 'is a vegetarian and believes in earth currents'. There is more attention to institutional politics, often manifest in scepticism towards postwar optimism about the new welfare state in Britain, the new Europe and colonial release abroad.

The writers' emphasis on constructed gendering invites materialist feminist readings and references to De Beauvoir occur in at least four chapters. Although my thematic arrangement does not offer a linear journey through women's social activities or developments in literary practice, the Chronology is intended to aid contextualising the works according to contemporary socio-literary events and trends. I could have arranged the chapters by genre, but the two on poetry and one on film and drama are swamped by the dominance of novel and short story. The non-fiction extracts tend to operate as secondary material but offer polemical anxieties and beliefs to accompany the literary works. The traditionally popular genres of romance, historical and detective fictions provide devices for examining current cultural conditions via dreamscape and fantasy; in poetry and drama the political impulse is obliquely manifest in the eschewal of the contemporary world, through idealisation, spiritual quest or the alternative realism of the past. This collection also provides the scope to concentrate on particular writers: Sylvia Townsend Warner features in three chapters and there are two on

Doris Lessing. The reputations of Barbara Pym and Elizabeth Taylor as uncritical recorders of middle class life are reconsidered by Clare Hanson and Linden Peach respectively.

The four sections – The Legacy of War; The Home; Love, Gender and Marriage; Across the Threshold: Spirituality, Colonisation and Subjectivity – indicate the dominant preoccupations of the writers, which do, of course, cut across my rather crude partitions. The immediate past of the war forms the first section of this book but psychological fragmentation and alienation are identified throughout. Home, a symbol of order and disorder, the stage on which the dynamics of old and new is played out domestically and globally, is an especially recurring signifier for women's competing impulses of advance and retreat. In Part One, Elizabeth Maslen's opening essay illuminates how old and new oppositions apply to postwar nostalgia for mythical prewar stability against dreams and disappointments concerning a new egalitarian era, to the difference between generations and to the review of class identities which had been muddled by the levelling experiences of war work and evacuation. As before the war, there were 'old' feminist drives for equality alongside 'new' impulses for celebrating emancipated and sexualised femininity. Additionally,

> Postwar women were not only concerned with domestic issues; the revelations of the Holocaust, Hiroshima, and the onset of the Korean War and, in Europe, the Cold War all helped to construct their visions of the future. (Maslen)

Women's involvement in war work had propelled their engagement with national and international politics, but they do not show symptoms of nationalistic fervour. The nostalgia which has characterised the postwar collective consciousness is both sustained and subverted, as Julia Briggs demonstrates in Elizabeth Bowen's fiction. Bowen's short stories, novels and essays which document the authentic struggle to retain a coherent psyche in postwar disillusion and dissolution are an antidote to sentimental depictions of community cheeriness in adversity. Briggs identifies the political resonances in Bowen's writing, even in the imaginative dimensions of the uncanny and inexplicable. Linden Peach's survey of crime writing identifies the tension between innovation and conservatism concerning traditional notions of Englishness and gender. He identifies how Agatha Christie's big house settings represent the confusion and complexity of postwar Britain. Christie was sceptical of the welfare state and utilitarian Britain in

4.50 from Paddington while *They Do It With Mirrors* unsettles gender constructions with androgynous and eccentric characterisation. Betty Kane in Josephine Tey's *The Franchise Affair* is a criminalised distortion of girlhood innocence which was prevalent in interwar schoolgirl fiction. St Trinian cartoons were first published as a book in 1947. In *Opening Night,* Ngaio Marsh similarly employs the transgressions allowed by the genre to ruffle society's drapes of decency.

Claire Tylee looks at adaptations of women's novels to film and particularly draws attention to conflicts over Jewish-British identities. The Ministry of Information was set up when war was declared to censor the media and women playwrights particularly encountered state control. Britain lagged behind America in adapting women's novels to stage and screen and in addressing racial tensions; anti-semitism was a closed subject in official British discourse. In 1946, the 43 group was formed by ex-service men and women to combat anti-semitic activity. Yvonne Mitchell's popular *The Same Sky* (1947) dramatises the culture of a working-class Jewish family in London. The peculiar difficulties of Jewishness and 'belonging' are also considered by Sarah Sceats in Betty Lee Miller's *Farewell Leicester Square* and by Alice Entwistle with reference to Denise Levertov.

As represented in Part Two, 'The Home: Retreat and Restraint', the domicile was the locus for enacting different models of marriage and family. The recurring motif is women's relationship with domesticated femininity; the absence of it in some works indicates denial or oppositional self-definition. John Brannigan identifies Elizabeth Taylor's manoeuvres between the conservative yearning for a mythical prewar security and a feminist critique of conservative ideologies of the family. Like Bowen's voyages into the mysterious, the features of gothic fantasy allow an uncertain narrative perspective which in turn allows an ambivalence about home – the sphere of paradoxical 'familial intimacy and patriarchal oppression'. The fantastic both displaces and exposes the characters' (and readers') alienation from the modern word. Sarah Sceats looks at the dynamic of belonging and homelessness by Bowen, Miller and Spark. In *Memento Mori* (1959) Spark especially intimates that 'at home' is an unachievable concept in this world. Alice Entwistle examines the 'terrible joy' of female authorship in Denise Levertov's knotty relationship with the domestic and her triple alienation as an Anglo-American woman and poet:

> For the (married) woman writer of the early postwar period, where the home offers emotional security it denies intellectual freedom. At

> the same time, however, enshrining the relationships and resources from which she draws material and spiritual inspiration, the domestic sphere prompts self-expression, paradoxically offering the chance of escape from its confines. For Levertov, the domestic was charged with subversive potential. As she says, 'My politics and my muse happen to get on very well together'.

Entwistle applies Levertov's poetics of the domestic to earlier writing. She also provides an incisive survey of the female postwar poetry scene, which has been dominated by the Movement.

Part Two runs into Part Three which magnifies the sexual politics in works where love is controversially often distinguished from marriage. Mary Joannou points to Nancy Mitford's *The Pursuit of Love* as a record of her readers' desire for glamour and excitement: 'the public appetite for narratives concerned with passion, adultery, feminine misconduct and the English aristocracy'. Mitford's novel offers a prototype of independent woman unencumbered by domestic responsibilities which prefigures the social and sexual revolution of the 1960s. Joannou also places Nancy Mitford in a neglected tradition of women's comic writing. Her irony distances romantic idealism from the dull and oppressive realities of women's lives which the escapades of wartime had exaggerated. Apart from Mary Joannou's chapter, romance is not the dominant template. As Diana Wallace points out, the tagging of 'romance' rather than 'fiction' to 'historical' has denigrated the wide corpus of women's historical fiction which bulged during and after the war. These novels investigate and connect the so-called 'popular' and 'serious' traditions. Like the tool of the gothic or uncanny, retreat into history is a device for both escaping from and evaluating the conditions which women experience at the moment of writing. It frees them to comment on taboo subjects, such as male and female homosexuality or patriarchal injustices, through the distance of the past. These works provide a vocabulary with which to interrogate contemporary concerns about gender roles and world affairs. Kathleen Bell discusses women's forays into male mindsets and activity through the adventurous cross-genderings of Cecil Woodham Smith, Rosemary Sutcliff and Mary Renault. These include intimate male partnerships, appropriately set in ancient Rome, which present men with conventionally female attributes. These writers also conflate ancient power systems with the colonisations familiar to their twentieth-century readers. 'Female masculinity', especially as a resistance to postwar ideals of femininity in marriage, is explored by Tammy Grimshaw in Iris Murdoch's fiction.

Part IV explores women's treatment of the socialised self; notably they dissolve the reductive opposition between 'private' and 'public' worlds and the myth of women's disengagement from global politics. Two enlightening chapters on Doris Lessing, by Kate Fullbrook and Susan Watkins, signal her importance to the 1950s, as to a canon of twentieth-century women's writing:

> Lessing's fiction can profitably be read in terms of questions of race, nationalism, postcolonialism, class, generational conflict and misapprehension, the treatment of those who violate expectations of normality (whether physical or mental), violence, and, of course, gender. (Fullbrook)

She was regarded as a radical realist, although Watkins suggests that she became more critical of the realist novel by the end of the 1950s. Subversively, Lessing indicates the war's positive effects of fragmenting complacent essentialising and hegemonising notions of the human: 'The "monstrosity" of Hitler's Germany is persistently seen as relative rather than absolute when set alongside the Soviet Union and the history of British colonialism' (Watkins). In this period, Lessing controversially examines hybridity, especially regarding inter-racial sexuality. (Sadly, the silence of black women writers prevails in the 1950s.[17]) She seems ahead of her time in presenting subjectivity as process, 'a confluence of the historical, the social, the sexual and the psychological, mixed with the peculiarly and often accidentally individual' (Fullbrook).

Clare Hanson argues that Barbara Pym appropriates anthropological enquiry 'to lay bare a society riven by conflict and power struggle, especially in relation to gender'. Pym engaged with contemporary debates about the divergent anthropological theories of Radcliffe Brown and Levi-Strauss which represent essentialist and constructivist versions of subjectivity. Pym also dramatises the period's dilemma between agnosticism and faith. In poetry, these poles were embodied by Philip Larkin and T.S. Eliot. I had to overcome my disinterest in this period's women poets and address the feminist avoidance of Elizabeth Jennings in particular. I concluded that her poetry transmutes the isolation of the woman artist who was acutely alienated from ideologies of domestic married femininity. For Jennings, as for other successful poets, Kathleen Raine, Ruth Pitter, Anne Ridler and Edith Sitwell, imaginative expression of spiritual quest asserts an autonomous subjectivity, albeit via mystical union. Likewise, the lyric's atemporality affords an alternative space for the female imagination and indicates the writers' distance from the worlds they inhabit. However, I have to acknowledge their unifying desire for intimate relationship.

Collectively, these essays record the rich texture of women's writing in the postwar period; they also add to the emerging history of twentieth-century women's literature, following on from *British Women's Comic Fiction, 1890–1990: Not Drowning, But Laughing* by Margaret Setz, Nicola Beauman's *A Very Great Profession: The Woman's Novel 1914–39,* Alison Light's *Forever England: Femininity, Literature and Conservatism Between the Wars,* Jenny Hartley's *Millions Like Us,* Gill Plain's, *Women's Fiction of the Second World War: Gender, Power and Resistance* and *British Women Writers of World War II* by Phyllis Lassner. The book is also confluent with Clare Hanson's *Hysterical Fictions: The 'Woman's Novel' in the Twentieth Century,* Elizabeth Maslen's *Political and Social Issues in British Women's Fiction 1928–68* and *Brave New Causes: Women in British Postwar Fictions* by Deborah Philips and Ian Haywood.[18] Most of the fiction analysed in *After the Deluge* strengthens the depiction of a 'woman's novel' as being written by and for a middle-class woman. However, detective fiction includes both male and female, 'high' and 'middlebrow', audiences. Theatre and film adaptations accommodate a universal public while poetry tends to avoid gender specificity. As Clare Hanson argues, since women's fiction is constituted by the range of discourses to which they had access, these discourses are in play within the level field of the texts: 'They thus not only raise crucial questions about women's lives but also offer a powerful critique of cultural assumptions about what "art" should be.'[19] These negotiations between the fantasy of popular genres and the suppressions of traditional literary realism produce a third space – between retreating from or returning to lived experience. Social and psychological complexities are neither reduced nor resolved by the idealism of popular fantasies; nor are they left unchanged. The intersection of a recognisable with a yet unrealised subjectivity allows both writer and reader an alternative state of consciousness in which to both indulge and scrutinise their desires.

Notes

1 See, for example, Alan Sinfield, *Literature, Politics and Culture in Postwar Britain* (Oxford: Blackwell, 1989).
2 Harry Hopkins, *The New Look: A Social History of the Forties and Fifties in Britain* (London: Secker and Warburg, 1963), p. 107.
3 See Steven Connor, *The English Novel in History 1950–1955* (London: Routledge, 1996).
4 Gill Plain, *Women's Fiction of the Second World War: Gender, Power and Resistance* (Edinburgh: Edinburgh University Press, 1996), p. x. See also,

Alison Light, *Forever England: Femininity, Literature and Conservatism Between the Wars* (London: Routledge, 1994).

5 Hopkins, 1963, pp. 320–21.

6 Hopkins, 1963, p. 328.

7 'Instructions for the Good Wife', *Housekeeping Monthly* (May 1955).

8 Eva Hubback, *Manchester Guardian* (21 September 1950); Elizabeth Wilson, *Only Halfway to Paradise: Women in Postwar Britain 1945–88* (London and New York: Tavistock, 1980), p. 48.

9 *The Report of a conference on the Feminine Point of View* drafted by Olwen W. Campbell (London: Williams and Norgate, 1952). I am grateful to Elizabeth Maslen for this information. Also, for her advice on the entire Introduction.

10 Gertrude Williams, *Women and Work,* The New Democracy Series (London: Nicholas and Watson, 1945).

11 For further details of career girl publications see 'Women Writers: Working Heroines', in Deborah Philips and Ian Haywood, *Brave New Causes: Women in British Postwar Fictions* (London: Leicester University Press, 1998).

12 'Special Number on Women', *The Twentieth Century*, Vol. 164, No. 978 (August 1958).

13 Simone De Beauvoir, *The Second Sex* (London: Jonathan Cape, 1988), p. 169.

14 Betty Friedan, *The Feminine Mystique* (New York: Dell Publishing, 1963), p. 314.

15 Stevie Smith, 'A London Suburb', printed in *Flowers of Cities*, 1949, in *Me Again: The Uncollected Writings of Stevie Smith* (London: Virago, 1988), p. 104.

16 Nicola Beauman, *A Very Great Profession: The Woman's Novel 1914–39* (London: Virago, 1983).

17 Elizabeth Maslen notes that Beryl Gilroy, the first black head teacher, wrote eloquently about how her writing was silenced by not only white publishers but by the men of her own community. Attia Hosain did get published, perhaps because she resided in Britain from 1947 or because she only wrote about India.

18 Margaret Setz, *British Women's Comic Fiction, 1890–1990: Not Drowning, But Laughing* (Aldershot: Ashgate, 2001); Beauman, 1983; Jenny Hartley, *Millions Like Us: British Women's Fiction of the Second World War* (London; Virago 1997); Plain, 1996; Phyllis Lassner, *British Women Writers of World War II: Battlegrounds of Their Own* (Basingstoke: Macmillan, 1998); Clare Hanson, *Hysterical Fictions: The "Woman's Novel" in the Twentieth Century* (Basingstoke: Palgrave, 2000); Elizabeth Maslen, *Political and Social Issues in British Women's Fiction 1928–68* (Basingstoke: Palgrave, 2000); Philips and Haywood, 1998.

19 Hanson, 2000, p. 7.

Part I

The Legacy of War: Continuity and Change

1
Legacies of the Past: Postwar Women Looking Forward and Back

Elizabeth Maslen

My purpose is both to explore a few of the ways in which postwar women look back and reassess their past and to examine some of the evidence for how they perceived their roles in the future. I shall be looking at both fiction and nonfiction to give some indication of how women saw their situation in the postwar world of the 1940s and 1950s.

The recent war inevitably meant that one favorite way of looking back was to recall wistfully what seemed a more innocent past – the past, that is, before both World Wars. So we find Rebecca West remembering (or, as theories of biography would have it, constructing a memory[1]) of her early childhood:

> When I was young ... I thought human beings were naturally good, and that their personal relations were bound to work out well, and that the law was a clumsy machine dealing harshly with people who would cease to offend as soon as we got rid of poverty. We were quite sure that human nature was good and would soon be perfect.[2]

Two World Wars served to destroy such innocence, if indeed it was ever more than a retrospective dream of childhood; Rosamond Lehmann's *The Ballad and the Source* (1944) shows how memory can be tailored more negatively, to reflect a bleak view of the human condition, offering a view of the past which disturbingly mirrors World War Two experience, as Phyllis Lassner has convincingly argued.[3]

Despite the triumph of gaining the vote, and subsequent preoccupations with domestic issues, the effects of war tend to dominate or at the very least colour women's writing in the interwar years (when the previous war and the growing fear of fascism were insistent issues) and both during and after World War Two.[4] Some writers look at ways in which war could scar young people for life; Rose Macaulay, for instance, in *The World My Wilderness* (1950), gives a haunting account of how a British child, Barbary, is brought up in France under the occupation, and is drawn into the fringes of the resistance, the *maquis*.[5] As a result, we see her judging her postwar world from the philosophical perspective she has learned in the French resistance movement and the moral choices it posed. She translates the enemies of those days into the English postwar society in which she finds herself (the ironies involved in this do not all rule out such a perspective). The chances of Barbary ever really emerging from this state of mind, and escaping from what the novel presents as the inevitably destructive barbarism which war generates are, it is implied, pretty remote. Such bleak assessments of the legacy of war are very common in the late 1940s and 1950s. Storm Jameson, for instance, charts the penalties for fraternisation and collaboration on the continent in a series of powerful novels, which explore the all too human dilemmas of ordinary people caught up in the extraordinary shifts and changes of their time. Jameson's *The Other Side* (1946) shows the wretched price a young French woman pays, both to her in-laws and to her compatriots in the army of occupation, for falling in love and marrying a German soldier who is later killed. *The Black Laurel* (1947) is set in the bleakly dangerous world of Berlin immediately after the war, where justice all too often recedes before vengeance; while *The Hidden River* (1955) develops a family situation in France akin to Greek tragedy, as one member is gradually revealed as having collaborated, betraying another. Crucially, too, Jameson championed, both during World War Two and later, the work of many European writers who had been persecuted, putting her readers in close personal touch with the realities in Europe both before and during the war. She frequently spent weeks rewriting the books and articles she received from refugee and overseas writers and translators, so that they would have a chance of being published in Britain; and her active support greatly enhanced their chances. For instance, in an issue of the journal, the *Adelphi*, in 1947, she writes a poignant introduction to an article by a Polish woman, Eugenia Kocwa, who had survived the horrors of Ravensbruck, the concentration camp for women. Describing her own postwar visit to Poland, Jameson tells how

> I learned quickly not to ask the woman who was showing me, smiling, her one dress, her single improvised pair of shoes: Have you a husband, a son, a brother, parents? The ruins of Warsaw, more alive

> than Paris at that time, taught me that men are able to endure the worst man can do.[6]

She then goes on to tell of the extraordinary response to suffering shown by Kocwa and other former inmates whom she encountered. At least three tell her that their suffering was so extreme that it could only be met by forgiveness, not revenge – and if that seems unlikely, there is the recent echo of such a solution proffered in South Africa. Be that as it may, Jameson herself does not claim that this was a typical reaction:

> I do not know how many of the survivors would answer as Eugenia Kocwa did. I know only that this answer was given to me three times in Poland, that country of broken lives, torn-out memories, survivors (p. 127).

Jameson's own commitment to exposing the appalling cruelties of Nazi oppression is matched by her passionate concern, mirroring what she learnt during that Polish visit, that justice, not revenge, is the only way towards a viable future. She is always haunted by the damage done by the retribution exacted from Germany after World War One, and many of her novels and articles reflect her concern. Such preoccupations serve to show (since these accounts sold well) that the need to come to terms with the war and its implications, if not always a predominant theme, is ever present among British writers and their readers. Postwar women were not only concerned with domestic issues; the revelations of the Holocaust, Hiroshima, and the onset of the Korean War and, in Europe, the Cold War all helped to construct their visions of the future. As a result, the doubts raised about the values of western civilization, the fear of the H bomb which made many wary of having families, the end of empire, the debacle of Suez, the Russian invasion of Hungary, were just some of the issues which made the late 1940s and the 1950s as complex and complicated as any previous decades in which to attempt to formulate definitive accounts of where women were feeling impelled to go. Storm Jameson can again be cited as a writer who charts postwar anxieties: as early as 1949, her novel *Moment of Truth* is set in a future World War Three, when decisions have to be taken as to those who will be deputed to survive in a fall-out shelter.[7]

And such visions of the future inevitably affect views on the domestic front, seeming in a fair number of cases to have contributed to the retreat into domesticity as a perceived alternative to engagement with an all too uncertain future in the world at large. For while many women had jobs in the war, both in the services and in civilian life, many of those who worked, as has been well explored (by Gill Plain and Jenny Hartley, for example), saw marriage as their ultimate goal and faced the likelihood of a return to domestic life without a career with few regrets. Many novels of the postwar years show the potency of conservatism about a woman's lot; whether this was an actual reversion to prewar conventions, or a return to the familiar as a reaction to an uncertain world situation is not always clear. The whole issue of what constitutes masculinity and femininity and the need for a clear line to be drawn between them seem very much alive and well in many works, both fiction and nonfiction, although there may be subliminal challenges to such conservatism. A writer like Elizabeth Taylor, for instance, does not, in many of her works, set out to upset the conservative model too obviously. Yet she shows in her novel *At Mrs Lippincote's* (1945), published as the war ended, how damaging a man's commitment to his uniform, or rather to the whole ethos behind militarism, could be for his wife. Betty Miller's novel, *On the Side of the Angels* (1945), explores the same theme, showing a husband distanced from his family by his absorption in the military life of the camp, and his wife's tight-lipped endurance of her domestic, subaltern role.[8]

But for many, such ambivalence to marriage and domesticity is not apparent. What is more, although there were many writers who deplored the drudgery of household chores, there were passionate advocates of domesticity, a cause that drew adherents throughout the late 1940s and the 1950s. For these were not only to be found amongst men, who might be expected to espouse the cause of woman's return to domesticity, partly in support of men returning from the war, and partly from an ingrained conviction about what a woman's role was. Many advocates could also be found among women; and where women were not advocates, they might none the less accept such domesticity as inevitable or, as I mentioned above, as a preferred option, given the uncertainty of a world after Hiroshima. There is also another reversion to conservatism which gives a further insight; a number of women writers take up the effects of the suffragettes on those of their children who are not by temperament disposed to fulfil the aspirations of their mothers. Elizabeth Taylor, for instance, in her novel *A Game of Hide and Seek* (1951), charts the career of Harriet, a suffragette's child, who distresses her mother by her apparent lack of interest in what the older generation endured to gain the vote.[9] It is not that Harriet positively disapproves of what her mother did as a suffragette, but that she is not academically gifted, and so has no chance of the brilliant career which her mother dreamed would be hers for the taking. But of course her mother's disappointment weighs on the girl. Not unnaturally, she counters this by shunning all references to the time her mother spent in prison for the suffrage cause, as all she really wants is to be married; her chosen career is to be domesticity. However, the novel does not end there; Harriet's daughter Betsy seems to be developing along the lines her grandmother dreamed of for Harriet. This raises an important issue, I think, for while it is certainly true that many women returned to domesticity after World War Two, and that many did so quite happily, the return to the home of one generation does not mean that the next may not reap the benefits for which their grandmothers fought.

For despite the apparent retreat into convention of many women after the war, this difference between generations is an illuminating feature of the late 1940s and the 1950s, as Deborah Philips and Ian Haywood have pointed out.[10] In their book, *Brave New Causes: Women in British Postwar Fiction*, they combat 'the prevailing popular idea of British society in the 1950s [as] a period of social stability [...] a touchstone of traditional moral virtues and "family" values' (p.1). They acknowledge that many postwar novels written by such women as Elizabeth Bowen, Barbara Pym, Doris Lessing and Iris Murdoch in the late 1940s and 1950s do not have working heroines – or if they do, work is set in the background to the main interests of the plot: relationships. Yet they also point to the number of less noted, popular romances, where the working girl and her career figure prominently; Mills and Boon heroines offer particularly striking examples, since they are shown in a wide range of jobs, many of them traditionally seen as exclusively male territory. Philips and Haywood point, too, to the 1956 conference of the Six Point Group and the Married Women's Association on the theme 'Married Women out of Work' as a sign that conservatism was being resisted, despite the remaining tensions between marriage and career. Yet, as they admit, abortion was still illegal, illegitimate birth frowned on, and so on; progress was indeed slow.[11] As always, continuity and change confront each other, and the contest between them can swing either way. Modernity cannot be pared down to change alone; the tension between old conventions and what struggles to replace them is the very essence of modernity since it insists on an articulation of definitions and distinctions – and change is not always the preferred way forward.

And this fact is clear when we review the struggles of the postwar decade when women attempt to reconcile the aims and aspirations of prewar 'old' and 'new' feminist priorities. As Marion Shaw has succinctly analysed, the 'old' order of feminists put a high value on equality between the sexes, while the 'new' order preferred to concentrate on such women's issues as rights in marriage and divorce, birth control, abortion and so on.[12] In the late 1940s and right through the 1950s, careers tend to be set against the urge to enjoy marriage and family, at a time when the pill was as yet out of reach. Yet, as I have suggested, life in these years is complicated by a great deal more than this, given the horror of the Holocaust and Hiroshima, the war in Korea and the unease of the Cold War.

Against the backdrop of such anxieties, women's future role is frequently debated in the period we are exploring. Gertrude Williams, for instance, in her book *Women and Work*, published in 1945, while acknowledging that most women still think of marriage and family as their ultimate goal, points to the gradual improvements in opportunities open to women since the beginning of the twentieth century, and to the ways women during World War Two have shown themselves capable of jobs once thought to be far beyond their capacity.[13] However – and this I think is important, as it will be repeated many times throughout the late 1940s and the 1950s – what Williams sees as the main obstacle to women continuing to improve their career prospects after the war is not only male opposition, but a mixture of female reluctance to assume public responsibilities together with a lack of confidence in the marketplace. Opportunity, then, is still operating against a subtext of Victorian values. Williams argues that

> the organised and articulate demand for equal opportunity for women to enter employments for which they could prove themselves competent has come from the small educated section of the middle class rather than from women as a sex (p. 34)

and that most women still subscribe to the Victorian convention that men must dominate in the workplace – and hence, by implication, in society at large. What Williams sees as a great gain for the future postwar woman is that she will have choice, but she also acknowledges the 'immense influence' of 'current ideas of right behaviour', seeing this as putting women under pressure to 'do what was expected of them', whether that is work during wartime or a return to the home afterwards (pp. 123–4). If women do return to the home, she says, she wants their role given the same prestige as any other career. What is more, while acknowledging the importance of the home, she warns that, while motherhood plays a crucial social role, children grow up quickly, and she urges women in the aftermath of war, 'against too intense a concentration on activity within the narrow boundaries of the home' (p. 126).

For as the Mills and Boon novels mirrored in their romances, opportunities for women in a range of jobs were there, if not yet at the highest level. Even amongst the wartime generation of women workers, there certainly were those who wanted to stay in the workforce. Victoria Sackville-West, for instance, in her book *The Women's Land Army* (1944), records how a fair number of girls working on the land wanted to continue in employment, either overseas or at home. In an appendix, she lists a wide range of possible postwar careers for women, giving the address of The Women's Employment Federation for those who wish for information. She does, however, warn that jobs for land-girls in Britain will be in short supply after the war, concluding that 'It ... seems extremely unlikely that women will oust men to any great extent on the farms, and indeed no reasonable person would wish them to do so'.[14] Here again, the old boundaries are implied. And despite the fact that daughters and granddaughters would pursue careers which the war had in part helped to make available to them, practically, culturally and psychologically, the lot of the women emerging from war work was not wholly encouraging.

We get further useful insights into how intelligent women saw the future of their sex when we turn to the conclusions of the Conference on The Feminine Point of View, which took place from 1947 to 1951; the impact of the war and its horrors is immediately obvious. The report on this conference describes its priorities interestingly. It announces that the conference decided to abandon an 'equalitarian' line, 'meaning by that women's right to do, experience and express the same kind of things as men', and instead concentrated on 'the ways in which women seem to differ from men, and have considered mainly the good elements in their outlook, since it is by virtue of these that they should be able to contribute towards a better world'.[15] There would seem to be a reaction here against a perception of too much emphasis on equality during the war; 'difference' is being re-emphasised (a point made in a number of the novels written at the time). Yet while the report does not suggest that women have a monopoly in what it defines as 'feminine' qualities, such as selflessness or dislike of cruelty, it does insist that women are the ones most likely to fulfil the need to inject 'feminine' qualities into the ruling ethos of the societies of their day, in the aftermath of World War Two. It is argued at one point,

> The deeply-rooted individualism of women makes them less likely to think in terms of masses at the cost of cruelty and cynical indifference towards the claims of the individual. A callous attitude to cruelty is the most horrible feature of the modern world. (p. 21)

Clearly, the human condition in general did not inspire much confidence in the conference. However, while delegates accept that many women have returned to the home after the war, they are not entirely conservative in their approach. They argue, like Gertrude Williams, for the housewife to be shown more respect, and for more part-time work to be made available for her. They argue for equal pay, more training and promotion for those in fulltime jobs, fairer tax provision for married women. They support contraception, and, while the majority finally come down in favour of traditional marriage, many see a role for what was termed 'companionate marriage', and there is strong support for single women who want to adopt children. However, their conclusions are not entirely optimistic:

> We came to the conclusion that the inequalities which still persist are due in the main to an attitude of mind – men's attitude to women, and a corresponding attitude of women to themselves; and such attitudes are not changed by heroic measures, but gradually and often almost imperceptibly.[...] The special sympathy and understanding which women so often acquire in their small circle should give them confidence to express their views more boldly and act up to them with more consistency whenever opportunity offers, both in private and public life. (p. 60)

So although there are some attempts to show masculinity and femininity as shifting their boundaries, what the report demonstrates is that attitudes of men and women to each other and to themselves remain much the same as ever; it seems that too little has changed since women gained the vote, twenty years earlier. Women, they conclude, still lack confidence; the traditional views on 'masculine' standards are still regarded as the norm. The delegates deplore, above all, women's lack of economic power, something that Gertrude Williams also deplores. They also deplore the lack of scope which, in practice, despite theoretical possibilities, they still see afforded to women when it comes to careers, although they do not undervalue women in the home. What they do stress is the importance of education for women, whatever their roles in life, if they are to have an impact on society as a whole. When reading this report, we can see that the conference has attempted to deal with women's responsibility to human society as a whole as well as with the improvement of women's lot. But, as I have argued elsewhere, the crisis of confidence in Western civilisation which resulted from World War Two clearly provides the motive power fuelling the debate.

Another revealing example of women's view of themselves is to be found in a special issue of the journal, *The Twentieth Century*, published towards the end of the 1950s, in 1958,[16] two years after the conference on 'Married Women out of Work'. In this 1958 periodical, as well as having a male editor who is a very good example of the conservative man coming to terms all too imperfectly with a changing view of women and their role in society, there are powerful contributions from many eminent women which clearly show the problems women are currently encountering in a society which is still, by and large, conservative about the proper role for women. Mary Warnock, for instance, seems to write positively when she asserts:

> Hostility to educated women may die hard, but it will presumably die in the end, except as an isolated matter of personal taste, and the reason for its death will be, more than anything else, the change in educated women themselves.[17]

Yet we soon find that she is addressing the stereotype of the 'unfeminine unwashed bluestocking', and insists that her female undergraduates may work hard, but on the whole enjoy their education as an extension of school; they very seldom seem to think that 'the whole point of coming up was to get a degree' (p.146). This style of argument comes perilously close to endorsing the image of the little woman, none too serious and slightly immature. The bulk of Warnock's argument stresses the value of education in marriage and child-rearing, which she assumes will be the primary goal of most of her Oxford women undergraduates; she is very concerned that there are still some of her women colleagues who fail to appreciate the 'non-academic qualities which people might have'. This is of course not to be scorned; but Warnock speaks from the top of her own profession, one of the few where women could have a satisfying career (which is not to say that they gained many chairs). Having, presumably, a fulfilling career herself, Warnock offers no answers to the points raised by Betty Miller, who sees the ablest young women of her day as continually frustrated in their attempts to use their skills to the full in the market-place beyond the university (a woman rarely reaches the top of her profession); such women tend, says Miller, to turn away in disgust, retreating into domesticity.[18] Nor does Warnock offer any response to the challenge which another contributor, Jenny Nasmyth, throws down. Nasmyth is an example of the kind of woman Miller has in mind, and she has indeed turned her back on a full professional life. She insists (although it is impossible to judge her tone) that, 'with few exceptions, able women are not as intellectually effective as able men',[19] and that work is just something a woman does until she learns how to be '100 per cent a woman in 1958', whatever that means (p. 143). Her argument receives not so much answers as disturbing echoes in Warnock's contribution. Instead, responses of a kind come from Naomi Lewis who, in the same issue, looks at the responsibility of literature in endorsing and perpetuating images of women as having some kind of inferior status.[20] In particular, she savages the kinds of stories that appear in popular women's magazines, positively insisting on marriage as a woman's ultimate goal. Then she invites us to look at the Letters section of these same magazines where we find 'letters from those who have taken this diet of Lit [sic] as a basis for life. [...] Nothing turns out like it does in books' (p. 125). In this, Lewis echoes Doris Lessing who, in *The Grass is Singing* (1950), portrays a woman who turns to an incompatible marriage, brain-washed by the expectations set up by magazine, romantic film and the chatter of similar-minded women around her.[21]

It is Jacquetta Hawkes's contribution on 'Women against the Bomb' which does actually show women taking action. She names a wide range of women present at the CND meeting she describes, including Rose Macaulay and Alice Meynell, together with messages of support sent by Elizabeth Bowen, Edith Evans, Barbara Hepworth, Moira Shearer and Edith Sitwell. She argues for CND that, 'while women are as various as men – of course they are', the meeting demonstrated that this 'at last is an issue which has brought the majority of thinking women a new unity'.[22] With hindsight, her 'at last' is somewhat poignant; it is still war together with its implications which is the binding force, not opposition as yet to the many inequities still endemic in a democratic society.

Yet clearly there are a good many women, despite these somewhat depressing publications, who can be seen as politically aware and active, and there are certainly a good number who can be seen as urging women to enter the struggle to better their lot and fulfil the hopes of the suffragettes. The popularity of writers like Storm Jameson, Doris Lessing, Elizabeth Taylor, Rose Macaulay, and Rosamond Lehmann, to name just a few, suggests that many readers during the late 1940s and 1950s were prepared to face the questions raised in their novels, and that the conservatisms of the society in which they lived were, albeit confusedly and sporadically, under pressure, even before the women's movements of the 1960s and 1970s. But it is important to see which priorities changed and which remained obstinately fixed over the decades, not only among men but among a fair proportion of women, if we are to understand some of the problems women faced when making decisions about their lives. For instance, Mrs Dighton Pollock's clear, suffragette view of women's way forward, expressed in an intelligent and optimistic pamphlet of 1929,[23] is all but lost sight of in the thirties and 1940s, as women contended, among other things, with the rise of Nazism; and the lessons of world war clearly influence the women's postwar conference. What seems to have happened is that many issues specific to women's needs and their perceived roles have been crowded out or at the least complicated by the events of the thirties and 1940s, and by the effect of these events on thinking in the 1950s. The novelist Ruth Adam, looking back through her life in the mid-1970s, concludes:

> A woman born at the turn of the century could have lived through two periods when it was her moral duty to devote herself, obsessively, to her children; three when it was her duty to society to neglect them; two when it was right to be seductively 'feminine' and three when it was a pressing social obligation to be the reverse; three separate periods in which she was a bad wife, mother and citizen for wanting to go out and earn her own living, and three others when she was an even worse wife, mother and citizen for not being eager to do so.[24]

New Wave feminism had a lot of barriers to break down – and even now, as we have daily proof, by no means all have given way.

Notes

1 As, for instance, in Nicola King, *Memory, Narrative, Identity: Remembering the Self* (Edinburgh: Edinburgh University Press, 2000).

2 Rebecca West, 'This I Believe', *This I Believe: The Personal Philosophies of One Hundred Thoughtful Men and Women in All Walks of Life*, ed. Edward Morgan (London: Hamish Hamilton, 1953) p. 100.

3 Phyllis Lassner, 'The Timeless Elsewhere of the Second World War: Rosamond Lehmann's *The Ballad and the Source* and Kate O'Brien's *The Last of Summer*', in Rod Mengham and N.H. Reeve, eds, *The Fiction of the Forties: Stories of Survival* (London: Palgrave, 2001) pp. 70–90. This collection of essays offers many valuable insights into the writing of the time.

4 See, for example, Vera Brittain's *Testament of Youth* (London: Gollancz,1933); Katharine Burdekin [Murray Constantine], *Swastika Night* [1937] (London: Gollancz, 1940). There are also admirable accounts of women's writing in Gill Plain, *Women's Fiction of the Second World War: Gender, Power and Resistance* (Edinburgh: Edinburgh University Press, 1996); Jenny Hartley, *Millions Like Us: British Women's Fiction of the Second World War* (London: Virago, 1997); and Phyllis Lassner, *British Women Writers of World War II: Battlegrounds of their Own* (London: Macmillan, 1998). See also Elizabeth Maslen, *Political and*

Social Issues in British Women's Fiction, 1928–1968 (London: Palgrave, 2001), which develops many of the above arguments.

5 Rose Macaulay, *The World My Wilderness* [1950] (London: Virago, 1983).

6 Storm Jameson, *The Other Side* (London: Macmillan, 1946); *The Black Laurel* (London: Macmillan, 1947); *The Hidden River* (London: Macmillan, 1955); *Adelphi*, New Series, Vols 23–4, pp. 127–8.

7 Storm Jameson, *The Moment of Truth* (London: Macmillan & Co., 1949).

8 Elizabeth Taylor, *At Mrs Lippincote's* [1945] (London: Virago, 1988). See also N.H. Reeve. 'Away for the Lighthouse: William Sansom and Elizabeth Taylor', in Mengham and Reeve, *The Fiction of the 1940s*, pp. 152–68. Betty Miller, *On the Side of the Angels* [1945] (London: Virago, 1985).

9 Elizabeth Taylor, *A Game of Hide and Seek* [1951] (London: Virago, 1986) p. 3. See also Doris Lessing, *Retreat to Innocence* (London: Michael Joseph, 1956), for a daughter who is utterly (and, in the event, disastrously) apolitical, in rebellion against her left-wing mother.

10 Deborah Philips and Ian Haywood, *Brave New Causes: Women in British Postwar Fictions* (London and Washington: Leicester University Press, 1998).

11 See Philips and Haywood, *Brave New Causes*, pp. 58–71; and, on Mills and Boon, pp. 80–88.

12 See Marion Shaw's classical article, 'Feminism and fiction between the wars: Winifred Holtby and Virginia Woolf', in Moira Monteith, ed., *Women's Writing: A Challenge to Theory* (Brighton: Harvester, 1986), pp. 171–91.

13 Gertrude Williams, *Women and Work* (London: Nicholson & Watson, 1945)

14 Victoria Sackville-West, *The Women's Land Army* (London: Michael Joseph, 1944), p. 91.

15 Olwen W. Campbell, ed., *The Report of a Conference on the Feminine Point of View* (London: Williams & Norgate, 1952), p. 15. See also my discussion of this report in *Political and Social Issues in British Women's Fiction 1928–1968*, pp. 186–9.

16 *The Twentieth Century*, August 1958, Vol. 164, No. 978: 'Special Number on Women'. See also my discussion of this issue in *Political and Social Issues in British Women's Fiction 1928–1968*, pp. 189–91.

17 Mary Warnock, 'Nymphs or Bluestockings?', *The Twentieth Century*, pp. 144–50, p. 144.

18 Betty Miller, 'Amazons and Afterwords', *The Twentieth Century*, pp. 126–35.

19 Jenny Nasmyth, 'The Wages of Freedom', *The Twentieth Century*, pp. 136–43, p. 138.

20 Naomi Lewis, 'In Spite of Lit', *The Twentieth Century*, pp. 114–25.

21 Doris Lessing, *The Grass is Singing* (London: Collins (Palladin), 1990).

22 Jacquetta Hawkes, 'Out and About: Women against the Bomb', *The Twentieth Century*, pp. 185–8, p. 188.

23 The Hon. Mrs Dighton Pollock, *The Woman of Today*, Routledge Introductions to Modern Knowledge, No. 14 (London: George Routledge & Sons, 1929).

24 Ruth Adam, *A Woman's Place: 1910–1975* (London: Chatto & Windus, 1975), p. 212.

2

Resisting Nostalgia: Elizabeth Bowen's *A World of Love*

Julia Briggs

> I wonder how you feel in the 1950s? personally I am enjoying this epoch – it is really the first time, it seems to me, in which I've enjoyed being 'grown up' as much as I expected to do when I was a child. The only sad thing is that, owing to the necessity to work so hard, I have altogether ceased to be able to write letters.[1]

Thus Elizabeth Bowen, writing to William Plomer from Bowen's Court, on 6 May 1958.

There is something of an air of adopted bravery, of somehow 'facing it out', in this letter which recalls one of her own characters, determined to be up-beat and cheerful in the face of accumulating difficulties. Her husband, Alan Cameron had died six years earlier, in 1952; little more than a year after she wrote this letter to Plomer, she took the difficult decision to give up Bowen's Court, her ancestral home, deep in the Irish countryside. Writing itself, and not merely letters, had become difficult for her. She found herself increasingly out of sympathy with the post-war, welfare state world – 'all these little middle-class Labour wets with their Old London School of Economics ties and their women', while the new cityscape also depressed her, 'the new soaring blocks of flats, the mushroom housing-estates ... the aching, bald uniformity of our urban surroundings, their soulless rawness',[2] though at the same time she could love New York for its vitality, its plugged-in quality.

For Bowen, the 1950s were overshadowed by the excitement and passion of the war years. Although her house at Clarence Terrace had been bombed, she told William Plomer that she had 'had such a good war',[3] living and writing at a pitch of great intensity, surrounded and assailed by heightened experiences that were a constant stimulus to her.

She found herself, she said, more at one with other people: 'In war, this feeling of slight differentiation [i.e. as a writer] was suspended: I felt one with, and just like, everyone else. Sometimes I hardly knew where I stopped and somebody else began ... Walls went down; and we felt, if not knew, each other. We all lived in a state of lucid abnormality.'[4] During the war, she became an ARP warden, and met and talked to ordinary local people. She also fell in love with a Canadian diplomat, Charles Ritchie, whom she met at a christening party given by the Buchans at Elsfield, near Oxford.

Out of the melodrama of her life during the war came a collection of short stories, *The Demon Lover* (1945), and arguably her greatest novel, *The Heat of the Day* (1949), which seems almost a culmination of the short stories, sharing with them the hallucinatory atmosphere and the theme of the impossibility of knowing another human being. In her final encounter with Robert, Stella, the novel's heroine, asks 'What is anyone? Mad, divided, undoing what they do',[5] in a distant echo of the short story 'Pink May', where a silly little woman betrays herself and can't understand how she has come to do so: 'Don't you see, can't you see there must have been *something*? Left to oneself, one doesn't ruin one's life!' [6] Though the setting is wartime London, we are here in Edgar Allan Poe country, a place of involuntary self-exposure and self-betrayal. In *The Heat of the Day*, as in the more experimental of her stories of wartime London, all certainties have been melted down, and the narrative of the love affair, grounded in the wordless communication of bodies, is matched and overlaid with the narrative of the spy story – the two are held in suspension, compared and contrasted, and the different learning curves associated with each is baffled and interrupted, giving place to a sequence of unanswered or unanswerable questions. These are epitomised in chapter 17, where Stella struggles to reply to the Coroner's questions about her relationship with Robert, leaving court with nothing but her reputation as 'a good witness' intact.[7] It's left to the reader to wonder what it is exactly that Stella has witnessed, and to recognise how dazzling is the bright light of being 'in love'. The two years of the love affair dissolve as if they had never been as both partners recognise the illusory nature of the trust, faith or merely suspension of disbelief on which their relationship had been grounded.[8] *The Heat of the Day*, as its title implies, is concerned with psychic heat, what Bennett and Royle in their book *Elizabeth Bowen and the Dissolution of the Novel*, term 'Thermo-writing', the writing of life tuned to the highest pitch of heat or intensity: 'There was a stir if not a kindling of exhausted senses, only now to be heated by being haunted ....'[9]

All Bowen's wartime writing is somehow 'heated by being haunted': camping out in her own bombed house, she described how the Nash Terrace, 'among the most civilised scenes on earth', is crumbling, its pediment fallen to the lawn. 'Illicitly, leading the existence of ghosts, we overlook the locked park.' Within, dahlias blaze, ducks mope unattended, and a boy cycles round and round, whistling "'It's a Happy, Happy day'. The tune was taken up by six soldiers digging out a bomb."[10] In the London of the Blitz, the lives of the living and the dead press upon one another. In Bowen's up-dated treatment of the ballad of 'The Unquiet Grave', a dead soldier from World War One carries off his former fiançée into the bombed-out streets of the Second World War. In her introduction to her collection, *The Demon Lover*, Bowen claims that 'the rising tide of hallucination' there reflected was 'the only diary I have kept' – 'This discontinuous writing, nominally "inventive" ... Transformed into images in the stories, there may be important psychological facts: if so, I did not realise their importance ... Through it all, one probably picked up more than can be answered for. I cannot answer for much that is in these stories, except to say that I know they are all true – true to the general life that was in me at the time'.[11]

Bowen thus authenticated her fictions from her own psycho-biography, and in doing so, she emphasised the inwardness of her war writing, its preoccupation with thought, memory and fictive worlds or shared dreams, imaginings that haunt other imaginations more powerfully, and perhaps more uncannily, than mere ghosts could do. The major story in the collection is thus 'Mysterious Kor', in which Pepita's imagination in the moon-drenched London park is focused not upon her soldier lover on leave, but upon Rider Haggard's imagined eternal city, from his novel, *She*. Broadcasting on this novel a few years later, Bowen explained 'I saw Kor before I saw London; ... I was inclined to see London as Kor with the roofs still on' (some of these had since, of course, been blown off). For the 12-year-old Bowen, *She* occupied something like the place that Tolkien's *Lord of the Rings* would hold for a younger generation: 'I read *She*, dreamed *She*, lived *She* for a year and a half ... After *She*, print was to fill me with apprehension. I was prepared to handle any book like a bomb.'[12] In her own story, it is the bombs that usher in Pepita's saving vision, for Kor is where she escapes to from the pain and sordidness of the present, and as the action progresses, and Arthur and Pepita return to the little flatlet she shares with Callie, it becomes steadily clearer that Pepita's imaginative escape reflects her stronger sensibilities, her deeper horror at the countless frustrations of day-to-day existence where, as Arthur says, 'To be human's to be at a dead loss'.[13] As the Yeatsian moon begins to set, so the powerful tide of imagination begins to wane in her.

In 'Mysterious Kor', it is the power of an identifiable text that simultaneously offers an escape from yet also a critique of actuality, reworking romantic or post-romantic debate about the function of art:

> A starlit or a moonlit dome disdains
> All that man is,
> All mere complexities,
> The fury and the mire of human veins.[14]

Elsewhere in Bowen's work, writing and documents become a generative source for the uncanny, heating (the imagination) through their haunting. It is tempting to read the stored or hoarded documents present in 'The Happy Autumn Fields' and *A World of Love* (though significantly missing, in her penultimate novel, *The Little Girls*) as figuring the return of the repressed, restoring a knowledge that had been concealed, only to resurface unexpectedly under the grotesque stimulus of the Blitz, as it dismantles skylines and lives, or the power of the heat wave that pervades *A World of Love*. If 'Mysterious Kor' is the most arresting treatment of this theme, 'The Happy Autumn Fields' is the most literally mysterious, a story possessing an extraordinarily clairvoyant quality, and with an uncanny twist in its tail. It begins with a Victorian family walking across ploughed fields one sunny September afternoon. The story is focused upon, though not quite related by Sarah, who is accompanied by her beloved sister Henrietta and her lover Eugene. As she walks between the two of them, Henrietta sings, heart-breakingly, and Sarah feels herself torn between her love for each of them. The tearing creates a different kind of tear into another fabric altogether, as Sarah gives place to Mary, apparently dreaming Sarah's story in a bombed-out house: 'her first thought was that it must have snowed'.[15] She awakes to find her lover Travis trying to persuade her to leave the house, but the twentieth century seems more like a dream than Sarah and the family to whom she longs to return. In an old leather box beside the bed are letters, photographs and a *carte de visite* of two young ladies whom Mary, with a sense of shock, recognises as Sarah and Henrietta. Having persuaded Travis to let her sleep a little longer, she slips back into the dream, where the family are now at home, and Sarah, who must say good-bye to Eugene, is full of presentiments that 'something may be going to happen'. A further explosion in the London of the Blitz wakes Mary: 'What has happened is cruel: I am left with a fragment torn out of a day, a day I don't even know where or when ... I cannot forget the climate of those hours'.[16]

Meanwhile, Travis has been reading through the letters from the old box, which Mary herself has not yet read, although in some unexplained way they seem to have occasioned her 'dreaming back'. There is no obvious connection between Mary and Sarah, who apparently never married and died young, and the uncanny twist lies in Travis's report that 'some friend', evidently Eugene, was killed riding back after a visit: 'Fitzgeorge wonders, and says he will always wonder, what made the horse shy in those empty fields'. His words recall Henrietta's hysterical warning to Eugene, that 'Whatever tries to come between me and Sarah becomes nothing ... You do not even know what you are trying to do. It is *you* who are making something terrible happen ...',[17] but also leaving us to wonder about Mary's presence in the story. Is she a witness, merely, or something more sinister?

'The Happy Autumn Fields', first published in November 1944, is a significant precursor to *A World of Love*, begun in 1952 and published in 1955. In the preface to her collection, *The Demon Lover*, Bowen wondered 'whether in a sense all wartime writing is not resistance writing? Personal life here, too, put up its own resistance to the annihilation that was threatening it – war. Everyone here, as is known, reads more: and what was sought in books – old books, new books – was the communicative touch of personal life. People whose homes had been blown up went to infinite lengths to assemble bits of themselves ... from the wreckage'[18] – or, as 'The Happy Autumn Fields' suggests, bits of other people's lives.

In a key essay of 1950, originally entitled 'Once Upon a Yesterday', and retitled 'The Bend Back' in Hermione Lee's key collection of Bowen's prose writings, *The Mulberry Tree*, Bowen examines nostalgia, not as a 'literary concoction' but 'a prevailing mood – to which, it may be, writers yield too much ... What is the matter with us, it may be asked ... Does our century fail us, or we it ? ... But confidence was broken by 1914: from then on, decline of love for the present went with the loss of faith in it.'[19] Later in the same essay she discusses the hankering for Victorian 'solidness, its faith, its energetic self-confidence, its domestic glow',[20] qualities evoked in 'The Happy Autumn Fields', only to disintegrate, within the story itself, and to be dismissed, perhaps as a vision conjured up in reaction to the dissolute nature of war-torn London, rather as Pepita had conjured up her vision of 'Mysterious Kor', as a kind of shield.

For Bowen herself, the more heroic act of resistance-writing lay not so much in her war stories but in the novel that followed: *A World of Love* focuses upon an exorcism of the past at a point in Bowen's own life when her yearning for the past must have oppressed her most painfully. If her wartime years were full of passion and creativity, her postwar years were increasingly disillusioned. Just how much she could hate some aspects of the modern world is reflected in a strange little fable called 'Gone Away', written in 1946. Here a certain Mr Van Winkle returns from the past to find the Vicar and the village ladies confined to 'The Reserve', 'demarcated by high-wire fencing, Whipsnade type'.[21] Beyond lies the soulless modern city of Brighterville, with its 'factories, sportsdromes, cafeterias and culture centres', now totally abandoned by its inhabitants who have fled, lemming-like, to the sea. Yet although her next novel includes elements of nostalgia, it is ultimately an exercise in resisting nostalgia. The past is, of course, directly implicated in an evocation of Bowen's Anglo-Ireland, for Ireland until recently had a habit of looking rather like England had looked some ten, or even 20 or more years earlier. And the past is embodied in the lost lover, Guy, killed in the First World War, one of the unforgotten dead who press so upon the living. Guy's love letters are rediscovered by the heroine, Jane, in the attics of an old Irish house, Montefort, for a while re-igniting his ghost in an atmosphere that is at once haunted and over-heated. Yet though the past is resuscitated, it is also laid, for this is the story of an exorcism, and not only within the novel, for Lilia and Antonia, Guy's former lovers: perhaps it was also an exorcism for its author, who four years later decided to sell Bowen's Court.

Her essay, 'The Bend Back' anticipates *A World of Love* in surprising detail. For Bowen, there are two routes back to 'the better days' – that of direct and that of factitious memory; remembering one's own childhood and reading about childhood restores us to the 'early morning' of our lives. Here, 'We are made to behold a landscape just after sunrise, a tract in which every feature not only stands up gleaming but casts a shadow which is unique, distinct...The semi-mystical topography of childhood seems to be universal'.[22] It includes streams, woods, thickets, hideout, attic, grandmother's treasure box and so on – I have slightly selected from Bowen's list, but precisely this dawn opens *A World of Love*, and this topography features largely in it. It is inside the cliché of the chest in the attic that Jane discovers an old muslin dress, and the bunch of letters jumps out of it. The novel opens theatrically, echoing Bowen's essay: 'The sun rose on a landscape still pale with the heat of the day before. There was no haze, but a sort of coppery burnish ... This light ...brought into being a new world – painted, expectant, empty, intense ... '[23] – southern Ireland during a heat wave (perhaps Bowen was recalling the oppressively hot summer of 1947). Her writing here is highly self-conscious – the reference to 'the heat of the day before' alluding to the title of her previous novel.

Clearly not only the topography, but many of the features of Montefort are intended to suggest nostalgic re-creation, and indeed, within the narrative itself, Guy's love-letters themselves attract Jane's attention through their referentiality, their redescription of Montefort. Her eye is initially drawn to the word 'obelisk',[24] within a text that is otherwise scarcely revealed to us, except for the sentence *'I thought ... if only YOU had been here!'*. As the narrator explains, 'The particular secret of the place where Jane lay was that it was pre-inhabited. An ardent hour of summer had gone by here – yes, here, literally where she was, to her certain knowledge ... it had been June then too.'[25] The events that follow take place over three days, as the beautiful 20 year-old Jane, her mother Lilia (once Guy's fiancée), and Guy's cousin Antonia bicker over who shall have the letters. In this overheated, haunted atmosphere, Guy appears to each of them in turn, and with his appearance, the expectations he had aroused, in some cases forty years earlier, are finally laid to rest, but the story is interestingly complicated by the fact that Antonia and Lilia have always known that there was 'someone else' in Guy's life, since the occasion when they saw him off on his final leave at Charing Cross Station,[26] and it is this unknown other to whom the love letters seem to have been addressed, though the logic of the book suggests that, unconsciously they were somehow addressed to Jane, who responds as if to a living suitor.

A World of Love is intricately claustrophobic, as the big houses of Ireland were, and as Montefort is within the novel. Yet a few sentences also suggest that Bowen's largely domestic tale was also intended as a fable with wider implications. Jane, as we are told, had 'an instinctive aversion from the past' – 'the world was in a crying state of exasperation ... The passions and politics of her family so much resembled those of the outside world that she made little distinction between the two.' In the past 'lay the root of all evil! – this continuous tedious business of received grievances, not-to-be settled old scores. Yes, so far as she was against anything, she was against the past.'[27]

Part of the family's unresolved problems are attributable to the dead who will not lie down, the neglected dead, and in particular those who, like Guy, died in battle, their lives meaninglessly interrupted at their outset: 'Meantime, another war had peopled the world with another generation of the not-dead, overlapping and crowding the living's senses still more with that sense of unlived lives. Antonia and others younger were creatures of an impossible time, breathing in wronged air – air either too empty or too full ....'[28]

Phyllis Lassner, in her writings on Bowen, has taught us to listen to the political resonances in Bowen's writing, here made explicit through 'the passions and politics' of the family and their transposition into the wider world beyond.[29] The long-drawn-out grievances and silences, the barely hidden domestic hostilities of the novel refer, among other things, to the Cold War. Here the cold war within the family, is acted out during a heat wave, carrying with it all the accumulated resentments, misunderstandings and self-deceptions that characterised international politics during the years after the war. Guy's letters, passed from hand to hand, are unreadable and unread by all but Jane, who must read them to overcome her aversion to the past, must fall in love with the past a little in order to find love at all. Only when Lilia and Antonia confront the past itself, in the form of Guy's ghost, are they released and able to begin afresh. Lilia, who has seemed the most emotionally becalmed of them all, not only goes to get her hair cut at Miss Francie's salon in Clonmore – she also decides that, she will, after all, visit London with Antonia on the grounds that 'the week will seem long ... to those left behind'.[30] In this way, she renews her compact with her husband, Fred. It is Jane's story that ends spectacularly, as she falls in love with Vesta Latterly's cast-off lover at Shannon airport, in the last line of the book.

Yet, as the narrator acknowledges, it is the small redemptive shifts, restricted in their significance, that are the hardest to achieve: 'A little redemption ... was felt. The alteration in feeling, during the minutes in which the two had been here, was an event, though followed by deep vagueness as to what they should in consequence do or say. Impossible is it for persons to be changed when the days that they still have to live stay so much the same – as for these two, what could now be their hope but survival? Survival seemed more possible now, for having spoken to one another had been an act of love.'[31] The future is not implausibly rosy for them – indeed it includes the comic-sinister figure of Maud, Jane's younger sister, with her imaginary companion, or possibly supernatural familiar, Gay David. As the narrator observes, 'Few are children for whom one feels no concern. Maud happened, however, to be one of them. Solicitude, in this case, went into reverse – what might the future not have to fear from her?'[32] So, in its characteristically indirect way, Bowen's novel *A World of Love* seems to be a coded message not only to herself, instructing her to confront the past and its ghosts and move on, but also to a wider world, to abandon its accumulated grievances and create something new – a message still relevant to Northern Ireland today, quite as much as when this book was written, half a century ago.

Notes

1 Elizabeth Bowen, *The Mulberry Tree*, ed. Hermione Lee (1986, London: Vintage, 1999), pp. 209–10. This essay is dedicated to Phyllis Lassner, the real expert.
2 Ibid., pp. 207, 59.
3 Ibid., p. 206.
4 Ibid., p. 95.
5 Elizabeth Bowen, *The Heat of the Day* (1949; London: Vintage, 1999), p. 287.
6 *The Collected Stories of Elizabeth Bowen*, intro. Angus Wilson (London: Penguin Books, 1983), p. 718.
7 *The Heat of the Day*, pp. 302–5.
8 Ibid., p. 272.
9 Andrew Bennett and Nicholas Royle, *Elizabeth Bowen and the Dissolution of the Novel* (London: Macmillan, 1995); Elizabeth Bowen, *A World of Love* (1955; London: Vintage, 1999), p. 67.
10 *The Mulberry Tree*, p. 24.
11 Ibid, p. 99.
12 Ibid., pp. 249, 250.
13 *Collected Stories*, p. 739.
14 'Byzantium', *Collected Poems of W.B. Yeats* (London: Macmillan, 1950), p. 280.
15 *Collected Stories*, pp. 675–6.
16 Ibid, p. 684
17 Ibid., pp. 685, 683.
18 *The Mulberry Tree*, p. 97.
19 Ibid., p. 54.
20 Ibid., p. 57.
21 *Collected Stories*, p. 761.
22 *The Mulberry Tree*, p. 55.
23 *A World of Love*, p. 9.
24 Ibid., p. 34.
25 Ibid., p. 48.
26 Ibid., p. 139.
27 Ibid., pp. 34, 35.
28 Ibid., p. 45.
29 Phyllis Lassner, *Elizabeth Bowen* (London: Macmillan, 1990); *British Women Writers of the Second World War* (New York: St Martin's, 1998).
30 *A World of Love*, pp. 89, 126.
31 Ibid., p. 104.
32 Ibid., p. 114.

3
'Criminal Desires': Women Writing Crime 1945–60

Linden Peach

Women's crime writing flourished in the period 1945–60, not least because established authors such as Agatha Christie, Margery Allingham and Ngaio Marsh continued to produce fiction featuring the detectives for which they had become famous. But is this work, or at least some of it, different from that which was written before the war? In this essay, I probe this question with reference to some of the most worthy or controversial crime texts by women, including, Christie's *They Do It With Mirrors* (1952) and *4.50 from Paddington* (1957), Josephine Tey's *The Franchise Affair* (1948), and Ngaio Marsh's *Opening Night* (1951).

With the obvious exception of Miss Marple, the investigators in women's crime fiction after the war, as before it, are men. Nevertheless, crime writing during these years, even in the case of the well-established figures, is characterised by a pronounced tension between innovation and conservatism that seems analogous of the wider postwar social and cultural confusion. The most interesting texts challenge and interrogate conventional symbolic categories; they raise issues about traditional notions of England and Englishness, regional identities, and the nature of gender identity. But they usually do so within a somewhat conservative aesthetic.

One of the first significant works of this period, Agatha Christie's Hercule Poirot mystery *The Hollow* (1946), encapsulates in its title the unease with conventional notions of Englishness that characterises much postwar women's crime writing. I say 'significant' because the novel was adapted for the stage by Christie herself and opened at the Fortune Theatre in London in June 1951. On a literal level, the title is the name of the big house which is the scene of the murder. Metaphorically, it emphasises the perceived emotional emptiness and lack of direction of postwar, and postempire, England. This is analogised by the Angatell family – Sir Henry is himself an ex-colonial governor. From one perspective, the murder of John Christow may be read as signifying a refusal to embrace postwar scientific Britain as he is a London-based scientist.

In fact, the big house becomes increasingly a symbol of the confusion and complexity of postwar Britain in Christie's 1950s fiction. This is evident in the way the Italian granddaughter in *They Do It With Mirrors* (1952) describes the large English house, Stonygates, to which Miss Marple goes to stay with Carrie Louise whom she met in Florence as a girl. The house is now the base for an education project in the rehabilitation of young delinquents where the family live alongside the boys together with psychologists and teachers:

> It was, as Gina had said, a vast edifice of Victorian Gothic – a kind of temple to Plutocracy. Philanthropy had added to it in various wings and outbuildings that, while not positively dissimilar in style, had robbed the structure as a whole of any cohesion or purpose.[1]

It is hard not to read beyond the literal text here and see a description of Britain 'robbed' of its structure and lacking 'cohesion and purpose'. Miss Marple's perspective on the gardens, metaphorically the Garden of England perhaps, implies that the postwar period is ushering in a utilitarian outlook with little respect for the past:

> Their condition distressed her. They had once been an ambitiously set out achievement. Clumps of rhododendrons, smooth slopes of lawns, massed borders of herbaceous plants, clipped boxhedges surrounding a formal rose garden. Now all was largely derelict, the lawns raggedly mown, the borders full of weeds with tangled flowers struggling through them, the paths moss-covered and neglected. The kitchen gardens, on the other hand, enclosed by red brick walls, were prosperous and well stocked. That, presumably, was because they had a utility value. (p. 536)

In the later novel *4.50 from Paddington*, the big house which is the crime scene displays similar signs of neglect. Acquired by a family that has made its money from biscuits, it is approached through an 'imposing pair of vast iron gates', the lodge is 'completely derelict', 'a long winding drive [leads] through large gloomy clumps of rhododendrons up to the house', and 'the stone steps in front of the door could have done with attention and the gravel sweep was green with neglected weeds'.[2] But while in *They Do It With Mirrors* the mansion signifies a lack of cohesion and direction, here the neglected house is an indictment of 1950s capitalism. In this text, Miss Marple proclaims: 'The trouble is ... that people are greedy. Some people. That's often you know, how things start. You don't start with murder, with wanting to do murder, or even thinking of it. You start by being greedy, by wanting more than you're going to have' (p. 704). In its quarrel with 1950s utilitarianism, the text almost slips into Gothic horror. On arriving at the front door, Lucy Eyelesbarrow, who is there at Miss Marple's instigation, has to pull on 'an old-fashioned wrought-iron bell' and, in keeping with gothic melodrama, 'its clamour sound[s] echoing away inside' (p. 556).

Basing her case largely but not exclusively on *They Do It With Mirrors*, Anne-Marie Taylor argues that Christie is sceptical of the postwar welfare state.[3] The scepticism and cultural pessimism, however, are attributed to various characters to whom Miss Marple herself does not always fully disclose her response. Ruth Van Rydock, for example, who first detects that something is wrong at Stonygates and encourages her friend to visit, believes: 'Soon, I expect, the fashionable thing to do will be not to educate your children, preserve their illiteracy carefully until they're eighteen' (p. 521). Gina complains:

> It's pretty ghastly, really ... A sort of Gothic monstrosity ... But it's fun, too, in a way. Only of course everything's madly earnest, and you tumble over psychiatrists everywhere underfoot. Enjoying themselves madly. Rather like Scout-masters, only worse. The young criminals are rather pets, some of them. One showed me how to diddle locks with a bit of wire and one angelic-faced boy gave me a lot of points about coshing people. (pp. 524–5)

At one level, Stonygates, the educational project apart, might be taken to connote nostalgia for an apparently stable, prewar England that never really existed. At another, it represents the way in which ostensibly insoluble, postwar social problems are giving rise to solutions which are short term and unconvincing. But the novel does suggest that there can be no return to the past. As Miss Marple herself advises: 'I'm afraid ... that we have all to the face the fact that conditions are different' (p. 543). Gina's story about the criminal expertise that the boys have tried to pass on to her, and presumably to each other, denotes a wider cultural pessimism about the way the country, and young people in particular, are deemed to have changed. Again it is Ruth Van Rydock who articulates the uncompromising viewpoint: 'Juvenile Delinquency – that's what is the rage nowadays. All these young criminals and potential criminals' (p. 515).

II

In this somewhat pessimistic social climate, it is not surprising that the criminal in Tey's *The Franchise Affair* is a teenage schoolgirl and that the murderer in Christie's *Crooked House* (1949) turns out to be a child. *They Do It With Mirrors* might appear to be a conservative novel in that it challenges the environmental explanation which was current at the time for criminal behaviour among the young, but it also takes issue with the concomitant myth that mothers are responsible for the way their children turn out. Gina muses: 'I mean they think it's repressed desires and disordered home life and their mothers getting off with soldiers and all that. I don't really see it myself because some people have had awful home lives and yet have managed to turn out quite all right' (p. 525). By implication, although Gina does not agree, it is widely believed that it is women 'getting off with soldiers' rather than the loose behaviour of the men that is to blame for some 'awful home lives'. This viewpoint is given more overt expression in Tey's *The Franchise Affair*.

The Franchise Affair, too, is generally regarded as a conservative novel. The status quo in a small, sleepy English country town is disrupted when a schoolgirl, Betty Kane, accuses an elderly woman and her daughter who live by themselves, of kidnapping and beating her. The status quo is restored when their house, The Franchise, is burned to the ground and, after being cleared of the offence, they are forced to flee to Canada. But, while it is less conservative in some respects than it might appear on a cursory reading, the novel suggests that the casual relationships that some women had during the war have led to sins visited on postwar society through their children. If Betty Kane is a victim at all the text suggests, she is the victim of her mother's casual moral behaviour during the Blitz, commented upon by the local tobacconist: 'But she was a bad mother and a bad wife, that's flat; and no one ever said anything to the contrary.' [4] The effect of this, of course, is to lend support to a dominant postwar discourse that a woman's place was in the home, as a good wife and mother, and that the moral and social life of the nation depended upon this.

Alison Light argues that the post-First World War years saw 'a move away from formerly heroic and officially masculine public rhetorics of national destiny ... to an Englishness at once less imperial and more inward-looking, more domestic and more private – and in terms of prewar standards, more "feminine"'.[5] A similar process of feminisation might be seen as projected more controversially by late 1940s and 1950s crime writing on to postwar Britain. Johnnie Restarick in *They Do It With Mirrors* is the worst kind of feminised man, at least in Mrs Van Rydock's assessment of him: 'Johnnie was a selfish, pleasure-loving, lazy hound ... All Johnnie wanted was to live soft. He wanted Carrie Louise to go to the best dressmakers and have yachts and cars and enjoy herself with him' (p. 514). In *The Hollow*, John Christow is not only a scientist, but is feminised as a victim of trauma who is helped by his mistress, Henrietta. She joins him at the house, shortly before his murder, along with his wife, and an impoverished relative Midge. The potential conflict between these two opposing female claims on him is exacerbated by the arrival of his former lover, Veronica. In itself, however, there is little positive about the strong female presence in *The Hollow*. The monument that Henrietta makes of John after his death would seem, in an understandably cryptic mode, to exemplify that strain of postwar thought that wished to preserve the past. John's wife, on the other hand, in her total commitment to her male heirs, would appear to exhibit the postwar trend that insisted on defining women in terms of the maternal and inculcated them into privileging the male over the female.

Although individual eccentricity is a recurring trope in crime writing around this time – Margery Allingham's *More Work for the Undertaker* (1948) features the rather bizarre Palinodes family, and Gina in *They Do It With Mirrors* describes the Serrocolds as 'bats' (p. 524) – it is less important than eccentricity in the structure of the family itself. At times writers seem to be vying with each other to conjure the most complicated web of family relations. Reflecting, cryptically rather than directly, the number of families having to deal with loss after the war, many of these families are constructed around significant absences.

The Serrocolds in *They Do It With Mirrors* (1952) are an extreme example of a family that has evolved around loss. However, somewhat unexpectedly, if we bear in mind the number of men killed in the war, this text is written around the absence and restoration of a female presence. Carrie Louise marries into a male-dominated family unit, the Gulbrandsens, as the name suggests (Gulbrandsons); she takes as her husband a widower with three grown-up sons. They adopt a two-year-old girl, Pippa, before Carrie Louise has a daughter of her own, Mildred.

Thus, Carrie Louise on three different levels, marriage, adoption and childbirth, restores the female presence to the Gulbrandsen family. Although in time Mildred marries a man in ill health and older than herself who leaves her a widow, Pippa and Mildred's life stories reinforce the concern with restoring the female presence. Mildred's husband's death brings her back to Stonygates. Pippa, having married an Italian, the Marchese di San Severiano, dies in childbirth and her daughter Gina is brought to live with her grandmother at Stonygates. Carrie Louise's second marriage repeats the pattern of the first; she marries a divorcee who already has two sons by a second marriage. This husband deserts her and she marries the idealist and philanthropist Lewis Serrocold.

III

Albeit cautiously, *They Do It With Mirrors* may be seen as projecting back to postwar Britain some of its anxieties, preconceptions and prejudices about women. In this respect, the title may well be taken as referring to the way in which at least one of its female characters appears to construct herself, as much as on another level she is culturally constructed, in the role of 'other'. Throughout the text, Gina, who when we first encounter her surprises Miss Marple with her appearance – in 'dirty corduroy slacks and a simple shirt open at the neck' – is a source of anxiety both for men and conservative women. Mildred, who looks 'exactly like a Canon's widow, respectable and slightly dull' (p. 532), criticises her because in her relations with men she is slippery and unpredictable: 'She does nothing but make trouble. One day she encourages the young man [Stephen Restarick] and the next day she snubs him' (p. 534). But half English and half Italian, Gina's Latin temperament enables her to elude the symbolic which in Mildred's acceptance of it defines and limits her. Gina's husband, the patriarchal law, is both suspicious of her and confused by her. His view of a wife is 'one who used to go along with the old pioneers, ready for anything, hardship, unfamiliar country, danger, strange surroundings ...' (p. 638). Although offering a more exciting version of womanhood than that embodied by Mildred, it is nevertheless not so dissimilar from one dominant, postwar expectation of women; a woman's place is with her husband. But, in contradistinction to this, Gina is associated with 'that eerie half light when objects lose their reality and take on the fantastic shapes of nightmare' (p. 637). This flirtation with an almost Gothic visioning of female sexuality, although not allowed its full reign, is not entirely displaced by the novel's conservative denouement in which

Gina decides to accompany her husband to the United States, vowing to 'forget all about Stonygates and Italy and all my girlish past and become a hundred per cent American' (p. 653).

In her theatricality, and shadowiness, Gina is very different from Christie's later 1950s representation of female independence, Lucy Eyelesbarrow in *4.50 from Paddington* and much closer to Tey's Betty Kane to whom I shall return in a moment. In a text which is critical of utilitarian Britain, Lucy achieves a pointedly entrepreneurial kind of independence, indicating the shift which occurred in Christie's own approach to female independence in the 1950s. Despite having taken a First in Mathematics at Oxford, Lucy eschews what promises to be 'a distinguished academic career' for her own business in which she accepts short-term, lucrative contracts as a housekeeper. At one level, Christie seems to compromise her portrait of the entrepreneurial female. Despite her intellectual brilliance, Lucy chooses to pursue what is conventionally women's work. But Lucy does resist another convention, the permanent housekeeper. In this sense, she may be seen as wriggling out from under the symbolic that tries to limit and define her: 'But Lucy had no intention of being a permanency, nor would she book herself for more than six months ahead. And within that period, unknown to her clamouring clients, she always kept certain free periods which enabled her either to take a short luxurious holiday ... or to accept any position at short notice that happened to take her fancy...' (p. 552). Lucy not only challenges social expectations regarding women, and professional domestic women, but the socioeconomic symbolic order in which women are expected to exchange themselves totally for a culturally and economically defined role.

The Franchise Affair, too, might be regarded as reflecting back to postwar society its anxieties and prejudices about independent women. Within its conservative framework, the novel raises disturbing issues and subjects. Even if, as in *They Do It With Mirrors*, they are not pursued to their ultimate conclusion, they are not entirely eradicated by the denouement. Even before being charged with abduction, Marion Sharpe and her mother are perceived by the community as a disturbing presence. Like the mother and daughter in Poe's 'Murders in the Rue Morgue', they arouse suspicion and gossip because they live alone without, apparently, the need for men. Even Robert Blair, their most sympathetic advocate, believes: 'The old woman had a fanatic's face if ever he saw one; and Marion Sharpe herself looked as if a stake would be her natural prop if stakes were not out of fashion' (p. 12). This comes from a man who later purports to be outraged by the way the community see the women as 'Foreign bitches' (p. 129). The threat posed by their independence and self-sufficiency is underlined by the small but not innocuous detail that they have taken over a property that had been owned by a man as long as anyone can remember. They represent an element of discontinuity in a text that regularly plays the tropes of continuity and discontinuity against each other.

Suspicion of independent women extends to Betty Kane herself who is the key disruptive presence in the text. Initially presented as the victim of a crime, she turns out to be the perpetrator. As a schoolgirl who picks up a business man, Chadwick, in the lounge bar of the Midlands Hotel with the aplomb of an experienced prostitute, she is one of the most slippery signifiers in the novel. But she draws into the work several motifs that increasingly figured in the representation of young women and crime in popular culture between the wars: the 'unadjusted girl', and the schoolgirl.

The concept of the 'unadjusted girl' acquired popularity in the 1920s and 1930s and can be found in popular culture right through to the 1950s. This motif dominated the way in which criminality among young women was conceived during this period and has never been fully challenged. It can be traced back to post-First World War criminology written by men and is associated with a text published in America in 1923 and in Britain in 1924, *The Unadjusted Girl* by W. I. Thomas. Thomas, who is associated with the Chicago school of criminology, argued that

> Fifty years ago we recognized, roughly speaking, two types of women, the one completely good and the other completely bad, – what we now call the old-fashioned girl and the girl who had sinned and been outlawed. At present we have several intermediate types, – the occasional prostitute, the charity girl, the demi-virgin, the equivocal flapper ... [who] represent the same movement, which is a desire to realize their wishes under the changing social conditions.[6]

The Franchise Affair explicitly invokes the concept of the unadjusted girl. The key perspective on Betty's criminality is provided by the barrister Kevin whose ideas unequivocally echo Thomas's: 'crime begins in egoism, inordinate vanity ... with an egoism like Betty Kane's there is no adjustment. She expects the world to adjust itself to her' (p. 222). Betty is contrasted with 'a normal girl ... [who could work things out] in sobs or sulks or being difficult, or deciding that she was going to renounce the world and go into a convent, or half a dozen other methods that the adolescent uses in the process of adjustment' (p. 222).

Betty Kane, though, is not simply an 'unadjusted girl' but a schoolgirl. The plot of *The Franchise Affair* has elements of schoolgirl fiction in which adventurous young women become involved in actual or threatened kidnapping, with isolated houses, and with gypsies. Not only does Tey's plot revolve around kidnapping, but the isolation of The Franchise is stressed throughout, and Marion Sharpe is 'given to bright silk handkerchiefs which accentuated her gipsy swarthiness' (p. 9). Given the cultural significance which the schoolgirl acquired in school stories from the turn of the century, its conflation with the trope of the 'unadjusted girl' was inevitable. Sally Mitchell argues: 'The new girl – no longer a child, not yet a (sexual) adult preoccupied a provisional free space. Girls' culture suggested new ways of being, new modes of behaviour, and new attitudes that were not yet acceptable for adult women.'[7]

As a schoolgirl, Betty is a criminalised version of a definition of girlhood, and ultimately womanhood, prevalent in interwar schoolgirl fiction. Gill Frith points out that, in this world of girls, 'to be assertive, physically active, daring, ambitious, is not a source of tension ... girls "break bounds", have adventures, transgress rules ... codes [are] broken, secret passages explored, disguises penetrated'.[8] The anxiety surrounding such a depiction of womanhood is evident in the concomitant shift in schoolgirl stories in the 1930s to which Rosemary Auchmuty draws attention.[9] These anxieties were popularised while Josephine Tey was working on *The Franchise Affair* in Ronald Searle's St Trinian cartoons. Published initially at the rate of one a month, they were first published as a book in 1947. As is clear from the ironic title of the second book, *The Female Approach* (1949), they portrayed the boarding school girl as not only violent and out of control, swigging gin and smoking cigars, but as embodying – quite literally in their short skirts and suspenders – an unadjusted, female identity and sexuality that are to be feared. Not coincidentally, the first novel that Ronald Searle wrote, with D.B. Wyndham, published a few years later, is called *The Terror of St Trinians*.

History has given Betty Kane's name an ironic inflection. In the 1950s, it became the name of Batgirl, an athletic, independent and adventurous eighteen-year old who accompanied her aunt, Batwoman, on her exploits. But the ironic link between Tey's Betty Kane and Batgirl is not coincidental. The name Betty Kane is one to conjure with. It would have been impossible for a 1940s reader not to think of Betty in relation to Grim Natwick's Betty Boop, the female protagonist in a series of pre-censorship American cartoons for adults including *She Wronged Him Right* (1934). By 1930s standards, Betty Boop, in short skirts and revealing cleavage, was an 'unadjusted girl'. She epitomised the promiscuity and liberated female sexuality that after the 1933 Hollywood code were repressed. Then Betty became a 'good girl', her skirts got longer, her garter disappeared, and eventually she became a housewife. What is especially intriguing given Betty's surname, however, is that Betty Boop was based on a Broadway singer of the 1920s whose name was also Kane. Helen Kane epitomised female sexuality in the Roaring Twenties with her song 'I Wanna be Loved by You' (1928).

Betty Boop's legacy can be found in the sexual and erotic films of the 1930s and 1940s featuring platinum blondes and cool seductresses. In this respect, too, Betty Kane is her heir. When Mrs Chadwick describes finding Betty in their holiday home, she recalls discovering her 'lying on the bed in the kind of negligée you used to see in vamp films about ten years ago ... Terribly nineteen-thirty, the whole set-up' (p. 244). The language – 'vamp', 'tramp', 'floo[sey]' – emphasises why she finds Betty different from all her husband's other women; she is the 'unadjusted girl', the 'occasional prostitute'. Betty's undressed but made-up body is both the cultural 'other' to the schoolgirl, yet also an 'other' within the schoolgirl.

In the novel as a whole, Betty Kane draws attention to the instability of numerous signifiers of respectability, including the lounge bar where she picks up Chadwick itself. The lounge waiter at the Midland so much as admits that the hotel's afternoon tea is something of a sham: 'But why the Midland, where the tea was the usual dowdy and expensive hotel exhibit, when she could wallow in cakes elsewhere?' (p. 111).

Why indeed? The lounge and its traditional afternoon teas are a facade behind which the hotel is something of a frontier location for an itinerant and morally more casual clientele than its locals. Here the boundaries between 'cheap' and 'respectable', 'prostitute' and 'client', 'professional' and 'occasional prostitute', 'child' and 'young woman' are blurred. Early in the novel, we learn that behind Milford's respectable High Street is Sin Lane. One version of its name accepts that it has always been Sin Lane while another suggests that 'Sin Lane' is a corruption of 'Sand Lane'. The debate, conflating sin with the instability of sand, encapsulates the text's primary concern with employing crime to destabilise society's so-called respectable conventions.

V

The slipperiness of signifiers in the case of gender, sexuality and identity is played out most convincingly in Ngaio Marsh's *Opening Night* (1951).

The novel concerns a protagonist with a deliberately androgynous name, Martyn Tame, who is introduced to us as a genderless and historyless character wandering in London. As Susan Rowland points out: 'The reader's orientation in the story is structured through Martyn's developing self.'[10] However, not only do we witness Martyn's entry into the symbolic – she is revealed to be an out-of-work actor – but the text explores how, as the late twentieth-century theorist Judith Butler argued, gender is constituted in performativity:

> Becoming a gender is an impulsive yet mindful process of interpreting a cultural reality laden with sanctions, taboos and prescriptions. The choice to assume a certain kind of body, to live or wear one's body a certain way, implies a world of already established corporeal styles. Less a radical act of creation, gender is a tacit project to renew a cultural history in one's own corporeal terms.[11]

In linking the performative nature of gender identity with the theatre, *Opening Night* is comparable to *They Do It With Mirrors*. In the latter, not only does Miss Marple encourage everyone to think of Stonygates as a stage, but also Gina is associated with its theatrical production. Stephen Restarick advises her that she has a 'flair for theatrical designing' (p. 532), and she is inseparable from 'the shadows by the theatre' (p. 637). As if to reinforce the connection between the construction of the female self and performativity in *Opening Night*, Martyn is taken on as a dresser before she assumes the pivotal role in the play.

Marsh, however, subjects the roles of agency and appropriation in the assumption of femininity to more scrutiny than Christie in *They Do It With Mirrors*. In doing so, she displays more engagement with the emancipatory possibilities in the performative nature of identity. Admittedly, the cultural construction of women as Woman is emphasised from the outset of Marsh's novel – when she is approached by one of the women exiting from the stage door, Trixie O'Sullivan, Martyn finds herself looking at 'for the second time that day, a too-large face, over-painted, with lips that twisted downwards, tinted lids, and thickly mascarated lashes'.[12] But, rather than simply oppose natural womanhood with the notion of womanhood as a masquerade, the text implies that there is freedom and possibility for women in the perfomativity of masquerade. Although, the tensions opened up within this liminal space are encapsulated in the increasingly violent relationship between Gay Gainsford and her dresser, the theatre itself serves to imply that it is in the possibilities of the feminine, freed from its restrictive and restricted cultural embodiment, that female identity is truly located:

> There is perhaps nothing that gives one so strong a sense of theatre from the inside as the sound of invisible players in action. The disembodied and remote voices, projected at an unseen mark, the uncanny quiet off-stage, the smells and the feeling that the walls and the dust listen, the sense of shimmering expectancy; all these together make a corporate life so that the theatre itself seems to breathe and pulse and give out warmth. This warmth communicated itself to Martyn, and in spite of all her misgivings, she glowed and thought to herself. 'This is my place. This is where I belong.' (pp. 88–9)

Marsh, though, is as aware as Christie, that the cultural constraints upon compliance and deviation are embedded in postwar society's insistence upon established gender affinities, and that these serve patriarchal interests. In projecting back to postwar Britain some of its views of women, the ostensible subject in much women's crime writing in the late 1940s and the 1950s is women, but ultimately the subject is masculinity. In *The Franchise Affair*, perhaps the waiter protests too much:

> 'Don't you believe it! [Chadwick] hadn't even thought of her when he sat down there. I tell you, sir, she didn't look that sort. You'd expect an aunt or a mother to appear at any moment and say: "So sorry to have kept you waiting darling." She just wouldn't occur to any man as a possible. Oh, no, it was the kid's doing. And as neat a piece of business, let me tell you, sir, as if she had spent a lifetime at it.' (p. 112)

The disguises that are penetrated in the novel are primarily those of men whose behaviour toward Betty Kane is more disturbing than her own. First, although Barney Chadwick is anxious to defend his legal position that he thought he had been picked-up by 'an inexperienced child of sixteen' (p. 238), he betrays the fact that he is not worried that, 15 or 16, experienced or inexperienced, he still had sex with a young girl he thought of as a child. Second, Betty Kane invokes in men fantasies of schoolgirl innocence, as is evident in the way Robert sees her: 'The blue outfit still made one think of youth and innocence, speedwell and camp-fire smoke and harebells in the grass' (p. 228).

Ultimately, in the work of Christie, Tey and Marsh, as Butler says of De Beauvoir, the 'analysis of the body takes its bearings within the cultural situation in which men have traditionally been associated with the disembodied or transcendent feature of human existence and women with the bodily and immanent feature of human existence'.[13] But for Christie, Tey and Marsh, it is the permeable space between these binarisms that threaten its stability and is an ever-present location of potential violence. Indeed, throughout women's crime writing, female independence and sexual aberration highlight women's vulnerability to male violence. Not only is this suggested in Tey's novel, through the violent justice even respectable men would inflict on the Sharpes or on Betty herself, but in *They Do It With Mirrors* where, at one point, Gina has a disturbing encounter with her husband:

> Gina stopped and looked up at her husband. Something in the effect of the shadows made him seem very big. A big, quiet figure – and in some way, or so it seemed to her, faintly menacing ... Standing over her. Threatening – what? (p. 637)

Not only in *Opening Night* do we have the lover-as-rapist in the figure of Helena, but further examples of the conflation of physical and psychic male violence. A case in point is Martyn's fear of Ben:

> She recognised this scene. She had dreamt it many times. His face had advanced upon her while she lay inert with terror, as one does in a nightmare. For an infinitesimal moment she was visited by the hope that perhaps after all she had slept and if she could only scream, would awaken. But she couldn't scream. She was quite helpless. (p. 102)

Like Christie, Marsh chooses traditional England in some of her texts to explore the way in which traditional notions of national and regional identity are being revisioned in 1950s Britain. But the rural England that she envisages in *Scales of Justice* (1955) and *Death of a Fold* (1956) is a darker place than Agatha Christie's St Mary Mead that is in many respects more suburban than rural. Even the names of the locations in Marsh's rural village in *Scales of Justice* conjure images of depravity, betrayal and violence: Nunspardon Manor, Jacob's Cottage, and Hammer Farm. In some crime texts by women in the 1950s, the sense of a masculine evil, which emerges but is never fully developed in the novels I have discussed, is quite pronounced. Margery Allingham's *The Tiger in the Smoke* (1952) concerns a vicious killer Jack Havoc on the run in fog-bound London, itself metynomic of postwar confusion, while *Singing in the Shrouds* features a serial killer who, in a grotesque, obverse parody of heterosexual romance, leaves flowers strewn on the faces and breasts of his victims, and broken necklaces beside their bodies.

The fusion, if not confusion, of real and symbolic violence in *Singing in the Shrouds* brings us once again to the way in which many postwar crime texts require the reader to read beyond the literal text. One of the most interesting aspects of postwar women's crime writing, despite their often fundamental conservativism, is the way it frequently challenges a range of interleaved symbolic categories. Marsh's concern with traditional notions of national, regional and gender identities epitomises how, even allowing for some very conservative denouements, women writing crime are writing difference. Difference, as in Christie's novels or Tey's *The Franchise Affair*, is usually part of a wider interplay between signifiers of continuity and discontinuity, analogous of larger postwar social and cultural uncertainities. In this space that the engagement with difference, even if it is not taken to its conclusion, opens, women crime writers frequently explore the slipperiness of definition and the performative nature of identity, especially gender identity.

Performance, masquerade and disguise are inevitably important elements in detective fiction where the plot afterall hinges on the unmasking of the criminal. In texts such as *They Do It With Mirrors* and *Opening Night*, performance and theatricality are not only an integral part of the story line but become themselves the novel's themes. Thus, the postwar crime novel becomes an appropriate medium in which to explore the twofold meaning of female corporeal identity which Butler, following De Beauvoir, summarises: 'a material reality that has already been located and defined within a social context' and 'a field of interpretive possibilities ... interpreting anew a historical set of interpretations which have already informed corporeal style'.[14] However, often in these texts, a concomitant concern is how the shifting nature of the female signifiers and the instability of gender identity make women vulnerable to male violence. Although halted by what is often the failure to embrace the radical implications of their own texts, postwar women crime writers begin to engage not only with the performative nature of femininity but the unravelling of traditional notions of masculinity.

Notes

1 Agatha Christie, *They Do It With Mirrors*, in *Agatha Christie: Miss Marple Omnibus*, Vol. 2 (London: HarperCollins, 1997), pp. 507–654 (p. 525). All subsequent references are to this edition and page numbers are included in parentheses in the text.

2 Agatha Christie, *4.50 From Paddington*, in *Agatha Christie: Miss Marple Omnibus*, Vol. 1 (London: HarperCollins, 1997), pp. 529–718 (p. 556). All subsequent references are to this edition and page numbers are included in parentheses in the text.
3 Anne-Marie Taylor, 'Home is Where the Hearth is: The Emptiness of Agatha Christie's Marple Novels', in Ian A. Bell and Graham Daldry, eds, *Watching the Detectives* (London: Macmillan: 1990), pp. 134–51 (p. 141).
4 Josephine Tey, *The Franchise Affair* (Harmondsworth: Penguin Books, 1951), p. 79. All subsequent references are to this edition and page numbers are included in parentheses in the text.
5 Alison Light, *Forever England: Femininity, Literature and Conservatism Between the Wars* (London and New York: Routledge, 1991), p. 8.
6 W.I. Thomas, *The Unadjusted Girl* (Boston: Little, Brown, and Company, 1923), pp. 230–31.
7 Sally Mitchell, *The New Girl: Girls' Culture in England 1880–1915* (New York: Columbia University Press, 1995), p. 3.
8 Gill Frith, 'The Time of Your Life: The Meaning of the School Story', in Carolyn Steedman, Cathy Unwin, and Valerie Walkerdine, eds, *Language, Gender and Childhood* (London: Routledge and Kegan Paul, 1985), pp. 121–2.
9 Rosemary Auchmuty, *A World of Girls* (London: The Women's Press, 1992), p. 127.
10 Susan Rowland, *From Agatha Christie to Ruth Rendell: British Women Writers in Detective and Crime Fiction* (London: Palgrave, 2001), p. 104.
11 Judith Butler, 'Variations on Sex and Gender: Beauvoir, Wittig and Foucault', in Philip Rice and Patricia Waugh, eds, *Modern Literary Theory* (London and New York: Arnold, 1996), pp. 145–59 (p. 148).
12 Ngaio Marsh, *Opening Night* (London: HarperCollins, 2001), p. 8. All subsequent references are to this edition and page numbers are included in parentheses in the text.
13 Butler, 'Variations on Sex and Gender', p. 149.
14 Butler, 'Variations on Sex and gender', p. 150.

4

Yvonne Mitchell's *The Same Sky*: Challenging World War Two Myths of Englishness

Claire Tylee

Between 1942 and 1952 there appeared on the British stage a number of plays that had been written by women in response to World War II. They included plays stirringly set in continental Europe close to the land battle-lines, such as: Mary Hayley Bell's *Men in Shadows* (1943), *Love Goes to Press* (1946) by Martha Gellhorn and Virginia Cowles, and Bridget Boland's *The Cockpit* (1948). Surprisingly, a far greater impact was effected by four domestic plays set on the British home front: Esther McCracken's *No Medals* (1944), Daphne Du Maurier's *The Years Between* (1944), Joan Temple's *No Room at the Inn* (1946) and, the most radical, Yvonne Mitchell's *The Same Sky* (1951).[1] The impact was not only achieved through long runs in West End theatres; these plays also later reached a wider audience through screen-adaptations for film or television soon after the war. The two by Du Maurier and Temple appeared as films with the same titles, *The Years Between* in 1946 and *No Room at the Inn* in 1948. McCracken's play took four years to appear as a film in 1948 (sarcastically renamed *The Weaker Sex*). The most notable, Mitchell's *The Same Sky*, found the television screen in 1952.[2]

Of the four, Yvonne Mitchell's play was the least sophisticated in terms of plot. It was her first and only play, an interruption to her long career as an actress for theatre, cinema and television.[3] Written in 1947, it did not reach the stage until 1951 and it had a shorter London run than the other three plays. Yet it had won a prize from the Arts Council in connection with the Festival of Britain Year, had been acclaimed by critics such as J.C. Trewin and was selected for publication in *The Plays of the Year (1951)*.[4] It may have reached a smaller commercial audience than the others but it achieved a different kind of success. Although not made into a cinema version it was broadcast several times on radio and television and it became a favourite with amateur companies.[5] The television adaptation provides a significant link between the prewar documentary tradition of British film, manifested during the war in *Love on the Dole* and *Millions Like Us*, and its apparent rebirth as postwar television docudrama in *Up The Junction* and *Cathy Come Home* in the 1960s.

Aesthetically interesting, *The Same Sky* is of particular importance in political terms. Like the other three plays it has implications for feminist politics: it is exceptional in expressing rebellious female desire in a realist mode. It also participates in the cultural politics of race, specifically in conflicts over Jewish-British identities. Whilst its direct outspokenness can still be immediately appreciated, a full sense of its cultural significance can only be gained by considering it in the complex historical context of the immediate postwar period. The play is set during the war, in 1940–41, but it was written in 1947, after the official cessation of hostilities yet when British society was still experiencing the aftershocks, and it was first produced in 1951 as part of the postwar celebration of Britain's modern identity: the Festival of Britain.

Despite receiving scant recognition from either film or theatre scholars (who seem unable to account for their success), the undoubted popularity of all four scripts arguably stems from the counter-hegemonic viewpoints they voiced. These can be distinguished by reference to the well-identified propaganda myths promoted by the British state as part of its World War Two effort. The hegemony of such myths was buttressed by the censorship of alternative views. Since the cinema played a prominent role in the state's propaganda campaigns and, like other ideological institutions, was male-dominated, it is significant that screen versions of these plays by women captured mass audiences once the stringent censorship controls were relaxed at the end of the war. Chosen for television adaptation in 1952 and revived several times on radio: Yvonne Mitchell's *The Same Sky* is of particular interest amongst this group of four plays. Mitchell may have been the least experienced of these playwrights yet she boldly opposed the establishment on two fronts. Going further than the other three plays in challenging state myths about femininity and women's role in wartime Britain, *The Same Sky* also tackled the state's concerted silence over anti-semitism in Britain both during and after the Second World War. In fact, to study the play leads on to a recognition of what Tony Kushner has called the 'collective forgetting' of the nationwide anti-Jewish riots of 1947, a deliberate amnesia he attributes to the myth of Englishness at the heart of British racism.[6] This chapter will examine Mitchell's play in relation to that mythology of Englishness.

The media's importance to state hegemony in the construction and control of ideologies was, of course, long recognised by the time of World War Two. Theatre censorship through the office of the Lord Chamberlain dated back to Shakespeare's time. Enduring till the late 1960s, it was supported by the Blasphemy and Obscene Publications Acts, which also covered written literature. Film censorship operated before the Second World War through the British Board of Film Censors. Originally founded in 1912, the Board took its lead from the Lord Chamberlain's office and from 1932 it examined scripts before the films were made, as well as finished films. Censorship's negative role with regard to the state control of ideas was used during the war to reinforce the active propaganda role of the so-called Ministry of Information (MoI), backed up by the Defence of the Realm Act.[7] Drawing on experience gained in the Great War, the MoI was re-established immediately upon the declaration of war, planning for it having begun in 1935.

Perhaps because its activity in the area of film and news was so marked, little has been written about MoI control of theatre. However, Mary Hayley Bell has outlined the special process of vetting she endured when trying to get *Men in Shadows* licensed for the stage.[8] Similarly, Joan Littlewood has revealed the Lord Chamberlain's continuation of MoI policies with regard to antisemitism even after the war.[9] MoI control of cinema was tighter than that of theatre because it could also control film stock through the Board of Trade. State control of television operated even more tightly. The only channel, BBC TV, which had commenced broadcasting in 1936, was closed down completely from September 1939 to June 1946. Although cinemas and theatres were also closed in 1939 they were re-opened by November, and not merely to entertain audiences. Like radio, sound cinema had not existed in 1914; from 1939 they became central to the British government's manipulation of opinion.[10]

The professional theatre, the variety stage and the music hall, as well as travelling groups, amateur dramatics and pageants had all been important to morale during the Great War, consolidating community spirit and diverting audiences.[11] The music hall was also used to promote jingoism and encourage enlistment, as satirically displayed 50 years later by *Oh What a Lovely War*.[12] Although the middle classes continued to go to the theatre, by the start of World War Two live performance had largely been replaced by cinema for working-class entertainment. The significance of film (especially at a time when there was no television in the home) can be judged from the fact that there were 4,000 cinemas in operation in Britain after November 1939. At that time 19 million people went to the cinema weekly; by 1945 the number had increased to 30 million, half the population.[13] And it was working-class opinion that civil servants and politicians were most anxious to reach and, again, not merely to raise morale. Agreeing with Goebbels that people were easier to influence when relaxed, the MoI did not merely aim to counteract boredom or to disseminate information and news. As wartime memos within the MoI make clear, subtle censorship and propaganda were seen as essential weapons of warfare, 'munitions of the mind' as Beaverbrook had called them – and of the heart, we might add. Cinema was used to engage 'ordinary' men and women and put them in sympathy with the government's war-aims.

Unlike in 1914, patriotism could not be taken for granted in the Second World War: women as well as men were registered, conscripted and indoctrinated.[14] In 1940 the first wartime Minister of Information, Lord Macmillan, circulated a memo identifying three themes for propagandist feature films: What Britain was fighting for; How Britain was fighting; The need for sacrifice. The MoI linked these into the myth of 'The People's War' – everyone determinedly pulling together to defeat a common foe.[15] But, *who* was 'everyone', who *were* 'the people'? Interwar class and gender conflicts were to be countered by an ideal of unity: unified by a common national identity (based on a common character of decency, a history of co-operation, and rooted in the national landscape[16]) the 'English', who were idiosyncratic, resilient and sympathetic to the underdog, would eventually win out over the essentially brutal, regimented German enemy.[17] Although the 'imagined community' thus created drew on books which were near mystical in nature, and in turn inspired what has been called the 'celluloid poetry'[18] of films such as *A Canterbury Tale* or *The Gentle Sex*, it did also draw on the documentary 'realist' tradition of English film-making to produce the success of films such as *Millions Like Us* (1943). Nevertheless, interwar racial conflict was countered by a near total disregard of ethnic difference. The long-term significance of such propaganda is indicated by Jeremy Paxman's use of two wartime films to indicate 'a clear and positive sense' of Englishness in 1998: David Lean's films of Noel Coward's scripts – *In Which We Serve* (1942) and *Brief Encounter* (1945).[19] Frequent retelevising of these classics, together with their video-marketing, continues to represent the British to themselves as self-denying, conservative about gender, and racially homogenous.

British audiences were subject to ideological offensives of two kinds. They experienced the blatant propaganda of American films long before America entered the war. (Eighty per cent of films seen in Britain were

US-made.[20]) The British campaign was more subtle; for instance it did not stress atrocities, having learned from the World War One fiasco about false allegations. Critics have divided the British wartime film-production into three categories: *information films*, such as newsreels, instructional films and documentaries; *'realist' feature* films (also called 'middlebrow'), which drew on the prewar documentary tradition; and 'lowbrow' *fantasy films*, which were pure escapist entertainment for the masses.[21] These last were mainly made by Gainsborough and seem to have operated outside MoI interest, whereas the first two kinds were often initiated from the MoI itself. The need to convince the home audience also produced unlikely results, such as permission for the 1941 feature film of Walter Greenwood's radical novel, *Love on the Dole* (1933), which articulated an authentic working-class perspective.[22] Greeenwood's example strongly influenced Mitchell.[23] But for MoI sponsored films aimed at female audiences the scripts were ventriloquised. This was the case, for instance, with the patronising *The Gentle Sex*, which is now greeted by students with incredulous laughter.

By contrast, American cinema, particularly MGM, did adapt women's novels to film. Amongst the novels by American women authors filmed by MGM was Ethel Vance's anti-Nazi thriller, *Escape* (1940). American films adapted from British women's writing included *The Mortal Storm* (1940) based on Phyllis Bottome's 1937 novel about Nazi anti-semitism, *Mrs Miniver* (1942) based on Jan Struther's writing about British women's fortitude on the Home Front, and *Mr Skeffington* (1944) based on a novel by Elizabeth von Arnim and directed to counter American anti-semitism. In fact *The Mortal Storm* was so outspoken on Nazi anti-semitism that Goebbels subsequently banned all MGM films in German-controlled territories.[24] These films may have been highly successful in the USA (*Mrs Miniver* was the most popular film of 1942 and apparently remained a favourite of Churchill and Eisenhower) but in Britain they seemed melodramatic. That may have predisposed British audiences to be receptive to the more conservative British products, which were neither anti-racist nor feminist. MoI-sponsored films did not seek female-authored work to gain an authentic female viewpoint. Nor did they promote women's ideas. The major exception was *The Lamp still Burns* (1943, starring Rosamund John) which was based on Monica Dickens's novel about probationary nurses in a war-hospital, *One Pair of Feet* (1942). This fitted the MoI's themes of 'self-sacrifice' and 'how we are fighting the war'.

Whereas American films like *The Mortal Storm* openly tackled issues of race, particularly anti-semitism, this remained a closed subject in

Britain during the war as far as officialdom was concerned. Indeed, the deliberate construction of an imagined island community, constructed as a national family, and polarised against continental Europe, precluded exceptions to a homogenous racial identity. Women's role was to support that family, especially through motherhood. In fact, film-critics such as Sue Aspinall and Marcia Landy have argued that the control of ideas of femininity and motherhood was central to MoI home-propaganda.[25] However, independently produced 'lowbrow' films such as *The Man in Grey* (1943) based on the novel by Lady Eleanor Smith, and Gainsborough's fantasy hit, *The Wicked Lady* (1946) which was based on the novel by Magdalen King-Hall, *The Life and Death of the Wicked Lady Skelton,* subversively revealed female sexual desire to be in conflict with maternal duty. The success of these films shows what the MoI was up against in its attempt to control women. The MoI was male-dominated, conservative and middle class. It did not want to know what women actually thought or wanted, but to tell them what to think and do. Furthermore, as cultural historians such as Tony Kushner and Jean R. Freedman have demonstrated, the British authorities were also anxious not to provoke racism which might foster support for fascist movements in Britain and divide the English family.[26] There was one British effort to make a serious feature-film centred on the positive figure of a Jewish man, *Mr Emmanuel* (1944) (based on a novel by the Jewish author, Louis Golding, that depicted Nazi anti-semitism in 1930s Germany); it provoked angry disturbances in the East End at the end of 1944.[27] The last thing MoI would have wanted during the war was to know what a British-Jewish woman thought – or to let anyone else know!

Accordingly, we can read women's wartime plays for the theatre as more likely to be voicing to a female audience – or at least a middle-class female audience – what women really thought and felt, in the face of the ideas promoted through the cinema and official publications. In fact, these plays were probably seen by other women as a direct rebuff to those ideas. But, by contrast with radio or cinema, the theatre was a relatively circumscribed means to permit opposition to steam-off. So, the filming of certain plays by women at the end of the war can be read as permitting muted voices finally to get a wider hearing. These voices used the conventions of popular genres to subvert the patriarchal mythology of the war years.[28] Thus *No Medals* is a farcical comedy 'sending up' propaganda about women's impossible home-duties in wartime; *No Room at the Inn,* about a wicked landlady taking in evacuees whilst running her home as a brothel, is a gothic satire on the idea of Englishwomen as good wives and mothers to the nation;

and *The Years Between* stretches the conventions of romance to show what use a woman given freedom from her husband might actually make of her wartime opportunities. These plays and films present very different images of mature womanhood from *Millions Like Us*, *The Gentle Sex*, or the American idea of *Mrs Miniver*. And what about *The Same Sky*? It confronts the wartime construction of younger women, re-telling the Romeo and Juliet story from the point of view of the Juliet figure, Esther. She openly stands up to her father and follows her own desire rather than an imposed duty of self-sacrifice. The play gives voice not just to an independently minded woman but to an unmarried working-class teenager, in fact to a young Jewish woman who insists on a sexual relation across what were seen as racial and religious barriers, in the face of opposition from the parents on both sides.

The Same Sky presents working-class life on the home front for an orthodox Jewish family in the East End during the Blitz. Concentrating on the metropolis, it not only counters the construction of Britain as a village community centred on the local church. It also writes Jews back into the national, collective family-history of 'the people's war'. Furthermore, through the daughter's marriage, the Jewish family (albeit reluctantly) becomes related to a non-Jewish family. A crisis is provoked when the gentile husband is killed in action. Benedict Anderson, in his analysis of the Imagined Community of the nation, has argued that a nation's identity is guaranteed by deaths, or rather by the writing of deaths as sacrifice for the national community, as 'the nation's deaths':

> The deaths that structure the nation's biography are of a special kind. The nation's biography snatches exemplary suicides, poignant martyrdoms, assassinations, executions, wars and holocausts. But to serve the narrative purpose, these violent deaths must be remembered/forgotten as 'our own'.[29]

The death in this play of 'one of our own', an English soldier-hero, not only validates the belief that Britain is worth dying for. His sacrifice is for the national community; so the poignant loss to the dead man's wife and child is also of national import. This guarantees that his Jewish widow and baby son will be accepted by his cockney mother and symbolically inducted into the National Family. A Jewish child thus becomes mythically part of the nation. What is particularly radical about Mitchell's play is that the Jewish grandfather is also persuaded to accept the child and thus to integrate. The *Radio Times* barely glimpsed the obstacles to this in 1955 when it stated:

> If there is a Jewish problem for Gentiles, there is a Gentile problem for Jews. The Brodskys and the Smiths have been brought up to a mutual distrust. But love ignores childhood prejudice and adult intolerance.[30]

Unfortunately, nations are not built by ignoring prejudice and intolerance.

Mitchell's postwar play reveals the limitations of the image of the 'national community' constructed by British wartime propaganda. Prime examples of wartime propaganda films would include Graham Greene's *Went the Day Well?* or *Mrs Miniver*.[31] These may be stories which cross class and gender barriers, revealing that even women can act heroically as mothers to the nation, but they are set in villages at a time in British history when the majority of the population lived in cities and it was cities that were bearing the brunt of the bombing. As Jean R. Freedman has recognised, by avoiding the city, wartime propaganda could avoid the actual ethnic diversity of the nation:

> Cities have always been problematic for romantic nationalists, containing too many foreigners, too many ethnic minorities, too many people who want to change the essence of the nation rather then preserve it.[32]

It seems the government deliberately intended to avoid raising what was called 'the Jewish issue', which was deeply rooted in British culture.[33] As Tony Kushner has shown, those few films which did have Jewish characters tended to recirculate the negative stereotypes widely found in novels, stressing connections with money-motives: the money-grasping poor of the East End versus the ostentatiously rich of North London, the oily old man and the wicked young woman, profiteers and cowards. (Even the American anti-anti-semitic film *Mr Skeffington* featured Jewish financiers.) British Jews were always presented as alien, not 'truly English' and films about refugees, such as *Next of Kin* (1942), fostered mistrust for Jews of German origin. Suspicion was reinforced by anti-German propaganda and the policy of internment. In feature films, Jews were mainly depicted as visibly different in ways that signified malevolence or foreignness; or else they were omitted. They were never just taken for granted or included as 'one of us'.[34]

So, *imaginatively* Jews were not seen as part of the National Community and MoI policies had exacerbated this. The fact that wartime films continued to be exhibited after the war meant that wartime propaganda carried over into peacetime and went on influencing attitudes. The socially divisive effects of this propaganda were to be evidenced in postwar race riots.[35] The British government was anxious not to encourage any fascist sympathies with Nazi Germany. Nor did it want to see a repeat of the racist-inspired street violence of the 1930s such as the battle of Cable Street in 1936 against the British Union of Fascists, recalled in Arnold Wesker's 1958 play, *Chicken Soup with Barley*.[36] Apparently this was why the presence of Jews was camouflaged. (This policy included turning a blind eye to the continuance of casual Jewbaiting.)[37] After the war one might have supposed that the indelible newsreel revelations about extermination camps would have raised sympathies for Jews. However, this was counteracted by postwar terrorist activity in Palestine to end the British Mandate and set up a state of Israel. In July 1947, photos on the front page of a daily newspaper showing the bodies of two British Army sergeants hanged by militant Zionist extremists, members of Irgun, triggered the worst race riots in Britain since World War One. (Ironically one of the sergeants was Jewish.) These riots were a more visible demonstration of the smouldering racial aggression, damped down during the war, that had been blown into new life by the release from internment of prewar fascists. Oswald Mosley commenced his plan to form a new 'Union Movement' in 1945, but already, as early as November 1944, the League of British Ex-servicemen and Women had held an anti-semitic rally in Hyde Park with ex-detainee speakers. Such meetings prompted the formation in April 1946 of the 43 Group by Jewish ex-servicemen and women who ran an underground commando organisation to infiltrate and disrupt fascist groups. The 43 Group lasted until April 1950, when Mosley finally gave up his bid for power.[38] The well-publicised campaign to make incitement to racial hatred unlawful may have been partly what prompted Mitchell to write her play in 1947; overt racial antagonism may also be what prompted her to shelve it. However, the play continued to be highly topical.

The 1947 riots were instanced by Panikos Panayi as part of his demonstration that 'no newcomers who have entered Britain in the last two centuries have escaped hostility on a significant scale'.[39] Of course, in Glasgow, Manchester and Liverpool, cities with a tradition of racial violence, where the rioting originated over the bank holiday weekend, as well as in London and towns all over Britain, where the rioting spread, the Jewish communities were not of recent origin. However, they were perceived as alien, as significantly different from the dominant norm. Such perceptions are part of what Robert Young has called 'an obsessive concern with difference (of culture, class, race and gender) and with the crossing and invasion of identities' which he claims characterises and unites English culture.[40] The ugly violence that results from that obsessive concern, part of an ever-present xenophobia, is invisible to romantic English nationalism. Panayi contrasts Orwell's (in)famous wartime praise of 'the gentleness of English civilisation ... with its basic underlying values of patience, tolerance and generosity' with Neal Ascherson's assertion at the time of the Tottenham riots of 1985, that 'rioting is at least as English as thatched cottages and honey still for tea'.[41] Panayi convincingly argues that it is the underlying racial hostility in Britain which, when exacerbated by particular socio-economic developments, enables such events as the Zionist activity in Palestine to 'spark off' riots. (Of course, riots also stem from political organisation as well as government policies and police response.) Mitchell's play can be seen as an attempt to make visible the continual low-key harassment of unthinking racism. Her pacific 'feminine' effort at the level of ideas should be set alongside the physical, 'masculine' response of Jewish organisations such as the 43 Group and the Manchester Union of Jewish Ex-servicemen and Women, who burned anti-semitic propaganda and confronted violence with violence. Ethnic coexistence required/s qualifications to the myth of tolerant, gentle Englishness.

In her autobiographical book, *Actress* (1957), Yvonne Mitchell stated that she had 'absolutely no political convictions'.[42] However, her account of the original inspiration for *The Same Sky* suggests otherwise. Apparently her sister had been working in a children's play-centre in the East End where the tiny children often yelled 'Dirty Jew!' One of the five-year old Jewish children had even tried to prevent her helping a gentile child who had hurt himself falling over: 'Don't help him, Miss, he's not one of Us' (pp. 55–6). Mitchell builds both of these remarks into the beginning of *The Same Sky*. The allusion to her sister is the closest Mitchell comes in her book to disclosing her own ethnic background. She was born in Cricklewood in North London in 1925 and educated at the prestigious boarding school, St Paul's Girls' School. Her father, Bertie Joseph, was an executive for a Jewish-catering firm. She never mentions her mother in her autobiography, although she adopted her mother's maiden name (Madge) Mitchell, when she went on the stage.[43] She married Derek Monsey in 1952 and had one daughter. Thus the play is not autobiographical: she clearly had a comfortable middle-class upbringing in North London and was well-integrated into British society. However, she may herself have been the product of a mixed marriage and thus have embodied the very hope her play transmits. She at any rate had more at stake in the play than a curious observation of East End life.

Racial antagonism when she was writing the play in 1947 went beyond the mutual intolerance identified by the *Radio Times*. She saw it as like what she called a 'Montague and Capulet type of feud' with bloodshed in the streets.[44] That, as she says, led to her basing the plot on *Romeo and Juliet*. But she placed it realistically in the modern day, in London's East End, with a love affair between a Jewish girl and a gentile youth disapproved of by both sets of parents. In fact, the play was so realistic she thought it would never get produced since, at a time when everyone was heartily sick of war, she had set it in wartime London. But it is its wartime setting, during the Blitz, that gives the play its peculiar resonance. It enables the play to tap into precisely what had been occluded by the official wartime propaganda and censorship. The enemy bombs which threaten Esther and Jeff during a Luftwaffe air-raid that drives them underground are the expression, both material and symbolic, of the racist hostility which prevents the normal, open, everyday expression of their mutual love. Their encounter in the Tube with a comic railway porter and a drunken woman enable Mitchell to display how endemic are the prejudices which affect Esther's acceptance: the old woman singing a belligerent hymn, 'Onward Christian soldiers', and the porter finding something 'as plain as the nose on a Jew's face'.

As a professional actress, Mitchell had often played not only the role of Juliet but also that of Jessica in *The Merchant of Venice*. Her autobiographical work *Actress* includes photographs of herself in such classical roles. In one photograph of her opposite Michael Redgrave as Shylock, his make-up and costuming, complete with hooked nose and greasy hair, promote one of the worst stereotypes of 'The Jew'.[45] References in *The Same Sky* to *The Merchant of Venice* underline the relation between the Jewish father and his daughter in her play and provoke comparisons with the classic text. There are productions and readings of *The Merchant of Venice* that confirm stereotypes of older Jewish men and younger Jewish women as egotistical monsters: money-obsessed tyrants and sexual adventuresses.[46] We can see Mitchell following the interwar tactics of Anglo-Jewish novelists such as G.B. Stern, Naomi Jacob and Louis Golding to oppose such stereotypical thinking.[47] Like them she attempts to 'normalise' the Jewish characters, partly by placing them at the centre of the plot rather than at the margins, and also by showing them amongst a diverse, loving family rather than in selfish isolation. Although the conflict between the Jewish father and his daughter over her choice of a gentile husband deliberately recalls Shakespeare's play, Mitchell sets up this parallel to highlight the different response to racial bigotry offered by her own play. Money is neither the motive for the marriage nor for the father's fury. Esther is not wickedly selfish and her father is deeply sincere in his religious beliefs. The play opens with a fight between Manny and George, the younger brothers of Esther and Jeff, over George calling Manny 'a Dirty Jew' but the bigotry is shown to be groundless and to operate on both sides. Separatism is practised both by Esther's father, an orthodox Jew who disowns her for 'marrying out', and by Jeff's mother, who refuses to acknowledge the marriage. As Lionel Hale said in his 1952 review: 'It has been said that there is no Jewish problem – only a Christian problem. In *The Same Sky*, a play which has tenderness as well as strength, the whole thing becomes a joint Jewish-Christian question.'[48]

The brave racial politics of a play which challenges both sides of the dispute are one reason for disinterring it; the feminist aesthetics are also striking. Whereas Shakespeare's *Romeo and Juliet* is dramatically presented mainly to express Romeo's sexuality, *The Same Sky* focuses on Esther's rather than on Jeff's. Shakespeare's plot shows Romeo continually active, competing and taking risks. This virile masculine sexuality is vividly staged for us in the scene where Romeo climbs up to invade Juliet's balcony. He displays his strength and ardour whilst she passively waits to welcome him into her father's house. The parallel scene in Mitchell's play takes place below ground during a bombing-raid. Despite the risk, Esther and Jeff have gone to the theatre (to see *The Merchant of Venice*) and when the sirens go off they take shelter in a tube-station. The staging shows them sitting together on the stairs down in a tunnel, a visual metaphor for her sexualised body and the mutuality of their relationship. It is Esther who suggests they anticipate the wedding and, as Jeff says, they let the ring marry them, pretending to her parents that they are already legally married. Later the play shows Esther in an advanced state of pregnancy, and she goes into labour on the stage. This is typical of Mitchell's frankness: an openness about women's physicality not seen since Webster and Shakespeare.

Thus, on the one hand Mitchell's play is significant for presenting a 'realistic' portrait of a working-class Jewish family, where the father is motivated not by greed but by strong religious convictions. On the other hand, Mitchell's play presents female desire in wartime, sympathetically portraying the plight of a young war-widow. However, unlike her original in *Romeo and Juliet*, the Jewish heroine does not herself have to die in order to bring about a reconciliation between the two families. The birth of her child embodies the birth of a new hope which, in hindsight when the play was performed, could also be seen to pre-figure the peace and a new beginning at the end of the war. A newly-born British identity and sense of Englishness still had a long way to go, but Mitchell's play was a brave, forward-looking choice for Festival of Britain year.[49]

Notes

1 Yvonne Mitchell, *The Same Sky* (London: Evans, 1953). The script for Daphne DuMaurier's play *The Years Between* is included with a critical introduction in Fidelis Morgan, *The Years Between: Plays by Women on the London Stage 1900–50* (London: Virago, 1994). The play by Joan Temple was discussed by Paul Webb in a talk, 'World War II Drama' given at the National Portrait Gallery, London, 26 November, 2000. The others are all discussed by Maggie B. Gale in *West End Women: Women and the London Stage 1918–62* (London: Routledge, 1996), pp. 162–71, where bibliographical details can be found. She does not, however, comment on their mass dissemination by cinema and television. This, the adaptation for screen, marks a major difference between British women's drama of the First and the Second World Wars. (Two acclaimed war plays by Bridget Boland, *The Cockpit* (1948) and *The Prisoner* (1954), were also made into films, but they did not have long theatre runs.)

2 None of the film versions of these World War Two plays by women was discussed in either of the two main critical assessments of British war films: Sue Harper, 'The Years of Total War: propaganda and entertainment' in Christine Gledhill and Gillian Swanson, eds, *Nationalising Femininity: Culture, Sexuality and British Cinema in the Second World War* (Manchester: Manchester University Press, 1996) or Jeffrey Richards, 'National Identity in British Wartime Films', in Philip M. Taylor, ed., *Britain and Cinema in the Second World War* (Basingstoke: Macmillan, 1988). On the rare occasion when British war films based on texts by women *are* discussed, the authors are ignored; for instance, in a crucial discussion of the film *Perfect Strangers* (Korda, 1945), Lant does not mention that it was scripted by Clemence Dane and based on her own story (Antonia Lant, *Blackout: Reinventing Women in British Wartime Cinema* (Princeton: Princeton University Press, 1991), pp. 117–27. Yet the American film based on the British newspaper column creation by Jan Struther, *Mrs Miniver* (William Wyler, 1942) nearly always receives attention, if only in a footnote. Alison Light discusses *Mrs Miniver* (both the novel and the film adaptation) extensively in *Forever England: Femininity, Literature and Conservatism Between the Wars* (London: Routledge, 1991), pp. 113–55.

3 There is a letter on file from the BBC to Mitchell, congratulating her and asking her to submit more plays (from Cecil McGivern, Controller of Television Programmes, 15 August 1952). She never did, although she did publish books such as novels, a biography of Colette and fiction for children. Jason Jacobs' study of early BBC television drama, *The Intimate Screen: Early British Television Drama* (Oxford: Oxford University Press, 2000), which discusses McGivern's policies (pp. 82–100), pays no attention to Mitchell's play, although it would have been a good example of the potentiality for television drama to 'exploit its visual mobility and transcend the drawing-room [of upper middle-class theatre drama]' (p. 125), which is the tenor of Jacobs' argument.

4 J.C. Trewin, 'Introduction' to J.C. Trewin, ed., *Plays of the Year Volume 6 1951* (London: Elek, 1952) which includes *The Same Sky* (pp. 233–311). See also: Francis Stephens, 'The Play Revealed Great Promise' in *Theatre World Annual 3* (1952).

5 Mitchell, p. 62. *The Same Sky* consistently attracted actors of a high calibre. It was first produced at Nottingham Playhouse in 1951 under the title 'Here Choose I', a quotation taken pertinently from *The Merchant of Venice*. It then showed at Brighton, and at the Lyric Hammersmith in January 1952, before moving to the Duke of York's in London, March to October 1952 and then on to The Embassy. In the London production the Brodski parents were played by Frederick Valk and Thora Hird, and Esther, their daughter, by Frances Hyland. Eric Porter played Jeff Smith. (Their contribution to the development of the play is discussed by Mitchell in *Actress*.) In the television production by Dennis Vance for Sunday Night Theatre, on 10 August 1952 (repeated the following Thursday), Yvonne Mitchell, in her television debut, herself took over the role of Esther, her parents being played by Joan Miller and George Colouris. She starred as Esther again when the play was adapted for radio by Peggy Wells for BBC Home Service Saturday Night Theatre on 14 May 1955 (repeated on Thursday 26 May), this time with David Kossof as Poppa Brodsky. Despite the somewhat sneering review by Stephen Williams in *Radio Times*, 6 May 1955 (p. 6), it was broadcast again on the Light Programme in January and February 1957, and on Remembrance Day 1961. A further version was broadcast on Radio 4, Saturday 19 February 1972.

6 Tony Kushner, 'Anti-Semitism and Austerity: the August 1947 Riots in Britain', in Panikos Panayi, ed., *Racial Violence in Britain 1840–1950* (Leicester: Leicester University Press, 2nd edn, 1996), p. 166.

7 Aided by the BBFC, MoI competed for ideological control with other institutions such as the Foreign Office, the War Office and the British Film Producers' Association. All were male-dominated. Aspects of this competition are discussed by Sue Harper, 'Years of Total War' (1996).

8 Mary Haley Bell, *What Shall We Do Tomorrow? An Autobiography* (London: Cassell, 1968), pp. 166–7.

9 See Joan Littlewood, *Joan's Book: Joan Littlewood's Peculiar History as She Tells It* (London: Methuen, 1994), pp. 284–9, as quoted in Kushner, Tony, 'Remembering to Forget: Racism and Anti-racism in Postwar Britain', in Bryan Cheyette and Laura Marcus, eds, *Modernity, Culture and 'the Jew'* (Cambridge: Polity Press, 1998), p. 235.

10 As Philip M. Taylor points out, the communications revolution provided a direct link between the government and people, and between the government of one nation and the people of another. Such a link was crucial to the waging of total war by enfranchised democracies. While the British government used film to raise morale in Britain, it also had one eye on persuading Americans of the strength and unity of Britain as a nation. Philip M. Taylor, *Munitions of the Mind: A History of Propaganda from the Ancient World to the Present Day* (Manchester: Manchester University Press, 2nd edn, 1995), p. 208.

11 L.J. Collins, *The Theatre at War, 1914–18* (Basingstoke: Macmillan, 1998) and see: Jane Potter, 'Hidden Drama by Women: Pageants and Sketches from the Great War', in Claire M. Tylee, ed., *Women, the First World War and Dramatic*

Imagination: a Collection of Essays (Lampeter: Edward Mellen Press, 2000), pp. 105–20.

12 Theatre Workshop, *Oh What a Lovely War* (London: Methuen, 1964), Act I, emphasised in the film version, directed by Richard Attenborough (GB, 1968).

13 Taylor, *Munitions*, p. 217.

14 Unlike Germany or USA, Britain mobilised women. Men were conscripted through the *British National Services Act* (2 September 1939) and from 10 December 1941, part 2 of that Act applied to women aged 20–31. Discussions of wartime film do not remark on the generational differentiation between women created by conscription. Like her heroine, Esther, Mitchell was apparently too young to be conscripted into the armed services, although her contribution to the war-effort is described in *Actress*.

15 Antony Aldgate and Jeffrey Richards, *Best of British: Cinema and Society 1930 to the Present* (London: Taurus, 1994), pp. 57–8.

16 David Mellor claims that by 1940, MoI propaganda exhibitions presented 'poetry, literature and the landscape' as 'the very identity Britain is fighting for' (in *A Paradise Lost* (London: Humphries, 1987) p. 12, quoted by Jenny Hartley *Millions Like Us: British Women's Fiction of the Second World War* (London: Virago, 1997), p. 6. That landscape was neither Northern industrial dereliction nor Southern suburban sprawl but the Romantic pastoral of Constable.

17 James Park, *British Cinema* (London: Batsford, 1970), p. 67.

18 Aldgate and Richards, *Best of British*, p. 60.

19 Jeremy Paxman, *The English: a Portrait of a People* (London: Joseph 1998), pp. 2–5.

20 Taylor, *Munitions*, p. 217.

21 E.g. Sue Aspinall, 'Women, Realism and Reality in British Films, 1943–53', in James Curran and Vincent Porter, eds, *British Cinema History* (London: Weidenfeld, 1983), p. 274.

22 Before the war, in 1936, film scripts for this book had twice been refused a certificate although it was adapted successfully to the stage. Nicholas Pronay and Jeremy Croft claim in 'British Film Censorship and Propaganda Policy during the Second World War', in Curran and Porter (ibid.) that the film adaptation was allowed in 1940 in a stronger form because of the perceived 'need to politicise ordinary people rather than dull them into passivity', p. 150.

23 Mitchell, *Actress*, pp. 56–7.

24 An attempt was also made to ban such propaganda films in USA too, see Taylor, *Munitions*, pp. 228–9.

25 'The contribution of women was vital': Aldgate and Richards, *Best of British*, p. 59. For a discussion of the 'fusion of femininity with the national interest' see Marcia Landy, 'Melodrama and Femininity in World War II British Cinema', in Robert Murphy, ed., *The British Cinema Book* (London: BFI, 1997), pp. 79–89; see also: Sue Harper, 'The Years of Total War: propaganda and entertainment', in Christine Gledhill and Gillian Swanson, eds, *Nationalising Femininity: Culture, Sexuality and British Cinema in the Second World War* (Manchester: Manchester University Press, 1996), Sue Aspinall, 'Women, Realism and Reality in British Films, 1943–53', and Antonia Lant, *Blackout*.

26 Tony Kushner, *The Holocaust and the Liberal Imagination: a Social and Cultural History* (Oxford: Blackwell, 1994), pp. 151–3; Jean R. Freedman, *Whistling in the Dark: Memory and Culture in Wartime London* (Lexington: University of Kentucky, 1999), passim.
27 Louis Golding, *Mr Emmanuel* (London: Rich & Cowan, 1939). See Tony Kushner, *The Holocaust and the Liberal Imagination: a Social and Cultural History* (Oxford: Blackwell, 1994), pp. 142–3 and 315; and Tony Kushner, *Persistence of Prejudice: Anti-semitism in Britain* (Manchester: Manchester University Press, 1989), pp. 115–19.
28 For a theoretical analysis of feminist modifications to generic conventions, see Anne Cranny-Francis, *Feminist Fiction: Feminist Uses of Generic Fiction* (London: Polity, 1990), pp. 195–6.
29 Benedict Anderson, *Imagined Communities: Reflections on the Origin and Spread of Nationalism* (London: Verso, 2nd edn, 1991), pp. 205–6.
30 *Radio Times*, 6 May 1955, p. 48.
31 Graham Greene's story 'The Lieutenant Died Last' was used for the film *Went the Day Well?* (*Forty-Eight Hours*, USA) dir. Albert Cavalcanti, GB, 1942, Ealing. For *Mrs Miniver* see footnote 2 above.
32 Jean R.Freedman, *Whistling in the Dark: Memory and Culture in Wartime London*, p. 113.
33 For a discussion of this embeddedness see: Tony Kushner, 'The Jewish Image in Britain in the War', in *The Persistence of Prejudice*, pp. 106–33.
34 Jewish writers and sympathisers did try to counter the dominant ideology, which explicitly vilified Jews or implicitly marginalised them as 'not really part of the Nation', as invisible, alien or extraneous to the national family. Two wartime radio plays, *Zero Hour* by Louis MacNiece (1943) and J.B. Priestley's *Desert Highway* (1944) had depicted Jewish heroes. They should be set against Dorothy L. Sayers' radio play *The Man Born to be King* (broadcast in 1941 and again in 1942 and 1943), which represented 'Matthew' to be 'as vulgar a little commercial Jew as ever walked Whitechapel'; see Tony Kushner, *The Holocaust and the Liberal Imagination*, p. 107.
35 See Tony Kushner, 'Anti-Semitism and Austerity: the August 1947 Riots in Britain', pp. 150–70.
36 Arnold Wesker, *Chicken Soup with Barley* in *The Wesker Trilogy* (Harmondsworth: Penguin, 1960). The battle is discussed in Richard Thurlow, *Facism in Britain: A History 1918–85* (Oxford: Oxford University Press, 1987), pp. 109–18.
37 Kushner argues that British anti-semitism continued right through the period 1918–45 and was never marginal to British culture: 'The Impact of British Anti-semitism, 1918–45' in David Cesarani, ed., *The Making of Modern Anglo-Jewry* (Oxford: Blackwell, 1990).
38 See Morris Beckman, *The 43 Group* (London: Centerprise, 2nd edn, 1993) for a first-hand account of this militant Jewish resistance to postwar Fascism in Britain. The enduring power of fascist anti-semitism is indicated by recent studies of racist British National Party, such as Kathy Brewis's interview with Mark Collett, leader of the Young BNP, 'National Affront' in *Sunday Times* magazine, 27 October 2002, pp. 54–61, which was an introduction to the Channel 4 *Dispatches* report by David Modell, 'Collett and the Young BNP' on 4 November 2002.

39 Panikos Panayi, 'Anti-immigrant Violence in Nineteenth- and Twentieth-century Britain', in *Racial Violence in Britain 1840–1950* (Leicester: Leicester University Press, 2nd edn, 1996), p. 3.
40 Robert Young, *Colonial Desire: Hybridity in Theory, Culture and Race* (London: Routledge, 1995), p. 2; as quoted in Tony Kushner, 'Remembering to Forget: Racism and Anti-racism in Postwar Britain', in Cheyette and Marcus, *Modernity, Culture and 'the Jew'*, p. 226.
41 Orwell and Ascherson are quoted by Panikos Panayi 'Anti-immigrant Violence in Nineteenth- and Twentieth-century Britain', pp. 1–2.
42 Mitchell, *Actress*, p. 110. This disclaimer was made specifically in the context of being accused of communism or anti-communism when starring with Peter Cushing in the controversial television version of *1984*. It should be read against a similar remark by Beckman with regard to the founding of the 43 Group as 'apolitical': *The 43 Group*, p. 25.
43 I assume her mother died when she was young and her father remarried, since she mentions having both sisters and a stepsister.
44 Mitchell, *Actress*, p. 55. The other observations by Mitchell in this paragraph are also taken from chapter 10 of *Actress*.
45 Plate 9, opposite p. 48. Frederick Valk, a refugee, who had played a stereotypical version of Shylock in London in 1943, was 'Poppa' in the London 1952 stage version of *The Same Sky*.
46 See John Gross, *Shylock: Four Hundred Years in the Life of a Legend* (London: Chatto, 1992). On the persistence of the Shylock stereotype see: 'A survey on the major influences affecting people's attitudes to Jews found that Shakespeare's play [*The Merchant of Venice*] was one of the most important': Tony Kushner, *The Persistence of Prejudice*, p. 111.
47 See for instance: G.B. Stern *Rakonitz Chronicle*, 5 vols (London: Chapman Hall, 1924–42); Louis Golding, *Magnolia Street* (London: Gollancz, 1932); Naomi Jacob, *The Gollantz Saga*, 7 vols (London: Hutchinson, 1936–58).
48 *Radio Times*, 8 August 1952, p. 35.
49 It was all the more important a choice since Kushner reveals that the catalogue to the Anglo-Jewish Exhibition which was part of the Festival of Britain, whilst referring to 'the unhappy period' at the end of the Mandate, could already claim that 'these memories have become dim', just four years later: Kushner, 'Anti-Semitism and Austerity: the August 1947 Riots in Britain', p. 165.

Part II

The Home: Retreat and Restraint

5

No Home of One's Own : Elizabeth Taylor's *At Mrs Lippincote's*

John Brannigan

> We have still to write the histories of the emotional and affective relations which women have with home-making as part of the histories of what we call 'class'. The idea of comfort, and the attitudes toward domestic labour, the whole panoply of relations which is covered by the word 'home' has formed a symbolic as well as literal interior which women inhabit: 'domesticity' is a complex knot of feelings, ideas and activities which have structured a sense of the feminine self ... Whilst we have begun as feminists to subject to historical scrutiny woman's place in the home, we have more to discover about the place of home in the woman.[1]

This essay is about the place of home in Elizabeth Taylor's first novel, *At Mrs Lippincote's*, published at the end of the Second World War. 'Home', as the epigraph from Alison Light explores, is a complex and potent term, rich in its symbolic and affective meanings for a wide range of social and cultural discourses. In the conservative political discourses of the postwar decades, 'home' is associated in particular with the ideology of separate spheres, and with the spatialisation of gender differences, so that even when women and men were 'at home', they were to behave in distinctly gendered ways.[2] 'Home' is, at one and the same time, charged with meaning as a private haven of intimacy and belonging, and made to function as an economic unit, both as a place of domestic labour and as the source of consumer desire and expenditure. The economic function of women at home acquired particular significance in the 1950s, for, as H. Hopkins argued in *The New Look* 'the woman of the Fifties possessed at once the time, the resources and the inclination to bring to perfection the new arts of continuous consumption. She was the essential pivot of the People's Capitalism and its essential heroine.'[3] Feminist critics and historians have explored in some detail the ways in which 'home' functions as an oppressive place for women, particularly in the first decades of the postwar period.[4] So too, recent work in cultural studies has explored the associations of 'home' with cultural and national identity, and with ideas of belonging and exile in the postwar period.[5] This essay draws upon such work to explain the significance of Taylor's novel as a representation of the 'place of home in the woman'.

At Mrs Lippincote's is a fiction about the meanings of home and dislocation. In this respect it shares with such writers as John Betjeman, Nancy Mitford and Evelyn Waugh a preoccupation with the significance of place and belonging at the end of the Second World War, and takes as one of its themes the peculiar sensation of unhomeliness, and the disturbed domestic arrangements, of England in the mid-1940s.[6] Taylor's novel tells the story of Julia Davenant, housewife to an RAF officer, who attempts to set up home for her family in a house rented from the austere and fearsome Mrs Lippincote. In part, *At Mrs Lippincote's* reflects on wartime experiences of displacement and social upheaval, and manages at the same time to anticipate much feminist criticism in the 1950s of the constraints of domestic life for middle-class women. In this sense, the novel is situated on the cusp between conservative nostalgia for a lost sense of security, and postwar feminist critiques of conservative ideologies of domesticity and the family.

Julia complains about having 'no home of one's own', an allusion, of course, to Virginia Woolf.[7] The novel is ambivalent, however, about whether this complaint of living in another woman's home reflects Julia's orthodox desire for the solidity of middle-class family life, or whether her sense of dislocation and unhomeliness empowers her with a radical critique of ideologies of 'home'. Taylor is usually known as the author of quiet, middle-class novels of genteel manners and modest style, similar to Angela Thirkell and Barbara Pym in her ability to produce well-made, Austen-like fictions of social observation. Frederick Karl, for instance, includes Taylor among a group of largely women novelists 'who aim at the well-made novel which neither surprises nor disappoints', and which lacks 'intensity, daring and range'.[8] The politics of such well-made novels are the subject of both Elizabeth Wilson's and Alan Sinfield's suspicions that Taylor's social perspective is ultimately that of a conservative leisured class. Sinfield includes Taylor among such company as Pym, Thirkell, Nancy Mitford, Pamela Hansford Johnson and Ivy Compton-Burnett, writers 'so situated that they found it natural to maintain the identification of the individual, the personal and the literary with the lifestyle and outlook of the leisured class'.[9] Elizabeth Wilson ponders the ambivalent narrative perspective of such novelists as Taylor and Elizabeth Bowen: 'It is not always clear at what point a minute and sensitive recreation in detail of the texture of daily life slips into snobbery and obsession with social nuances.'[10] Here we might think of Julia Davenant's frequent attempts to imagine the life of a domestic servant, or her susceptibility to thinking of 'titles' as 'everything ... a world of difference' (p. 22). Such details lead Deborah Philips and Ian Haywood, in their wide-ranging revision of the literary history of women and women's writing in the post-1945 period, to observe that there is little evidence in Taylor's novels of the 'social revolution' taking place in England after the war.

This is a reputation which I intend, in the following discussion, to revise, and to counter with the specific argument that Taylor's first novel, in proto-feminist fashion, explores the home as an ambivalent space of both familial intimacy and patriarchal oppression. I argue here that two significant characteristics of Taylor's early writings are central to the novel's exploration of this theme: firstly, the attention given in the narrative to landscape, or physical space, as a determinant of action; and secondly, the tendency of Taylor's characters to splice their own feelings of alienation and loneliness with an immersive, imaginary existence which centres around the meanings of home and belonging. What emerges from this consideration of the meanings of home in *At Mrs Lippincote's*, I hope, is the recognition that Taylor's depictions of middle-class women are appreciably more ambivalent and potentially more critical than previously suspected.

To begin, then, with the house, which forms not just the background setting for the novel, but plays a central role in how the characters behave and relate towards each other, and which is imagined in meticulous detail in *At Mrs Lippincote's*. Julia remarks on its careful delineations according to social divisions, between the dark basement rooms of linoleum and varnished deal, and the 'other world' upstairs of plush curtains, carpets and mahogany. An arch separates the middle-class comforts from the bleak interiors of the working-class world of the servants:

> This room, she supposed, represented what was fitting and decent for the working class. On this side of the arch, varnished deal was preferred, wallpaper of brown and pink flowers, a brown tablecloth reaching to the floor and a plant with thick grey velvety leaves. Then

> down a hollowed stone step into a brick scullery where a refrigerator whirred and water dropped bleakly and with regularity into a bowl. (pp. 8–9)

This is a journey of discovery for Julia, who can only 'suppose' that what she observes in the 'other world' through the arch belongs to a different class. Julia seems preoccupied for much of the novel with imagining how this upstairs-downstairs world functioned, spatially as well as socially. The space in which Julia performs her role as housewife is represented as the site of routine, domestic practices, but we are constantly reminded that this is also a haunted space: 'The ghosts of servants seemed to hover in the place – Mrs Beeton's servants, with high caps and flying bows to their aprons. But the ghosts haunted; they did not help or encourage' (p. 9). The house also has its own gothic turret and locked attic room, in which we find, to no surprise, a ghostly, and vaguely frightening madwoman, whom Julia's bookish son, Oliver, associates immediately with Mrs Rochester. The gothic theme of the novel, intensified through its frequent allusions to the novels of the Brontë sisters, is established at an early point in the narrative in descriptions of 'clammy and unfamiliar walls', 'blood-red glass' in the front door, and 'beads of moisture' which trickle down the kitchen walls. The kitchen is likened to the 'baser side of someone's nature', and suggests dark secrets, such as 'a soup tureen the size of a baby's bath' (pp. 8–9). These gothic features are all, of course, comic exaggerations, which serve to illustrate Julia's heightened sense of estrangement from the house.

Mrs Lippincote, along with all her interior furnishings and décor, serves only one purpose in the novel, which is to represent for Julia an image of the constant presence of the past. The house, for Julia, is haunted by the Lippincotes and their servants, with every artifact and fabric a ghostly reminder of past lives. It becomes, then, a kind of ruin, a decayed memorial to other lives and loves. Julia's experiences of the house, and her imaginative engagement with its history, are thus tinged constantly with melancholy. This air of melancholy pervades representations of landscape in the novel, so that excursions out of the house always seem to end up at ruined abbeys, run-down streets, or crumbling façades, or, indeed to meet up with people, such as Mr Taylor, who have themselves fallen from grandeur into illness or ruin. This is the case not just for Julia, but also for Eleanor, Roddy's devoted cousin, who lives with the Davenants. The beginnings of what might be a romantic escape from domestic drudgery for Eleanor turns quickly to dust, a word repeated frequently in the description of her interlude with Mr Aldridge. As he confesses to her that he has just three months to live, which later turns out to be a sham, the landscape she inhabits seems decayed and futile:

> She walked back along the gritty pavement feeling overwhelmed. The spring seemed to have become smudged and rotten, the trees dully bluish green, railings coated with dust, lilac dead, laburnum dead, guelder roses dying, pink may was a little sickly, white may quite overpowering. From the playing fields a solid click at intervals, but no noise. No whistles in the summer. (p. 55)

This melancholic landscape, of decay, sterility and ruin, which Ian Baucom argues is central to modern English literature and culture, is the unrelieved setting onto which Taylor's characters project their own fictions of loss and desire.[11]

Melancholy, and the related sentiments of mourning and nostalgia, are perhaps the inevitable outcome of the unsettled geography of wartime England, in which people and their homes were dramatically transformed and transported.[12] One approach to the novel's representations of Julia's concern for how past inhabitants lived and worked in the house is to argue that the war invites an imaginative engagement across social and cultural divides, and encourages anxiety about how the past erupts into the present in uncanny and disturbing ways. The wartime setting, in other words, may go some way to explaining Julia's experience of the house as a haunted, uncanny space, and so might suggest some thematic overlaps between Taylor and Elizabeth Bowen (to whom early reviewers of Taylor's work frequently compared her). In Julia's case, it is not so much that the war has brought her into contact with the experience of another class, but that the unhomely, unsettled experience of domesticity in the war compels her into imagining the 'other world' of working-class existence much more closely. To put it another way, it is the absence of domestic servants in Julia's house, and her experience of the emptiness of the house as a result, that obliges her to engage imaginatively with other forms of social existence. The house functions, in this regard, to contain and bring into focus the relationship between the familial and the other, between intimacy and estrangement, and hence the gothic tropes deployed within the novel.

The house is disturbing not just for what it suggests about the past, or about Mrs Lippincote, who turns out to be far less frightening than Julia has come to suspect. But the house also disturbs Julia for the ways in which it registers uncomfortable truths about her own life and marriage.

In particular, a photograph of Mr and Mrs Lippincote on their wedding day haunts Julia throughout the narrative:

> Julia gazed as if lost. There they stood, young, surrounded by prosperous-looking parents, all pleased, sure and comfortable. Yet did not one set of parents look milder, on a smaller scale than the other? Had she, in fact, married a little beneath her? ... 'And now it's all finished', Julia thought. They had that lovely day and the soup tureen and meat dishes, servants with frills and streamers, children. They set out that day as if they were laying the foundations of something. But it was only something which perished very quickly. (p. 10)

The photograph isolates a moment of both happiness and unease in Mrs Lippincote's life, which Julia comes to know only through the letters, photographs and memorabilia which adorn the house, but it produces a shock of recognition in Julia too. The idea that Mr and Mrs Lippincote were mismatched in some way, that a promising moment of happiness 'perished very quickly', seems to correspond with the crisis in Julia's life. Her husband, Roddy, is having an affair, and has moved his family into their new house in order to conceal his infidelity. We discover at the end of the novel that Julia has known this all along, or, at the very least, has had good cause to believe that her marriage is threatened. The marriage is in crisis not just for Roddy, however, but for Julia too, who begins to wonder if she can continue to love a man in whom there is little sense of compassion or sensitivity. Julia lies to Roddy when she visits an old acquaintance who is dying, fearing that 'there was no longer any room in his heart for the weak or unsuccessful' (p. 179). This compels Julia into the realisation that she is unhappy in her marriage, and that it is the fate of women to endure marriage long after it has ceased to have any meaning. This is the significance of Julia's preoccupation with the photograph of the Lippincotes: it functions as an uncanny projection of Julia's sense of alienation and unhappiness. For Julia, the photograph is a fundamentally melancholic representation, which registers the future anteriority of its object, and which, as Thomas Docherty argues, 'produces "presence" only if that term is understood as carrying the sense of "ghostly" presence'.[13] Julia is surrounded by such figurations of historicity and spectrality in the novel, which signal her own feelings of being out of place and time.

The photograph for Julia constitutes a site of loss, of mourning, figured even more clearly when she confronts the hoards of her own photographs. Mrs Lippincote's house functions in part for Julia as the storehouse of memories which belong to someone else, and thus Mrs Lippincote's 'belongings' – the photographs, furniture, ornaments and décor – serve to remind Julia of her estrangement. But this feeling is compounded for Julia by the fact that her own hoarded belongings serve equally to estrange her. Among them, her photographs seem to function paradoxically as both forms of registering and dissolving identity:

> Julia, in her picture, was only one of four hundred other girls in white linen tunics and stood near the end of the strip rather blurred and unfocussed. She looked merely cheerful and healthy, as far as one could see anything of her. And so did Roddy in his football group. His lip curled more in those days, his hair hung in a fringe above his eyes, his rather square-shaped knees were as if sculped; but the hands (which were spread round a football on which was whitewashed 'Ist XI 1926') were the same, and she recognised with a little shock the wide fingers, the shape of the nails, the man's hands before the man. 'Oh, Roddy!' she cried aloud, but softly, kneeling before the drawer, mourning Roddy's boyhood for him. (p. 203)

As with the photograph of the Lippincotes on their wedding day, the photograph of Roddy symbolises a moment of possibility for Julia, a figure of openness towards the future, to contrast with the closure of hope which Julia experiences in the present. The photograph represents a time, now lost, of hope, to which Julia can only respond melancholically. 'Why keep all this?' Julia wonders, thinking of her hoarding of photographs, letters from old lovers, memorabilia of times past, and she asks specifically of the letters from a man she would once have married, 'why any longer desire the remembrance of having been cherished – however meagrely – by other men than Roddy?' (p. 203). Such memorabilia, or the acts of mourning before such memorabilia which Julia undertakes, serve within the novel to figure a crisis in Julia's sense of self, and in the emotional security of her family life. The domestic space cannot but register the disrupted emotional lives of those within it. More than this, however, Julia's contemplation of the 'other time' figured in photographs and letters is an indication of her constant awareness of the spectral displacement of her own time, of the ghosts of the past which emerge to trouble the security of the present. It is for this reason that Julia attempts towards the end of the novel to burn her letters and photographs, purging the other selves of her past so that she can become 'a good mother, a fairly good wife, and at peace' (p. 204). Thus, one of the ways in which Taylor's novel discloses the restrictive ideologies of femininity and family is to represent the roles of mother and wife as necessarily involving the closure of possibility, and the denial of desire. Julia remains the 'blurred and unfocussed' subject at the edge of her photograph, a marginal figure within her own story.

There is, then, an important process of what Homi Bhabha calls 'time-lag', or 'the projective past', occurring in the novel, in which past and present are sutured together, in which the past is given 'the circulatory life of the "sign" of the present'.[14] It is a process which recurs in many of Taylor's novels, in the fiction of Bowen and, more recently, Pat Barker, and, in somewhat different forms, in the novels of Peter Ackroyd and Iain Sinclair. In Taylor's novels, only certain characters perceive or experience the spectral presence of the past. In *At Mrs Lippincote's*, the capacity – or perhaps, the sensitivity – to perceive the ghostly trace of the past serves to distinguish the sympathetic characters from the less sympathetic ones.[15] As Avery Gordon argues, haunting involves a particular kind of visibility and perception, and an openness to alterity, to change: 'Being haunted draws us affectively, sometimes against our will and always a bit magically, into the structure of feeling of a reality we come to experience, not as cold knowledge, but as a transformative recognition'.[16] Julia is affected by the house and its ghosts in precisely the way that Gordon describes, drawn into and then transformed by them. Her openness to the 'projective past' of the house is one of the principal ways in which the novel registers her desire to connect and empathise with others. This is signalled from the very beginning of the book, in a difference in outlook between Julia and Roddy. Julia ponders whether old Mr Lippincote died in the house, a thought which leads her to consider if the dead 'communicate with the living, or do harm to them' (p. 5). She suspects not, but pauses anxiously before proceeding into one of the rooms. Her hesitation indicates her difference from Roddy, who entertains no such concern for others, and for whom death and the dead can be dismissed clinically and coldly. It is a mark too of the difficulties between Julia and Roddy that Julia remains unsettled and haunted by the house, and its various, hidden and imagined stories, while Roddy expects the house to function mechanically as a family home. The house remains peculiarly resistant to becoming a home, however, partly because, as Julia perceives, it is haunted by the ghosts of the Lippincotes, and partly too because Julia's marital and family relations are increasingly strained and fraught. In this sense, the novel explores the ideologies of home in terms both of territorial identity and family unity.

For the Davenants, 'home' remains an elusive ideal, and an illusory object of desire and nostalgia. 'Home', in its various meanings as dwelling and belonging, space and identity, takes on particular significance in the novel as a mark of loss and disempowerment. Julia is unable to make a home, unable to find happiness, love, or familial unity, because she cannot command the house as her own. The novel comes close to implying, then, a cosmic connection between woman and home, which is disturbed and thrown off balance in the upheaval caused not just by the war but also by Roddy's deceptions. There are some uncomfortable, reactionary implications here: that homeliness and family unity are interlinked, that woman serves as a kind of gravitational centre of 'home' and belonging, and, more widely, that women are essentially concerned with the private, domestic sphere. Moreover, the narrator suggests that it is not Roddy's infidelity which is to blame for upsetting the home life of the Davenants. The narrator directs us instead to examine Julia's culpability:

> Could she have taken for granted a few of those generalisations invented by men and largely acquiesced in by women (that women live by their hearts, men by their heads, that love is woman's whole existence, and especially that sons should respect their fathers), she would have eased her own life and other people's. She did not probably never would now realise that generalisations are merely conveniences, an attempt to oil the wheels of such civilisation as we have. (p. 26)

The narrative tone here is borrowed from Austen, and, like Austen in places, too, there is a certain indeterminacy in how we should read the narrative perspective. The narrator appears to blame Julia for making life for herself and those around her more difficult by her stubborn refusal to acquiesce in those convenient stereotypes of femininity. If we are to read this as the moralising perspective of an omniscient narrator, then the novel apportions much of the blame for the domestic discontent of the Davenants to Julia. At this point the narrator seems to endorse Roddy's point of view, and to marginalise Julia as an eccentric, stubborn woman who fails to fit into sociable patterns of behaviour. But it is also possible to read this passage for its ventriloquism of Roddy's view. The anxiety that 'sons should respect their fathers' seems more appropriate to his perspective than any other, for example. We also find Roddy articulating or thinking these same criticisms of Julia's refusal to conform to or accept social conventions later in the novel (p. 105). A recurrent feature of the narrative is that it tends to shift perspective cinematically from one character to another. To think of the passage in these terms would make it an ironic imitation of how Julia is seen through Roddy's eyes, and would draw attention to the ways in which Julia is constantly constructed and represented as a failure by Roddy, and by his cousin, Eleanor.

Eleanor serves as a recalcitrant foil to Julia, always quick to observe and criticise Julia's failings as a wife. She plays with the illusion that she would make a better wife for Roddy, and wishes that Roddy had 'some woman behind him to make his career her life's work, and to be an inspiration and incentive to him' (p. 20). Eleanor is, of course, disillusioned about Roddy's suitability as a husband when she learns about his deceptions, but for much of the novel she contributes to the notion that Julia has failed to make her marriage work, and has failed also to make a home for her family. When she learns that Roddy has been unfaithful, she shifts the blame away from Julia. 'There's no love in this house', she cries, which seems to echo Julia's suspicions that the building itself registers some sense of psychic or emotional disturbance.

Taylor's novel thematises this connection between 'home' and love, between the symbolic meanings of 'home' and the desire for security, warmth, family. It is a theme which preoccupies much feminist writing of the postwar period, in various guises, from the narratives of marital breakdown in Macauley's *The World My Wilderness* (1950), Lessing's *Children of Violence* novels (1952–69), or Lehmann's *The Echoing Grove* (1953), to literary representations of single mothers in Delaney's *A Taste of Honey* (1958), Lynne Reid Banks' *The L-Shaped Room* (1960), and Margaret Drabble's *The Millstone* (1965). The idea of home as an ambivalent space of identity and alienation, of belonging and oppression, became central to postwar representations of women. My argument here is that Taylor figures home as an ambivalent space through gothic tropes of displacement and the uncanny, or unhomely, and through themes of marital failure and domesticity. Biddy Martin and Chandra Mohanty argue that there are political connotations to these experiences of home and the unhomely:

> 'Being home' refers to the place where one lives within familiar, safe, protected boundaries; 'not being home' is a matter of realizing that home was an illusion of coherence and safety based on the exclusion of specific histories of oppression and resistance, the repression of differences even within oneself.[17]

In *At Mrs Lippincote's*, Julia's experience of the unhomely enables her to begin to construct an oppositional perspective on the practices of oppression and exclusion which revolve around notions of 'home'. She recognises, for example, that marriage entails both making a home and being deprived of her home: 'I am a parasite', Julia tells Roddy and Eleanor bitterly, 'I follow my man round like a piece of luggage or part of a travelling harem' (p. 199). She knows too, at the end of the novel, that her fate is to endure her marriage, to do what 'women have to' (p. 214). The concluding image of the novel, as the Davenants prepare to leave the house, is, as Jenny Hartley has argued, a fitting finale, in this respect.[18] The novel closes with Julia pulling the heavy damask curtains across Mrs Lippincote's window for the last time, a gesture which conceals the false intimacy of their marriage from the street outside, and which draws a thick veil over the failures and discontents of ideologies of 'home'.

Notes

1 Alison Light, *Forever England: Femininity, Literature and Conservatism Between the Wars* (London: Routledge, 1991), p. 219.

2 See Lynne Segal, 'Look Back in Anger: Men in the Fifties', in Rowena Chapman and Jonathan Rutherford, eds, *Male Order: Unwrapping Masculinity* (London: Lawrence and Wishart, 1988), pp. 68–96.

3 H. Hopkins, *The New Look* (London: Secker and Warburg, 1963), p. 324.

4 See Birmingham Feminist History Group, 'Feminism as Femininity in the Nineteen-fifties?', *Feminist Review*, 3 (1979), pp. 48–65; Elizabeth Wilson, *Women and the Welfare State* (London: Tavistock, 1977); Elizabeth Wilson, *Only Halfway to Paradise: Women in Postwar Britain 1945–1968* (London: Tavistock, 1980); Martin Pugh, *Women and the Women's Movement in Britain 1914–1959* (Basingstoke: Macmillan, 1992). For discussion of women's writing in this period, see Niamh Baker, *Happily Ever After? Women's Fiction in Postwar Britain, 1945–60* (New York: St Martin's Press, 1989), Deborah Philips and Ian Haywood, *Brave New Causes: Women in British Postwar Fictions* (London: Leicester University Press, 1998), and Maroula Joannou, *Contemporary Women's Writing: From* The Golden Notebook *to* The Color Purple (Manchester: Manchester University Press, 2000).

5 See in particular Rosemary Marangoly George, *The Politics of Home: Postcolonial Relocations and Twentieth-Century Fiction* (Berkeley, CA: University of California Press, 1996) and Wendy Webster, *Imagining Home: Gender, 'Race' and National Identity, 1945–64* (London: University College London Press, 1998).

6 See for a discussion of Taylor in relation to Waugh, Betjeman, Mitford and others in 1945, specifically on the theme of place and nation, my *Orwell to the Present: Literature in England, 1945–2000* (Basingstoke: Palgrave, 2002).

7 Elizabeth Taylor, *At Mrs Lippincote's* [1945] (London: Virago, 1988), p.12. For critical and biographical sources on Elizabeth Taylor, see Florence Leclercq, *Elizabeth Taylor* (Boston: Twayne, 1985) and Robert Liddell, *Elizabeth and Ivy* (London: Peter Owen, 1986).

8 Frederick Karl, *A Reader's Guide to the Contemporary English Novel* (New York: Octagon Press, 1972), p. 274.
9 Alan Sinfield, *Literature, Politics and Culture in Postwar Britain* (Oxford: Blackwell, 1989), p. 63.
10 Elizabeth Wilson, *Only Halfway to Paradise: Women in Postwar Britain, 1945–1968* (London: Tavistock, 1980), p. 150.
11 Ian Baucom, *Out of Place: Englishness, Empire, and the Locations of Identity* (Princeton, NJ: Princeton University Press, 1999), p. 175.
12 See David Matless, *Landscape and Englishness* (London: Reaktion Books, 1998), pp. 173–200.
13 Thomas Docherty, *After Theory: Postmodernism/postmarxism* (London: Routledge, 1990), p. 77.
14 Homi Bhabha, *The Location of Culture* (London: Routledge, 1994), p. 254.
15 Jane Brown Gillette makes a similar argument about the function of creative illusions in Taylor's novels: 'her less sympathetic characters only use their imaginations to aggrandize and protect their egos, while her more sympathetic characters, although equally isolated, express through their illusions a solidarity with other lonely people' (Jane Brown Gillette, '"Oh, What a Something Web We Weave": The Novels of Elizabeth Taylor', *Twentieth Century Literature*, Vol. 35, No. 1 (Spring 1989), pp. 94–112, p. 94).
16 Avery Gordon, *Ghostly Matters: Haunting and the Sociological Imagination* (Minneapolis, MN: University of Minnesota, 1997), p. 8.
17 Biddy Martin and Chandra Talpade Mohanty, 'Feminist Politics: What's Home Got to Do with It?', *Feminist Studies/Critical Studies*, ed. Theresa de Lauretis (Bloomington, IN: Indiana University Press, 1986), pp. 191–212, p. 191.
18 Jenny Hartley, *Millions Like Us: British Women's Fiction of the Second World War* (London: Virago, 1997), p. 137.

6

Souls Astray: Belonging and the Idea of Home: Elizabeth Bowen's *The Heat of the Day*, Betty Miller's *On the Side of the Angels* and *Death of the Nightingale* and Muriel Spark's *Memento Mori*

Sarah Sceats

The notion of stable personal identity has all but disappeared: called into question by the modernists, fragmented by postmodernism and more recently almost entirely metamorphosed into acts of performance. Vikki Bell cites Judith Butler's claim that: '[i]dentity is the effect of performance, and not vice versa' as a basis for her own view that '[b]elonging is an achievement at several levels of abstraction'.[1] She is surely right to emphasise complexity: by and large, one never simply 'belongs', for there are processes at work, involving, according to your viewpoint, interpellation, reiteration, discursive practices, incorporation, and so on. But I think I want to quarrel with the other term she uses, at least in relation to the texts I will be discussing, in which the 'achievement' of belonging is at best questionable. Elspeth Probyn's encapsulation of belonging as a process of 'becoming' rather than a fixed state is useful, but it seems to me that for women writers in the middle of the twentieth century there is both more and less than Probyn's description encompasses, for they see belonging itself as inherently problematic.[2]

Much twentieth-century theory stresses provisionality, privileging fluctuation, difference and diversity over continuity, and this is perhaps not surprising, given the history of the period. In the period in question, the chaos of the Blitz, the tragedy and upheavals of war, the ongoing material and social disruptions of wartime and its immediate aftermath, and the postwar measures aimed at re-establishment of 'normality' bespeak a troubled and insecure existence. In the light of such historical trauma and uncertainty, how *do* we locate ourselves; how, where and to whom or what do we belong? A consciousness of one's identity (necessary for the function of self) depends on some *sense* of belonging. We define ourselves or are defined both in contradistinction to others and in terms of our attachments – love objects, material surroundings, family, neighbourhood, social group, country and so on – and a potent manifestation and major focus here is the idea of home. Indeed, in the postwar period domesticity – and specifically the re-establishment of the home as 'woman's place' – played a major part in what Deborah Philips and Ian Haywood describe as a distorting, ideologically-conceived myth 'in which women returned to the home after their war labours and set about replenishing the nation'.[3] Their point is that the myth was not only coercive (enshrining patriarchal dominance) but is descriptively incorrect, since many women continued to work. Certainly for the writers considered here the home is by no means an evident source of nourishment or place of belonging. I shall explore how, against the background of mid-twentieth century upheavals, 'belonging' emerges as a crucial issue, mediated through representations of home or homes.

For a novel with only a handful of characters, *The Heat of the Day* contains an extraordinary number of homes: Stella's prewar houses and the lodgings and flats in which she lives during the war, Holme Dean and its precursors, Louie's parents' home and Louie's and Connie's rooms in Chilcombe Street, Mount Morris in Ireland, and Wistaria Lodge, the home for 'tranquil uncertified mental patients' in which Cousin Nettie takes refuge.[4] Yet – as though to feel at home is an impossibility – the prevailing ethos of the novel is one of *homelessness*. The opening description of the Regents Park concert stresses uncertainty and dislocation, sketching exiles and people without purpose somehow tenuously held together outdoors in twilight community only by the music. The presence of Louie, adrift and seeking vaguely for some affirmation of her existence reinforces the mood: 'her object was to feel that she, Louie, *was*' (p. 15).

Clearly, the setting of the novel – London, 1942, the middle of the war – provides adequate explanation for the prevailing sense of dislocation. Louie, for example, has lost her home in multiple senses: married and displaced from Seale on Sea, she is brought to London by her new husband Tom; her parents and her childhood home are subsequently obliterated by a bomb, the husband in whose presence she locates her sense of home is removed to serve in India, so that all that her room in Chilcombe Street offers is an uncommunicative photograph of Tom and the faint ghost of his presence. In comparison with Connie upstairs, Louie is 'a Kentish sea-coast orphan' (pp. 144–5), feeling like a day-tripper stranded in town.

The central character of the novel, Stella, is similarly nomadic for ostensibly topical reasons, giving up her house at the outbreak of war and living in furnished accommodation, a move she experiences as a liberation. She does not really inhabit her flat, however; it 'expresse[s] her unexceptionably but wrongly' (p. 24), the narrator observes, and her son Roderick thinks it does not even look like home, though it does look 'like something – possibly a story' (p. 47). We are given a clue here, I think, about self-narrativisation. The dislocation in Stella's living arrangements not only suggests the precariousness of civilian life in wartime but mirrors the re-location of her self in a lovers' story (as well as gesturing towards some more profound sense of homelessness). Stella's 'habitat' is not that of bricks and mortar, ashtrays and sofas, but her investment in Robert, her absorption in what Bowen calls the 'hermetic world' of lovers. She is so far from rooted in her surroundings that even coming home – that is, entering the flat – with the enigmatic Harrison is preferable to coming in alone. Harrison, who by this stage has revealed to Stella both Robert's treason and his own desire for her, is able to observe that *he* begins to feel 'quite at home' in her flat. Harrison fails to perceive Stella's absence within her surroundings.[5] Caressing a flowered ashtray he murmurs, 'Pretty ... All your things are so pretty'. Though she quickly tells him nothing is hers, he continues to feel that the room is imbued with her presence; 'They might not be her ... [possessions]', he reasons to himself, 'but she had, still, employed them' (p. 137). Although he works in Intelligence and observes acutely, Harrison is so intent on capturing the essence of Stella that he misreads her. Himself homeless by design and profession, when Stella asks out of politeness where he lives, he equivocates:

> 'There are always two or three places where I can turn in.'
> 'But for instance where do you keep your razor?'
> 'I have two or three razors', he said in an absent tone. (p. 140)

Yet despite his elusiveness it seems his interest in Stella is symptomatic of some inescapable desire to belong somewhere. 'Is it so odd I should want a place of my own?', he asks Stella, to which she shrewdly replies 'What seems to me most odd is the way you expect me to make one' (p. 34).

Stella barely even provides a suitable home for her son Roderick. On leave from the army, he seems adrift in her flat. Sensing her lack of presence, he is unable to decide even where to put down the coffee tray. Indeed his very identity seems at risk, and although he seeks to re-establish their connections with some care he feels displaced. His pyjamas, the only property of his not in store and thus themselves a sort of home, seem to have disappeared from Stella's flat. The impersonality of the environment ('the absence of every inanimate thing they had had in common' (p. 55) places a burden on the relationship, so that it becomes flavoured by a 'sense of instinctive loss' (p. 55), of the 'impoverishment of the world' (p. 56). The impersonality of life in the army is compensated for by order (everything has its place) and comradeship; in his mother's flat, which should be 'home', he can find neither.

Two substantial homes in the novel do appear to contrast with Stella's nomadic perches. Robert's family house, Holme Dean, situated in the Home Counties and described as a 'considerable manor', is a solid English upper-middle-class dwelling. It soon becomes apparent, however, that this family home is deeply flawed. The driveway is significantly 'concealed' and Robert's mother Mrs Kellaway – in the xenophobic spirit of an Englishman in his castle – does not like people coming down the drive. The house itself is a fake, described ominously as featuring passages like 'swastika arms' (p. 258); the atmosphere is stultifying, 'time-clogged'. What goes on within the house, devoid of joy or spontaneity, provides Robert with no sense of belonging.[6] Though his boyhood room is preserved and adorned with photographs of him at various stages, it is shrine-like and seems empty, as Stella instantly notices; it makes him feel he does not exist, but has simply 'gone through the motions' (p. 118). This 'home' in Robert breeds a traitor; the combination of repression, subterfuge and expectation producing a withdrawal that seeks extremes of order and redefines home as an illusion. Those who live at Holme Dean perpetuate its tyrannies and idiocies: none of Stella's 'uncertainties of the hybrid' for them (p. 114). Mrs Kellaway poisonously and self-righteously presides, while Robert's sister Ernestine keeps herself frantically busy. Overall, a restrictive and chauvinistic code of behaviour stifles sincerity and results in such absurdities as the threat that Germans would *make* you eat cake for tea. Even the garden – emblem of innocence – is described as 'betrayed'.

If home is, as I suggest, a problematic concept in this novel whose principal characters are marked by their homelessness, then what sense of belonging do they manifest? Roderick's inheritance brings the idea of belonging and a material building together to offer both home and purpose. In this sense Mount Morris might be considered to represent the novel's optimistic response to the problem. Mount Morris is certainly different: outside England, away from the war, marginal, a mythologised antithesis to Holme Dean, perhaps. When Stella first revisits the place, she experiences a strange dislocation: 'what she was forced to grope for, as though for her identity, was the day of the week, the month of the year, the year ...' (p. 176). Later that same day she feels a 'rapture of strength' a 'breathless glory' and 'an unfinished symphony of love' in the woods, the sublimity here suggesting some kind of epiphany. For his part, Roderick is cheerfully enthusiastic about his role; arriving at night, he is nevertheless anxious to discover the outside, how the house fits into its context. Again, the place has a profound effect, 'concentrate[ing] upon Roderick its being' (p. 312), an experience described as a 'consummation', which awakens in him an awareness of death and succession.

The force of this home, then, is dynastic, as Stella recognises when she finds herself speculating about Roderick's future wife. Roderick has been given a lifetime's project and trajectory; he is installed in the 'master's' bedroom. There is some ambiguity about the place, however. Although Roderick is amenable to Uncle Francis's intentions, he is exercised by the equivocal phrasing of the will, unsure to what extent he has freedom within the traditions enshrined in the property. It has to be said, too, that reversion to an Anglo-Irish 'big house' offers an idiosyncratic and anachronistic solution to mid-twentieth century dislocation.

The degree to which Mount Morris invites belonging is further complicated. Uncle Francis's cousin-wife Nettie unequivocally does *not* want to be there (p. 216). Stella, too, is less than enthusiastic, 'not sorry' when work keeps her from accompanying Roderick. On her solo visit Stella considers the rooms to be 'without poetry'. She imagines Cousin Nettie and her predecessors 'pressed back', 'not quite mad', but 'in vain listening for meaning' in the passing of time (p. 174). This passage is quite obscure, suggesting obliquely that the women suffered an enforced passivity, that they observed, understood but felt constrained to maintain their painful, knowing silence. Cousin Nettie indicates something similar when she says that men 'may keep going, going, going and not notice', and attributes her depression to the fact that she 'could not help seeing what was the matter' (p. 217). For women at least, Mount Morris and its patriarchal tradition appears as a prison, not at all somewhere to want to belong.

Of course, homes do not necessarily or exclusively offer a sense of belonging, in wartime any more than peacetime. As I suggested earlier, Robert and Stella seek their sense of belonging in each other. Both are nomadic. Robert feels antipathy to Holme Dean and we see him in no home of his own, just as Stella lives in furnished flats. But belonging to a person is a fragile contract. When Stella questions Robert's loyalty to his country, he places a terrible burden on her in asserting that *she* is his country. Stella herself is bereft in the wake of Harrison's disclosures about Robert's treachery; it is after the conclusive interview with him that Louie, seeing Stella (and recognising, perhaps, a kindred spirit), dubs her a 'soul astray'. It is no surprise that after Robert's death Stella moves again, this time across London, to another anonymous flat.

There is one further 'home' in this novel, and that is the institution, Wistaria Lodge. Here is an insular, introverted, tidy and controlled little world, which the proprietors, the Tringsbys, do not want disrupted. They are, to use a contemporary colloquialism, on to a good number. Speaking on behalf of her charges, Mrs Tringsby patronises with oppressive benevolence: 'Here, we are so careful not to have dreadful thoughts', she says, 'we quite live, you see, in a world of our own' (p. 204). The décor and atmosphere are alike stiflingly 'nice', and the Tringsbys evince little humanity – and no sense of humour. But for Cousin Nettie Wistaria Lodge provides a refuge from Mount Morris; she has feigned madness to remain there and is described as 'well placed' and 'possibly never ... [having been] as happy as she now was' (p. 68). Wistaria Lodge thus has a peculiar place in the novel. It is a home without homeliness, anodyne in its tastefulness, subject to rules and control – and its residents largely incapable of feeling they belong or otherwise. Cousin Nettie lives here precisely because she need not struggle with the dilemma of belonging; it is sufficient that she is not at Mount Morris. It is also, perhaps not coincidentally, a place into which contemporary history does not intrude.

Taken as a whole, the novel's drift does seem to suggest that locating oneself and feeling 'at home' is profoundly difficult at this time, and not only because of the material circumstances of war (troop movements, bombed buildings and so on). Emotional investment of any sort – whether in people or possessions or traditions or even in the form of loyalty to one's country – is represented as something absent or at best insecure. Homes are anonymous or sinister and personal relationships severely tested. Nothing, it seems, can be relied upon, except perhaps death – and birth. And yet the novel is not gloomy. It is, rather, sceptical, which can also be said of Betty Miller's somewhat different take on the Home Front in her wartime novel *On the Side of the Angels* (1945). Instead of radical uncertainty, this novel suggests a polarisation of genders: that masculinity seeks to attach itself to the military and to action, in contradistinction to all that is 'female', domestic and stresses continuity.

The novel focuses on two sisters and their partners: the domesticated and maternal Honor, married to Colin, a doctor posted to a provincial military hospital, and her independent, schoolteacher sister Claudia whose fiancé Andrew has been invalided out of service. The wartime situation exposes considerable strains in these relationships. Honor is a domesticated young middle-class mother, her life devoted to Colin, 'the lynch-pin around which all her thought, her emotions, her smallest daily actions revolved'.[7] She is portrayed very much in terms of her domestic setting, is associated with food and eating, bathing and grooming, nurturing and dependence. When she goes out she gets homesick for her babies, the youngest of whom she is still breastfeeding. Although conforming to the conventions of mid-twentieth century middle-class behaviour, she is disordered and instinctual; even the garden of their billet is going slightly wild, as though to reflect 'a certain fertile disorder' (p. 119). Her husband, by contrast, is increasingly repelled by domesticity and infatuated by the military as embodied in the person of the CO, with whom he continually but ineffectually attempts to curry favour. Colin's desire is to locate himself absolutely in this masculine world of the army – though Honor's image of the CO is as a sheikh with a 'harem of competitive wives' (p. 169) suggests it may be less masculine than he thinks. Hence the seemingly irresolvable tensions in their marriage.

Claudia and Andrew are more complex. Andrew is not only sickly, and sceptical, but struggling with the implications for his masculinity of a weak heart and exclusion from active service. Claudia is sharp, independent-minded and troubled. She resents pressures to locate herself domestically. She is irritated by Honor's formlessness and her emotional dependence on an unseeing husband, while Honor sees Claudia as 'hounded by impulses so contrary that it took every available ounce of will-power and energy to control them' (p. 202). The other domestic model Claudia is presented with is even less appealing to her than Honor's and that is the upper-middle-class self-preservation of Andrew's mother, who remains in her country home and manages more or less to ignore the war, keeping her old retainers, traditions and (selfish) way of life under the cover of supporting wartime fundraising activities. Inevitably, when the 'commando' Captain Heriot comes onto the scene, Claudia – resisting what she perceives as the oppressive and deadening comforts of home – is drawn to the energy, decisiveness and associations with order of a dashing military man. She becomes confusedly infatuated. Heriot appears to be the antithesis of Andrew, embracing war and fighting as an exciting challenge and opportunity for action. But it turns out that he is an impostor and the excitement is merely that of the gambler. He, like Colin, wants to belong to a *Boy's Own* world of male camaraderie and risk.

As with Stella's self-location in a lovers' story, Heriot – a dutiful husband, bank manager and the father of three grammar-school boys – recasts himself into a more exciting story and one that eschews a domesticated belonging. Heriot does not truly seek to locate himself in the reality of army life (which he avoids), but in a heroic and sexual fantasy. Claudia believes that it is wartime that makes for the peculiar behaviour of people like Colin (and Heriot): 'Surely none of these people would behave like this in ordinary civil life. What is it that this situation has brought out in us all?' (p. 47). The answer, perhaps, lies in Andrew's view that war is a form of escapism, 'a flight from reason, from everyday duties and responsibilities' (p. 141). This is not to say it is avoidable, for civilization is so costive, he says, that it needs 'a regular dose of high explosive' for catharsis (p. 72). Claudia's ambivalence and Andrew's appreciation of the desires embodied in Heriot's fake persona, and of its attraction, all serve to emphasise the threat posed to family and society, not only by the devastations of war but by the charismatic spell cast by 'belonging' to the military. Like *The Heat of the Day*, *On the Side of the Angels* implies that the disruptions of the Second World War went much further and much deeper than its manifest effects. With hindsight, of course, and the experience of half a century in evidence, it is easy to draw such conclusions, but given that these novels were written up close, as it were, to the effects of war, the suggestion of a far-reaching dislocation is prescient.

Elsewhere, Miller does not offer such a simple or reductive view of domesticity and belonging. Her final novel, *The Death of the Nightingale* (1948), reverses the gender implications suggested above, opposing rationality and the instinctual in such a way that belonging is connected with passion and politics and domesticity is characterised as a facet of repressive masculinity. The story turns upon the hostility of Professor Newman Cain to the love between his daughter Léonie and a young Irishman, Matthew O'Farrell, not long discharged from service in the RAF. The plot is complicated by Newman Cain's personal history, his rancorous separation from Léonie's mother and ambivalent personal and political involvement with Matthew's family during the Troubles. For the purposes of my argument here, what is interesting is that it is Cain who is associated with domesticity and that this domesticity is represented as effete, xenophobic and life-denying.

The house in which Cain and his daughter live is carefully evoked. A scene in which Cain manipulates Léonie's loyalty by placing Matthew as an outsider to 'the inner life of a family, its stealthy continuity of growth and custom' is followed by an evocation of the smell of the dining room from Léonie's perspective, 'a mellow date-like smell, as of old furniture, of preserves and spices, of table-linen packed freshly glazed in a paper-lined drawer', which suggests continuity as well as sensuousness.[8] The house – Bishop's House – is Cain's home, his refuge and the place he feels he belongs:

> This was his own home: a frame so moulded by the constant thrust and pressure of his own desires that, despite its proportions, it seemed at that moment to conform as intimately to the contours of his own body as the interior of its shell to the snail whose coils, retracting, replenish it to the very brim. (p. 140)

This sense of intimacy applies only to the house, however. Though he lives in a village, Cain is aloof, and his neighbours are merely polite, not friendly. He may walk for the sake of fitness but it is so that he can ignore his body, and he loathes the country and especially rain. His preference is for winter and electric light and he is bothered by open doors and animals. In short, he is a man of intellect, a cerebral creature who needs to feel he is in control.

Matthew, by contrast, is a man of instinct, destined to become a farmer. While Cain huddles deeper into his snail shell, Mattew goes to see his mother in Ireland and is able – despite the pressures of history, maternal persuasion and the overwhelming sensations of childhood evoked by a rug on the lawn – to revisit and then leave the only home he has ever had. He no longer wishes to belong to an enshrined and mythologised past. Léonie meanwhile finds it difficult to resist the pull exerted by her father and their cosy domestic history, but she is nevertheless positioned on the side of resistant life (as indicated by Cain's disturbing dream of a single blade of grass pushing aside a paving stone). The opposition between Cain and the young people is further emphasised by the juxtaposition of Cain's sanctuary in the British Library with a visit Matthew and Léonie make to the London Zoo.

This perhaps all sounds rather schematic, but the polarisation of instinct and intellect is tempered by the revelation that Cain's inwardness results from repression of what he feels is a 'shameful avidity' (p. 63) in himself. His young wife was French and the love of his life Irish; his retreat to the English countryside and adoption of frigidity is a desperate defence, a willed internal exile from his feeling past. To put it in the terms of current pop psychology, he is 'in denial'. Not only does he seek to exclude from his home (and daughter) a young man he sees as an undisciplined, passionate interloper, scion of a troublesome Irish Republican. He wants to protect Léonie from any knowledge of the personal past, and thus to shield her (and himself) from ignominy – and he wants her to remain unchanged. He seeks to excise feeling. Home is not for him so much a place of positive belonging as a place where the world is absent. Just as in *The Heat of the Day* Mount Morris remains untouched by the upheavals of the war years, so Bishop's House here represents a place of escape, from personal pain and political responsibility, where Cain can immerse himself in abstract texts and repudiate painful involvement with human complications. What is interesting is that although Léonie does manage, with difficulty, to extract herself, marry Matthew, and go off to expand on a farm (suggesting, perhaps, some reconciliation in Anglo-Irish relations) Cain recoils from the opportunity to reconnect with Matthew's mother, the object of his youthful desire, and retreats to his own hearth and his books. This Englishman's home is a retreat, and something of a prison.

The final novel I want to consider, Muriel Spark's *Memento Mori*, comes a full decade later, in 1959, when the shadows of war have receded and the country has, as Harold Macmillan put it, 'never had it so good'.[9] Spark's focus is not so much on the disruptions brought about, directly or indirectly, by the strains and upheavals of twentieth-century history, as on the appropriateness or otherwise of material attachments in a burgeoning affluent society.[10] The novel, a moral fable, features a variety of ageing characters, whose sense of belonging is characterised by obsessive concern with money and its manipulative potential, sexual dalliance (past and present), spiteful rivalries (ditto) and the increasingly desperate lottery of their own survival. Most of them at some time or another receive anonymous telephone calls telling them to remember that they must die; how they respond to the calls is indicative of their spiritual condition.

The general force of 'home' in this novel is thus that it relates to this world rather than the next, but there are also at least three particular and significantly typified residences. The first is the house of an uncaring and materialistic member of the upper middle classes. The selfish, bullying committee woman and hanger-and-flogger, Dame Lettie, who spends much of her time rewriting her will in order to manipulate her nephew, lives alone in a large house in a 'posh part' of Hampstead. She is not only unnerved but also enraged when the telephone calls begin and as well as threatening all kinds of action against the ineffectualness of the Police she takes on a young maid for protection. The degree of her self-righteousness and her all-consuming egocentricity soon transform her response into paranoia, however, and her home becomes a nightmarish prison as she engages in a nightly ritual of poking into every corner of house and garden before bed, for fear of the intrusion of death. Her fears become self-fulfilling, for the maid, leaving in disgust, tells her boyfriend about the situation; from him word spreads to a violent burglar, and a sort of poetic justice is meted out.

The second home belongs to Eric Mortimer, retired Chief Inspector turned private investigator, who is called in to investigate the mysterious telephone calls. He lives in suburban contentment in Kingston upon Thames, under the watchful eye of a tactful and caring wife. They tend their garden, love their grandchildren and in a spirit of helpfulness play host to the recipients of the telephone calls for an investigative discussion. Mrs Mortimer's indignation at the lack of younger family to help the old people, the provision of afternoon tea, the tactful orchestrating of the occasion and the couple's subsequent quiet evening and Eric Mortimer's prospective retirement pursuits all suggest an unquestioned homeliness and calm acceptance in which the notion of belonging is not remotely problematic. Significantly, Mortimer is self-reflective and unafraid of death.

The final home is an institution, of which there are two types in this novel: the public medical ward and private nursing home. Jean Taylor lives uncomplainingly in the Maud Long Medical Ward, where she experiences feelings of 'desolate humiliation' and loneliness. The ward is filled with 'Grannies', for whom it is home, but where none feels she belongs; they connect only superficially, and suffer the demise of their fellows. By the time we meet Jean Taylor, it is, she says, too late for her to relocate to 'a home in Surrey' with her ex-employer Charmian. 'I've made friends here', she says, 'it's my home'.[11] The implication is that she locates herself in relation to people rather than places, a fitting sentiment, perhaps, for an ex-'companion'. But although she is unwilling to desert her fellows, the point is really that the worst of Taylor's mental suffering is over; she has begun to move beyond worldly attachment.

Moving into an Old People's Home is often seen as threatening; it may involve loss of owner-occupation and mark a move from autonomy to passivity and dependence. While in more recent years, in a work-dominated culture, there is a stigma attached to being functionless, in the 1950s there was a sense of disgrace to do with not being cared for by one's family, as suggested by Mrs Mortimer's indignation at the old people being left to their own resources.[12] The prospect of being 'put in a home' is certainly menacing in this novel. The threat to Charmian by both her husband and the blackmailer Mrs Pettigrew is one of the things that incapacitates her – though ironically the pressure she suffers helps reverse her dementia. But Charmian's ultimate decision to move into the home allows her to realise how much she longs for the release: 'In the nursing home she could be a real person again ... instead of a frightened invalid. She needed respect and attention. Perhaps she would have visitors' (p. 161). As indeed she does. Her room, like the home itself, recalls her school, rekindling a sense of innocence and suggesting not simply senility but another, less corrupted layer of belonging.

The novel as a whole plays with the contradiction that to hold on you must let go. Those who most attach themselves to earthly possessions have least sense of happy belonging: Dame Lettie, abusing the power of wealth, effectively transforms her luxury home into a prison and brings about her own demise; Mrs Pettigrew, the blackmailer, gets rid of Charmian but in the process unwittingly undermines herself. Alec Warner is attached in a rather different way, to gerontology and fixation on his own survival. During a visit to Jean Taylor Alec witnesses a Granny's hundredth birthday. Noting 'an almost cannibal desire' in his gaze, Taylor observes, 'We all appear to ourselves frustrated in our old age, Alec, because we cling to everything so much. But in reality we are still fulfilling our lives' (p. 218). And here is the moral of the tale, as proclaimed by the mystery voice on the telephone: remember that you must die. Those who take the calls in their stride are those who already do so (Jean Taylor, Charmian, the aptly named Henry Mortimer); it is the unmindful who are put into a panic.

Ostensibly, then, the novel proposes that belonging is unimportant, home is where you find yourself, and that what the old should be about is detaching themselves from material concerns. Knowledge, power and houses are no protection – in fact invite trouble – but a dispassionate loyalty to fellow sufferers may nourish a suitably temporary sense of home. Far from a rejection of belonging, however, I would argue that the 'message' – underlined by the epigraph from the *Penny Catechism* and references to Catholicism sprinkled through the novel – proposes a redeeming *attachment*, a sense of spiritual belonging fostered by religious practices.

Such a sense of belonging, like the lived love story or the desire for heroic adventure, is a form self-narrativisation, one of the means through which we put together a sense of ourselves, in terms of the past, in relation to other people, or in particular roles. The domestic narrative is particularly potent inasmuch as it intersects with all the others and because the desire to belong somehow is so very strong. As these novels suggest, though, the possibility of feeling at home in the modern world is fraught with difficulties. To achieve a sense of belonging without retreating from the world into a narrow domesticity on the one hand or losing one's bearings on the other seems almost impossible. What all these novels intimate, one way or another, is a mid-twentieth century unease with the idea of feeling 'at home' and a questioning uncertainty about belonging itself.

Notes

1 Vikki Bell, ed., *Performativity and Belonging* (London: Sage, 1999), p. 3.

2 Cited in Anne-Marie Fortier, *Migrant Belongings: Memory, Space, Identity* (Oxford: Berg, 2000).

3 Deborah Philips and Ian Haywood, *Brave New Causes: Women in British Postwar Fictions* (London and Washington: Leicester University Press, 1998), p. 2. Their point is that the myth was not only coercive (enshrining patriarchal dominance) but is descriptively incorrect, since many women continued to work.

4 Elizabeth Bowen, *The Heat of the Day* (1948) (London: Vintage, 1998), pp. 67–8. All further references will be to this edition.

5 Harrison is barely a character, as Bowen has Stella perceive: 'By the rules of fiction, with which life to be credible must comply, he was as a character "impossible" – each time they met, for instance, he showed no shred or trace of having been continuous since they last met', p. 140.

6 Robert's perception of the life of his niece Anne presumably reflects his own. He perceives it as: 'without rapture or mystery, grace or danger' and concludes 'This was demeaning poverty', p. 263.

7 Betty Miller, *On the Side of the Angels* (London: Robert Hale Ltd, 1945), p. 46. All further references will be to this edition.

8 Betty Miller, *The Death of the Nightingale* (London: Robert Hale Ltd, 1948), p. 41. All further references will be to this edition.

9 At a garden fête in Bedford in 1957, Macmillan said 'Let us be frank about it. Most of our people have never had it so good.' William Keegan, *The Observer* (20 May 2001).

10 John Kenneth Galbraith's *The Affluent Society* was published in 1958.

11 Muriel Spark, *Memento Mori* (1959) (London: Penguin Books, 1961), p. 73. All further references will be to this edition.

12 In Doris Lessing's *The Diaries of Jane Somers* (1983–84), for example, characters rail against the possibility of being 'put in a home', speculating about what kind of society it is that so tidies old people away from general sight.

7
'At Home Everywhere and Nowhere': Denise Levertov's 'Domestic' Muse

Alice Entwistle

Denise Levertov died at home in Seattle, over Christmas in 1997. She was 74 and had been suffering from cancer. During a career which almost spanned the second half of the century, this distinguished writer published some 25 books, 18 of them volumes of poetry, and earned herself many national and international honours along the way.[1] It is not always remembered that Levertov, regarded at the time of her death as one of America's leading twentieth-century poets, was in fact born and raised in Essex, and published her first collection in London. An exact contemporary of several of the writers who came to dominate British postwar poetry, Levertov left home in 1946 and ended up living in America: her literary career took shape – and her poetic reputation was secured – outside the parameters of the British intellectual and critical scene. Today, she is hardly ever mentioned in critical accounts of the development of British poetics from 1945–60. Then again, few women poets are.

Despite changing her nationality, throughout her life Levertov retained a deep-seated and affectionate sense of connection with the country of her birth, and fiercely defended her right to enjoy the cultural ambiguities generated by her emigration. Her exclusion from the postwar record of British poetics is unjust to a poetry which frequently returns to the people and places of her childhood, wistfully rendering them with the distinctive phraseology and inflections of her native idiom. Indeed, the anomalies of her never whole-heartedly American idiom make for a poetry which, in its cultural unresolvedness, was both of its time and farseeing. Reintegrating Levertov into the literary narrative of the country of her birth commemorates the cultural intermixing which, by 1950, two world wars had visited on Europe as a whole: in refusing to narrow her sense of cultural place, Levertov re-enacts the restless internationalism of the postwar world and also contrives to presage the postcolonial sensitivities of late twentieth-century literature. At the same time, her resistance to a singular 'domestic' national context is echoed and replayed in her ambivalent attitude towards the domestic space in which, as woman and writer in the socio-political climate of the Anglo-American mid-century, she both is and is not 'at home'.

To tidy Levertov and her female peers out of this period is to efface the response of the postwar woman poet to the tensions of an important historical moment. For women of this generation seeking professional independence in a unforgivingly gendered social milieu, the responsibilities of house and home were inescapable. At the same time however, to the woman writer in the 1950s, the domestic interior was often, ironically, the only place available in which to work. Paradoxically, the self-determined reconceiving of home as workplace can be liberating, as Simone De Beauvoir begins to argue in 1949, in her seminal study *The Second Sex*:

> confined within the conjugal sphere[,] it is for [woman] to change that prison into a realm. Her attitude towards her home is dictated by the same dialectic that defines her situation in general: she takes by becoming prey, she finds freedom by giving it up: by renouncing the world she aims to conquer a world ....[2]

Levertov's poems affirm how 'home' like 'homeland' confines but also underwrites her multiple identity – as wife, mother and poet. Her poetic wrestles with the conflicting exigencies of home and family sympathetically dramatise the dilemmas of the woman compelled to find or make room for creativity in the relentless domestic routine. Refusing to moderate or reconcile the tensions which define her own daily existence, her work attests to the complexities of what might be called the *domestic* muse of her poetry, and makes her more important to a literary discourse still circumscribed by the homogeneities of the Movement.

By the early 1950s Britain, like America, was growing deeply conservative. As economic prosperity increased, the idealised well-kept household, equipped with automatic washing machine, vacuum and demure young mother styled in the overtly sexy New Look, helped to re-seal women into the gendered spheres of activity which their mothers had prised open. Against this backdrop, it was particularly difficult for the woman writer to make her way in the prevailingly masculine, casually misogynist atmosphere of a university-dominated literary-critical world.[3] The scientific evaluative methods of the New Criticism emanating from Cambridge complemented the discursive, witty, self-restrained poetry of the so-called Movement, a loose grouping of young Oxbridge graduates, at their centre Philip Larkin, Kingsley Amis and Donald Davie, now synonymous with postwar British poetics.[4] To some extent, Levertov's absence from this literary context is explained by the effects of emigration on her developing poetics: in its choice of subject matter, its American-influenced imaginative energy and 'open' forms, her poetry had little in common with the traditionalist forms, guarded idiom, and apparently neutral (but essentially conservative) outlook with which her British contemporaries displaced the florid, highly metaphoric, 'neo-Romantic' writing made popular during the war by Dylan Thomas and his ilk. Moreover, though, the Movement's mostly white, male, middle-class writers traded on a defensive elitism which was hard for any woman to contest, even those working within postwar Britain. As the only female poet represented in their definitive anthology *New Lines*, edited by Robert Conquest and published in 1956, Elizabeth Jennings observed with hindsight that her inclusion in the Movement 'was positively unhelpful, because I tended to be grouped and criticized rather than be grouped and praised ...'.[5]

Jennings' association with the group gave her a public profile which marked her out from other women poets. Elaine Feinstein, for example, could be relaxed about a poetic style she never admired:

> My resistance to mainstream English poetry in the 1950s was that of an outsider, albeit a Cambridge-educated outsider, born in Liverpool, into a family of Jewish immigrants from Russia. The cautious, ironic tone of the movement ... did not excite me. It sounded smugly self-protective, and far too determined not to expose the indignities of emotion.[6]

From the contents of Al Alvarez' 1962 anthology, *The New Poetry*, you could not tell that Feinstein was not the only woman poet whose existence might disrupt the accepted profile of a predominantly male, intellectual, unsettlingly nationalist postwar 'British' poetics. Partly in response to Conquest's anthology, Alvarez' equally influential anthology 'attempt[s] to give [his] idea of what, that really matters, has happened to poetry in England during the last decade.' He includes no women at all. Of the 28 poets who appeared in an expanded edition published the following year, only two are female, both – ironically for Levertov – American: Anne Sexton and Sylvia Plath. They are allowed just 13 poems of 190 in total. It comes as little surprise to find that the poet Alvarez approves for an 'ability and willingness to face the full range of *his* experience with *his* full intelligence' is resolutely male: like so many of his literary generation, this editor does not really expect *women* to write *New Poetry* 'that really matters'.[7]

Like Feinstein, Denise Levertov's poetry always fell outside the British 'mainstream' even though, born in 1923, she was barely a year younger than Amis, Davie and Larkin. As Blake Morrison notes, the central figures of the Movement began publishing in the mid-1940s, after completing their studies.[8] In contrast with them, Levertov was never formally schooled and was working as a nurse in London when the war ended. Even so, her first collection, *The Double Image*, was published by Cresset Press in 1946 just as she departed for Paris. By 1961, the year she achieved international recognition, she had also raised a ten year old child. However, had she stayed, Levertov would have had even less reason to feel 'at home' in 'English poetry in the 1950s' than Feinstein. Her parents were, in her words, 'exotic birds in the plain English coppice of Ilford', where the poet and her elder sister were raised: 'he a converted Russian Jew who, after spending the First World War teaching at the University of Leipzig ... settled in England and was ordained as a priest of the Anglican Church; she a Welshwoman who had grown up in a mining village and later in a North Wales country town ...'.[9] Their blended backgrounds made for a set of affiliations which complicated Levertov's sense of cultural place from the outset:

> Among Jews a Goy, among Gentiles (secular or Christian) a Jew or at least half Jew ..., among Anglo-Saxons a Celt, in Wales a Londoner who not only did not speak Welsh but was not imbued with Welsh attitudes; ... all of these anomalies predicated my later experience.[10]

Having left London for Europe, Levertov never really returned to Britain. By 'spring of 1948, I was living in Florence, a bride of a few months, having married American literature, it seemed, as well as an American husband'.[11] She went on travelling with her new husband, the writer Mitchell Goodman, and their baby son all over Europe and the States for several more years, before settling in America. She eventually adopted US citizenship in 1955. The itinerant years between were crucial to the rapid reconstruction of a poet who started out, an early biographical note diffidently explains, as 'a British Romantic with almost Victorian background':[12] Looking back on this period, Levertov later observed, 'The early '50s were for me transitional, and not very productive of poems; but I was reading a great deal and taking in at each breath the air of American life.'[13] Barely two years after she changed nationality, *Here and Now* (1957), the first of three collections to appear in just over four years, was published by City Lights to widespread acclaim.

The transformation of Levertov's idiom was catalysed, as her biographical note in Allen's anthology freely admits, by the example of the leading American poet William Carlos Williams, whose work she had discovered in Paris. At first his poems, though attractive, seemed inaccessible:

> I literally didn't know how they would sound. I couldn't read them aloud. I couldn't scan them ... I didn't understand the rhythmic structure ... After I had lived here for a little while, I picked them up again, and I found to my joy that I could read them – and I think it was simply that my ear had gotten used to certain cadences.[14]

In time, Williams' relaxed idiom and radical prosodic techniques would significantly affect the way in which Levertov wrote, especially in teaching her how to put the unfamiliar resources of her new surroundings to use:

> Williams showed me the way, made me listen, made me begin to appreciate the vivid and figurative language sometimes heard from ordinary present-day people, and the fact that even when vocabulary was impoverished there was some energy to be found in the here and now.[15]

Her mentor's presence is readily discernible in much of the early work collected in *Here And Now* and the companion volume, *Overland To The Islands*, which appeared in its wake. For example, the easy manner of 'Laying the Dust' ('What a sweet smell rises / when you lay the dust –', *H&N*) clearly recalls Williams' courteous and understated idiom, not least in the muscular lineation which looses 'the water' from the left hand margin in a suddenly physical movement:

> The water
> flashes
> each time you
> make it leap –
> arching its glittering back. (ll.5–9)

Elsewhere, Levertov's growing sensitivity to the American vernacular emerges in the muted consonants, generous assonance and languid, musical pace of a poem like the much-anthologised 'Scenes from the Life of the Peppertrees' (*OTI*), which captures the drowsy mood of the siesta: 'Branch above branch, an air / of lightness; of shadows / scattered lightly'.

At the same time, however, both poems also testify to the new by accidentally betraying the old. Halfway through 'Laying the Dust', the (English) bucket becomes the more American 'pail', while the self-conscious reference to 'Someone / getting the hell / outta here' in 'Peppertrees' seems frankly clumsy. Years later, Levertov complained that the 'Americanisms' in these early poems 'is extremely obtrusive ... It doesn't sound all that natural. When I reread them I can see myself enthusiastically and strenuously making myself over.'[16] By contrast, the clipped rhythms, attenuated vowels and sharper consonance of the contemporaneous 'The Instant' ('"We'll go out before breakfast, and get / some mushrooms", says my mother ...', *OTI*) sound immediately more English and, somehow, less studied:

> up the dewy hill, quietly, with baskets.
>
> Mushrooms firm, cold;
> tussocks of dark grass, gleam of webs,
> turf soft and cropped. Quiet and early ... (ll.8–10)

Set in Wales, where the poet spent many childhood holidays, 'The Instant' reminds how the complexities of an already unusual background must have been deepened by emigration. Here again, Williams' example (his own pen name flagging his French mother's Spanish ancestry) helped to endorse Levertov's own cultural diversity as well as her decision to settle in the States. In a tribute entitled 'Great Possessions', Levertov remarks that 'what [Williams] was after was origins, springs of vitality: the rediscovery, wherever it might turn up, of that power of the imagination which first conceived and grasped *newness* in a new world'.[17] To amplify, she goes on to summon an essay, 'The American Background', in which Williams pictures the first settlers finding

> that they had not only left England but that they had arrived somewhere else: at a place whose pressing reality demanded ... great powers of adaptability, a complete reconstruction of their most intimate cultural make-up, to accord with the new conditions.

As a twentieth-century emigrée, Levertov learned to value 'newness in a new world', amid the 'pressing reality' of her 'new conditions'. In 'Laying The Dust', her attentive, respectful interest in an unfamiliar activity reconfigures a routine chore as a moving ritual of husbandry. She quietly confers on mundanity the status and significance of ceremony, enriching, sweetening and re-invigorating it, just as the water restores beauty and fertility to a dusty backyard, transformed into 'this / wet ground, suddenly black.' In the fleeting 'here and now' of 'The Instant', old and new, in the form of past and present, converge: the poet's memory revives the expedition as a journey crowded with exquisitely near sensations made sudden and surprising by mist. When the cloud breaks and the left hand margin shifts to expose 'Eryri', the mountain becomes both gateway and barrier to yet another homeland, the 'core of Wales' brought nearer and made more remote:

> 'It's Snowdon, fifty
> miles away!' – the voice
> a wave rising to Eryri,
> falling.
> Snowden, home
> of eagles, resting-place of
> Merlin, core of Wales.
>
> Light
> graces the mountainhead
> for a lifetime's look, before the mist
> draws in again. (ll.20–30)

The prize-winning *The Jacob's Ladder* appeared in 1961, confirming a success which would eventually see Levertov's reputation outstrip all the Movement poets except Larkin. Significantly however, it is in this superb collection, which includes some of her best-known poems, that the poet proudly chooses to re-advertise her un-American background. The exhaustive detail of 'A Map of the Western Part of the County of Essex' romanticises a childhood spent roaming the rural byways in which she grew up. It begins by forcefully reminding us of 'Something forgotten for twenty years: though my fathers / and mothers came from Cordova and Vitepsk and Caernarvon',

> and though I am a citizen of the United States and less a
> stranger here than anywhere else, perhaps,
> I am Essex-born: ... (ll.3–5)

Amid the ambiguities of this statement (especially 'less a / stranger here than anywhere else, perhaps',) the decision to emphasise her cultural distinctiveness at this moment may well have been deliberate. A year before the publication of *The Jacob's Ladder*, a letter from Williams, by now a close friend, dared to query what he called the 'disastrously' 'staid iambic' of its title poem. Levertov responded with this impassioned defence of her cultural plurality:

> for me personally, I cannot put the idea of 'American idiom' *first* ... [W]hen I came to the U.S., I was already 24 years old – so tho' I was very impressionable, good melting-pot material, the American idiom was an acquired language for me ... It may perhaps not be a *good* thing to be without deep local roots, to be at home everywhere and nowhere, but if one's life has made one be such a person, & one is a poet ... one must surely accept it: ... my *daily* speech is *not* purely American – I'm adaptable & often modify it to fit whoever I'm with ... And I believe fervently that the poet's first obligation is to his own voice-- ... with all the resources of one's life whatever they may be ... I'm a later naturalized, second-class citizen, not an all-American girl, & I'm darned if I'm going to pretend to be anything else or throw out what other cultural influences I have in my system, whatever *anyone* says.[18]

Levertov would never lose her conviction that 'all the resources of one's life whatever they may be', were usable. Ten years later, she would tell William Packard, 'It was an unconscious thing, but in fact my language has always moved back and forth between English and American ... I feel that I'm genuinely of both places, and that has simply extended my usage. I'm glad to have a foot in more than one culture.'[19] The essay which accompanies the poems in Jeni Couzyn's *The Bloodaxe Book of Contemporary British Women Poets* (1986) repeats 'I so often feel English, or perhaps European, in the United States, while in England I ... feel American' and insists, 'these feelings of not belonging were positive, for me, not negative.'[20]

If these words summon Virginia Woolf's *Three Guineas* ('As a woman, I have no country. As a woman I want no country. As a woman my country is the whole world'), the determination to retain 'a foot in more than one culture', mirrors Levertov's equivocal attitude to gender issues.[21] Her preference, in the letter to Williams, for 'citizen' over 'all-American girl' seems almost feminist. Yet she tells an interviewer in 1979, 'I object to the term and the concept "Women's poetry." ... I feel that the Arts always have and must transcend gender.'[22] In 1990, she stoutly refuses to concede any 'feminist' consciousness ('it just isn't part of it. I am a human being. And I am *me*. Of course if you stop to think about it I am a woman ... But ... as a poet I'm a poet. I'm not a woman poet; I'm not a man poet. I'm a poet'). But in the same interview, she also concedes that 'when a woman is writing something out of their own outer or inner experience it will bear the mark of ... their gender'. Thus 'of course if you speak honestly for yourself, then you find that you have, as it turns out, spoken for others too'.[23]

This ambivalence reflects Levertov's paradoxical claim to feel 'at home everywhere and nowhere', and is replayed in those poems which seem to have been written out of her 'own outer [and] inner experience' of what is typically, in the late 1950s and early 1960s, the narrowly gendered environment of the family home. The woman poet's relationship with her domestic world has long been problematic: down the centuries, she has been repeatedly attacked and disparaged for writing about it. Arguably, critical impatience with this recurring theme explains her low profile in the mid-century. However, Levertov's poetry proves that the often fraught relationship between the woman poet's aesthetic and home life can make for rich and resonant writing.

Although used lightly, often as a term of critical abuse, the notion of the 'Domestic' Muse is knotted, blurring the distinction between life and art, linking and dividing the world of the creative imagination and humdrum reality. Gender has always complicated the relationship between the woman poet and the Muse. In her controversial book *Slipshod Sibyls*, Germaine Greer reminds that the nine female ancient Muses were all themselves expert poets. However, as Greer shows, the 'rhetoric of musedom' gradually contrived to exclude women as writers in their own right from the delicate intercourse – since to inspire and to be inspired is in both cases at once penetrative and passive – between the conventionally male poet and his classical, conventionally female, Muse. Further, as Greer notes, 'conscious efforts to weaken this gender-specificity seem to be ineffectual ... Either [women poets] must impersonate the muse herself or impersonate the male poet ...'.[24] The female poet, distorting and subverting the traditional working partnership between author and source of inspiration, is therefore condemned to 'subject-matter [which] seems in some limiting and stifling way to be herself. Whereas the male poet might be thought to be projecting a separate identity (the work) the female poet is invariably seen to be projecting herself in an unavoidably immodest way.'[25]

Although Greer does not acknowledge it, the figure of the *domestic* Muse offers one way round this impasse. Authorising the aesthetic potential of the traditionally feminised domestic sphere, the Domestic Muse oversees the construction of a pragmatic, exclusively female and highly self-aware creative dynamic which is based on respect rather than romantic devotion and precludes the need for male impersonation. When her quasi-mythical figure makes an early appearance in English poetry, in Anna Laetitia Barbauld's mock-heroic 'Washing Day', cited by Greer in passing, it is with a not unironic lack of ceremony. Summoned by an unapologetically female voice, Barbauld's Muse is not a distant or exotic figure, but an understanding companion, a kindred spirit implicated by her own gender in the domestic grind. Her disarmingly shambolic presence, in 'slipshod measure loosely prattling on / Of farm or orchard, pleasant curds and cream', cheerily legitimates the weekly wash as creative activity, and converts tedious labour into imaginative resource.[26]

Poised between the prosaic realm of household work and the rarified world of the poetic imagination, the self-deprecatingly 'slipshod measure' and 'prattling' of the Domestic Muse should not be underestimated. Nor is her appearance amid the confused and confusing socio-political construction of gender in the 1950s and 1960s, surprising. Betty Friedan's *The Feminine Mystique* (1963) contextualises this period of political hiatus in which great numbers of Anglo-American women voluntarily exchanged the chance of independent working life for the 'dailiness' involved in running the home. As Friedan's famous study of the 'problem that has no name' bleakly records, 'In the fifteen years after the Second World War, [a] mystique of feminine fulfilment became the cherished and self-perpetuating core of contemporary American culture':

> By the end of the nineteen-fifties ... fourteen million girls were engaged by 17. The proportion of women attending college in comparison with men dropped from 47 per cent in 1920 to 35 per cent in 1958. A century earlier, women had fought for higher education; now girls went to college to get a husband ... Women who had once wanted careers were now making careers out of having babies ... They baked their own bread, sewed their own and their children's clothes, kept their new washing machines and dryers running all day. They changed the sheets on the beds twice a week instead of once, took rug-hooking classes in adult education, and pitied their poor frustrated mothers, who had dreamed of having a career.[27]

The world described here mirrors the one Simone De Beauvoir was romanticising in 1949:

> With her fire going, woman becomes a sorceress; by a simple movement, as in beating eggs, or through the magic of fire, she effects the transmutation of substances: matter becomes food. There is enchantment in these alchemies, there is poetry in making preserves; the housewife has caught duration in the snare of sugar, she has enclosed life in jars.

But De Beauvoir sternly warns,

> writers who exalt [domestic work] are persons who are seldom or never engaged in actual housework ... If however, the individual who does such work is also a producer, a creative worker, it is as naturally integrated in life as are the organic functions.[28]

Accordingly, amid precisely the 'dailiness' tracked by Friedan some 300 years later, Barbauld's *domestic* Muse dares to reproach the masculine literary traditions which demean and diminish her. Male poets leave no place for the Wash Day in the discourse of inspiration, despite the potential of the suggestively beautiful bubbles that the speaker is left symbolically contemplating at the poem's close; because it is not a world they know how to value. In contrast, as far as Barbauld herself is concerned, the Muse belongs amid the dispiriting labour of 'red-armed washers'; her presence sanctifies the task as well as supplying relief from it. Even laundering can inspire: in doing so it offers freedom from itself; drudgery, deflected, is transformed.

For the (married) woman writer of the early postwar period, where the home offers emotional security it denies intellectual freedom. At the same time, however, enshrining the relationships and resources from which she draws material and spiritual inspiration, the domestic sphere prompts self-expression, paradoxically offering the chance of escape from its confines. For Levertov, the domestic was charged with subversive potential. As she says, 'My politics and my muse happen to get on very well together.'[29] Surveying mid-twentieth-century US poetry, *The American Moment*, Geoffrey Thurley notices a 'generation of phenomenalist poets' who conflate 'the private world of poetic experience... and the grubby world of social living' in what he terms 'a unified continuum.' He homes in on the work of 'the poet-housewife / mother (Denise Levertov), whose living-space coincides with [her] aesthetic space' to demonstrate the importance of the domestic, as both setting and theme, in her earlier ouevre.[30] For example, in 'The Five-Day Rain' (*WEBH*), Thurley compassionately detects 'the predicament of the woman who wants to accept the role of mother and wife, with all the curtailments and sacrifices it involves, without losing contact with that other self that writes poetry and lives intensely':

> Wear scarlet! Tear the green lemons
> off the tree! I don't want
> to forget who I am, what has burned in me,
> and hang limp and clean, an empty dress – (ll.9–12)

For Thurley, the 'unifying continuum' makes each self into a version of the other, and 'the poetry comes out of the conflict of the two roles'.[31] A similar conflict underpins my earlier examples. Does 'Laying the Dust' offer relief from a sterile interior or commend the healing effects of domestic activitity on the arid yard? Is the clumsy off-stage row in 'Peppertrees' to be pitied, or is it a warning? In 'The Instant' the 'square house' lies behind all the worlds experienced by the expedition; the 'lifetime's look' at Eryri which affirms the rapt mother's cultural roots also ruefully affirms her distance from them. Her wistfulness reflects a lifetime spent *merely* looking. In the version of the poem published in *Origin xiv* in the autumn of 1954, her watching daughter ends by wryly observing that 'To pick mushrooms with you was / not only to pick mushrooms.'

Perhaps Levertov learned to negotiate the conflict-ridden 'continuum' of her own daily experiences from watching women like her mother make creative space for themselves in, not outside, domesticity. Interlacing pragmatism with romantic rhetoric, 'Zest' (*H&N*) underlines how intimately housework, intellectual stimulation and imaginative freedom are related:

> work by a strong light
> scour the pots
> destroy old letters
>
> finally before sleep
> walk on the roof here
> the smell of soot recalls a
> snowfall.
>
> Up
> over the red darkness dolphins
> roll, roll, and tumble, flashing the
> spray of a green sky. (ll.5–15)

This poem suggests that it is *only* in the aesthetic that the fruitful tensions inherent in the so-called 'Domestic Muse' can be fully staged. If there is something puritanically invigorating about so anti-intellectual a regime, the prescribed distractions seem intended not so much to suppress as *nourish* the alternative sensual existence which attends (or follows) the nightly 'walk on the roof'. Yoking work and play, industry and 'inspiration', 'Zest' evokes the interdependence of the apparently opposed worlds of the imagination and reality in the (implicitly female) creative experience; the presence of the domestic muse hovers, liminally, between them. Likewise, the clearly female speaker of a later and much longer poem, 'Matins' (*JL*), detects poetry in the unlikely materials – knocking pipes, a broken hairbrush, breakfast cereal – of a 'new day.' 'Matins' goes further than 'Zest' in asserting the creative potential of 'the authentic', in 'rhythms it seizes for its own', in daily routine. In closing, the poet insouciantly invokes an incontrovertibly domestic Muse, only admitting the friction between mythic and quotidian in a final, fleeting oxymoron:

Marvellous Truth, confront us
at every turn,
in every guise,
...
dwell
in our crowded hearts
our steaming bathrooms,
kitchens full of
things to be done, the
ordinary streets.

Thrust close your smile
that we know you, terrible joy. (ll.81–93)

Rooted in the domesticity by which she finds herself – in the prosperous and complacently gendered socio-political conditions of the late 1950s – both privately and publicly defined, Levertov's poems constantly review the 'terrible joy' of female authorship. James Breslin notes, '[she] locates her muse within the domestic world, but without domesticating her. The muse in fact manifests the presence of the mysterious within the house, "within you", within a newly conceived domestic order.'[32] Freshly reconceived, that order is invested with surprising potential. 'From the Roof' (*JL*) openly links domesticity with physical and emotional escape. Wrestling with 'playful rebellious linen' on a 'wild night', another female speaker delights in the good fortune which finds her living 'now in a new place', and a task which suspends her, literally and liberatingly, between earth and sky, interior and exterior, domesticity and commerce.

The continuum of female experience outlined here is matched in the archetypes of the early poem, 'The Earthwoman and the Waterwoman' (*H&N*). The practical instincts of the former, who 'by her oven / tends her cakes of good grain', highlights the more whimsical approach of the latter, who 'sings gay songs in a sad voice / with her moonshine children.' In a highly coloured, mythopoeic atmosphere, the two visions and versions of woman and motherhood co-exist in a strangely contented harmony. Each pole has its advantages: the earthwoman's stamping shouting children seem as restlessly animal as their 'spindle thin', 'moonshine' cousins seem fey. As in 'Zest', and 'From The Roof', night-time proves definitive; the slow-fermenting powers ('dark fruitcake sleep') of the 'oak-tree arm[ed]' mother parallel and invert the artistic talents of her more ethereal counterpart (precursor of the water nymph-like Muse of poems like 'The Well' and 'The Illustration' (*JL*):

> When the earthwoman
> has had her fill of the good day
>   she curls to sleep in her warm hut
>   a dark fruitcake sleep
> but the waterwoman
>   goes dancing in the misty lit-up town
>   in dragonfly dresses and blue shoes. (ll.12–18)

Together the two figures imagine womanhood itself, to borrow Thurley's term, as a continuum: each reifies a different but complementary version of domesticity; each finds a different form of satisfaction from her lifestyle; neither mode of motherhood is judged or favoured over the other. Thus, as in all the other poems, the incipiently generative 'conflict' between living space and aesthetic space which fuels Thurley's 'continuum' is smoothly transformed into the 'doubleness' to which Albert Gelpi, glancing at the title of Levertov's first collection, *The Double Image*, draws our attention. Gelpi applauds hers as poetry

> more remarkable for its centredness: its tenacious grasp of the one grounding the two. For her, the double propounds not contradiction but paradox, aspects of relationship twinned in concentricity. If the two adhere as one, the one inheres in doubleness.[33]

His brilliant analysis is echoed in one of the fragmented memoirs of *Tesserae*, published posthumously, in which Levertov can be found contemplating 'how intimately opposites live, their mysterious simultaneity, their knife edge union: the Janus face of human experience'.[34] The 'simultaneities' of Levertov's poetics, her resolutely double sense of herself as both earth and waterwoman (both figures reappear elsewhere in her oeuvre), as mother and writer, woman and poet, Anglo-American 'at home everywhere and nowhere', can seem, frustratingly, evenly balanced in their ambiguities. But to some extent, this equipoise simply reminds that her idiom was forged amid the tensions of a highly gendered and uneasily international postwar world. Levertov's friend the leading US poet Robert Creeley, fearing 'that the particular sense and fact of Denise [are] being overwritten by a meager generalizing "appreciation"', insisted to me:

> She was not, to my mind, a team player, despite association with peace groups and feminist interests ... She was not trying to mediate: she was intent on adherence to principles she believed in – and would brook no compromise or failure to comply.[35]

Amid all the 'doubleness', as Creeley warns, what Gelpi calls her 'centredness' derives chiefly from Levertov's absolute determination to reconcile the contrasting elements of her aesthetic and political life *without* compromise. In an unpublished tribute delivered in her memory to the American Academy late in 1999, Creeley explained:

> She had a way of seeing the world that was perhaps without a usual shading. But what use the endless accommodation, the temporizing, the irresolution? She would have none of it ... there is no one who writes more particularly of what being a woman constitutes ...

For no other reason, then, we should perhaps resent Al Alvarez' overlooking of a poet who deserves to be more widely read on this side of the Atlantic, not least for the articulate doubleness which signals a formidable 'ability and willingness to face the *full range* of [her distinctively female] experience with [her] *full* intelligence.'

Notes

1 In this chapter I refer only to poems collected in those works published prior to 1962. Titles are abbreviated as follows: *H&N* (*Here & Now*, San Francisco:

City Lights, 1956); *OTI* (*Overland To the Islands*, Highlands, NC: Jonathan Williams, 1958), *WEBH* (*With Eyes at the Back of Our Heads*, New York: New Directions, 1960), *JL* (*The Jacob's Ladder*, New York: New Directions, 1961).

2 Simone De Beauvoir, *The Second Sex* (London: Jonathan Cape, 1963), p. 469.

3 It was only in the 1950s that Oxford and Cambridge stopped limiting the number of women undergraduates they admitted. See Harry Hopkins, *The New Look: A Social History of the Forties and Fifties in Britain* (London: Secker & Warburg, 1963), p. 320.

4 According to Kingsley Amis: 'All the people writing it were dons, and all the people who were reviewing it were dons, and all the people reading it were dons ... So you've got a kind of donnish poetry.' See Peter Firchow, ed., *The Writer's Place* (Minneapolis: University of Minnesota Press, 1974), pp. 22–3.

5 Quoted by Edward Lucie-Smith in *British Poetry Since 1945* (Harmondsworth: Penguin, 1970), p. 136. Her remark is borne out by Lucie-Smith himself, who complains that her writing is 'rather prissily decorous ...'. Interestingly, Blake Morrison's seminal study of the group (see below), although covering Jennings alongside her contemporaries, devotes much less space to her, and while acknowledging the sexism inherent in much Movement writing fails to provide any wider examination of the kind of gender issues which might illuminate her own experiences.

6 Elaine Feinstein, 'The Voice of Pound', *P.N. Review*, Vol. 138 (2001), p. 31.

7 Al Alvarez, ed., *The New Poetry* (Harmondsworth: Penguin, 1962), p. 24.

8 Larkin's first collection, *The North Ship*, was published by Fortune Press in 1945. The same publishers brought out Amis' *Bright November* two years later. See Morrison's *The Movement: English Poetry and Fiction of the 1950s* (Oxford: Oxford University Press, 1980), p. 16.

9 Jeni Couzyn, ed., *The Bloodaxe Book of Contemporary Women Poets: Eleven British Writers* (Newcastle: Bloodaxe, 1985), p. 75.

10 Ibid., p. 76.

11 See 'Some Duncan Letters: A Memoir and a Critical Tribute (1975)', in Denise Levertov, *New And Selected Essays* (New York: New Directions, 1992), p. 194.

12 Donald Allen, ed., *The New American Poetry* (New York: Grove Press, 1960), p. 441.

13 Denise Levertov, 'The Sense of Pilgrimage', in Denise Levertov, *The Poet in the World*, (New York: New Directions, 1973), p. 67.

14 'Interview with Walter Sutton (1965)', *Conversations with Denise Levertov*, ed. Jewel Spears -Brooker (Jackson: University Press of Mississippi, 1998), p. 7.

15 'Some Duncan Letters', in Levertov, *New and Selected Essays*, p. 199.

16 'Interview with Terrell Crouch (1986)', Spears-Brooker, p. 153.

17 Denise Levertov, 'Great Possessions', *The Poet in the World*, p. 91.

18 21 September 1960, *The Letters of Denise Levertov and William Carlos Williams*, ed. Christopher MacGowan (New York: New Directions, 1998), p. 100.

19 'Interview with William Packard, (1971)', Spears-Brooker, 1998, p. 41.

20 Couzyn, 1988, p. 76.

21 Virginia Woolf, *Three Guineas* (Florida: Harcourt Brace & Co, 1938), p. 109.

22 'Interview with Fay Zwicky (1979)', Spears-Brooker, 1998, p. 117.

23 'Interview with Nancy Gish (1990)', Spears-Brooker, 1998, pp. 172–8.

24 Germaine Greer, *Slipshod Sibyls: Recognition, Rejection and the Woman Poet* (Harmondsworth: Penguin, 1996), p. xv.

25 Ibid., p. 18.
26 Anna Barbauld, 'Washing Day', in Jennifer Breen, ed., *Women Romantic Poets 1785–1832: An Anthology* (London: J.M. Dent & Rutland, Vermont: Charles Cuttle Co, 1992) pp. 81–3.
27 Betty Friedan, *The Feminine Mystique* (Harmondsworth: Penguin, 1965), pp. 14–16.
28 De Beauvoir, 1963, pp. 472–3.
29 'Interview with Janet Tassel (1983)', Spears-Brooker, 1998, p. 132.
30 Geoffrey Thurley, *The American Moment: American Poetry in the Mid-Century* (London: Edward Arnold, 1977), p. 119.
31 Thurley, 1977, p. 121.
32 James Breslin, 'Denise Leverton', *Denise Levertov: Selected Criticism*, ed. Albert Gelpi (Ann Arbor: University of Michigan Press, 1993), p. 79.
33 Gelpi, 'Centering the Double Image', *Selected Criticism*, 1993, pp. 1–3.
34 Denise Levertov, 'Janus', *Tesserae: Memories and Suppositions* (Newcastle upon Tyne: Bloodaxe Books, 1997), p. 56.
35 Robert Creeley, letter to Alice Entwistle, November 1999.

Part III

Gender, Love and Marriage

8
Nancy Mitford and *The Pursuit of Love*

Maroula Joannou

In Libby Purves' novel *Home Leave* (1997) the married daughter of a diplomat returns to France where she lived as a girl and meets a childhood friend. He quips, 'You are an English woman now, very respectable, and you think that because I am a French man. I want to dress you in fur coats and make you my mistress in the middle of the afternoon.' Chretien knows this because his father gave him books to read by Nancy Mitford. Moreover, he knows that English women think French men are very dangerous and consider themselves invited to bed at all times.[1]

Nancy Mitford has provided us with one of the unforgettable moments of twentieth-century romantic fiction; the point at which the heroine of her best-known novel, *The Pursuit of Love* (1945), wearing a fur coat and sitting upon a suitcase, encounters her lover-to-be, a short, stocky, very dark Frenchman in a black homburg in the Gare du Nord: Linda who has entertained fantasies about being spirited away into the white slave trade ('Je ne suis pas,' she said, 'une esclave blanche' (*POL*, p. 126) willingly delivers herself to become Fabrice's adoringly compliant mistress:

> Linda was feeling what she had never so far felt for any man, an overwhelming physical attraction: It made her quite giddy, it terrified her. She could see that Fabrice was perfectly certain of the outcome, so was she perfectly certain, and that was what frightened her. How could she, Linda with the horror and contempt she had always felt for casual affairs, allow herself to be picked up by any strange foreigner, and, having seen him for only an hour, long and long to be in bed with him? (*POL*, p. 129)[2]

The romantic ingredients here are all deeply conventional, replicating the national stereotypes and imbalances of power which are the stock in trade of romantic fiction; the overpowering and immediate heterosexual attraction between a powerful man who doubles as a war hero and an impressionable younger woman who lives only for his love by which her life is transfigured. Gallic charm and insouciance are juxtaposed to Anglo-Saxon naiveté and French sophistication to English prudery and earnestness.

As Nicola Beauman has put it, *The Pursuit of Love* is the 'apotheosis of the woman's romantic novel about love'.[3] But the comic tone of the novel immediately differentiates it from many popular works of romantic fiction which often contain the word love in their titles thus vitiating the obvious comparisons which the title invites. Moreover, both the comic and romantic elements in *The Pursuit of Love* take their place alongside an insistent note of melancholy and loss to which generations of readers have responded. In Rosamond Lehmann's autobiographical fragment, *The Swan in the Evening* (1967), for example, Lehmann recollects the young woman to whom her autobiography is dedicated 'buried in a Penguin, which has caused her recurrent collapses into laughter'. The book is *The Pursuit of Love*. The reader's comment on finishing it is 'a very sad book'.[4]

The romantic novel has traditionally centred on woman's subjectivity and has presupposed that women are destined to express their femininity and sexuality through male agency as the 'other' of a man. Mitford adheres to the *res gestae* of the romance while introducing disturbing, unconventional and unpredictable elements including failed marriages, death, and abandoned children. Moreover, she deployed the romance format in *The Pursuit of Love* at a historical moment in which women had distinguished themselves actively in wartime in ways which had opened up new social, political and cultural horizons and challenged the assumptions on which the love story was formulated.

I wish to examine a number of issues raised by *The Pursuit of Love* including its relationship to its historical moment of production, its attitudes to mothering, to adultery, its humour, the difficulties of pinpointing Mitford's social attitudes, and the dangers and pleasures which she finds in the pursuit of romantic love. I shall also situate the sexual politics of *The Pursuit of Love*, and particularly the heroine's quest for romantic intensity and the birth outside marriage of her baby son, in the context of the struggles about women's identity and sexual behaviour in the 1940s. Nancy Mitford's writing, which offers a critique from within of the English aristocracy while investing their lives with glamour and excitement, also provides important contradictions: *The Pursuit of Love* is not only light-hearted distraction from postwar despondency but also a powerful locus of women's emotional intensity and anguish. The modernist playfulness and concern with surface brilliance which characterise Mitford's writing also sit somewhat uneasily with traditional impulses antithetical to modernity which I shall discuss.

The Pursuit of Love was published in December 1945 followed by its sequel, *Love in a Cold Climate* in July, 1949. Nancy Mitford's career as a novelist purveying with inimitable wit and style the mannered, extravagant and arcane behaviour of the English aristocracy among whom she grew up began in 1931 with *Highland Fling* and finished in 1960 with *Don't Tell Alfred*. But it was in the 1940s with *The Pursuit of Love* produced in a wartime economy format of 195 pages of poor quality type and paper that her reputation was established. The novel was an immediate bestseller which sold over 200,000 copies in its first year[5] and produced the lavish sum in those days of £4,500 for its author in its first six months of publication.[6] It has subsequently never been out of print.

As Selena Hastings has pointed out, *The Pursuit of Love* was the 'perfect antidote to the long war years of hardship and austerity, providing an undernourished public with its favourite ingredients: love, childhood and the English upper-classes'.[7] Although the dominant mood of the nation was of austerity and retrenchment interest in the latest French fashions reflected a longing for glamour that had been missing from the lives of women habituated to unbecoming uniforms, trousers, utility garments, and 'make-do-and-mend'. The Paris fashions shown in the spring of 1946 exhibited narrow waistlines, padded hips and expensive, voluminous dress materials. The New Look, which was launched in February 1947, daringly accentuated the bosom and the full, feminine, billowing skirt.

If the external appearance of *The Pursuit of Love* reflected wartime conformity and regulations its contents, particularly the tempestuous love affair between an aristocratic Frenchman and a well-born Englishwoman, satisfied the desire for the glamour and excitement of which its readers had been deprived. Nancy Mitford's hallmark as a novelist was a 'special sort of flippancy and lightness of tone' in which 'the rest of the world, and everything that happens in it' was often regarded as 'a huge joke'.[8] Amid the postwar sobriety which followed the election of Atlee's government, *The Pursuit of Love* appeared, as a 'gloom dispelling rocket'.[9] The public's appetite for narratives concerned with passion, adultery, feminine misconduct, and the sexual behaviour of the English aristocracy which helped to account for the sales of *The Pursuit of Love* was also reflected in the popularity of the film, *The Wicked Lady*. Featuring the cross-dressing Margaret Lockwood in the role of a swashbuckling highwayman, and based on Magdalene King-Hall's eponymous novel (1944), this was the greatest box office success of 1946. The historical novel also came into prominence as a way of exploring illicit sexual desire and feminine rebellion in books like Kate O'Brien's *That Lady* (1946) about romantic intrigue in the court of Philip II of Spain, made into a successful film starring Olivia de Havilland in 1955, and the popular romances of Georgette Heyer with their Regency settings such as *Friday's Child* (1944) and *The Reluctant Widow* (1946).

Romance reading for wartime and postwar audiences often became a form of complex self-fashioning involving the reformulation of national and gendered identity. Moreover, the return to the romance, often through the mediation of history, as with *The Wicked Lady*, was sometimes a way of camouflaging forbidden desires and longings at the same time as it gave the authors of historical romantic fiction the freedom to portray sexual behaviour which might be censored were it to take place in the present. The distinction between history, romance, and fiction was sometimes difficult to maintain as Mitford herself was to demonstrate in writing her biography of Louis XV's mistress, Madame de Pompadour (1954) 'exactly as though it were one of her novels, with herself as the Pompadour and Colonel as Louis XV'.

Evelyn Waugh, who gave *The Pursuit of Love* its name, tellingly described Nancy Mitford as a 'fifth-columnist',[10] that is, someone who makes calculated use of her membership of the ruling classes in order to give away their trusted secrets to outsiders and thus to undermine the dominant order from within. There is much in her writing which could be cited to substantiate the notion of a nation governed by effete aristocrats in terminal decline. As Harold Acton has observed, to certain readers at the time of publication *Love in a Cold Climate* 'appealed as a portrayal of aristocratic England in full decadence and of pedigreed poodles in a corrupt menagerie'.[11] Mitford's depiction of the aristocracy would certainly have provided fuel for those who had returned from the war to demand reform of Britain's antiquated social structures – the parliament returned after the Labour landslide in 1945 began with an impromptu rendition of the Red Flag. But in *The Pursuit of Love* the author's sympathies are largely with those whose privilege she depicts; while she delights in pouring ridicule on the upper classes she simultaneously highlights the attractiveness of their leisured way of life.

Mitford was always chary of political commitment deeply regretting that the lives of her friends, the Duchess of Atholl and Nancy Cunard had been so deeply affected by the Spanish Civil War: 'Women', she wrote, 'should never take up causes.'[12] Yet she herself went to Perpignan in France in the 1930s to help refugees from Franco's Spain, enthusiastically taking on the republican politics of her husband at the time in much the same way that Linda embraces the Communist politics of the ironically named Christian in *The Pursuit of Love*. The importance of the human tragedy she witnessed was later to be minimised as it was for her heroine in *The Pursuit of Love*.

Tendentially light-hearted ('darting about in the society of the fashionable and the intellectual like a magnificent dragon-fly', 'a delicious creature, quite pyrotechnical ... and sometimes even profound')[13] she was unhappy in a milieu in which (much like her heroine of her semi-autobiographical novel) she 'saw nothing but serious people trying to put the world to right' (*POL*, p. 134). Mitford certainly enjoyed teasing and hyperbole – *The Pursuit of Love* is a *jeu d'esprit*, playful, delighting in wit and verbal dexterity, concerned with surfaces rather than depth. But its author was far more than an aristocratic gadabout. Even her celebrated essay on the 'English Aristocracy' (1955)[14] with its mock-solemn pontification on 'non-U' language which pandered mischievously to the innate snobbery of the socially aspirant middle-class reading public, can be read tongue-in-cheek. Mitford fell out of fashion in the 1960s after changing tastes made readers uncomfortable with her upper class diction and affectation. The recent revival of interest in her work after the BBC's dramatisation of *Love in a Cold Climate* (February, 2001) as a period piece was sufficiently far away from the time of the publication of the original novel to make derision of its outmoded social attitudes appear unnecessary.

In a review of Nancy Mitford's novel, *Don't Tell Alfred* (1960) Evelyn Waugh refers to the coded question between Jessica and Nancy, 'have you been committing again?'[15] The noun to which commit referred was adultery. Adultery is central to *The Pursuit of Love* and was of topical concern at the time of publication. Waugh humorously concludes that 'Miss Mitford is the last of the committed novelists'.[16] The experiences of intense romantic love and separation were common during the Second World War in which the illegitimacy rates rose dramatically. A public survey in Birmingham observed that during the last two years of the war, nearly a third of all illegitimate children were born to married women.[17] 1947 was to be the peak recorded year for divorce of which adultery, much of it committed in wartime, provided *prima facie* grounds. While adultery has traditionally been viewed as a matter of public as well as private concern, potentially destructive of the morale of the nation as well as of the family, it generated specific anxieties at a time when men were enlisted away from home. In this context, adultery exposed the vulnerability of patriarchy at two critical points; its power to ensure the 'legitimate' lines of descent of absent men and to control the behaviour of women through marriage when close surveillance was not possible. In *The Pursuit of Love* Fanny reflects on Linda's adultery with Christian noting that 'he, at least was English, and Linda had been properly introduced to him and knew his surname. Also, Christian had intended to marry her. But how much less would Aunt Sadie like her daughter to pick up an unknown, nameless foreigner and go off to live with him in luxury' (*POL*, p. 137).

In David Lean's film of *Brief Encounter* which went on general release in February, 1946, two months after the publication of *The Pursuit of Love*, two middle-aged married characters played by Trevor Johnson and Celia Johnson also meet for the first time on a railway station beginning a relationship which is never physically consummated. Their peculiarly English emotional reserve is intimated in Raymond Durgnatt's witty summary of the film's sexual morality in *A Mirror for England*: 'True affection is restrained and asexual. "Make tea not love".'[18] The comparisons and contrasts between the libidinal Linda and the *roué* Fabrice in *The Pursuit of Love* and the impeccably behaved Laura and Alec in *Brief Encounter* would have been obvious to readers and viewers in 1946.

In *Forever England*, Alison Light suggests that the ironic stance to romance of writers like Ivy Compton-Burnett, Agatha Christie and Daphne Du Maurier is one of the ways in which women of their generation rejected the image of a woman's role confined to emotionality: 'Ironic dismissal, worldly wisdom, brisk competence and heroic disavowal could all be part of that reaction to the legacy of representations which had seen ladies as the softer and the frailer sex, the medium of the emotions and of '"higher things".'[19] But as Light concedes, the woman writer's rejection of romance did not mean that either the impulses which underpin it, or the solace which women knew it to provide, would go away.[20] In *The Pursuit of Love* Linda is romantically besotted and is neither ironically dismissive, preturnaturally wise, nor briskly competent; the qualities reserved for the high-minded Christian and his awful partner who had 'never lived in a dream of love' and epitomised 'everything that the Radletts considered most unromantic' (*POL*, p. 121). If, as Light argues, the anti-romantic qualities of the woman writer must be recognised as part of a project of modernity between the wars, and by extension afterwards, the question becomes how we position romantic writers in whom these qualities are absent?

Nancy Mitford's sense of humour accounts for much of her popular appeal as a writer but the humour is in tension with a deep strain of sadness. However, the usual comparisons between *The Pursuit of Love* and the bestselling *Brideshead Revisited* published a little earlier in 1945 ('everyone will say what a copy cat')[21] miss the important point that Brideshead has nothing to compare with the emotional intensity and anguish underlying Mitford's humour. *The Pursuit of Love* belongs to a strong but as yet undertheorised tradition of women's comic writing. In *Comedy and the Woman Writer* Judy Little has identified a radical strain of comic writing by women which 'implies, or perhaps even advocates, a permanently inverted world, a radical reordering of social structures, a real rather than temporary and merely playful redefinition of sex identity'.[22]

In some respects, all comic writing which deals, as Mitford does, with instinct versus its social expression or with the eccentric versus the socially conventional mocks some standards and affirms others. As Umberto Eco has put it, 'In humour we smile because of the contradiction between the character and the frame the character cannot comply with. But we are no longer sure that it is the character who is at fault. Maybe the frame is wrong.'[23] Yet the reader of *The Pursuit of Love* is left with no sense of its author or narrator as outsiders at variance with their culture or of the characters' frustrations at having to live by rules they did not make. In as much as it relishes the privilege which it describes, *The Pursuit of Love* fits uncomfortably within the radical traditions of women's humour which Little and others have discussed.[24]

Before she chases the will-o'-the-wisp of love with 'one of the wickedest men in Europe, as far as women are concerned' (*POL*, p. 145) the twice-married heroine of *The Pursuit of Love* has recklessly abandoned the boorish, Conservative husband who was an approved parental choice for an emotionally desiccated Communist who was not, and has also abandoned her baby daughter in the process. When Jessica Mitford, who did not know about her sister's relationship with the philandering Gaston Palewski, to whom the book is dedicated, read *The Pursuit of Love* she assumed that as all her novels were autobiographical she must be having an affair with a French officer. Nancy answered briefly confirming this fact.[25]

The Pursuit of Love is of more interest as a register of a transitional moment for women in cultural history (between their visibility in wartime and the wholesale return to the home in the 1950s) than it is as erotic confessional. But Mitford's doomed relationship with a hero of the French Resistance certainly provided her with the template for the relationship between Linda and Fabrice. Linda dies tragically in childbirth at the very moment in which the father of her baby is about to be shot by the Nazis. Palewski, who appears to have been fond of Nancy but never to have reciprocated the grand passion that the latter felt for him ('I say to him, "d'you know what Colonel – I love you" & he replies, "that's awfully kind of you"'),[26] eventually married another woman. A devastated Nancy died of Hodgkin's disease in 1973.

The protagonist in *The Pursuit of Love* is a mobile woman, a term used officially by the authorities in the Second World War and one with pre-existing connotations of fickleness (*la donna mobile*). Linda is from a good, respectable family ('je suis la fille d'un tres important lord anglais', *POL*, p. 226) and is conducting an affair abroad with a foreigner. Her adultery disrupts her family in England in ways which allow differences, conflicts and abiding loyalties to surface. Linda is visited in Paris by two concerned male envoys dispatched by her family to protect her reputation and by extension theirs. Despite the fissures and challenges to its authority occasioned by the blatant indiscretion of its *femme errante* Linda's family is ultimately supportive and resilient. Her cousin, Fanny, takes in Linda's son on her death as the Alconleighs had earlier taken in the Bolter on her return to the fold.

The relationship between Fabrice and Linda is essentially erotic and invested with desire. What kindles this in Linda is a foreign man and a different type of sexuality. Englishmen as Linda observes are 'hopeless as lovers' (*POL*, p. 139) because 'their minds are not on it, and it happens to require a great deal of application' (*POL*, pp. 139–40). Such strangeness provides the terrain on which the English can fantasise about the old conundrum of what it is that a woman wants. Thus women's disobedience posits a conflict between what women represented for society and their specific conditions of existence and potential desires. In invoking a guiltless female sexuality that exceeds reproduction, ideological contradictions and tensions are activated distorting a narrative which is strained to contain these excesses.

The symbolic figure of the mother was pivotal to the construction of national unity and identity during the Second World War helping to override differences such as region and class. In their responses to war-related traumas – separation, bereavement, loss, homelessness and geographical displacement – mothers exercised the power to wield symbolic national unity out of disparate elements at an ideological level constructing new familial forms, consolidating older ones, shifting class boundaries, and constructing new social unities. Denise Riley has described 'the particular concentration on "the mother"' in 1945–46, the time of the publication of *The Pursuit of Love*, as 'symptomatic/ indication of the impossibility of holding together, at the level of language, the unity of "the family" once the end of the war had dissolved its rhetorical appeal'.[27]

The Pursuit of Love, which ends with the simultaneous pregnancies of Louisa, Linda and Fanny might appear to affirm the inescapability of motherhood as the destiny for women. But Mitford's representation of motherhood is conspicuously different from the hegemonic ideas of the 1940s. Moreover, *The Pursuit of Love* offers prototype of independent women unencumbered by domestic responsibilities which prefigure the social and sexual revolution that was to come later in the 1960s. The pursuit of love in the novel is emphatically not the pursuit of marriage but that which propels the women for whom it is a *raison d'être* in vertiginous directions. Moreover, maternity and chaos in the novel go hand-in-hand.

The refusal of Mitford's more attractive women characters to be 'good' mothers because they are able to recognise and define their own sexual and relational needs with acuity reinforces women's resistance to the notion of compulsory motherhood. As Helene Deutsch observed in *The Psychology of Women* written in 1945, 'Many women express their fear of motherhood by becoming psychologically incapable of it.'[28] In *The Pursuit of Love* both the central protagonist and the narrator's mother are too self-centred to wish to be saddled with the responsibilities of children. However, the freedoms they crave are class-specific. The freedom to walk away from responsibility is predicated on the existence of family money and is not an option open to women of other social classes. The refusal of motherhood, although radical for its period, perpetuates the old dichotomy found in art, for example in paintings of the Italian Renaissance, between the lively, sexualised woman and the sexless maternal one. Indeed, the attitudes to mothering of many of Mitford's women characters run counter to current psychological thinking on women. The object relations theory favoured by American theorists such as Nancy Chodorow,[29] for example, presents women as having fluid ego boundaries and seeking to define and experience themselves relationally with others, affirming the importance of motherhood as being more than a biological phenomenon and as something which crucially defines the sense of self and the day-to-day experience of a woman.

Nancy Mitford's own mother, Lady Resedale, had a somewhat cavalier attitude to mothering: 'These were the simple days of family upbringing, before the ideas of modern psychology had taken hold, saddling parents with the additional uneasy and frustrating burden of the unknowable.'[30] Fanny in *The Pursuit of Love* dismisses the wives of progressive academics who insist on bringing up their children without nannies, 'they would gradually become morons themselves, while the children looked like slum children and behaved like barbarians' (*POL*, p. 185).

In T*he Pursuit of Love*, Moira functions as an unwanted reminder of a brief, unhappy marriage and is calculatingly abandoned by Linda: 'I didn't want to get too fond of Moira, or to make her too fond of me. She might have become an anchor, and I simply didn't dare let myself be anchored to the Kroesigs' (*POL*, p. 159). Emotionally still a child, the mother can see no resemblance between this, plaintive, unadventurous little creature and her risk-taking self. According to Deutsch, a 'feeling of insufficiency with regard to the great emotional demands of motherhood', is one of the principal reasons why women have found it difficult to mother.[31]

A second and more flamboyant upper-class defector from motherhood, home and duty is the 'Bolter', Fanny's mother[32] who has confidently 'doorstepped' her daughter for a disastrous succession of lovers – 'doorstepping' being the upper-class slang for the practice of abandoning an unwanted child on a doorstep where they are likely to be taken in. Ironically, Fanny who was herself deprived of maternal love takes on the upbringing of young Fabrice on his mother's death despite the fact that none of her father's subsequent three wives had wanted to bring her up when she had been abandoned as a child.

Mitford at once suggests and resists the obvious connections between the 'Bolter' and the more idealistic Linda, both of whom have jettisoned their daughters in the pursuit of sexual fulfilment. If acceptable modes of sexual behaviour are always socially constructed, recognisable products of the interaction between the individual's formative influences and sexual preferences, but also reflecting the dominant expectations of men and women in a specific historical time, so Fanny's mother is an epitome of the sexually liberated behaviour and the androgynous looks fashionable among sections of the rich in the 1920s.

Fanny is reunited with her mother on the outbreak of the Second World War to discover the latter still spiritedly resisting all outward signifiers of propriety and that her old fashioned attire and deportment signifies her formation in an earlier sexually rebellious decade: 'She had a short canary-coloured shingle (windswept) and wore trousers with the air of one still flouting conventions, ignorant that every suburban shopgirl was doing the same.' Moreover, the 'Bolter', who is given no first name, has transgressed taking a 'ruffianly-looking Spaniard' (*POL*, p. 168) who is not only from a different nationality but also of a lower social class.

Despite the older women's refusal to conform to the stereotype of the caring, comforting maternal figure, the daughter seeks out the company of her natural mother to seek out an understanding of how to negotiate life. Adrienne Rich has described this desire for maternal connection as 'the mutual confirmation from and with another woman that daughter and mother alike hunger for, pull away from, make possible or impossible for each other'.[33] Fanny sensibly regards the aunt who brought her up as her 'real mother' and greatly as she 'might hanker after that glittering evil person' who bore her it is to her aunt whom she turns for 'the solid, sustaining, though on the face of it uninteresting relationship that is provided by motherhood at its best' (*POL*, p. 24). But she also comes to like her biological mother, the 'adulterous doll' whom she compared to Helen of Troy. Although she appears to Fanny as 'silliness personified' she nevertheless earns her daughter's respect for her 'frankness and high spirits and endless good nature' (*POL*, p. 169). Their mutual recognition signifies the 'need to say goodbye to maternal omnipotence and establish a woman-to-woman relationship of reciprocity' which Luce Irigary sees as the 'indispensable condition for our liberation from the authority of fathers'.[34]

Despite the inauspicious example of her biological parents' marital unhappiness, Fanny arrives at an improbably contented marriage with an Oxford academic. Yet Fanny's domestic life, satisfying though it might be, also strikes her as a 'series of pin-pricks': 'the endless drudgery of housekeeping, the nerve-racking noise and boring, repetitive conversation of small children'. Such components of marriage constitute the 'wholemeal bread of life, rough, ordinary, but sustaining'. In contrast, Fanny reflects that 'Linda had been feeding on honey dew, and that is an incomparable diet' (*POL*, p. 159).

A consistent thread running through the novel and through much of Nancy Mitford's fiction is the incompatibility of marriage and passion. Characters like Linda, Louisa and Jassy opt for marriage in a context where girls are chaperoned 'with Victorian severity' (*POL*, p. 65). The 'principle was that one never saw any young man alone, under any circumstances, unless one was engaged to him' (*POL*, p. 58). Marriage was still the only escape route from a restrictive parental home: 'To become engaged was the most daring, inflammable act yet attempted by any of us, one that inevitably signalled a call to arms.'[35] As Jessica Mitford has put it, 'it seems incredible that in those already modern, liberated times a woman in her middle and late twenties – especially one as brilliantly talented as Nancy – could be totally subject to parental discipline'.[36] The same is true of her characters.

Marriages like Linda's to Tony Kroesig, a 'first-class bore' who chooses a subject and drones around it 'like an inaccurate bomb-aimer around his target' (*POL*, p. 76) are socially sanctioned while passion outside marriage is by its nature illicit. Divorce may also on occasion be socially sanctioned if it helps to keep up appearances. Linda's leaving Tony means that he can marry his mistress without having a scandal or upsetting the Conservative Association. In contrast, the pursuit of love is dangerous and self-destructive – it literally kills Linda – but such brief intensity is nevertheless preferable to marital contentment' ('eleven months of perfect and unalloyed happiness, very few people can say that, in the course of long long lives', *POL*, p. 159). Mitford's descriptions of Linda's childhood makes clear the correlation between her emotional neglect and the bizarre upbringing which she experienced as a girl. Her desperate emotional need and insecurity as an adult women underpins her insatiable craving 'for love, personal and particular, centred upon herself' (*POL*, p. 109). Moroever, the reasons why love is elusive for the central protagonist are clearly gender specific

The reader of *The Pursuit of Love* is asked to choose between security versus uncertainty, safety versus danger, dullness versus excitement, conformity versus rebellion. In the end, there is no real contest, even if it is clearly signalled that lasting love will forever be unattainable. The novel finishes with the prosaic Fanny's romantic speculation that had she lived Linda would have been happy with Fabrice which is undercut by the realism of her mother.

> 'But I think she would have been happy with Fabrice,' I said, 'He was the great love of her life, you know.'
> 'Oh, dulling,' said my mother, sadly, 'One always thinks that. Every, every time.' (*POL*, p. 192)

Notes

1 Libby Purves, *Home Leave* (London: Sceptre, 1997), p. 240.
2 Nancy Mitford, *The Pursuit of Love* (1945; Harmondsworth: Penguin Books, 1949). All quotations are from the Penguin edition and are contained in the main body of my text.

3 Nicola Beauman, *A Very Great Profession: The Woman's Novel 1914–1939* (London: Virago, 1984), p. 198.
4 Rosamond Lehmann, *The Swan in the Evening: Fragments of an Inner Life* (1967; London: Virago, 1982), p. 137.
5 Letter from Nancy Mitford to Diana Mosely 15 June 1946, in Charlotte Mosely (ed.), *Love from Nancy: The Letters of Nancy Mitford* (London: Hodder and Stoughton,1993), pp. 169–71, p. 171.
6 Harold Acton, *Nancy Mitford: a Memoir* (London: Hamish Hamilton, 1975), p. 65.
7 Selena Hastings, *Nancy Mitford* (London: Hamish Hamilton, 1985), pp. 165–6.
8 Jessica Mitford, *A Fine Old Conflict* (London: Michael Joseph, 1977), p. 20.
9 Acton, *Nancy Mitford: a Memoir*, p. 9.
10 Evelyn Waugh, 'The Last Committed Novelist', undated MS (probably 1960) John Lehmann collection, Harry Ransom Center for Research in the Humanities, The University of Austin, Texas. This was later published in *The London Magazine*, December, 1960.
11 Acton, *Nancy Mitford: a Memoir*, pp. 75–6.
12 Letter from Nancy Mitford to Raymond Mortimer, 19 June 1960, in *Love from Nancy: The Letters of Nancy Mitford*, p. 453.
13 Mitford, *A Fine Old Conflict*, p. 9.
14 This article was reprinted in book form a year later as *Noblesse Oblige* (London: Hamish Hamilton, 1956).
15 Evelyn Waugh, undated MS, loc. cit.
16 Ibid.
17 Rayner Minns, *Bangers and Mash: The Domestic Front 1939–45* (London: Virago, 1980), p. 183.
18 Raymond Durgnatt, *A Mirror for England: British Movies from Austerity to Affluence* (London: Faber and Faber, 1970), p. 181.
19 Alison Light, *Forever England: Femininity, Literature and Conservatism Between the Wars* (London: Routledge, 1991), p. 210.
20 Ibid., p. 163.
21 Letter from Nancy Mitford to Evelyn Waugh, 17 January 1945, in Charlotte Mosely (ed.), *The Letters of Nancy Mitford and Evelyn Waugh* (London: Hodder and Stoughton, 1996), pp. 16–17, p. 17.
22 Judy Little, *Comedy and the Woman Writer: Woolf, Spark and Feminism* (Lincoln: University of Nebraska Press, 1983), p. 2.
23 Umberto Eco, 'Frames of Comic "Freedom"', in Thomas A. Sebeok (ed.), *Carnival!* (Berlin: Mouton, 1984), pp. 1–9, p. 8.
24 See also Nancy A. Walker, *A Very Serious Thing: Women's Humour and American Culture* (Minneapolis: University of Minnesota Press, 1988).
25 Mitford, *A Fine Old Conflict*, p. 197.
26 Nancy Mitford to Lady Diana Cooper, quoted by Charlotte Mosely in *Love From Nancy: The Letters of Nancy Mitford*, p. 124.
27 Denise Riley, 'The Free Mothers: Pronatalism and Working Mothers in Industry at the end of the Last War', *History Workshop Journal*, No. 11 (Spring 1981), pp. 58–119, p. 98.
28 Helene Deutsch, *The Psychology of Women*, vol. 2, *Motherhood* (New York: Grune and Stratton, 1945), p. 292.

29 Nancy Chodorow, *Feminism and Psychoanalytic Theory* (New Haven: Yale University Press, 1989).
30 Jessica Mitford, *Hons and Rebels* (1960; London: Victor Gollancz, 1989), p. 85.
31 Deutsch, *The Psychology of Women*, p. 47.
32 'The Bolter' is an upper-class sobriquet still applied to women like Frances, the mother of Diana, Princess of Wales, who leave their home and children to be with a lover.
33 Adrienne Rich, *Of Woman Born: Motherhood as Experience and Institution* (New York: Norton, 1976), p. 218.
34 Luce Irigaray, Interview, 'Women-mothers, the Silent Substratum of the Social Order', in Margaret Whitford (ed.), *The Irigary Reader* (Oxford: Basil Blackwell, 1991), p. 50.
35 Mitford, *Hons and Rebels*, p. 37.
36 Mitford, *A Fine Old Conflict*, p. 22.

9

Retreating into History?: Historical Novels by Women Writers, 1945–60

Diana Wallace

The writing of the immediate postwar period is often characterised as retrospective. The image is of a literature escaping from the immediate concerns of a contemporary history which was all too dangerously close into a reassuringly stable past: a retreat from history into history. In *Only Halfway to Paradise* (1980), Elizabeth Wilson, for instance, notes the 'general sense of retreat and nostalgia' as many writers 'took flight into the past'.[1] Wilson does not mention the historical novel *per se*, but it seems to be the unspoken exemplar behind her comments. This in itself reflects a more general omission of the genre in critical accounts of the period which tend to move from Modernist experimentalism through the social realism of the 1930s to that of the1950s.[2] The assumption seems to be that the historical novel, which by its very nature looks back at the past, is escapist, nostalgic and reactionary in content, and formally unadventurous. Seen therefore as both anti-experimental and anti-realist it stands outside the traditional critical mapping of the twentieth century.

There is, however, a gender issue here. Most critics locate the golden age of historical fiction in the nineteenth century, beginning with Scott and ending with Rafael Sabatini at the beginning of the twentieth century. Crucially, they treat it as an almost exclusively male tradition.[3] Yet in 1958 Peter Green noted an 'unmistakable renaissance' in the historical novel, particularly as written by women, while in 1961 Helen Cam drew attention to the current 'vogue' for historical fiction.[4] The years between 1945 and 1960, so often regarded as a fallow period, are in fact particularly rich in historical fiction by women writers, among them Georgette Heyer, Margaret Irwin, Norah Lofts, Naomi Mitchison, Mary Renault, Sylvia Townsend Warner, Daphne Du Maurier, Phyllis Bentley,

Bryher, Margaret Kennedy, Doris Leslie, Anya Seton (American but with an English-born father), H.F.M Prescott and Eleanor Alice Hibbert (née Burford, writing as 'Jean Plaidy'). It is only when this fiction is taken into account (as both Green and Cam do) that we can see that the genre does not suddenly die at the beginning of the twentieth century but, on the contrary, becomes, as Alison Light has remarked, 'one of the major forms of women's reading and writing in the second half of the twentieth century'.[5]

I would go further and argue that it has been a major form of women's reading and writing throughout the twentieth century. As I have shown elsewhere, women writers turned to the historical novel from the 1920s onwards, partly in response to the war, and partly because their new status as enfranchised citizens gave them a consciousness of participating in history for the first time.[6] Gill Plain has suggested that 'The historical novel is in some respects the ideal form for the feminist writer' because it 'offers the opportunity to revise, even to rewrite, the past; to imagine and include what has been excluded by the chroniclers of patriarchal history'.[7] In this sense the historical novel is a potentially subversive, rather than reactionary, form. For women writers during the 'consensus' ideology of the postwar years,[8] as I will argue here, the historical novel offered a form into which they could retreat and under cover of which they could express and explore subversive ideas which might otherwise have been regarded as unfeminine, or even unpatriotic.

It is partly the neglect of this material that has led to the perception of this period as an empty one for women's writing. It has also meant that there has been no recognition of the continuing importance of the genre for women writers across the twentieth century, and no sustained examination of the way in which women writers negotiate, extend and subvert the traditional parameters of historical fiction.

This postwar renaissance in historical fiction can be partly attributed to the way in which the Second World War, perhaps even more than the First World War because of its direct effect on civilians, focused attention on the processes of history. Churchill himself was not only a maker but a prolific writer of history.[9] Peter Hennessy has called the years between 1945 and 1951 the 'golden age of history not just in the British Universities but among a wider reading public'.[10] These were the years, he reminds us, of the *Penguin History of Britain*, and G.M. Trevelyan's *Social History of Britain* (1944) which went on to sell over 300,000 copies. Women also contributed influential works such as Elizabeth Jenkins' biography of Elizabeth I.[11]

Within this context it is not surprising that women turned to historical fiction. What is more surprising is that this body of work has received so little attention.[12] To a large extent this can be attributed to the downgrading of the genre as 'popular' and 'escapist' precisely at the point when it was being appropriated by women writers. Sue Harper has drawn attention to the emergence of 'costume fiction' as a new form during the war years,[13] and her analysis has important implications for women's historical fiction after that point. The readership for these novels was 'exclusively female, in work, and almost always middle-class'.[14] This is the point when the market for women's popular historical novels became established and where the genre becomes associated with women readers, but it is also the point where it becomes stigmatised as 'popular'.

Women readers themselves saw these novels as escapism, a 'bromide' during trying times.[15] Yet Harper's comment that the historical novel 'was the most heavily subscribed type of *light reading* among those classified as "*serious*" readers'[16] is especially interesting. The two key terms being deployed here – 'popular' ('light') and 'serious' – are, as Alison Light has noted, 'relational' – they only *mean* by differentiation from each other.[17] But it's worth historicising them further because the association of women's historical novels with the 'popular' has been particularly limiting.

In 1958 Margaret Kennedy bemoaned the destructive influence of a division between 'serious' novels and other novels written for commercial reasons, which she dated to the appearance of the phrase 'the serious novelist' around 1947.[18] It was no longer possible to call someone 'a good novelist', she noted. Instead, reviewers praised writers for their moral seriousness. The kind of lazy reviewing that Kennedy lambasts seems to have its roots in the work of F.R. Leavis who, while he may not have initiated its use, deploys the word 'serious' as a kind of litmus test for greatness in *The Great Tradition* (1948).[19] Leavis, of course, did not include Sir Walter Scott in this tradition, dismissing him as 'a kind of inspired folk-lorist' who 'made *no serious attempt* to work out his own form'.[20] In arguing that 'out of Scott a bad tradition came',[21] Leavis sets the stage for the dismissal of the historical novel as a genre characterised neither by moral seriousness nor a serious concern with form.

I don't think that it is an accident that this downgrading of the historical novel (often simply by omission from critical accounts) happens precisely at the point where, as Sue Harper shows, the genre had become associated with women writers. The slippage between 'historical novel' and 'historical romance' at a point where 'romance' had come to signify only a mass-produced, popular love story aimed at a female readership reinforced this. In contrast to the almost aggressively documentary-style social realism of the 'Angry Young Men' of the 1950s, with their preference for working-class heroes, women's historical fiction of the period might indeed *look* escapist, conservative and nostalgic because it does not deal with urgent contemporary issues in a direct way but this is deceptive.

While I would agree with Alison Light that we should pay attention to the 'popular' historical writing of this period (the novels of Anya Seton, Jean Plaidy, Daphne Du Maurier, Georgette Heyer and Margaret Irwin) it's equally important to note that the tendency to ignore *all* women's historical fiction has led directly to the neglect of some of the most interesting 'serious' writers working at this time, including Naomi Mitchison, Margaret Kennedy, Mary Renault, H.F.M. Prescott, Sylvia Townsend Warner, Phyllis Bentley, Sybille Bedford and Bryher. The pigeonholing of writers as 'serious' or 'popular' is itself somewhat arbitrary,[22] in part because the categories themselves are fluid. It is tempting, though it might be overly cynical, to argue that the main marker of a 'serious' historical novel is that it has a male protagonist and that it is the use of a female protagonist which condemns a novel to the 'popular' category.

To return to Sue Harper's comment that the historical novel was the 'most heavily subscribed type of *light reading* among those classified as "*serious*" readers', she adds that, 'high praise for it as a genre came from female students and the occasional female lecturer'.[23] Noting their 'air of learning', Alison Light categorises the woman's historical novel as falling into the 'good bad group' of literature.[24] Historical fiction has always been regarded as a hybrid, even bastard, form ('vulgar fiction, impure history' in Dean Rehberger's phrase [25]), but these oxymorons – 'serious light reading', 'good bad books' – suggest its especially problematic position when written by women.

By reading across these categories and looking at women's historical fiction as a whole, it becomes possible to see that in a period when feminism was ostensibly *passé* because all the battles were allegedly won and it had become increasingly hard to argue for women's rights, this was one area where women were still agitating against the status quo.

In this sense, then, women writers do retreat into history but they do so for complex reasons. Firstly, there is the retreat that is escapism in the light of a historical present which, in the face of Hiroshima and the Holocaust, is almost too much to bear. Secondly, there is a desire to examine the past to discover how it led to the present, and to prevent such violence occurring again. Thirdly, the past is used as a cover for the treatment of issues which are too contentious to be dealt with directly, often in what Elizabeth Maslen has called Aesopian writing.[26] The use of a historical setting, even in a popular novel, entails at least some consideration of historical process. Of particular concern to women writers between 1945–60 were issues of gender construction, especially the relationship between gender, power, sexuality and violence, and the relation of this to historical process, particularly in times of war.

For many women the words 'historical novel' immediately summon up the work of Georgette Heyer, the progenitor of the much-imitated sub-genre of the Regency romance. At the 'popular' end of the spectrum, her works are on the surface pure escapism. However, Heyer's work is more sophisticated than it has been given credit for and she has some unexpected admirers, including A.S. Byatt and Carmen Callil.[27] Her romantic comedy of manners is, in fact, exquisitely written and given the appearance of realism by an accurately-detailed historical setting, seasoned with Regency slang. From the 1940s on, Heyer was increasingly, as Byatt recognises, 'playing romantic games with the novel of manners',[28] and she pays her readers the compliment of assuming that they are perceptive enough to appreciate this.

It was in the 1940s that Heyer settled on the Regency period for the setting of her novels, and it's worth asking why it proved so particularly appealing. Kathleen Bell's essay on *The Corinthian* (1940) usefully sets the novel in its wartime context, noting that the occasional references to the Napoleonic Wars offered readers the 'happy conclusion of Allied Victory at Waterloo'.[29] Wellington's victories ensured Britain's reputation as a power in Europe – the only country able to check Napoleon's progress, as wartime Britain saw itself standing alone against Hitler. Equally reassuring in the postwar novels, this background is most overt in *The Grand Sophy* (1950) though even here it is conveyed through the Sophy's casual references to the 'Iron Duke', her Spanish horse, Salamanca, and the handsome scarlet-coated officers who are her admirers.[30] A peripheral character Bell notes – the young man who seeks military service as a 'means to personal redemption' [31] – also persists after the war. The hero in *Arabella* (1949), for example, intends to assist the heroine's genteelly-impoverished family by helping one brother to achieve his 'burning ambition to be a second Nelson' and the other to join a cavalry regiment.[32] The notion of enduring English military and naval supremacy here had obvious comforts during the beginning of the Cold War period when Britain was readjusting to no longer being a powerful player in world affairs.

The Regency setting also capitalises on the popularity of Jane Austen during these years. This popularity, Wilson argues, reflected the desire for an ostensibly more ordered, cultivated and civilised time.[33] Heyer uses the glamour and elegance of the Regency setting as a distancing device, paradoxically giving her texts both the status of fantasy and the 'realism' of history, but also endowing them with the comforting glow of that supposedly more ordered time. Like Austen, however, Heyer also uses the romance plot to centralise and explore women's needs and desires and the ways in which these have to be made congruent with what society allows. As both Lillian Robinson and Helen Hughes note,[34] Regency women actually had far more freedom than Heyer implies. It is through exaggerating social conventions that Heyer's work expresses women's anxieties about such historically imposed limitations and implicitly draws their attention to the limitations of their own position.

Kathleen Bell suggests that Heyer's use of a cross-dressing heroine in *The Corinthian* implies that during wartime 'women prepared to be lesser men can be trained to obey male commands and absorbed into male hierarchies without danger'.[35] In contrast to this teacher-pupil model of gender relations, the novels Heyer published after the war – among them *Arabella, The Grand Sophy, Bath Tangle* (1955), *Sylvester* (1957), *Venetia* (1958)[36] – are less conservative, at least in their treatment of gender (Heyer's party politics were staunchly Tory). They offer strong, individual, indeed 'liberated', heroines who rebel against the conventions which confine them, and whose relations with the hero are often cast in terms of struggle or contest. Arabella masquerades as an heiress to put the hero in his place; Sophy undermines her high-handed cousin's rigid control over his siblings; Phoebe in *Sylvester* writes a Gothic novel satirising the over-proud hero; and Venetia virtually proposes to the rake she loves, telling him that if he must continue to hold orgies she can always retire to bed. Most importantly of all Heyer's heroes and heroines *talk* to each other. When they marry it is after a process where both heroine *and* hero have been educated into an understanding of themselves and their desires. Ultimately, Heyer offers the ideal of a marriage of equals where love is an educative force which overcomes the limitations gender roles impose on both sexes.

It is easy to sneer at 'popular' historical fiction as 'escapist' but one of Heyer's fan letters pays testament to its very real value during these years. The letter, quoted in Jane Aiken Hodge's book on Heyer, was from a woman who had been jailed in 1948 and spent 12 years as a political prisoner in Romania.[37] By retelling the plot of Heyer's *Friday's Child* (1944) to her fellow prisoners she had managed to give them, at least for a few hours, an escape from their surroundings, and wrote to Heyer to thank her for this.

While real historical figures have only walk-on parts in Heyer's romances, a second type of popular historical fiction recreated the lives of women who actually existed. These books often assert their historical credentials as 'serious' popular fiction by including a list of sources and asserting their fidelity to the facts of these women's lives. Many, like Margaret Irwin's well-regarded series about Elizabeth I (1944–53), or Jean Plaidy's *Royal Road to Fotheringay* (1955)[38] about Mary Queen of Scots, focus on well-known royal women. Reflecting the concerns of the period in which they were written rather than set, these texts are centrally concerned with the emotional and sexual lives of their protagonists and especially the tension between desire and their public position. Alison Light has written about the way in which such texts offered 'fantasies of power' by depicting powerful and sexually-autonomous women.[39] While she acknowledges their conservative politics, Light points out that these texts do at least give femininity 'the lead role in the national drama'.[40] They articulate modes of resistance and the possibility of alternative constructions of subjectivity, specifically 'a femininity where sexual desire is taken as crucial and mobilising'.[41] They also offer a far more 'plural and perverse model of desire', including teenage sexuality, than one normally associates with these years.[42] That sexuality, however, is almost always heterosexual.

Slightly different are the books – such as Anya Seton's *My Theodosia* (1945), about the daughter of American Vice-President Aaron Burr, and *Katherine* (1954) about Katherine Swynford, wife of John of Gaunt, Doris Leslie's *A Toast to Lady Mary* (1955) about Lady Mary Wortley Montagu, or Kate O'Brien's *That Lady* (1946) about Ana de Mendoza and the King of Spain[43] – which focus on less well-known figures whose importance usually lies in their role as wife, mistress, mother or daughter to a famous man.

Aware of the lack of information about women's lives because of their exclusion from mainstream history, these writers offer a woman's eye view of history which in itself asserts a potentially subversive critique of traditional accounts and their implicitly patriarchal values. Seton's 'Author's Note' to *Katherine* sets out what looks like the beginnings of a proto-feminist analysis:

> ... in the great historians Katherine apparently excited scant interest, perhaps because they gave little space to the women of the period anyway.
>
> And yet Katherine was important to English history.[44]

Here the historical novel becomes a way of imaginatively retrieving women's lost history, continuing a project which had begun in the 1920s, and making women the subjects and sometimes the instruments of history.

In his 1924 defence of the historical novel Herbert Butterfield argued that it 'emphasizes the influence of personal things in history, it regards man's life as a whole and runs his private actions and his public conduct into each other, as it ought to do'.[45] This emphasis on the personal element in history makes it a particularly attractive form for women writers and readers. Although it is true that the weakest of these novels reduce all motivation to the personal, the best of them dramatise and critique the exclusion of women from the public sphere. Furthermore, many of them revalue the personal to offer a critique of masculine conduct, questioning the convention that separates public from private in moral judgments of men's actions and absolves them of responsibility for private wrongs in pursuit of public aims. By acting as advocates for the wrongs of women within history, these novels begin to create a vocabulary with which to explore anxieties about gender roles. Ironically, they often use the techniques of romantic fiction to do this.

In *Katherine*, Seton, like Heyer, offers romantic love as an equalising force: 'I am no duchess, no queen', Katherine tells John of Gaunt, 'but I have been your equal in love.'[46] But other texts expose the romance plot as delusionary. The opening scenes of Seton's *My Theodosia* (1945), for example, use the language of romance to centralise Theodosia as a desiring female subject, but Seton subverts this plot to produce what might be more accurately called an anti-romance. Like Irwin's Elizabeth and Plaidy's Mary, Queen of Scots, Theodosia is depicted as a woman with desires recognisable by a twentieth-century readership. But lacking their power as Queens, she is trapped by the historical constraints of her time and the ambitions of a father who marries her off to further his own aims. In the description of Theodosia's death at sea the sinking boat acts as an image for her own weariness of a life over which she has had so little control: 'The *Patriot* rolled sluggishly for the last time as though weary of her fruitless struggle. With a long sigh she nestled slowly into the welcoming depths of the tranquil, omnipotent sea.'[47] This is hardly the escapism usually associated with women's historical fiction. Instead,

Seton offers a biting analysis of the way that women's desires and needs have historically been sacrificed to men's ambitions.

This theme is also central to Norah Lofts's *The Luteplayer* (1951), an account of the marriage of Richard I and Berengaria of Navarre centered around the abortive Third Crusade.[48] This takes Lofts into the territory Sir Walter Scott mapped in *Ivanhoe* (1819), and *The Talisman* (1825). Retaining the concept of conflict which Scott placed at the heart of the historical novel, Lofts shifts the focus on to the conflict between male and female needs, and to the exclusion of women from the spheres of public and political action. Having fallen in love with Richard at first sight, Berengaria is determined to wed him, but his actions are dominated by his crusading ambitions. This collision of the female romance plot and the male quest plot is further complicated by the fact that Lofts presents Richard as a homosexual man who, once wedded to Berengaria for diplomatic reasons, finds repeated excuses to avoid consummating the marriage. Lofts shows how male homosexual desire reinforces the homosocial structures which ensure that Richard and Berengaria occupy different worlds. Women find homosexuality 'disgust[ing]', Lofts suggests, because 'it threatens something that women stand for. It cuts out, disowns, disinherits them'.[49] The book is actually sympathetic to Richard but Lofts's portrayal of his homosexuality is a startling antidote to the usual heroic picture of Richard Coeur de Lion as the quintessentially 'manly' English King.[50]

The second theme from Scott's work which Lofts reworks is the tension between legend and historical fact. By using three narrators – Blondel the luteplayer; Anna, Berengaria's hunchbacked illegitimate half-sister; and Richard's mother, Eleanor of Aquitane – Lofts undermines the possibility of a single 'history', showing how other histories have been dismissed as legend or myth. The 'legend' of the luteplayer who finds the imprisoned Richard is shown, through Blondel's narrative, to be 'the truth'.[51] Blondel and Anna are both liminal figures – Anna unsexed by her disability, Blondel feminised by his role as luteplayer. Both move across the boundaries between the confined private world of the women and the active public world of the men. In traditional historical accounts they would be either excluded (like Seton's Katherine), or dismissed as 'legend' but Lofts reimagines these marginal figures and their possible influence on public history. Her text may look like 'popular' historical fiction but it is addressing complex questions of historiography and the construction of gender in wartime in ways that might be more associated with 'serious' fiction. A 'good bad book' or 'serious light reading', it blurs categories as Blondel and Anna themselves do.

These categories, as I have suggested, have led to the neglect of some of the most interesting books from this period, often texts which explore transitional moments in history as the pre-history of the present. Dedicated to Winston Churchill, Hope Muntz's *The Golden Warrior* (1948) is a saga-like narrative of the Norman invasion of Britain. The parallel with the present is made explicit in a foreword by G.M. Trevelyan, who notes that Canadian-born Muntz 'has a deep knowledge of the island she has twice seen threatened with invasion'. [52] This is not, however, a simple celebration of England's glorious past. The sympathies of the text are with Harold, who is presented as a deeply religious and loving family man, flawed not only by masculine ambition but by his own heritage of violent conquest as a Saxon. 'Saxon dogs, dogs of Saxons, all your land is ours',[53] spits the Welshwoman who represents this repressed Celtic underclass, and whose curses are represented as leading to his downfall. Harold's casting-off of his hand-fast wife, Edith Swan-neck, in order to marry the daughter of a potential ally is presented as being as serious a betrayal as his breaking of his oath to William. By citing the dying words of William I – 'By wrong I conquered England ...'[54] – Muntz suggests continuing cycles of violent conquest closely linked to patriarchal values. Her sympathy with the conquered, like that of Naomi Mitchison in *The Bull Calves* (1947),[55] anticipates the beginnings of a postcolonial and feminist analysis of England's own past as a conquered and conquering nation.

The historical novel emerges here as one of the few genres which has allowed women writers to write about men and the public sphere, including war and politics, and thus directly to criticise patriarchal value systems. Margaret Kennedy's *Troy Chimneys* (1953)[56] has been compared to Austen's work but it is the kind of book that Austen might have written had she been able to escape the romance plot and take as her protagonist a self-made male politician. Although it looks back to Regency England, this is not a nostalgic, reassuring text. It deals with a schizophrenic duality which lies at the heart of a protagonist who has two existences, one as Miles Lufton, well-meaning and morally upright, and one as Pronto, the self-interested social butterfly whose easy charm oils his political passage. Like Seton, Lofts and Muntz, Kennedy judges her male character by the effect of his behaviour on the woman he loves, whose life he ruins not maliciously but by thoughtless delay, and suggests that the separation of public and private spheres damages men as well as women.

These texts are also interesting formally in ways that suggest that the experimentalism/social realism dichotomy which has dominated debates about this period is overly simplistic. *The Golden Warrior* uses a saga-like narrative structure, while Kennedy uses a series of documents (memoir and letters). The latter suggests the difficulty of understanding a past which can only be accessed through texts, as well as the constructed nature of identity, both insights which anticipate the concerns of the 1980s and 1990s.

One of the outstanding novels of the period, H.F.M. Prescott's *The Man on a Donkey* (1952),[57] uses a chronicle form gradually to weave together the stories of five characters whose lives are affected by the sixteenth-century dissolution of the monasteries culminating in the ill-fated Pilgrimage of Grace. In contrast to the usual focus on the glamorous personal lives of Tudor royals, Prescott focuses on the ordinary people whose lives are disrupted and destroyed as a result of Henry VIII's marital and political maneouverings – an illegitimate gentlewoman, a lapsed priest, a Prioress. Inasmuch as there is a hero, it is Robert Aske, the one-eyed Yorkshire lawyer, who unwillingly became leader of the Pilgrimage and was betrayed by Henry to an appalling death as sentence for treason. (Betrayal and treason are themes which, not surprisingly, occur frequently in the postwar period.) The novel is also unusual in its sympathetic presentation of Catholicism, (often treated as an irrelevance in the 'popular' historical novel) as the underpinning faith of the people, woven into the very fabric of the society which is being destroyed. This is expressed in the visions of Malle the serving-woman, which provide a symbolic subtext to the otherwise realist novel.

Finally, women writers used historical fiction during this period in order to explore issues that could not be treated directly. Particularly interesting here is their treatment of male homosexuality, which is often used (as Lofts uses it) to destablise gender roles and boundaries. In the hands of Mary Renault and Sylvia Townsend Warner it also suggests the even more tabooed subject of lesbianism.

The fate of Mary Renault's fine novel *The Charioteer* offers a striking illustration of why writers turned to historical fiction to code such issues. Set during the Second World War, it is historical in the sense of self-consciously depicting what Lukács calls 'the present as history' or 'self-experienced history'.[58] Its protagonist is Laurie Odell, a soldier in hospital after Dunkirk, learning to live with both a disabling knee wound and a growing realisation of his homosexuality. The 'charioteer' of the title is Socrates's image in *The Phaedrus* of the soul as a charioteer driving two mismatched horses. This controlling metaphor directs the reader to the classical world where love between men was regarded as a high form of love. The novel was published in Britain in 1953, the year in which three socially prominent men were tried and imprisoned for homosexuality, an event which led to the Wolfenden Report of 1957.[59] Its publication in the US was delayed until 1959 as a result of Renault's frank treatment of homosexuality. What this experience seems to have shown Renault was that radical material could be slipped past the censor much more easily in a historical setting and after this point all Renault's novels are set in the classical world.

The critical neglect of Renault, which is only just starting to be addressed,[60] can be attributed not only to the fact that she writes historical fiction but also to her use of male protagonists in a largely male-centred world. The focus on femininity has meant that feminist criticism has been slow to address the ways in which women writers such as Renault, as well as Sylvia Townsend Warner, Naomi Mitchison and Bryher, have used male narrators and characters, particularly within historical fiction, to explore issues of gender.

As critical accounts of the interwar years have been re-drawn, Sylvia Townsend Warner's novels have looked increasingly important, and her postwar work is equally innovative. In *The Corner that Held Them* (1948),[61] for instance, a novel which has interesting parallels with *The Man on a Donkey*, Warner set out to write a Marxist novel, the story of a community rather than an individual. In *The Flint Anchor* (1954)[62] Warner takes her experimentation with form further. The novel has no hero and no plot, and includes none of the large public events which traditionally make up 'history'. Instead, it gives us the histories of a single nineteenth-century bourgeois family in the remote Norfolk port of Loseby where historical events, including the Napoleonic Wars, impinge only indirectly.

Warner uses this to offer an analysis of patriarchy as a kind of Fascism which damages both women and men. The text opens with the public record of John Barnard's life: the inscription on his tombstone records a man 'Deeply conscientious in the performance of every Christian and social duty', and a 'devoted husband and father'. [63] The novel then fills in the 'private' truth behind these platitudes and exposes John Barnard as a domestic tyrant and a religious hypocrite, who has driven his wife to drink, five children to an early death, and his surviving children, as well as his son-in-law Thomas Kettle, to varying states of unhappiness.

Like other men in these texts (Kennedy's Lufton, Lofts' Richard I, Renault's Laurie), Barnard is trapped within structures which force him to be something he is not temperamentally suited to be, and thus damage and deform him. His house, with its flint anchor motif and the high spike-topped walls which keep the family in and the working classes out, functions as a metaphor for these patriarchal structures, and gives the novel a symbolic unity.

Opposed to these rigid structures is the fluidity of the sea, and another kind of writing on stone – a piece of graffiti suggesting that 'Thomas Kettle goes with Dandy Bilby'[64] – indicating the possibility of a more plural acceptance of desires within the working-class community. Reminded that 'For a man to love a man is a crime in this country',[65] Crusoe, who chalked up the graffiti in recognition of his own desire for Thomas, asserts:

> 'Not in Loseby, Mr Thomas ... Nor in any kind of sea-going place, that I've heard of. It's the way we live, and always has been ... in Loseby we go man with man and man with woman and nobody think the worse'.[66]

Loseby's liminality as a 'sea-going place' suggests a freedom to cross the kinds of boundaries Barnard is so determined to enforce. Moreover, Crusoe indicates the historical continuity of this possibility, although it has gone unrecorded (like Richard I's homosexuality) in the official documents of history. Significant in its absence here is the even more radical possibility that women might 'go with' women.

Warner's diaries record the contemporaneous 'howdydo about homosexuality' which produced her publisher's request that she take out the 'whole of the Crusoe conversation', as well as her amused scorn at their suggestion that 'no one could call it provocative ... it was a period story – like *Forever Amber*, no doubt'.[67] It is hard to think of two novels more unalike than *The Flint Anchor* and *Forever Amber*, Kathleen Winsor's bestselling bodice-ripper.[68] The fact that they could be so cavalierly lumped together and dismissed as 'period stories' is indicative of the failure to take the woman's historical novel of this period seriously.

In fact, as I hope I have shown, the historical novel was used by women writers during these years in a variety of different and extremely fertile ways. What looks like a conservative and nostalgic retreat into history, then, is actually a strategy which allows them to explore a far wider range of issues and anxieties, especially around gender (masculinity as well as femininity) and sexuality, than the traditional accounts of this period suggest.

Notes

1 Elizabeth Wilson, *Only Halfway to Paradise: Women in Postwar Britain, 1945–68* (London and New York; Tavistock, 1980), p. 147. Similarly, D.J. Taylor notes that the tendency of postwar novels is 'retrospective' in *After the War: The Novel in England Since 1945* (London: Flamingo, 1994), p. 5.

2 In *No, Not Bloomsbury*, for instance, Malcolm Bradbury writes of 'the relative silence [in the writing] of the period from 1939 toward the end of the 1940s', until the emergence of a new form of social realism in the 1950s (London: Andre Deutsch, 1987), p. 69. Andrzej Gàsiorek frames his account in *Post-war British Fiction: Realism and After* (London: Edward Arnold, 1995) around the dichotomy between realism and experimentalism which, again elides the historical novel until it resurfaces in the historiographical metafiction of the 1980s and 1990s.

3 The founding text in this area, Georg Lukács's *The Historical Novel* (1937; London: Merlin Press, 1962) mentions no women writers at all. Avrom Fleishman's *The English Historical Novel: Walter Scott to Virginia Woolf* (Baltimore and London: Johns Hopkins Press, 1971), Harry E. Shaw's *The Forms of Historical Fiction: Sir Walter Scott and His Successors* (New York and London: Routledge, 1983), and Harold Orel's *The Historical Novel from Scott to Sabatini: Changing Attitudes toward a Literary Genre, 1814–1920* (London: Macmillan, 1995) all treat historical fiction as an overwhelmingly male tradition, which ends at the beginning of the twentieth century. Margaret Scanlan's *Traces of Another Time: History and Politics in Post-war British Fiction* (Princeton: Harvard University Press, 1990) is an account of the '"other" historical novel: sceptical, ironic and discontinuous' as written by Elizabeth Bowen, Iris Murdoch and Doris Lessing, but most of the novels she discusses deal with the history of the twentieth century. Ruth Hoberman's valuable *Gendering Classicism: The Ancient World in Twentieth-Century Women's Historical Fiction* (New York: State University of New York Press, 1997) is a theoretically-informed treatment of how women have subverted historical narratives to include issues of gender but it focuses only on those novels which are set in Ancient Greece or Rome. Helen Hughes's *The Historical Romance* (London and New York: Routledge, 1993) is useful on the historical romance developed by Georgette Heyer and her many imitators. Critical attention has returned to historical fiction in another form in the interest in the 'historiographical metafictions' published by writers such as John Fowles and A.S. Byatt in the latter half of the twentieth century. What is missing, however, is a sense of the continuity of the genre throughout the century and it is here that an attention to gender, and particularly to women's writing between 1940 and 1960 is especially useful.

4 Peter Green, 'Aspects of the Historical Novel', *Essays by Diverse Hands*, 31 (1962), pp. 53–60; Helen Cam, *Historical Novels*, published for the Historical Association by Routledge and Kegan Paul, p. 3.

5 Alison Light, '"Young Bess": Historical Novels and Growing Up', *Feminist Review*, No. 33 (Autumn 1989), pp. 57–71, p. 60.

6 Diana Wallace, '"History to the Defeated": Women Writers and the Historical Novel in the 1930s', *Critical Survey*, forthcoming.

7 Gill Plain, *Women's Fiction of the Second World War: Gender, Power and Resistance* (Edinburgh: Edinburgh University Press, 1996), p. 154.

8 Wilson, *Only Halfway to Paradise*, p. 2; Alan Sinfield. *Literature, Politics and Culture in Post-war Britain* (London: Athlone, 1997, 2nd edn), pp. 13–19.
9 See Churchill, *The Second World War* (6 vols, 1848–54) and *A History of the English-speaking Peoples* (4 vols, 1956–58).
10 Peter Hennessy, *Never Again: Britain 1945–51* (1992; London: Vintage, 1993), p. 323.
11 Elizabeth Jenkins, *Elizabeth the Great* (1958; London: Companion Book Club, 1959).
12 Alison Light, Gill Plain, Sue Harper and Kathleen Bell have all written illuminatingly about aspects of women's historical fiction or individual texts during and after the war. What has been lacking is an overview which would demonstrate how important the genre as a whole has been for women writers.
13 Sue Harper, 'History with Frills: "Costume" Fiction in World War II', *Red Letters*, No. 14 (1983), pp. 14–23.
14 Ibid., p. 21.
15 Ibid., p. 20.
16 Ibid.
17 Alison Light, 'Towards a Feminist Cultural Studies: Middleclass Femininity and Fiction in Post Second World War Britain', *English Amerikanische Studies*, No. 1 (1987), pp. 58–72, p. 65.
18 Margaret Kennedy, 'The Goosefeather Bed', in *The Outlaws on Parnassus* (London: Cresset, 1958), pp. 200–14.
19 F.R. Leavis, *The Great Tradition* [1948] (Harmondsworth; Penguin, 1962). He notes, for instance, a 'seriousness of concern' (p.19) with essential human issues as the marker of a great novelist. Austen's 'moral seriousness' (p. 25) ensured her importance while Dickens' *Hard Times* is the only one of his novels which is 'a completely serious work of art'(p. 249) and therefore worth including in the great tradition.
20 Leavis, *The Great Tradition*, p. 14 (my emphasis).
21 Ibid.
22 Daphne Du Maurier, for instance, seems to be in the process of moving from one category to another as her work is given more scholarly attention.
23 Harper, 'History with Frills', p. 20.
24 Light, '"Young Bess": Historical Novels and Growing Up', p. 60.
25 Dean Rehberger, 'Vulgar Fiction, Impure History: The Neglect of Historical Fiction', *Journal of American Culture*, Vol. 18, No. 4 (1995), pp. 59–65.
26 Elizabeth Maslen, 'Naomi Mitchison's Historical Novels', *Women Writers of the 1930s*, ed. Maroula Joannou (Edinburgh: Edinburgh University Press, 1999), pp. 138–50.
27 See Byatt's 'An Honourable Escape', *Passions of the Mind* (1991; London: Vintage, 1993), pp. 258–65; Carmen Callil, *Subversive Sybils: Women's Popular Fiction This Century* (London: The British Library, 1996).
28 Byatt, 'An Honourable Escape', p. 261.
29 Kathleen Bell, 'Cross-dressing in Wartime: Georgette Heyer's *The Corinthian* in its 1940 Context', Pat Kirkham and David Thomas, eds, *War Culture: Social Change and Changing Experience in World War Two* (London: Lawrence and Wishart, 1995), pp. 151–9, p. 152.
30 Georgette Heyer, *The Grand Sophy* (1950; London: Arrow, 1999).

31 Bell, 'Cross-dressing in Wartime', p. 153.
32 Georgette Heyer, *Arabella* (1949; London: Arrow, 1999), p. 313.
33 Wilson, *Only Halfway to Paradise*, p. 148.
34 Lillian Robinson, 'On Reading Trash', *Sex Class and Culture* (Bloomington and London: Indiana University Press, 1978), pp. 200–22; Hughes, *The Historical Romance*, Chapter Seven.
35 Bell, 'Cross-dressing in Wartime', p. 158.
36 Georgette Heyer, *Bath Tangle* (1955; London: Pan, 1967); *Sylvester* (1957; London: Mandarin, 1992); *Venetia* (1958; London: Arrow, 1992).
37 Jane Aiken Hodge, *The Private World of Georgette Heyer* (1984; London: Pan, 1985).
38 Margaret Irwin, *Young Bess* (1944; London: Allison and Busby, 1998), *Elizabeth Captive Princess* (1948; London: Allison and Busby, 1999), and *Elizabeth and the Prince of Spain* (1953; London: Allison and Busby, 1999), Jean Plaidy, *The Royal Road to Fotheringay* (1955: London: Pan, 1967).
39 Light, '"Young Bess": Historical Novels and Growing Up', p. 61.
40 Ibid., p. 5
41 Light, 'Towards a Feminist Cultural Studies', p. 68.
42 Light, '"Young Bess": Historical Novels and Growing Up', pp. 63, 64.
43 Anya Seton, *My Theodosia* (1945; London: Coronet, 1965); *Katherine* (1954; London: Hodder, 1961) Doris Leslie, *A Toast to Lady Mary* (London: Companion Book Club, 1955); Kate O'Brien, *That Lady* (London: Heineman, 1946).
44 Seton, *My Theodosia*, p. 9.
45 Herbert Butterfield, *The Historical Novel: An Essay* (Cambridge: Cambridge University Press, 1924), p. 74.
46 Seton, *My Theodosia*, p. 270.
47 Ibid., p. 314.
48 Norah Lofts, *The Luteplayer* (London: Michael Joseph, 1951).
49 Ibid., p. 393.
50 Lofts's depiction of Richard's sexuality is supported by historical evidence. See, for instance, James Reston Jr, *Warriors of God: Richard the Lionheart and Saladin in the Third Crusade* (New York: Doubleday, 2001).
51 Lofts, *The Luteplayer*, p. 490.
52 Hope Muntz, *The Golden Warrior* (London: Chatto and Windus, 1948), p. v.
53 Muntz, *The Golden Warrior*, p. 52.
54 Ibid., p. 389.
55 Naomi Mitchison, *The Bull Calves* (London: Cape, 1947). See Gill Plain, *Women's Fiction of the Second World War*, Chapter 8 for a suggestive analysis of this novel.
56 Margaret Kennedy, *Troy Chimneys* (1953; London: Virago, 1985).
57 H.F.M. Prescott, *The Man on a Donkey* (1952; Harmondsworth: Penguin, 1969).
58 Lukács, *The Historical Novel*, pp. 83, 84.
59 Wilson, *Only Halfway to Paradise*, pp. 101–2.
60 In addition to Hoberman (1997), see also the next chapter of this book, Kathleen Bell 'Writing a Man's World'.
61 Sylvia Townsend Warner, *The Corner That Held Them* (1948; London: Virago, 1988).

62 Sylvia Townsend Warner, *The Flint Anchor* (1954; London: Virago, 1997).
63 Ibid., p. 1.
64 Ibid., p. 177.
65 Ibid., p. 183.
66 Ibid.
67 Claire Harman, ed., *The Diaries of Sylvia Townsend Warner* (1994; London: Virago, 1995), p. 206.
68 Kathleen Winsor, *Forever Amber* (1944; Chicago: Chicago Review Press, 2000).

10

Writing a Man's World: an Exploration of Three Works by Rosemary Sutcliff, Mary Renault and Cecil Woodham Smith

Kathleen Bell

Throughout the twentieth century there have been women who wrote chiefly about men and male relationships. While such subjects may have offered advantages in terms of audience, or simply have reflected a personal interest, the decision to write a man's world offered additional advantages in the way it permitted women to contemplate politics, history and even romantic friendships without the immediately complicating factors of an explicitly gendered position or perspective. Most obvious, perhaps, in terms of appeal, are books in which women wrote about male friendships in terms that paralleled male/female romance, offering women readers as well as men an enjoyment of romantic content. Examples include D.K. Broster's interwar historical novels[1] and something similar is found in the early science fiction novels of Marion Zimmer Bradley in the 1960s[2] – before she became committed to the Women's Movement and began to introduce strong and complex female characters.

Women readers may find benefits in exploring romance between men, rather than adhering to the conventional heterosexual pattern. In an all male or largely male environment the policing of gender boundaries need not be vigorous. What is more, conventionally feminine attributes can be shared between male characters when there are no women to lay claim on them. Qualities such as sensitivity, beauty and spirituality have to be allocated to male characters, since these are qualities we expect to find somewhere in the world. And since we see these qualities as good, they are often allocated to sympathetic male characters.

However, the predominantly male world in fiction has still more to offer the female writer and reader. Following the Second World War, when the crucial involvement of women had provided new chances for participation in both politics and history, the war was being reimagined as a male preserve in which men defended freedom while women kept 'the home fires burning'.[3] Democracy might admit women but they were certainly not seen as equals in the field of political debate.[4] Historical fiction, however, especially when it was centred around masculine experience, allowed writers to initiate and recreate a political debate in which readers could participate imaginatively. In particular, the three books which are the subject of this chapter permit their readers to consider questions of war and empire, and ambivalent attitudes to both. Moreover these questions are at times implicitly related to the perception and construction of gender roles, with conventionally feminine attributes of the 1950s relocated in a world peopled largely by men.

Cecil Woodham Smith's *The Reason Why*, Rosemary Sutcliff's *The Eagle of the Ninth* and Mary Renault's *The Last of the Wine*, although not directed primarily at a gendered audience, provided their women readers with a space in which they could confront some of the problems and anxieties of the 1950s with both reason and imagination. The balance is different in each book, partly because of the difference of genres. Cecil Woodham Smith is writing a history centred around a brief incident in the Crimean War, and, while all three writers cared passionately about accuracy and careful research, for her, imaginative engagement had to be secondary. Rosemary Sutcliff's book about Roman Britain is for children while Mary Renault's *The Last of the Wine* is an adult historical novel set in the Peloponnesian War, starting after it had begun and ending shortly before the trial and execution of Sokrates.

The opening of each book is concerned to establish the difference between then and now. Woodham Smith starts with the praise not of war but of military glory:

> Military Glory! It was a dream that century after century has seized on men's imaginations and set their blood on fire. Trumpets, plumes, chargers, the pomp of war, the excitement of combat, the exultation of victory – the mixture was intoxicating indeed. To command great armies, to perform deeds of valour, to ride victorious through flower-strewn streets, to be heroic, magnificent, famous – such were the visions that danced before men's eyes as they turned eagerly to war.[5]

but she establishes it as a dream, gradually undermining it. She makes it clear that this dream is restricted to the aristocracy (she doesn't mention gender) and, by the third paragraph, undermines it by 'the sombre realities of history' reminding the reader that 'Great armies in their pride and splendour were defeated by starvation, pestilence and filth, valour was sacrificed to stupidity, gallantry to corruption.' These 'sombre realities' play the conflicts of the mid-nineteenth century against the mid-twentieth. And further reference to the miseries of war shows that the as-yet-unnamed central characters of the narrative – Lord Cardigan and Lord Lucan – are possessed by a particular blindness which, although this is not stated, is a blindness reserved for men. Already the trajectory of the narrative is clear – the absurd dream of military glory, and these two aristocrats who hold to it, will be found to blame for the catastrophic charge of the Light Brigade.

Military glory was a particularly absurd dream in the early 1950s, when Woodham Smith was researching and writing. It had been the dream of fascist armies but the allied troops, rarely presented as glorious, had found themselves increasingly armies of occupation whether in Europe or in the decreasing number of colonial possessions. The Second World War had been presented as a war of stolid endurance rather than a glorious adventure.[6] National Service had created a conscript army.

Occupation and colonial possession is of course the subject of *The Eagle of the Ninth*, although it is easy for readers to forget this since Britain is the colonial possession in question.[7] Sutcliff deals with the absorption of Roman values into British ways through her hero, Marcus, who arrives in Britain as a centurion but is set up as one of the implied ancestors of 1950s Britain. However, she also addressed the oppression of colonialism through the important character of Esca, a British slave who is to become Marcus's friend. However, *The Eagle of the Ninth* opens by establishing difference from the present by using Roman names and describing the strange British inhabitants of the wilderness:

> From the Fosseway westward to Isca Dummoniorum the road was simply a British trackway, broadened and roughly metalled, strengthened by corduroys of logs in the softest places, but otherwise unchanged from its old estate, as it wound among the hills, thrusting further and further into the wilderness.
>
> It was a busy road and saw many travellers: traders with bronze weapons and raw yellow amber in their ponies' packs; country folk driving shaggy cattle or lean pigs from village to village; sometimes a

> band of tawny-haired tribesmen from further west, strolling harpers and quack-oculists, too, or a light-stepping hunter with huge wolf-hounds at his heel ...[8]

Yet, once the defamiliarisation has been achieved, the familiar is introduced and the idea of continuity:

> On they went, following the road that now ran out on a causeway between sodden marsh and empty sky, now plunged into deep boar-hunted forest, or lifted over bleak uplands where nothing grew save furze and thorn scrub. On with never a halt nor a change of rhythm, marching century by century, the sun bright on the Standard at their head, and the rolling dust-clouds kicked up over the pack-train behind.[9]

The landscape is recognisably English while the phrase 'marching century by century' suggests more than its primary meaning. While at a surface level a century is a division of a hundred soldiers under a centurion, the phrase cannot help but suggest the passage of time and the ghostly presence of Roman legions marching on Roman roads in the present day. This ghostly mingling of past and present is suggested elsewhere in the novel. It is clear from Sutcliff's writing on Kipling that she values this sense of continuity, seeing history as 'living roots' on which the understanding of the present depends.[10]

Perhaps most concerned to divide past from present is *The Last of the Wine*. The opening two paragraphs cannot help but take the present-day reader by surprise:

> When I was a young boy, if I was sick or in trouble, or had been beaten at school, I used to remember that on the day I was born my father had wanted to kill me.
>
> You will say there is nothing out of the way in this.[11]

This reference to the custom of exposing new-born babies – a decision made by the father or his appointed representative and taken on such grounds as the child's physical weakness or the family's economic circumstances – is one which recurs in the novel. Alexias, the narrator, feels guilt that he has not exposed his half-sister as his father wished but has, instead, allowed her to live. And later, when Athens is suffering from siege and starvation, he takes his baby half-brother to expose him in an earthenware pot.

But despite the difference established here, we are soon taken into a more familiar world of refugees and contagious illness:

> The country people, whose farms were being burned, poured into the City, and lived like beasts, wherever they could put up a few boards, or a roof of hide. They were even sleeping and cooking in the shrines, and in the colonnades of the wrestling schools. The Long Walls were lined with stinking huts all the way to the harbour.[12]

And it is this novel, with its debates on democracy and demagogues, and its reflection on what by the 1950s were being termed 'war-crimes', which is perhaps the most relevant to the time when it was first published – and even our own.

So before these books begin to touch on gender in a man's world they indicate an engagement with the problems of the times – with big international questions which even in the 1950s were often regarded as beyond women (despite women's involvement in the democratic process).

But at times gender does overlap with these large questions, as in *The Eagle of the Ninth* in which metaphorical associations with gender roles are extended to other oppositions – in particular, the colonisers and the colonised. To examine this it is helpful to focus on two passages. In the first, the British slave and ex-gladiator Esca tries to explain to Marcus the difference between British ways and Roman ways, comparing the metalwork of a dagger-sheath and a shield. In the second, Marcus and Esca enter the sacred cave in which the lost Eagle of the ninth legion is held – they must retrieve it to prevent a rising against the occupying forces but Marcus is also bound to retrieve it from duty to his father, who commanded the legion and vanished with it.

The first passage is a significant one in the novel, since it occurs when Marcus tries, for the first time, to understand something which has been puzzling him – why the colonised resent their colonisers. In the preceding discussion it is established between Marcus and Esca that Rome offers four things: merchandise (which can make people fat and lazy), justice, order and good roads. (These are not unlike the offerings of the British Empire.) Marcus can understand that the northern tribes want their freedom but Esca says that 'other things than freedom' are involved. It is only through the metaphor of artwork that the crucial difference can be understood. The Roman design consists of, in Esca's words:

> ... a tight curve, and ... another facing the other way to balance it, ...between them is a little round stiff flower; ... all repeated here, and here again ...[13]

By contrast, the British design offers:

> ... bulging curves that flow from each other as water flows from water and wind from wind, as the stars turn in the heaven and blown sand drifts into dunes. These are the curves of life; and the man who traced them had in him knowledge of things that your people have lost the key to – if they ever had it.[14]

Esca amplifies this by using it as the key to understanding the difference between Briton and Roman:

> You are the builders of coursed stone walls, the makers of straight roads and ordered justice and disciplined troops. We know that, we know it all too well. We know that your justice is more sure than ours, and when we rise against you, we see our hosts break against the discipline of your troops, as the sea breaks against a rock. And we do not understand, because all these things are of the ordered pattern, and only the free curves of the shield-boss are real to us.[15]

Obviously Sutcliff's descriptions are historically accurate, and may apply to actual archaeological finds. But the contrast she draws between the stiffness, order and repetition of the Roman design and the flowing curves, like sea-water, wind, stars and blown sand seems to offer a masculine/feminine opposition as well as an opposition between artistic styles and coloniser and colonised. What Marcus must learn to see is a 'formless yet potent beauty' allied with freedom and what is to him a barbarous way of life. The novel's point of view is that of the coloniser but we are asked to see the limitations of that view – limitations which may have been even more evident in the 1950s when totalitarianism, in whatever form, seemed the most acute problem facing the world. Formlessness on a shield offers beauty and freedom allied to barbarism, the colonised and, by the implications of the metaphor, women. However, it would be overly simple to praise the beauty of formlessness against Roman stiffness. Much theorising about Hitler's rise to power saw him harnessing the human desire for the irrational, so that formlessness as well as order offers danger.[16] Nonetheless, this passage, which shows the limitations of Marcus's world – already suggested by the description of gladiatorial combat – is more sympathetic to the freedom desired by the British people. It is a suggestive conjunction of ideas which is left in the reader's mind with the idea of the damage the coloniser can do: 'when ... we begin to understand your world, ... we lose the understanding of our own'.[17]

But this implied conjunction between femininity, the colonised and barbarism is not always so easily explored. At the climax of the novel, Marcus sees the cave where the eagle is kept in terrifying and female terms. The darkness of the cave, known as 'the Place of Life' as if to underline its womb-like properties, is 'horribly personal' and 'the centre of a dark worship'. Within the central chamber is an amber cup filled with blood that gleams 'darkly and stickily red'.[18] And it is only when he has gone beyond this that he can lay his hand on the shaft of his father's lost eagle.

At this point, the feminine seems to have shifted from its earlier associations with beauty, formlessness and freedom. It is no longer sympathetic but threatening and scary – and it is at this point in the narrative that we are asked to be most in sympathy with the Roman cause since Esca, now freed from slavery, has given his support to Marcus if not the colonisers. Together they stand for light against darkness and finally, after a moment when Marcus is taken over by a series of orgasmic shuddering gasps, they release the Eagle and are able to begin their journey south. In this passage it is as though Esca has been claimed from the disturbingly linked ideas of barbarism and feminine power for Rome, order and masculinity. But the metaphorical values are insufficiently fixed for this. Esca may have been won over to support Marcus, but he supports him as a wife might support a husband, taking on, voluntarily, more excitement and risk than would usually be imagined for a 1950s woman. For the rest of their escape south the two are mutually dependent in the face of danger, each risking his life for the other and both showing the conventionally male virtue of courage. Although femininity has appeared metaphorically and offered parallels to the reader, because its name has been unspoken it remains, despite the overpoweringly biological metaphor of the cave scene, a set of qualities which may be found in either gender.

This split between femininity and the female is more apparent in *The Last of the Wine,* in which all the major relationships – of comradeship, friendship, love, and enmity – are between men. Indeed, Alexias has to display tact to Xenophon when he realises, with pity, that his friend may be exclusively heterosexual and thus denied the fulfilment of loving a man or boy. Additionally, in the historically accurate situation of the novel, we see the male narrator trying to deal with his own attractiveness, to fend off unwanted suitors and use his beauty as a commodity when he is forced to work as a sculptor's model. In other words, the problems girls and women face are seen from the point of view of someone who is also powerful as a man within society. Intentionally or not, the novel imagines a world in which the roles women conventionally take in sexual and emotional relationships are occupied by men who will also fight, take political decisions and run their families.

In this situation the differences which usually exist between women and men can be found elsewhere, for instance, between Spartan and Athenian. Athenian men have their legs shaved while Spartans do not. But for the Spartan man, long hair is a sign of adulthood while the Athenian man cuts his hair short. Thus aspects of masculine appearance taken for granted in the 1950s are called into question. The graceful Athenians with their shaven legs and reverence for physical beauty are seen as the most acceptable model of masculinity while the hairy Spartans, who neglect beauty and praise physical endurance are seen as limited and, later, easily susceptible to corruption because of the limited lives they lead. What the novel recommends, by implication, is a rounded life, in which both beauty and strength are prized – a life in which the aim is not a specialised person, but a person who can take part in all forms of activity.

This search for roundedness is perhaps most apparent in the appearance of Sostratos, the wrestler, at the Isthmian games. In the novel Sostratos is drawn to wrestle with Lysis, Alixias' lover, in the pankration and we are invited to share Alexias' sense of shock at this over-specialised (and arguably over-masculine) man, this 'mountain of gross flesh, great muscles like twisted oakwood gnarling his body and arms; a neck like a bull's; his legs ... thick and knotty, ... bowed by the weight of his ungainly trunk'.[19] Sostratos, who nearly kills Lysis in the subsequent bout, has chosen to develop his body in a way that fits him only to compete in the pankration – he can win, but only at the cost of his all-round ability. He cannot defend his city if this is required of him – and in the Classical Greek world, this is one of the defining tasks of a free man (along with, in Athens, voting on decisions that affect the city and serving on juries). The ideal man in this world must develop himself in many ways. And it is also suggested that a proper relationship with a male lover (not necessarily consummated and not necessarily exclusive) as well as marriage is a vital part of a rounded man. On one of the rare occasions in which Renault looks beyond the classical period, she has a Theban soldier, Tolmides, anticipate in imagination the famous Theban 'army of lovers' who were to fight to the death against Alexander the Great.

What this suggests is that love is a crucial part of the male – and hence, I think – the human condition. It is not surprising that Sokrates' famous oration in praise of love from Plato's *Symposium* is also used and that his teachings from the *Phaedrus* are echoed through the book.[20] The imagination of humanity is perhaps fuller in this male-dominated world, in which men embody humanity and women are marginalised, than it is when characteristics are assigned simply on the basis of gender.

Woodham Smith has no such idea but demonstrates, with historical evidence and, I suspect, some pleasure, the absurdities of Lord Cardigan – beautiful, athletic, fearless and 'unusually stupid'. She lavishes some pity on him as a boy brought up in a feminine world, growing up spoilt among his seven sisters and protected from danger by his family because he is the only male heir. But he too is seen in conflict with men in a way which demonstrates a difference both of class and gender. He despises the 'Indian officers'[21] – that is, officers of a lower social class who had seen active service in India – preferring inexperienced young men of higher social standing. With no chance of fighting, he concerns himself with parade-ground manoeuvres and the design of a suitable uniform for his hussars. She quotes the *Times* description of the 11th hussars:

> The brevity of their jackets, the irrationality of their headgear, the incredible tightness of their cherry-coloured pants, altogether defy description; they must be seen to be appreciated.[22]

In other words, what is often seen as the feminine concern with costume and outward appearance, is here allied with masculine stubbornness and stupidity. And it is the masculine bodies that are put on display here and later as the bodies of the 17th Lancers are torn to pieces by gunfire in the charge of the Light Brigade. But Cardigan, with his stubborn concern for military etiquette coupled with stupidity and insensitivity to others 'led the Light Brigade down the valley as if he were leading a charge in a review in Hyde Park' and 'avoided any undignified appearance of haste by riding back very slowly'.[23] It is from a mixture of conventionally masculine and feminine characteristics that his absurd courage is born.

The Reason Why, as a history, perhaps finds it easiest to reach a conclusion. However, in its conclusion it has to reflect on the past and, as it does so, relate it to subsequent events. It is here that the relation of history to the present becomes most apparent. The final paragraphs move away from the two absurd aristocrats who have been at the centre of the book to eulogise 'the private soldier' and to look at the improvements in 'Army welfare and Army education, Army recreation, sports and physical training, the health services' which occurred. Written shortly after a war in which civilians had been involved and praised for their endurance and at the beginning of a new Welfare State with all that involved, the conclusion of *The Reason Why* seems to refer to the present as well as the past when it offers 'almost ... a happy ending'.[24]

But while *The Reason Why* is fairly clear cut in its sense of right and wrong, *The Eagle of the Ninth* has set up a much more complex problem in the oppositions it has created between coloniser and colonised, opening up a gulf in the common phrase 'Roman Britain'. As the novel reaches its conclusion it too anticipates a future in which the legions – the colonisers – will withdraw but leave their traces on the colonised, as was happening throughout Britain's old Empire. A story for children, told from the Roman point of view but with strong sympathy for the native Britons, requires some reconciliation at the end, not merely between the characters but between the different views taken by Roman and Briton. By the end of the book, Esca has been granted Roman citizenship – although he can understand this only through a parallel from gladiatorial contest – and Marcus is to marry Cottia, brought up by her Romanised aunt but proud of her Iceni heritage. (She is descended from the female-led tribe who had fought the 9th legion under Marcus's father.) First, however, Marcus has encountered Guern, an ex-legionary who has chosen to live as a Pict and can tell him the story of the lost 9th Legion, its indiscipline and the effect of Boudicca's curse. In their last meeting, Guern seems to offer an image of a way forward – he is both a 'half-naked, wild-haired tribesman, with a savage dog against his knee' and 'all Rome' in the 'iron discipline and pride' of the parade ground.[25] Instead of one world replacing another we are offered a vision in the mist of the trace of one culture upon another, a kind of cultural palimpsest. And this is what seems to be offered in Marcus's final decision. The Roman recognises a new sense of home and decides to stay in Britain. This sense of home, as anticipated in the book's opening, is derived from the landscape as Marcus's visual sense adjusts to recognise the subtle beauties of the British landscape:

> He could go home.
>
> Standing there with the last cold spattering of the shower blowing in his face, he thought, I can go home, and saw behind his eyes the long road leading south, the Legion's road, white in the Etruscan sunlight; the farmsteads among their terraced olive-trees, and the wine-darkness of the Apennines beyond. He seemed to catch the resiny, aromatic smell of the pine forests dropping to the shore, and

> the warm mingling of thyme and rosemary and wild cyclamen that was the summer scent of his own hills. He could go back to all that now, to the hills and the people among whom he had been bred, and for whom he had been so bitterly home-sick, here in the North. But if he did, would there not be another hunger on him all his life? For other scents and sights and sounds; pale and changeful northern skies and the green plover calling.[26]

While learning to love a new landscape in this way is something with which many readers of the book will be familiar, it also, in part aestheticises questions of unjust power and colonial rule which have previously been raised. For us as readers, our strong sense of Marcus, the Roman coloniser, as ancestor may tend to displace our awareness of other fictional ancestors – the colonial subjects, Esca, Cottia and Guern – because Marcus has learned the love of English landscape so often associated with deeply-held patriotism.[27]

The most difficult problem in achieving closure is that faced by *The Last of the Wine* because the political problems it has advanced are so acute. Running through the novel is a sense of the danger of demagogues, informed no doubt not just by past events in Europe but also by the introduction of apartheid in South Africa, where Renault had made her home. The romantic, dangerous figure of Alkibiades stalks through the novel as both hero and villain. While he retains his glamour and fascination, he is also presented as the demogogue who swayed the people in the agora to punish Melos by massacring all men of fighting age and enslaving the rest of the population. There were many stories of brutality in the Second World War but the much told story of Lidice[28] would probably have been most potent to readers at the time. The figure of Phaedo, sold into a boy-brothel after witnessing the death of his lover in the massacre, doubting all yet recognising wisdom and goodness in Sokrates, stands for the Melian outrage in the novel. Phaedo's experience raises the question of whether democracy can be trusted – and even Sokrates' followers find themselves unable to agree on the right answer. The question was particularly resonant at the time – democracies, such as they were, had seen people swayed by Mussolini, by Hitler, by the National Party in South Africa – and democracy as a system was plainly open to such abuse.

The Last of the Wine does not end with an easy solution, or even with an obvious closure. An italicised note from Alexias' grandson says that Alexias had died suddenly and that it is unclear whether the book is finished.[29] It ends instead with an argument about the nature of the

Demos (the people), about whether democracy is possible or desirable and Alexias remembering what Lysis had said much earlier in the book, after quoting Perikles' oration for the first dead of the war.[30] It's a modest version of democracy – 'a City where I can find my equals and respect my betters' and 'where no one can tell me to swallow a lie'.[31] But it also depends on the presence of Sokrates in the agora and the novel's last image is of 'Sokrates talking to Phaedo, with the cup in his hand'.[32] This image begs us as readers to continue questioning because it anticipates the image from the account of Sokrates' death, which takes Phaedo's name. Sokrates is soon to die, in Phaedo's company, drinking hemlock from a cup, sentenced to death by that same democracy to which he was so vital. Without Sokrates, perhaps we should ask, what is our own responsibility to a democratic society.

The conclusions to all three books omit women, although there are references to Cottia in the conclusion of *The Eagle of the Ninth*. But characteristics which we are accustomed to attach to gender have not been firmly fixed in the preceding narrative. Consequently, as women readers, we may feel ourselves less firmly gendered than with many texts. Gender identity can be a strength but in the 1950s – and perhaps today too – it could also be a limitation. By concentrating upon the world of men the women authors of these texts have at least made it possible for women, through imagination and reason, to enter debates about war, democracy and colonisation. Perhaps, in the process, women have been able to feel ever so slightly more confident in entering such debates outside the world of historical writing while the constraints of gender identity may also have become a little less secure.

Notes

1 See *Mr Rowl* (1924) which deals with the Napoleonic Wars and the trilogy concerned with the Jacobite rising of 1745–46 and its aftermath: *The Flight of the Heron* (1925), *The Gleam in the North* (1927) and *The Dark Mile* (1929). These novels, which include male-female romance, nonetheless take relationships between men as their focus. Interestingly, these novels, concerned with the effects of war and the actions of the conquerors, were written at roughly the same distance in time from the First World War as the works I discuss are distant from the Second World War.

2 Her Darkover series beginning with *Planet Savers* (1962), *Sword of Aldones* (1962) and *The Bloody Sun* (1964).

3 Although I have no detailed, statistical information on which to base this, I have observed that films made during the war – including, of course, *The Gentle Sex* (1943: Leslie Howard and Maurice Elvey) – depict women as war-workers in a variety of fields while this depiction seems less common in films about the war made during the 1950s.

4 This might be demonstrated by the roles offered to women in the Cabinet. Between 1945 and 1963 only two women (Ellen Wilkinson, Labour, 1945–47 and Florence Horsbrugh, Conservative, 1953–54) served as Cabinet ministers. Both were Ministers of Education.

5 Cecil Woodham Smith, *The Reason Why: the Story of the Fatal Charge of the Light Brigade* (1953; London: Penguin, 2000) (henceforward *Reason*), p. 9.

6 Consider, for instance, Humphrey Jennings' *London Can Take It* (1940), aimed at an American audience or Noel Coward and David Lean's *In Which We Serve* (1942).

7 Instead of perceiving Roman Britain as subject to imperial rule, there was a nineteenth-century tendency to use Rome as a model for imperial prowess and governance. Elements of this may be detectable in such works as Macaulay's *Lays of Ancient Rome* (1842) – still recommended for schoolchildren in the 1950s.

8 Rosemary Sutcliff, *The Eagle of the Ninth* (1954; Oxford: Oxford University Press, 2000) (henceforward *Eagle*), pp. 1–2.

9 Ibid.

10 Rosemary Sutcliff, *Rudyard Kipling* in *Threee Bodley Head Monographs: Arthur Ransome (Hugh Shelley), Rudyard Kipling (Rosemary Sutcliff), Walter de la Mare (Leonard Clark)* (London: The Bodley Head, 1968) (first published in individual volumes, 1960), pp. 67–109. Sutcliff writes, 'Children are prone to grow up seeing history as a series of small static pictures, all belonging to Then and having nothing to do with Now. The two Puck books, stories and songs alike, with their history of past and present in one corner of England, must help them to feel it as a living and continuous present of which they themselves are a part, must help them to be at least a little aware of their own living roots behind them, and so see their own times in better perspective than they might otherwise have done', p. 100.

11 Mary Renault, *The Last of the Wine* (1956; London: Longman, 1972) (henceforward *Wine*), p. 1.

12 Ibid.

13 *Eagle*, pp. 89–90.

14 Ibid.

15 Ibid.

16 A trend of scholarship can be observed, including the work of philosopher, R.G. Collingwood, which saw the need to harness both rational and irrational elements and in E.R. Dodds' influential 1950 study of Ancient Greece, *The Greeks and the Irrational*.

17 *Eagle*, p. 90.

18 Ibid., pp. 199–201.

19 *Wine*, pp. 178–9.

20 The teachings of love from the *Symposium*, based on Sokrates' speech which he in turn attributed to the teachings of Diotima, are read by Renault as recommending unconsummated homosexual love as the highest type of love. In the novel Alexias and Lysis try to follow Sokrates' teaching but eventually consummate their love. The most famous image from the *Phaedrus* is that of the charioteer who tries to control two horses which, roughly speaking, represent the body and the soul. It is this image which provided the title for Renault's earlier novel of male homosexual love.

21 *Reason*, p. 60.
22 Ibid., p. 62.
23 Ibid., p. 249.
24 Ibid., pp. 273–4.
25 *Eagle*, p. 243.
26 Ibid., pp. 288–9.
27 Consider, for instance, the elision made between patriotism and a nurturing English landscape in Rupert Brooke's famous sonnet, 'The Soldier'.
28 In 1942 Reinhard Heydrich was assassinated in the Czech village of Lidice. In reprisal the Germans killed all the men, deported the women and children and destroyed the entire village.
29 *Wine*, p. 381.
30 Derived from the second book of Thucydides' history of the Peloponnesian War.
31 *Wine*, p. 237.
32 Ibid., p. 381.

11
Female Masculinity in Iris Murdoch's Early Fiction

Tammy Grimshaw

New philosophical and literary movements proliferated both in Britain and on the Continent after the Second World War, fuelled by the pervasive societal demand for change and renewal. Continental thought influenced many British writers, including Iris Murdoch, who often acknowledged her fascination with French Feminism. In a 1976 interview, Murdoch spoke openly of her admiration of Simone De Beauvoir and her work: 'Simone de Beauvoir is someone I admire enormously. *The Second Sex* is a very good book and makes me like her as a *person*'.[1] In addition, Murdoch's affinity with De Beauvoir may have had its bases in similarities of a more personal nature between the two writers, both of whom had unconventional views on marriage and family life.[2]

The views on marriage which De Beauvoir and Murdoch shared stand in stark contrast to the socio-political circumscription of family life as a necessity for women during this epoch. While *The Second Sex* laments in particular the plight of women in postwar France, the conditions which De Beauvoir decried were also affecting women in Britain during this period. For example, in France, motherhood was regulated through both abortion and birth control, which were illegal until 1967 and 1974, respectively, while in Britain, the family allowance was introduced to encourage marriage and new births, both of which rose steadily from 1945 to 1965.[3]

Women's fiction of the postwar period often depicts home and family life, illustrating that femininity was primarily constructed within the institution of marriage. Murdoch likewise depicts the deployment of femininity in the marital home in two of her early novels, *The Sandcastle* (1957) and *The Bell* (1958). Because of Murdoch's affinity with *The Second Sex*, I shall utilise it as a critical framework in this chapter to explore the manner in which the married female protagonists in these novels embrace postwar ideals of femininity. I shall then analyse her female characters' attempts to shirk these feminine ideals and become independent as they align themselves with the masculine.[4]

In *The Sandcastle*, Murdoch portrays Nan Mor as a strong woman who attempts to conform to the postwar construct of domestic femininity. De Beauvoir asserts that because marriage is enjoined under this construct, women are required to care for the man's household (*SS*, p. 416).[5] However, domesticity is not a positive experience for a woman since she 'is doomed to the ... care of the home ... She reaches out beyond herself toward the social group only through her husband as intermediary' (*SS*, p. 419). In the same way, Nan 'deliberately related herself to the world through ... [her husband, Bill] only and then disliked him for it. She had few friends, and no occupation other than housework' (*TS*, p. 14).[6] Nan's primary activity is looking after the family home, a modern semi-detached house filled with 'large and glossy' furniture, situated in a new housing estate (*TS*, p. 7). In Nan's characterisation, then, Murdoch illustrates the manner in which women lived vicariously through their husbands and home lives during this era. By portraying the dislike which Nan feels towards her husband, Murdoch also demonstrates that femininity restricted women and often caused them to resent their husbands.

De Beauvoir asserts that femininity and the related construct of female domesticity are the result of social forces which work together to make women dependent upon men. Her statement 'One is not born, but rather becomes a woman' is one of the most often-cited quotations in criticism analysing her work. Judith Butler concludes that De Beauvoir's use of the verb 'become' implies an interplay between individual action and acculturation which is an ongoing process.[7] De Beauvoir's assertion therefore means that gender is 'a project of constructing ourselves' which consists of strategies of performance that individuals tacitly, insistently and repeatedly take up.[8] Murdoch illustrates gender performance at length in this novel. Indeed, she portrays predictable, 'recurring patterns' of gender performance in Nan and Bill Mor's 20-year marriage (*TS*, pp. 12, 202). While predictable and thus providing domestic stability and comfort, these patterns can nevertheless undermine the success of a marriage. According to De Beauvoir, this potential for failure exists because of the 'curse' in the marital home:

boredom (*SS*, p. 456). This phenomenon also materialises in the Mor's household, and while Bill once found this 'homely ennui' reassuring, he admits to being overwhelmed by 'a soporific feeling of conjugal boredom' (*TS*, pp. 9, 274). Accordingly, he begins to seek out pleasurable diversions to mitigate his domestic monotony and ultimately embarks on an affair with Rain Carter, a younger woman.

Nan also acts out against the drudgery of her home life. De Beauvoir states that becoming a 'shrewish matron' is one 'avenue of escape' open to women (*SS*, p. 460). Women engage in this strategy of feminine gender performance because of the oppressive nature of marriage, an institution which engenders their passivity. Since the housewife is reluctant to admit the redundant nature of her domestic drudgery, 'she is ... led to impose her services by force: she changes from mother and housewife into ... shrew' (*SS*, p. 442). Murdoch portrays Nan as a shrew who openly expresses her resentment towards her husband by constantly condemning him. Shrewishness then is one possible strategy or performance of femininity, albeit an undesirable one from the male perspective. Bill responds negatively to Nan's undesirable gender performance, and when she repeatedly imitates and mocks him in the conversation they have about their son and daughter, he entreats her not to nag. She then abruptly retorts, 'Don't use that word at me' (*TS*, p. 8).[9] Nan responds acerbically because Bill, having labelled her 'a nag', has implicitly criticised her gender performance and, therefore, impugned her femininity. Such responses are common among those who receive negative receptions to their gender performance. As Butler points out, 'most people feel deeply wounded if they are told ... that they have failed to execute their manhood or womanhood properly'.[10]

During the postwar years, women were expected to execute their femininity 'correctly' by being passive in the marital home. De Beauvoir emphasises that since a woman is 'given' in marriage while a man actively 'takes' a wife, a woman is required to submit to her husband (*SS*, p. 418). Yet a woman sometimes reacts against her feminine passivity and disempowerment by refusing merely to accept her husband's point of view (*SS*, p. 449). In other words, a woman negotiates not only her gender, but also the power dynamics inherent in the marital relationship while performing as a wife and mother. Murdoch also illustrates the feminine experience of passivity and disempowerment. Experiencing such disempowerment while sorting out how properly to perform her gender, Nan's mockery of her husband is a rejection of his viewpoints and a reaction against her passivity. Nan then expresses a predilection for control over her husband and children in order to feel that she has gained power over them. Upon learning of her husband's affair, for example, she 'knew ... she would have to hold this situation as she had held all other situations, controlling Bill' (*TS*, p. 195). As Toril Moi explains, De Beauvoir's 'problematic is one of *power* ... a domination of the other's freedom is always intolerable'.[11] Thus Nan tries to obtain power in the relationship to preserve her own potential for freedom because she feels that her husband too often dominates her and forces her into submission.

Significantly, the desire for freedom, like Nan's, is a masculine trait according to De Beauvoir. Attributing productivity and activity, which she equates with freedom and independence, to the masculine, De Beauvoir states, 'a man is ... an independent and complete individual ... a producer' (*SS*, p. 416). In turn, these male traits are paramount to both men and women since De Beauvoir repeatedly maintains throughout *The Second Sex* that masculinity represents the universal human condition. She asserts that 'woman's situation inclines her to ... [live] marginally to the masculine world ... she sees it not in its universal form' (*SS*, p. 662). De Beauvoir therefore suggests that since the masculine is the accepted, universal gender, women should strive to become more masculine in order to overcome their marginalisation. Being heavily influenced by the existentialist tradition, Murdoch also believed in masculine universality. She explicated this belief in an interview, stating that 'a male represents ordinary human beings ... whereas a woman is always a woman!'.[12]

Undoubtedly, the professional experiences of these two women writers deeply shaped their views on masculine universality. Murdoch's own life experiences, such as her life as an Oxford don and the press's inclusion of her as the token female novelist in the Angry Young Men of the Movement, aligned her professional pursuits with those which were decidedly masculine.[13] De Beauvoir was also involved throughout her lifetime in what was then a male-dominated intellectual and creative milieu. While Murdoch asserted that her characters were often 'androgynous' or 'genderless', a detailed examination of her work reveals that she did not truly endorse genderlessness or androgyny as she claimed.[14] Rather, in aligning the universal with masculine, male experience, and encouraging women to gain independence through such experiences, Murdoch promoted 'female masculinity' instead of 'genderlessness' or 'androgyny'.

Murdoch deploys her construct of 'female masculinity' in this novel in her depiction of Nan's predilection for freedom and independence. She writes: 'one day Mor made the discovery that he was tied for life to a being ... who could withdraw herself from him and become independent. On that day Mor had renewed his marriage vows' (*TS*, p. 11). Thus Murdoch demonstrates that a woman who is capable of independence is to be feared from the male perspective since she undermines the stability of the home and disrupts prescribed gender performances. Greatly fearing his wife's freedom and intuiting the potential threat to his marital home, Bill re-enacts the marriage ceremony to remind his wife of her marital responsibilities. In so doing, he attempts to squelch her desire for independence and reinstitute domestic stability.

Women could also pursue independence during the postwar years by shirking maternity since having children was promoted as integral to building a stable and satisfying home life. As De Beauvoir points out, 'through childbearing ... the institution of marriage gets its meaning and attains its purpose' (*SS*, p. 466). However, De Beauvoir laments maternity as restricting the freedoms of women. Motherhood is to be shunned according to De Beauvoir since it is disempowering; it confines woman to the home, limiting her ability to become liberated.[15] Being independent women who had unconventional domestic arrangements, neither De Beauvoir nor Murdoch had the personal experience of motherhood.[16] Ineluctably, this lack of personal experience impacted upon the views of motherhood which these two writers expressed in their works: Murdoch's fiction lacks the intimate, day-to-day details of maternity, while De Beauvoir's personal view of motherhood in *The Second Sex* has been described as that of a potentially horrific and threatening experience.[17]

De Beauvoir explains that motherhood creates an especially precarious and threatening situation in the relationship of a mother to her daughter since the mother may view the daughter as a rival, a constant source against which to assess her own ageing. The mother thus develops highly ambivalent attitudes towards her daughter (*SS*, p. 559). Murdoch depicts a similar scenario in the Mors' household. Nan and Bill's 14-year-old daughter Felicity strongly resembles her mother (*TS*, p. 16). Felicity is therefore a tangible reminder to Nan of her own ageing femininity. Perhaps because of Nan's ambivalence towards her daughter, Felicity has been sent away from the family home and resides in a boarding school (*TS*, p. 7). Donald, Nan and Bill's son, also lives in a school dormitory, in spite of the school being within walking distance of the family home (*TS*, p. 128). Hence, the children do not figure prominently in Nan's life because she attempts to shun some of the responsibilities and restrictions of motherhood. Since being a mother is often considered to constitute the *sine qua non* of femininity, it could be argued that women also evade the feminine as they shun motherhood.

In her portrayal of Nan's aversion to certain of the duties associated with motherhood, Murdoch illustrates that women can desire independence. Since the pursuit of independence was a masculine trait according to De Beauvoir, this character seems to represent Murdoch's belief in 'female masculinity' at this point in the narrative.

This character continues to be aligned with the masculine through the clothing she chooses to wear. Butler analyses in depth the use of clothing in the performance of gender, particularly the use of clothing as an empowering form of gender transgression.[18] On the other hand, De Beauvoir laments that conforming to prescribed feminine modes of adornment and attire only spuriously enable women to take possession of themselves (*SS*, 505). Murdoch depicts Nan as having an aversion to feminine clothing and, accordingly, demonstrates that this character refuses fully to take on her femininity, thereby transgressing prescribed gender norms. She portrays this early in the narrative as Nan laments having to get 'flossied up' for an evening at Demoyte's, the headmaster (*TS*, p. 10). Bill later muses that his wife 'could look handsome ... at an evening party, [but] ... never managed to look like anything' in the clothing she usually wore (*TS*, p. 53). Murdoch uses the word 'handsome' in this passage, a word generally associated with the masculine, to underscore Nan's failure to execute her femininity 'correctly'. This failure brings about Bill's attraction to Rain Carter, whose delicate appearance he associates with desirable feminine attributes. He is attracted to Rain's dress sense, particularly when 'she was wearing a close-fitting blue silk dress which made her look ... feminine' (*TS*, p. 70).

Murdoch thus characterises this female protagonist as masculine in certain ways. Nevertheless, the author depicts Nan ultimately returning to femininity. At the school's end-of-term dinner at the close of the narrative, Nan wears 'an extremely *decolleté* black nylon evening-dress, with a very full skirt and sort of bustle at the back. She also had on ... ear-rings ... Her fine bosom, extensively revealed, was rounded and powdery smooth. Her hair was sleekly curled' (*TS*, p. 288). Adorned in this fashion, Nan's gender performance exudes femininity as she has carefully selected this garment to accentuate her breasts, womanly hair and radiant skin. In addition, clothing is integral to woman's sexual allure and often makes them erotic objects (*SS*, p. 506). Nan also chooses clothing which exudes sex appeal; she wears a low-cut, bustled dress, specifically designed to exaggerate her curvaceous womanly figure.

Echoing Joan Riviere's essay 'Womanliness as Masquerade', Murdoch also illustrates masquerade in this scene. Viewing his wife's gender performance, Bill 'was amazed at her capacity to put on this act. He would not have suspected her capable of such a masquerade' (*TS*, p. 297). Nan's ultimate return to femininity is predicated upon the presence at the dinner of Rain Carter, the romantic rival for her husband. This depiction further highlights Murdoch's deployment of the concept of gender performance, particularly the theory that 'masquerade' can be used as a means of conflict resolution.[19] The conflict which Nan seeks to resolve at this juncture is her husband's attachment to Rain, who threatens the stability of her marital home. De Beauvoir asserts that 'in order to tear her husband way from an alarming rival, [a wife] will ... try to offer him diversion' (*SS*, pp. 453–4). Nan presents such a diversion to Bill as she gives her speech after the meal. Although she has vehemently opposed her husband's intention to stand as an MP candidate up to this point, she announces her support of Bill's Labour candidature during her speech. Bill will now be required to stand as a candidate, although he had been vacillating on the issue and had not yet made a definite decision. Further, since Bill has not told Rain the truth about his political aspirations, Nan's announcement indirectly effects Rain's termination of her husband's affair because she reveals his failure to be honest to his mistress. As the family move to London at the close of the novel, Nan remains completely dependent upon Bill. She continues to view marriage as her sole career and occupation, a phenomenon which, according to De Beauvoir, should be prohibited in order to promote women's common welfare (*SS*, p. 465). In her representation of Nan, Murdoch therefore illustrates her belief that women give up the possibility of achieving independence through 'female masculinity' when they continue to adhere to the feminine ideal of living vicariously through their husbands.

Murdoch continues to explore the deployment of domestic femininity in her next novel, *The Bell*. Depicting Dora Greenfield's admiration of her husband, Paul, and her willingness to please him, Murdoch again illustrates the concept of gender performativity.[20] Butler explains that 'becoming' a woman in De Beauvoirian terms 'is a purposive ... set of acts, the acquisition of a skill'.[21] One of the key skills which mothers taught their daughters during the postwar period was how to 'catch' a husband (*SS*, p. 422). Having 'caught' Paul, Dora is keen to make what her mother called a 'good marriage' and accordingly performs her gender by acquiring the skills necessary for domestic life with him (*TB*, p. 8).[22] Dora 'becomes' a woman as she performs the feminine by striving to be servile to Paul and embracing her passivity and dependence in the marital home. She was attending the Slade School of Art on a scholarship when she met Paul (*TB*, p. 7). Yet she discontinues the pursuit of her artistic endeavours upon marrying him because he 'had assumed that she would give up her art studies, and she had given them up with some regret' (*TB*, p. 8). Because having a career is essential for women's independence under De Beauvoir's vision, Dora becomes completely passive and dependent upon her husband as she relinquishes her professional pursuits. Butler argues that De Beauvoir reformulates gender as a choice, 'whereby 'choosing' a gender is understood as the embodiment of possibilities within a network of deeply entrenched cultural norms'.[23] Dora too chooses her femininity as she decides to give up independent work of her own. In addition, Dora's choice illustrates the influence of cultural norms during this epoch which dictated that women shun careers of their own in order to focus on the stability of the home.

As Dora relinquishes her independence and embraces passivity, she, like Nan, becomes disempowered. Moi explains that 'for De Beauvoir ... when we alienate ourselves in another thing or person, we deprive ourselves of the power to act for ourselves'.[24] Giving up her career and therefore her power to act independently from her husband, Dora alienates herself as she 'becomes' Paul's wife. Further, becoming a wife often means that 'the husband succeeds in making his wife an echo of himself' (*SS*, p. 456). Dora similarly muses that her marriage to Paul will be a successful one only if she continues 'to be enclosed in ... [his] aims' (*TB*, p. 18). Once Dora and Paul are married, and she moves into his Knightsbridge flat, she begins to experience more profoundly the problems associated with femininity. Indeed, she 'discovered that it was not so easy as she had imagined to grow into being Paul's wife' (*TB*, p. 8). Hence, Murdoch demonstrates that the performance of feminine passivity can be a very onerous task. Continuing to illustrate the postwar emphasis on the feminine interest in the home, Murdoch depicts Dora, like Nan, attempting to ward off her consternation by concentrating on domestic pursuits. In De Beauvoirian terms, she attempts to renounce the world and conquer her home (*SS*, p. 437). She occupies herself with keeping the flat 'meticulously clean' and with making 'long preparations for dinner parties with Paul's friends' (*TB*, p. 9). She also 'becomes' a woman through her use of clothing to perform the feminine. De Beauvoir suggests that a woman changes the image of herself if her lover wishes it (*SS*, p. 616). In the same way, Dora alters her appearance, wearing outfits only of which Paul approves (*TB*, p. 9).

At first blush, it appears that Murdoch's depiction of Dora's failure to provide Paul with children conflicts with the postwar construct of domestic, maternal femininity. Dora experiences no maternal feelings in spite of her husband's desperate wish for a child: 'Paul wanted children ... He yearned for a little Paul whom he could instruct and encourage' (*TB*, p. 10). On the other hand, Dora is 'alarmed at the thought of children', consistent with De Beauvoir's assertion that maternal instinct is 'a cultural fiction'.[25] However, Dora's evasion of maternity is only a specious attempt to shun femininity since she avoids motherhood merely by chance. Murdoch writes: 'it was typical of the paralysis which affected her dealings with Paul that she made no effort to prevent conception' (*TB*, p. 10). Murdoch thus depicts Dora's actions as at odds with De Beauvoir's view that control over fertility and decisions about whether or not to become a mother should be 'conscious choice[s] rather than a passive yielding to tradition'.[26] Since Dora is not proactive about birth control, she does not actively ensure her freedom from maternity and continues to yield passively to her husband.

Decisions about maternity also invariably impact upon sexuality in marriage. Being passive about contraception, it is not surprising then that Dora is also passive during the sex act itself. She 'submits' to Paul's love making 'without enthusiasm' (*TB*, p. 182). In portraying Dora's sexual submission to Paul, Murdoch illustrates De Beauvoir's belief that 'the act of love is ... a *service* rendered to the man ... [who] *takes* his pleasure' (*SS*, p. 420). Patriarchal masculinity assigns value to sexuality and freedom, further aligning the male with activity and power and the female with passivity and disempowerment.[27] In other words, for the male, sexual desire for a woman is inextricably linked to power over her. It therefore follows under De Beauvoir's view that if a husband can no longer dominate his wife, he will cease to experience sexual desire for her. Thus, when Paul ultimately is unable to control Dora and loses power over her, he tells her, 'I'm not sexually attracted to you' (*TB*, p. 289).

Paul's inability to exploit his power to control his wife leads to a great deal of ferment in the Greenfield's marital home. De Beauvoir asserts that 'there are many marriages that 'go well' – that is to say, in which man and wife reach a compromise. They live side by side without too much mutual torment' (*SS*, p. 456). Murdoch does not depict such a compromise, but rather portrays Paul and Dora existing in 'mutual torment', often having heated arguments which leave Dora 'humiliated and exhausted' (*TB*, p. 9). Acrimony takes place in the marital home because 'very often it is not enough for the husband to be approved of and admired ... He enacts violence, power [and] unyielding resolution' (*SS*, p. 450). In the same way, Paul is violent and possessive towards Dora, who is often afraid of him and flees their home in fear of his violent outbursts (*TB*, pp. 7, 11). Butler asserts that domestic oppression 'is a dialectical force which requires individual participation ... in order to maintain its malignant life'. It could be argued that Dora similarly participates in her own oppression by being drawn to Paul's violence. From the beginning of their relationship Dora was aware of, if not attracted by, Paul's violent tendencies, which she considered 'a sort of virile authority' (*TB*, p. 11). It seems that she perpetuates her own oppression as she repeatedly returns to Paul after their bitter quarrels. However, De Beauvoir also infuses such oppression with 'emancipatory potential'.[28] Murdoch depicts Dora beginning to experience her own potential for emancipation as she comes to see Paul's power differently; Dora realises that 'she was returning, and deliberately, into the power of someone whose conception of her life excluded or condemned her deepest urges' (*TB*, p. 18).

Indeed, Murdoch does not portray Dora as completely powerless. As she looks in the mirror just after her arrival at Imber Court, she is astonished by the image of the strong woman who confronts her. She muses: 'How very much, after all, she existed; she, Dora, and no one should destroy her' (*TB*, p. 45). Ursula Tidd argues that, in *The Second Sex*, 'power is not represented as monolithic, repressive or as the unique preserve of men ... but as a potential for action which, in most cases, can be grasped by either women or men'.[29] Acknowledging 'a wish to punish' Paul, Dora experiences 'the need to show him that she could still act independently. She was not his slave' (*TB*, p. 184). Dora's musings about her domestic slavery demonstrate that she has understood the extent of her oppression in the marriage. She then experiences the desire to exercise power in the relationship, taking action to display to Paul her ability to be independent. De Beauvoir emphasises that in an ideal relationship, the independence of both partners is the essential basis of love (*SS*, p. 631). However, the impetus for Dora's action is not love, but rather the desire to exact revenge on her husband. Murdoch therefore portrays this character's quest for independence in opposition to De Beauvoir's vision of love.

Believing that it was generally impossible for love to exist within the institution of marriage, De Beauvoir claimed that 'marriage finds its natural fulfilment in adultery. This is woman's sole defence against the domestic slavery in which she is bound' (*SS*, p. 80).[30] In order to alleviate her own feelings of marital unfulfilment brought on by the constraints of her domestic slavery, Dora commits adultery with Noel Spens, an acquaintance of her husband. In so doing, she attempts to cast off her oppression and gain independence.[31] However, Paul continues to exercise power over her as he phones Noel's flat, thereby thwarting her plans for a romantic rendezvous with her lover. Having abruptly fled from Noel, Dora then goes to the National Gallery. The ecstatic transports she experiences upon viewing the pictures show that she now realises that empowerment can be gained through art, rather than adultery (*TB*, pp. 190–92). Significantly, De Beauvoir asserts that art is powerful because it is aligned with the masculine: 'Woman is still astonished and flattered at being admitted to the world of thought, of art – a masculine world' (*SS*, p. 666). As an antidote to gender inequality, Murdoch similarly stressed that women should be allowed to join men in the 'great main stream of thought and art'.[32]

Modelled on Murdoch's views on 'female masculinity', Dora shuns femininity, the home and marriage and ultimately becomes masculine. De Beauvoir repeatedly emphasises that 'independent work of her own' is essential in the process of women's liberation (*SS*, p. 459). Dora too establishes a career for herself before she begins her new single life. She finally makes the decision to leave Paul for good and feels a new-found sense of liberation (*TB*, p. 315). Alone at Imber, she grows much more self-confident. While Paul suppressed Dora's creative powers throughout their marriage, Dora now displays the masculine affinity with art. She 'flourished remarkably' as she made daily water-colour sketches out beside the lake (*TB*, pp. 186, 308). At the close of the novel, Dora leaves Imber to live with her friend Sally in Bath, where she has decided to re-train as an art teacher (*TB*, p. 306).[33] Using the masculine pursuit of art as a road to freedom, she thus fulfils her ambition 'to live and work on her own and become ... an independent, grown-up person' (*TB*, p. 305). De Beauvoir explains that 'it is agonizing for a woman to assume responsibility for her life' (*SS*, p. 610). In spite of similar agonies, Dora ultimately assumes responsibility for her own life: she is productive and active and seeks to express herself artistically, all of which are masculine traits according to De Beauvoir. Dora is therefore a representation of Murdoch's notion that independence from the constraints of marriage can be achieved through 'female masculinity'.

While Murdoch believed that De Beauvoir's views on masculinity were positive and empowering for women, many feminists have expressed ambivalent reactions to this belief in masculine universality. Indeed, certain Anglo-American feminists' responses to *The Second Sex* have been highly negative, particularly with respect to De Beauvoir's viewpoints on the experience of maternity. For instance, Mary Evans indicts De Beauvoir's male-centred approach, lamenting that it suggests 'a set of values that place major importance on living like a childless, rather singular, employed man'.[34] Mary O'Brien claims that *The Second*

Sex does not value highly enough uniquely female experiences, such as women's ability to reproduce.[35] Carol McMillan likewise presents a sustained critique of what she sees as De Beauvoir's denigration of pregnancy and motherhood.[36] However, after De Beauvoir's death in 1986, feminists began to change dramatically their views on her life and works following the posthumous publication of many of her letters and other previously-unpublished writings. Toril Moi sees much to admire in De Beauvoir's work, particularly what she considers to be the fashioning of a political agenda for later generations of feminists.[37] Ruth Evans praises the book's 'untimeliness', particularly what she and other feminists see as its anticipation of later postmodern concerns.[38] Similarly, Ursula Tidd asserts that De Beauvoir's work continues to offer much to contemporary debates on gender and sexuality.[39]

Would contemporary feminist responses to Murdoch's early depiction of 'female masculinity' then be as positive as these more recent views on De Beauvoir's work? Judith Butler has commented that, although De Beauvoir seems to reinforce 'the masculine project', she ultimately reveals it as 'self-deluding ... and unsatisfactory'.[40] Yet it seems that Murdoch's fictional depictions of 'female masculinity' do not likewise reveal it as unsatisfactory. Dora seems highly fulfilled, her life full of new possibilities, upon taking up her new gender. By portraying masculinity so positively as the path to freedom from the constraints of femininity, it could be maintained that Murdoch reasserts the societal pervasiveness of patriarchal power in her fiction. Further, in her depiction of Nan's presentation of femininity as a complement to her husband's masculinity, Murdoch could also be accused of reiterating the circumscription of compulsory heterosexuality. Finally, in illustrating compulsory heterosexuality and 'female masculinity' as seemingly universal templates to which any woman can adhere, Murdoch, like De Beauvoir, could also be subject to the charge of denying the importance of sexual, class and racial differences in her fiction.

Notes

1 Sheila Hale and A.S. Byatt, 'Women Writers Now: Their Approach and Apprenticeship', *Harpers and Queen*, October 1976, pp. 178–91, p. 180.

2 See Kate Fullbrook and Edward Fullbrook, *Simone De Beauvoir and Jean-Paul Sartre: The Remaking of a Twentieth-Century Legend* (Hemel Hempstead: Harvester Wheatsheaf, 1993); Peter Conradi, *Iris Murdoch: A Life* (London: HarperCollins, 2001).

3 Ursula Tidd, *Gender and Testimony*, Cambridge Series in French, 61 (Cambridge: Cambridge University Press, 1999), p. 34; Martin Pugh, *Women*

and the Women's Movement in Britain, 1914–1999, 2nd edn (Basingstoke: Macmillan, 2000), pp. 293–5.

4 In spite of the postwar prescription of marriage, Murdoch's first two novels, *Under the Net* (1954) and *The Flight from the Enchanter* (1956) do not contain any married characters.

5 Simone De Beauvoir, *The Second Sex*, (London: Jonathan Cape, 1953). All references will be given in the body of the text with the abbreviation '*SS*'.

6 Iris Murdoch, *The Sandcastle* (London: Chatto and Windus, 1957). All further references will be given in the text using the abbreviation '*TS*'.

7 Judith Butler, 'Sex and Gender in Simone De Beauvoir's *Second Sex*', *Yale French Studies*, 72 (1986), pp. 35–49, p. 35.

8 Ibid., p. 41.

9 For a witty and insightful analysis of the literary deployment of the trope of the shrew, see Mary Ellmann, *Thinking about Women* (London: Virago Press, 1968).

10 Butler, 'Sex and Gender', p. 41.

11 Toril Moi, *Simone De Beauvoir: The Making of an Intellectual Woman* (Oxford: Blackwell, 1994), p. 184.

12 Jean-Louis Chevalier, 'Closing Debate' in *Recontres avec Iris Murdoch* (Caen: Centre de Recherches de Litterature et Linguistique des Pays de Langue Anglaise, 1978), pp. 73–93, p. 82.

13 Conradi, p. 288; Blake Morrison, *The Movement: English Poetry and Fiction of the 1950s* (Oxford: Oxford University Press, 1980), pp. 1–2.

14 Hale and Byatt, 'Women Writers Now', p. 180.

15 Jo-Ann Pilardi, 'Feminists Read *The Second Sex*', in Margaret A. Simons, ed., *Feminist Interpretations of Simone De Beauvoir* (University Park: Pennsylvania State University Press, 1995), pp. 29–43, p. 35.

16 Beauvoir avoided motherhood on one occasion by having an illegal abortion, which she publicly proclaimed by signing the *Manifeste de 343*. See Mary Evans, *Simone de Beauvoir: A Feminist Mandarin* (London: Tavistock, 1985). Murdoch likewise supported the avoidance of motherhood through abortion, and on several occasions, helped friends arrange to have unwanted pregnancies terminated. See Conradi, *Iris Murdoch: A Life*.

17 Moi, *Simone de Beauvoir*, p. 173.

18 Judith Butler, *Gender Trouble: Feminism and the Subversion of Identity*, 2nd edn (London: Routledge, 1999), pp. 174–7.

19 Ibid., p. 64.

20 Perhaps Murdoch recalled Freud's most famous female hysteric, who was also called Dora, when naming this character.

21 Butler, 'Sex and Gender', p. 36.

22 Iris Murdoch, *The Bell* (London: Chatto and Windus, 1958). All further references to this novel will be given in the body of the text, using the abbreviation '*TB*'.

23 Butler, 'Sex and Gender', p. 37.

24 Moi, *Simone De Beauvoir*, p. 161.

25 Butler, 'Sex and Gender', p. 42.

26 Yolanda Patterson, 'In Memoriam', *Yale French Studies*, 72 (1986), pp. 203–5, p. 105.

27 Pilardi, 'Feminists Read *The Second Sex*', p. 34.

28 Butler, 'Sex and Gender', p. 41.
29 Tidd, *Simone De Beauvoir*, p. 57.
30 Since sexuality is associated with masculinity, sexual expression through adultery also enables women to become more masculine.
31 It appears that both De Beauvoir and Murdoch utilised Hegel's master-slave dialectic in their writings. Much criticism exists on De Beauvoir's deployment of this dialectic. See, for example, Eva Lundgren-Gothlin, *Sex & Existence: Simone De Beauvoir's 'The Second Sex'*, trans. Linda Schenck (Hanover: University Press of New England, 1996). However, a detailed analysis of De Beauvoir's deployment of the conventions of Sartrean or Hegelian existentialism is beyond the scope of this chapter.
32 Chevalier, 'Closing Debate', p. 83.
33 Dora's relationship with Sally also illustrates Adrienne Rich's notion of 'woman identification'. See Adrienne Rich, 'Compulsory Heterosexuality and Lesbian Existence', in *Blood, Bread and Poetry, Selected Prose 1978–1985* (London: Virago, 1987), pp. 23–75.
34 Mary Evans, *Simone De Beauvoir*, p. 57.
35 See Mary O'Brien, *The Politics of Reproduction* (London: Routledge, 1981).
36 See Carol McMillan, *Women, Reason and Nature* (Oxford: Blackwell, 1982).
37 Moi, *Simone De Beauvoir*, passim.
38 Ruth Evans, 'Introduction: *The Second Sex* and the Postmodern' in Ruth Evans, ed., *Simone De Beauvoir's The Second Sex* (Manchester: Manchester University Press, 1998), pp. 1–30, p. 3.
39 Tidd, *Simone De Beauvoir*, p. 31. For an excellent summary of critical responses to *The Second Sex*, see Joseph Mahon, *Existentialism, Feminism and Simone De Beauvoir* (Basingstoke: MacMillan, 1997).
40 Butler, 'Sex and Gender', p. 43.

Part IV

Across the Threshold: Spirituality, Colonisation and Subjectivity

12
The Presentation of the Self in Doris Lessing's *Martha Quest*

Kate Fullbrook

In the second volume of her autobiography, *Walking in the Shade*, Doris Lessing, with her usual engaging honesty, describes her situation in 1950 as she began to compose her third book and second novel, *Martha Quest*. Although Lessing was only in her early thirties at the time, she had packed an astonishing amount of experience into her life. Born in what was then Persia in 1919, she was raised on an unsuccessful farm in Southern Rhodesia (now Zimbabwe) by parents whose lives had been traumatically blown off course by the violence of the First World War. Resolved to find ways to live which did not mirror those of her parents (and especially those of her mother), Lessing left school at 14 and moved to Salisbury. There, in 1939, she married Frank Wisdom, a civil servant, with whom she had a son and a daughter. By the time of her divorce in 1943, Lessing's strong anti-racist politics led to her involvement with a group which became the Communist Party in the Southern Rhodesian capital. Leaving her children with her first husband, Lessing married the group's leader, Gottfried Lessing, a refugee from Nazi Germany, in 1945, to save him from deportation. The couple divorced in 1949, and Lessing, taking Peter, her two-year-old son from her second marriage, with her, left Africa for London. Despite the dire conditions in postwar London, Lessing's move to England proved a success and London became her permanent home. Her first novel, *The Grass is Singing*, set in Africa and concerned with racism, appeared in 1950, while her first collection of short stories, *This was the Old Chief's Country*, again deeply concerned with Africa, race, and the iniquities of colonialism, came out in 1951. Still connected to the Communist Party, which she wouldn't leave until 1956 in the aftermath of the Soviet invasion of Hungary and the horrifying revelations regarding Stalin's mass murders, purges, death camps, and general reign of terror, Lessing was regarded as an important new politically radical realist writer, with illuminating things to say about race, the colonial experience, and Africa in particular.[1]

It was at this juncture in 1950, thinking about what to write next, that Lessing reflected on the potential of working directly on her own life as the topic of her next novel. As she explains in *Walking in the Shade*:

> There was a point when it occurred to me that my early life had been extraordinary and would make a novel. I had not understood how extraordinary until I had left Southern Africa and come to England. *Martha Quest*, my third book, was more or less autobiographical, though it didn't start until Martha was fourteen, when her childhood was over. First novels, particularly by women, are often attempts at self-definition, whatever their literary merits. While I was seeing my early life more clearly with every new person I met ... I was nevertheless confused. While I certainly 'knew who I was' ... I did not know how to define myself as a social being. In parenthesis ... this business of 'finding out who I am' has always left me wondering. What do they mean? Surely they can't be without a sense of self. A sense of: Here I am, inside here. What can it be like, to live without that feeling of me, in here; of what I am?[2]

The 'confusion' Lessing mentions with regard to defining herself had to do with the intersection of the intimate personal identity, whose absence Lessing cannot even imagine, with the self as an epiphenomenon of social factors and forces. As she elaborates, this historically and collectively derived aspect of the self was still unclear to her:

> What I did not know was how to define myself, see myself in a social context. Oh yes, easy enough to say I was a child of the end of the Raj – but that phrase had not yet come into use. The end of the British Empire, then. Yes, I was one of a generation brought up on World War I, and then as much formed by World War II. But there was a hiatus, a lack, a blur – and it was to do with my parents and particularly my mother. I had fought her steadily, relentlessly, and I had had to – but what was it all about? Why? And I was not able to answer that, entirely, until I was in my seventies, and even then perhaps not finally.[3]

Martha Quest, the novel that Lessing produced in the light of these confusions and questions, was published in 1952, and consolidated the author's reputation. Further, it inaugurated Lessing's explicit and trademark presentation of the self as a confluence of the historical, the social, the sexual, and the psychological, mixed with the peculiarly and often accidentally individual, which would form the foundation of her presentation of characters throughout her fiction. The selection of this specific configuration of factors for the examination and explanation of the self is that, of course, of classic realism. It is also that which has often proved most friendly to those writers whose primary literary interest tends toward the social and the political rather than the aesthetic or formalist. It is entirely in keeping with Lessing's political affinities, her keen sense of moral responsibility, and her scrupulous honesty in terms of social reportage that in her first volume of explicitly autobiographical fiction, as would be the case in her later novels, the self should be explored in these realist terms.

As Lessing herself insisted in her important essay of 1957, 'The Small Personal Voice', written for *Declaration*, a collection of essays and manifestos which also included contributions from other significant radical members of Lessing's British literary generation such as John Osborne, Colin Wilson, John Wain, and Kenneth Tynan,

> For me the highest point of literature was the novel of the nineteenth century, the work of Tolstoy, Stendhal, Dostoevsky, Balzac, Turgenev, Chekhov; the work of the great realists. I define realism as art which springs so vigorously and naturally from a strongly held, though not necessarily intellectually defined, view of life that it absorbs symbolism. I hold the view that the realist novel, the realist story, is the highest form of prose writing; higher than and out of the reach of any comparison with expressionism, symbolism, naturalism, or any other ism.[4]

Lessing's five-volume *Children of Violence* series (which *Martha Quest* inaugurates in 1952, and *The Four-Gated City* completes, 17 years later, in 1969) with its themes of psychological disturbance and apocalyptic catastrophe, concludes, is governed by a single overriding concern. As Lessing explained, exasperated that no critic had understood it, the series is 'a study of the individual conscience in its relations with the collective'.[5] That collective is composed, said Lessing, 'of people like myself, people my age who are born out of wars and who have lived through them, the framework of lives in conflict'.[6] For Lessing, all of us who have been denizens of the twentieth century are Children of Violence, conceived and raised in the interstices of the cataclysms that have categorised our era, haunted, even in the periods we have called peaceful, by the Cold War, the atomic bomb, continual episodes of barbarism, continual practice of war. Against this, Lessing counterpoises what she thinks of as 'a complex of ideas which could be described as left – and which were born with the French Revolution. And they're all to do with freedom. They are revolutionary ideas that are no longer revolutionary and have been absorbed into the fabric of how we live.'[7]

And it is this general commitment to tracing the fortunes of the great political idea of freedom (as well as its duplicitous, counterfeit manifestations) in an era dedicated to its suppression, which is always justified in the name of the special, extraordinary demands of times of war and conflict, that is one of Lessing's great topics. When Lessing's interests in the individual conscience in relation to the collective, in the formation of the self as a nexus of collective forces and intimate, enclosed ontological conviction, and in the progress of freedom in a time of continual war are pulled together, the sources of the strength of her realism are obvious. What is also clear is the reason for her repeated refusal to be labeled as a writer working for any one discernible cause or social movement: her topic is greater than that of any single area of change, no matter how desirable. And it is clear that Lessing has often been annoyed by readers who attempt to recruit her for political or social causes with which she is in sympathy, but which would represent a narrowing of her field of vision if taken as the full extent of her practice.

Thus, Lessing's fiction can profitably be read in terms of questions of race, nationalism, postcolonialism, class, generational conflict and misapprehension, the treatment of those who violate expectations of normality (whether physical or mental), violence, and, of course, gender. It is the later topic and its exemplary treatment in *Martha Quest* that the rest of this essay will consider. What I want to argue is that in devising her female rebel as the central point of conscience in her fictional presentation of the eddies of violence that wash through the experience of modernity, Lessing provided a deeply influential paradigm for the ways in which women would be represented by many women writers in English for the remainder of the century. Writing in the slipstream of modernism, and therefore intensely sensitive to the representation of psychological formations, but honing the realist practice she so admired, which was also so deeply characteristic of the politically 'committed' writer of her generation, Lessing's *Martha Quest* offered a way to present women's experience of the self in ways attentive to the pursuit of freedom and to a concomitant revision of the relations between men and women.

In constructing her exemplary rebel, Martha Quest, from the starting point of her own experience (and it must be emphasised that, for Lessing, everyone's experience is exemplary) Lessing captured the cultural ambience of Southern Rhodesia between the wars with remarkable faithfulness. However, the ambience of London during the book's composition also needs to be noted, as it forms the furthest extremity of the temporal horizon towards which the novel looks. In *Walking in the Shade*, Lessing points out a number of significant elements which dominated her life in London during the writing of *Martha Quest*. The first of these is a technological change which she describes as 'the end of an era, the death of a culture', so great is the significance Lessing ascribes to the arrival of television in the ordinary household in which she rented a flat. The arrival of the television set saw the instant death of conversation in a household which had been vibrant and lively. 'It was the end of an exuberant verbal culture.' says Lessing.[8] Meanwhile, she notes, Britain, still exhausted by the Second World War, was nevertheless characterised by inexplicable and maddeningly innocent convictions of hope and success. Summarising the shibboleths of the *zeitgeist* which pertained in London in 1950–51 as she worked on her novel, Lessing comes up with a list that includes the belief that 'a new world was dawning', and in this world 'Britain was still best' (in 'education, food, health, anything at all – best. The British Empire, then on its last legs – the best'). British prisons, however, were disgusting. 'Charity was for ever abolished by the welfare state.' 'Everyone from abroad, particularly America, said how gentle, polite – civilized – Britain was.' Lessing witnessed a display of bullying toward a newly arrived West Indian immigrant which reminded her of the racism of Southern Rhodesia.[9] The new dawn, then, was decidedly murky, but a postwar feeling of hope (however misplaced, fantastical, or simply deluded) characterised the cultural climate of the London in which *Martha Quest* was produced. When one adds to this the general atmosphere of the 1950s, notable, above all, for a passion for conformity, complacency, and by a fear of violating all norms that emanated from the paranoia generated by the Cold War, and by the success of the McCarthy witch hunts in the United States, which were at their peak as Lessing was writing *Martha* Quest, the need to address the question of freedom is apparent in all its dangerous urgency.

It was important for Lessing in composing her text that she stuck by her commitment to realism. *Martha Quest*, she said, was

> a conventional novel, though the demand then was for experimental novels. I played in my mind with a hundred ways of doing *Martha*

> *Quest*, pulling shapes about, playing with time, but at the end of all this, the novel was straightforward. I was dealing with my painful adolescence, my mother, all that anguish, the struggle for survival.[10]

Lessing's memory of literary trends is not entirely accurate. This was the era of the Angry Young Men (a group with which Lessing was sometimes associated), and the fashion for social realism was strong among the politically engaged authors of the day. However, her sense of the threat her mother posed to her identity is all too accurate. In the middle of her agonising engagement with her material, Lessing's mother announced that she was joining her daughter in London. Lessing simply collapsed at the prospect of her mother's arrival. She was rescued by a friend who, seeing how desperate Lessing was, introduced her to the therapist who served as the template for Mother Sugar in *The Golden Notebook* and who first aroused Lessing's interest in the work of Jung.

All these elements of experience feed directly into *Martha Quest*, with its great, exemplary tale of a woman's quest for freedom which would be, in its many varieties, *the central* story women writers would tell for the rest of the century. As Lessing so clearly understood, this was one aspect of the greater story of the pursuit of freedom which constitutes the positive contribution of the progressive philosophy that fired the French Revolution and of which we are all the inheritors. However, for Lessing, as much as for her contemporary, Simone De Beauvoir – the English translation of whose groundbreaking study of women, *The Second Sex*, would appear in 1953 – a year after *Martha Quest*, freedom was only valuable when practised in terms of reciprocity. And, given Lessing's views on the nature of individuals, who are as much complex manifestations of the collectivities to which they belong as they are atomised and singular agents, the question of freedom is not only one of extreme complexity, but comprises a state which can never be grounded in the other's unwilling surrender of their own freedom. Simply trading positions won't do. One cannot secure freedom by inverting old patterns of oppression and control (and this is one reason why Lessing has never been willing to align herself with contemporary feminism, as she sees it as simply inverting traditional sexist views by self-indulgently castigating men. Her analysis is, of course, arguable, but then, Lessing's relish of her position as a thought-provoking iconoclast must never be underestimated). For Martha Quest, as she begins her attempt to find a kind of freedom as a woman which accords with her necessary attachment to the collectivity, the way is definitively blocked by the immersion of her entire way of life in the violence which characterises her era.

For Martha's very existence has arisen from a concatenation of abuses and oppressions which, in the course of the novel, the young Martha, slowly and incompletely, comes to understand. Her education regarding freedom will continue through the remaining four volumes of the *Children of Violence* series, but the key elements of *Martha Quest* are those which speak most clearly to the preliminary stages of the classic woman's quest for freedom. Set in Africa, in the closing decades of the British Empire (although, of course, the unwitting inhabitants of the colony have no way of knowing history is about to extinguish their way of life) *Martha Quest*, says Lessing in *Under My Skin*, the first volume of her autobiography:

> has a simple plot. She has a childhood in the bush, quarrels with her mother, is taught politics by the Cohen boys, reads, escapes into the big town, Salisbury, learns shorthand typing, plans all kinds of attractive futures, but is swept away into dancing and good times, and marries a suitable young civil servant while the drums are beating for the Second World War.[11]

Lessing's helpful synopsis of her novel points to several classic components of postwar fiction concerned with women's quests for freedom. First, there is the stress on the need for the quester to escape the mother, who is construed, with absolute typicality, as the figure who insists on the daughter's replication of her own life of female self-sacrifice to the intimate family, and to the conventions of the collectivity. There is a great deal that could be said about Lessing's complex and shifting portrayal of the maternal figure in her fiction, but in *Martha Quest*, Mrs Quest, herself a fascinating and brilliantly-drawn character, is a force set against freedom and, as such, is one that Martha must overcome. The Cohen boys, the intellectually-accomplished sons of a Jewish shopkeeper, are important to Martha as representatives both of a group which suffers from bigotry and of the subset of fellow human beings who see life as governed by mind and ideas as much as by the exigencies of the body. Martha's reading is treated in the novel as the emblem of her allegiance to this group. All this represents an alternate source of power which is almost unknown, and certainly seems ineffectual, in the colony, but which is immensely attractive to Martha as it links her, in ways that overcome both space and time, to intellectual traditions which operate in pursuit of truth and justice. Lessing also emphasises the importance of the city in Martha's pursuit of freedom. As the characteristic environment of modernity, with its gifts of variety, excitement, and opportunity for self-refashioning, and its curses of temptation to decadence, loneliness and indifference to the fate of the individual, the city has always served, in fiction, as much as in fact, as the most likely location for bids for personal freedom. Importantly, too, the success of Martha's drive for freedom is linked to her becoming (and remaining) a self-sufficient economic agent. Her work is important as an element of her quest, and Lessing's attentiveness to paid employment and its significance is a particularly pleasing feature of the novel given the tendency of fiction to underplay or even omit its centrality for women who wish to exercise control over their lives. Finally, and I shall return to this, Lessing carefully delineates the reasons for the disastrous initial failure of Martha's quest. Martha fails in the face of the lure of pleasure which combines with the collective attentiveness to the coming of the next great bloodbath that will engulf the world inhabited by the children of violence.

The dream that Lessing counterpoises to the world inhabited by Martha Quest, a world in which force ultimately determines all elements of the culture's structure, is beautifully presented in young Martha's utopian vision which features strongly in the first section of the novel, and which is probably the most often-cited passage in all of Lessing's fiction. The preparation for the passage is interesting. It describes the flood of pity Martha refuses to expend on herself flowing out from her to a small, almost naked black child, walking at the head of a team of oxen driven by a harsh native man with a whip. In contradistinction to this multiply-layered display of control through violence, Martha imagines how things could be radically other:

> There arose, glimmering whitely over the harsh scrub and the stunted trees, a noble city, set foursquare and colonnaded along its falling flower-bordered terraces. There were splashing fountains, and the sound of flutes; and its citizens moved, grave and beautiful, black and white and brown together; and these groups of elders paused, and smiled with pleasure at the sight of the children – the blue-eyed, fair-skinned children of the North playing hand in hand with the bronze-skinned, dark-eyed children of the South. Yes, they smiled and approved these many-fathered children, running and playing among the flowers and the terraces, through the white pillars and tall trees of this fabulous and ancient city ...[12]

Martha's utopian vision, which outlines a stately and exquisite pacific counterpoint to the activities of the children of violence, remains a point of reference for Lessing throughout the *Children of* Violence series. And, as young Martha discards 'the heroines she had been offered'[13] by her mother and her mother's generation of colonists and substitutes her dream of the city of harmony, her aesthetic principles, her anti-racist politics, her sexual and cultural openness, her desire for tranquility, and her wish for transgenerational harmony all blend in her ravishing vision. Throughout the series this combination of aspirations will characterise Martha, and govern her choices and her behaviour, when Martha is at her best. However, Lessing is nothing if not thorough in her realism, and her characters, Martha included, only intermittently live up to their own ideals.

Further, like most novelists, Lessing is at her best as a writer when describing bad behaviour. And for Lessing, that behaviour most characteristically occurs when individuals lose all sense of the singular self and subsume themselves in the mass activities of the collectivity. This is precisely what happens to Martha as her first attempt at freedom fails. Easily abandoning her initial interest in the dully earnest Left Book Club, Martha is drawn first to the dancing and drinking at the Sports Club which exists to drown out the individuality of the younger generation of colonists in a loud, rough but pleasurable mindlessness. She is then caught in a marriage which is one driving manifestation of the great urge to replenish the species which presages the upcoming slaughter of the Second World War. In all this, Martha truly functions as an exemplary figure of her generation as she loses what she had managed to construct of her individuality in the great waves of collective pressure of world events which drench even the remote, provincial, colonial city. Lessing ends her novel with maximum foreboding, with news of Hitler's seizure of Bohemia and Moravia first mentioned at Martha's wedding. As a coda, following the ceremony, some of Martha's drunken friends from the Club, roaring after the newlyweds, are involved in a car crash which knocks over but does not kill, a black man, who is showered with money before the drunken, mechanical chase begins again. The conclusion is both heavy-handed and exactly right. The Children of Violence lurch recklessly toward their next collective spasm of aggression, and death is most definitely an expected part of the company.

Lessing's conviction of the difficulty of maintaining the integrity of any aspect of the self that diverges from the collective is one of the most distressing elements of her presentation of Martha Quest's initial failure to secure the freedom that she sought in her move to the city. That this is particularly the case for women is stressed by Lessing, who takes care to present the number of ways in which Martha is construed as a relative being by those who surround her, and the continuing strength of mind that she needs to resist complete subsumption in one or another of these classifications. Whether she is classified as a daughter, the new girl in town, a typist, a marriageable young woman, a female member of the colonial ruling class, Martha is rarely in focus for anyone as an individual. And, given that Lessing has never subscribed to the idea that each human possesses a core 'self' which can be 'discovered', and therefore does not present characters in this way, this makes it all the harder for Martha to define herself in any way that contravenes the dictates of one or another of the identities generated for her by the collectivity. And because Martha cannot understand, much less control, the rules which govern the multiple identities which are used to define her, she collapses, at the end of the novel, exhausted but also removed and indifferent, into the role most heavily overdetermined by the *zeitgeist*, that of war bride, though this is an identity she will vehemently reject later in the series as she becomes better at developing and enacting that part of herself which is most singular and individuated, that aspect of herself which is what led her to make her quest in the first place.

That this is particularly difficult for women is something Lessing understands well. The brilliantly-selected epigraph from Proust, which heads Part Three of *Martha Quest*, puts the point perfectly: 'In the lives of most women everything, even the greatest sorrow, resolves itself into a question of "trying on".'[14] And it is precisely because, in her best moments, Martha resolves that she will not be satisfied with the traditional, relative condition of women, that she will not co-operate with being content to take on the colouring of the lives of the men who have appended her nor the traditions of female behaviour to which the collectivities to which she belongs subscribe, that she serves as an exemplary figure of rebellion for the postwar women who made up the first audience for Lessing's novel. As much as *Martha Quest* begins the story of the refusal of a young woman of the 1930s, in a corner of the soon-to-be-dismantled British Empire, to inhabit the roles prepared for her, so the novel addresses the conformity, the paranoia, and the complacency of the postwar era in which it was composed. It forms part of the literature of subversion which is so characteristic of the progressive writing of the Cold War era, and one of its cardinal areas of subversiveness (along with its anti-racism, anti-imperialist, anti-war tendencies) resides in its complex challenge to the norms of gendered behaviour for women, which were, in the aftermath of the Second World War, in the process of seriously eroding the gains that had been made by women in the West earlier in the twentieth century.

And, unless the underlying structure of society changes, Lessing suggests, not only in *Martha Quest*, but throughout her work, there will be no ascent of freedom of the kind that does not mean the violation of the other, but simply the ebb and flow of oppression and subservience, backed by the violence that characterises modern culture. And, if Lessing chose an epigraph from Proust to summarise one of the most salient points about the experience of women as relative beings, she heads Part One of the novel with a quotation from one of her most significant literary precursors, the South African novelist, Olive Schreiner. 'I am so tired of it', says Schreiner as she is given the first words of the *Children of Violence* series, 'and also tired of the future before it comes'.[15] This fatigue in the face of futurity is altogether fitting as a starting point of extreme ethical weariness in response to Lessing's anatomisation of an era which is governed by its love affair with violence. And, although *Martha Quest* is doubly a postwar novel, written after the Second World War about characters who are maimed and deformed by their and their parents' experience of the Great War, for Doris Lessing there is no period which comes 'After the Deluge'. There is, as she has remarked again and again in interviews and in her writing, always a war, the deluge of horror is always with us. We remain Children of Violence struggling, when we are at our best, to build the new selves which constitute the precondition for a world in which things might be otherwise.

Notes

1 Information on Doris Lessing taken from her autobiographies: *Under My Skin: Volume One of My Autobiography, To 1949* (London: HarperCollins, 1994) and *Walking in the Shade: Volume Two of My Autobiography, 1949–1962* (London: HarperCollins, 1997). Additional material taken from the following useful studies of Lessing: Ruth Whittaker, *Doris Lessing* (London: Macmillan, 1988); Jeanette King, *Doris Lessing* (London: Edward Arnold, 1989); Elizabeth Maslen, *Doris Lessing* (Plymouth: Northcote House, 1994); Jenny Taylor, ed., *Notebooks, Memoirs, Archives: Reading and Rereading Doris Lessing* (London: Routledge and Kegan Paul, 1982); Lorna Sage, *Doris Lessing* (London: Methuen, 1983); and my own *Free Women* (London: Harvester Wheatsheaf, 1990). Lessing is very interesting on her refusal to display guilt at leaving her first two children in her autobiography. 'On the contrary,' she says, 'I'm very proud of myself that I had the guts to do it. I've always said that if I hadn't left that life, if I hadn't escaped from the intolerable boredom of colonial circles, I'd have cracked up, become an alcoholic. And I'm glad that I had the bloody common sense to see that' (Barbara Ellen, 'I Have Nothing in Common with Feminists. They Never Seem to Think that One Might Enjoy Men', *The Observer Magazine* (9 September 2001), p. 12.

2 *Walking in the Shade*, pp. 14–15.

3 *Walking in the Shade*, p. 15.
4 'The Small Personal Voice' in Doris Lessing, *A Small Personal Voice: Essays, Reviews, Interviews*, ed. Paul Schlueter (London: Flamingo, 1994), p. 8.
5 'The Small Personal Voice', p. 18.
6 Roy Newquist, 'Interview with Doris Lessing', *A Small Personal Voice*, p. 18.
7 Florence Howe, 'A Talk with Doris Lessing', *A Small Personal Voice*, p. 85.
8 *Walking in the Shade*, p. 16.
9 *Walking in the Shade*, pp. 12–13.
10 *Walking in the Shade*, p. 32. The importance of escaping from her mother cannot be overemphasised. As Lessing explained in an interview in 1994, 'What oppressed me was not class or convention ... but my mother's insistence on being like her. It's one thing which seems to have gone now – women have their own careers and there is not this terrible identification with their children' (Lesley White, 'Pages from Her Own History', *The Sunday Times, Culture Section* (9 October 1994), p. 5).
11 *Under My Skin*, p. 162.
12 Doris Lessing, *Martha Quest*, 1952 rpt (London: Grafton Books, 1966), p. 17.
13 *Martha Quest*, p. 17.
14 *Martha Quest*, p. 145.
15 *Martha Quest*, p. 7.

13
Going 'Home': Exile and Nostalgia in the Writing of Doris Lessing

Susan Watkins

'Children of Violence'

Doris Lessing's postwar fiction is obsessed by war. The key novels of the period 1945–60 examine the years leading up to the Second World War or the early to middle years of the war itself. Like Lessing, her heroines, Mary Turner and Martha Quest, grow up in a British colony in Africa in this period. The umbrella title of the five volume novel sequence focusing on Martha is 'Children of Violence'. This is indicative not just of Lessing's preoccupation with the war, but also of her wider analysis of its connection with the violence of the colonial encounter. The sharpest irony for Lessing is occasioned by the patriotic willingness of white 'Zambesians' (Southern Rhodesians) to fight with England against Hitler, the 'monster across the seas ... whose crimes consisted of invading other people's countries and forming a society based on the conception of a master race'.[1] Lessing's controversial suggestion of a continuity between British and German imperialism resembles her detailing of the frank uncertainty in the immediate prewar period about who exactly the adversaries would be. When asked what he will do when the war starts, Solly Cohen remarks: 'I shall be a conscientious objector if they turn the war against the Soviet Union, and I shall fight if it's against Hitler' (*PM*, p. 57). Lessing demonstrates that the enemy fluctuates in the popular press also: 'the newspaper had warned them that an enemy (left undefined, like a blank in an official form to be filled in later as events decided) might sweep across Africa in a swastikaed or – the case might be – hammer-and-sickled horde' (*PM*, p. 114). The 'monstrosity' of Hitler's Germany is persistently seen as relative rather than absolute when set alongside the Soviet Union and the history of

British colonialism. This chapter will argue that in Lessing's fiction of the 1950s the war is not unequivocally negative because it begins a process that ultimately splits apart white British colonial supremacy and fragments stable conceptions of race and gender. Lessing's novels in this period mark the tentative emergence of more plural, fluid notions about race and gender and the interconnections between them, which force their way through the 'crack in the white crust'[2] of a strictly segregated society like the African desire for uplift in *A Ripple from the Storm*.

Going 'home'?

A narrative voice that might almost be characterised as 'nostalgic' for those aspects of the war that created an impulse for decolonisation is important in the fiction of this period. This can be instructively compared with the narrative perspective in Doris Lessing's 1957 essay, *Going Home*, which details her first return to Southern Rhodesia (now Zimbabwe) after an absence of eight years. Lessing's English parents had settled in Rhodesia when Lessing was a young child and she remained there until 1949 when she came to live in England.[3] At the time of Lessing's visit, Southern Rhodesia had become part of the Central African Federation (1954–63) with Northern Rhodesia and Nyasaland (now Zambia and Malawi). 'Partnership' between black and white was, despite continuing racial segregation, the official rhetoric of the white government. Both Federation and Partnership were suspected as attempts to prolong white supremacy against emerging nationalist movements (the Southern Rhodesian African National Congress was formed from various protean groups in 1957). As Christine Sylvester suggests: 'SRANC capped a period of increasing unrest about the cynical half-measures of racial partnership.'[4] Federation was also intended to collapse the differences between Southern Rhodesia and the historically more independent Northern Rhodesia and Nyasaland. Colin Stoneman argues that Federation was 'strongly opposed by the blacks, particularly in the latter two countries' and that it 'operated greatly to the benefit of the industrial economy of Southern Rhodesia'.[5] *Going Home* thus appears to occupy an unusual historical moment of stasis and consolidation of colonialist forces, which, I will suggest, is apparent in its narrative voice.

Going Home situates 'home' as a wandering site of nostalgia, exile and alienation. At the opening of the essay, Lessing attempts to construct a Romantic African landscape, which can unite people of all races and political persuasions. She begins by acknowledging that after a year of 'horrible estrangement' in London, a 'nightmare city'[6] of cold, damp and weak sunlight, it has finally become her home. Of her return to Africa Lessing writes that she had 'turned myself inwards, had become a curtain-drawer, a fire-hugger, the inhabitant of a cocoon' (*GH*, p. 12). Yet, confronted with the heat and light of Africa the adjustment 'outwards' again is easy because 'this was my air, my landscape, and above all, my sun' (*GH*, p.12). However, ownership of the landscape can only ever be provisional in a country where white people are the descendants and beneficiaries of settler-invaders: 'Africa belongs to the Africans; the sooner they take it back the better' (*GH*, p. 12); yet Lessing also suggests: 'a country also belongs to those who feel at home in it' (*GH*, p. 12) and expresses the utopian hope that 'the love of Africa the country will be strong enough to link people who hate each other now' (*GH*, p. 12). She concludes, however, that 'this passion for emptiness, for space, only has meaning in relation to Europe' (*GH*, p. 13). Acknowledgement of relativity and specificity in relation to history and racial difference questions any absolute understanding of the landscape of Africa as 'home' for the narrator, or anyone.

As *Going Home* progresses the narrator is forced to confront further her status as exile and alien. She is refused entry to the Union of South Africa, discovering that she is a prohibited immigrant on arrival at Jan Smuts airport. She is then informed that she was only granted permission to enter Rhodesia after intervention from a senior official and that if she attempts to visit Northern Rhodesia and Nyasaland (part of the Federation) she will be deported. Lessing writes: 'to be refused entry into a country one knows and loves is bad enough; but to be told one is on sufferance in a country one has lived in nearly all one's life is very painful' (*GH*, p. 89). Lessing manages to visit Northern Rhodesia, but not Nyasaland before returning to London, at which point she is informed that she is now prohibited from entering the Federation. These events render her homeless and alien, a status she also occupied during the war because of her marriage to a German refugee. Regular reporting to the Aliens' Office was, for the narrator, a 'useful apprenticeship' (*GH*, p. 112) for her postwar experience. *Going Home* concludes: 'I don't feel very optimistic. I don't see how the next decade can be anything else than stormy, bitter and unprofitable' (*GH*, p. 248). The title *Going Home* thus becomes increasingly ironic as the reader progresses through the essay. Losing a secure sense of home is regretted by the narrator and associated with loss of faith in a secure identity. As Edward Said suggests, exile creates an 'unhealable rift forced between a human being and a native place, between the self and its true home'.[7] This regret for home and self is explicitly related to the uneasy political situation in Rhodesia in the 1950s.

Home and exile in the fiction

A Ripple from the Storm, first published the following year, constructs such loss in very different ways. In this text, set during the war, the colony is being used to train the British airforce, the arrival of which has disturbed many of the certainties of Zambesian society, including previously secure sexual, racial and class categories. The heroine, Martha is at this point fiercely engaged in left-wing politics (in an environment broadly sympathetic to communism and the Soviet Union as 'Our Allies' against Hitler) and much of the novel deals with the activities and alliances of the nascent communist group in the colony. However, an important episode in the middle of the text tells of the experiences of one of the British air crew, a fitter named Jimmy, as he struggles to adapt himself to the colony's way of life. Returning to the RAF base after an argument at the communist group meeting, the men joke 'back to the concentration camp' (*RS*, p. 144). However, once Jimmy is at the base, he begins to feel the reality of his imprisonment and persuades one of the African camp guards to lift a broken bit of perimeter fence and let him 'escape'. The freedom of lying in the grass outside the camp is a revelatory epiphany for him, which is severely undercut by the discovery that the grass is full of insects, which are also crawling all over him.

After this initial and important experience of abjection and displacement, Jimmy decides to take the opportunity to visit the Native Location and the Coloured Quarter, partly as a challenge to communist group decisions against this. When he arrives in the Location, he is struck by the fact that the perimeter fence is rusty and much lower than the RAF camp fence. He concludes: 'fences, fences, everywhere you look, concentration camps everywhere and fences. He thought of the concentration camps in Europe and without any feeling of being alien' (*RS*, p. 154). Reluctantly admitted to a room in the Location, he concludes: 'I feel at home here. This is the only place in this bloody country I've felt at home' (*RS*, p. 155). Jimmy makes putative attempts here to equate the Location with 'home', but also to place the experiences of exile and alienation as universal. These impulses arise from a feeling of working-class solidarity with black Africans (as he says later, watching men and women from the Location cycling to work: 'at home I'd join in, I'd be one of them' (*RS*, p. 163)) and a sense of the global existence of economic exploitation. However, his confidence in finding a home in shared oppression is only shortlived. His host's obvious fear forces Jimmy to recognise that his white skin makes him an extremely dangerous (in fact prohibited) houseguest and thus profoundly separates him from the people in the Location. Jimmy then visits the Coloured Quarter and attempts to find somewhere to sleep for the night, but the woman, a prostitute, will only let him into her home if he pays for sex. The only (unofficially) sanctioned relation between 'coloured' woman and white man in the colony is that of prostitute and client.

Jimmy's superior position in the hierarchies of gender and race and his position in the RAF fragment his notions of home, which are based on an attempt to recapitulate his subordinate class position in Britain: 'just because I've got a white skin ... He remembered his uniform – he was doubly separated from them' (*RS*, p. 163). Indeed, all the events of the night are triggered by his exploitation of the black camp guard, who would doubtless have born the brunt of the punishment if he had been discovered enabling Jimmy's 'escape'. Jimmy is forced to accept his own position as part of the white elite in the colony and recognise the provisional nature of home for its black populace, whose civil rights are nonexistent. In *A Ripple from the Storm*, home and exile are split and fragmented as they are in *Going Home*. Overall, the narrative displays a sense of the futility and inevitability of what happens to Jimmy which resembles the tone of *Going Home*: immediately after the events just described the airmen who attend the communist group are posted from the colony as the result of a terrified black informant involving the local magistrate. However, the memorable episode of Jimmy's 'escape' tends to positively disrupt and subvert those naïve certainties that function elsewhere in the text (such as the communist group's reliance on economic explanations and class categories which substantially ignore gender and race). In addition, rather than solely creating a sense of regret on the part of the narrator, the fragmentation of securely established ways of perceiving subjectivity is seen as productive, generating what Said terms the exile's 'contrapuntal' vision, where 'habits of life, expression, or activity in the new environment inevitably occur against the memory of these things in another environment' (Said, 2000, p. 186). He argues that there is a 'unique pleasure in this sort of apprehension, especially if the exile is conscious of other contrapuntal juxtapositions that diminish orthodox judgement and elevate appreciative sympathy' (ibid.).

Colonial desire

Lessing's work of the 1950s is permeated by the mobility of concepts like home, exile, refugee and alien. In *In Pursuit of the English* (1960), for example, Lessing turns from Southern Rhodesia to an examination of the shifting nature of postwar English national culture and mores. Here, she focuses on her own position in London as an outsider and analyses how she is perceived in this way precisely because of her colonial background. Yet Jimmy's night-time excursion in *A Ripple from the Storm* suggests, in addition, a further important way in which home is defined in Lessing's work of this period: as a place apparently removed from, yet actually underpinned by, inter-racial sexual desire. Jimmy is seeing a woman from the Coloured Quarter, against the agreed rules of the communist group. Jimmy views this relationship as one of class solidarity: 'I've got myself a real working girl, a girl like myself' (*RS*, p. 141). Anton, the leader of the group asks:

> Would it help matters if every single man here married an African or a coloured girl tomorrow – not that it would be possible. Or if we all took coloured mistresses? There's nothing new about white men sleeping with coloured and African girls. Is there? The basic problem is economic and not social. (*RS*, p. 140)

Jimmy's use of the term 'working girl' implies prostitution to an early twenty-first-century reader; indeed, in the episode we have just examined, Jimmy finds that despite his efforts to relate to 'coloured' women as equals and friends, the only relationship that is possible is one that combines and conflates the sexual and the economic: '"How much?" she said ... Jimmy, his throat thick, half with lust and half with a longing to cry, said, "But listen, I just wanted to..."' (*RS*, p. 162).

Lessing's work in this period acknowledges and analyses the workings of what Robert Young has termed 'colonial desire'. Young's aim is to demonstrate that notions of racial difference have always been bound up with inter-racial desire: 'racial theory, which ostensibly seeks to keep races forever apart, transmutes into expressions of the clandestine, furtive forms of what can be called "colonial desire": a covert, but insistent obsession with transgressive, inter-racial sex, hybridity and miscegenation'.[8] The term 'hybridity' has been used by Homi Bhabha (and others subsequently) to suggest the mutual implication of colonising and colonised voices, which ultimately enables the contestation of colonial discourses by revealing their lack of purity, or inevitable 'contamination' by the colonised voice.[9] However, for Young, the term hybridity carries with it echoes of nineteenth-century racial theories about inter-racial sex and miscegenation (the 'fertile fusion and merging of races'),[10] which makes it a more suspicious term than theorists like Bhabha allow: 'there is no single, or correct, concept of hybridity: it changes as it repeats, but it also repeats as it changes' (ibid., p. 27).

What strikes any reader of Lessing's writing of this period is her willingness to address the controversial question of inter-racial sexuality. In *Martha Quest* we are presented with several scenes of colonial desire, including a heated conversation between Martha and her mother about whether or not she should be allowed to walk to the station:

> 'What would happen if a native attacked you?'
> 'I should scream for help,' said Martha flippantly.
> 'Oh, my dear ...'
> 'Oh, don't be ridiculous,' said Martha angrily. 'If a native raped me, then he'd be hung and I'd be a national heroine, so he wouldn't do it, even if he wanted to, and why should he?'
> 'My dear, read the newsapapers, white girls are always being ra – attacked.'
> Now, Martha could not remember any case of this happening; it was one of the things people said. She remarked, 'Last week a white man raped a black girl, and was fined five pounds.'
> Mrs Quest said hastily, 'That's not the point; the point is girls get raped.'
> 'Then I expect they want to be,' said Martha sullenly; and caught her breath, not because she did not believe the truth of what she said, but because of her parents' faces: she could not help being frightened.'[11]

This passage makes a number of dangerous suggestions: first, that inter-racial desire is a routine part of colonial discourse and second, that it is permissible (if illicit) only in the case of the white man for the black woman. Thirdly, Martha implies that the black man's desire for the white woman is phantasmatic: a displacement of its phantasised opposite: the white woman's desire for the black man, or the white man's fear of/desire for that possibility. Ironically, when Martha makes the trip to the station, she is actually propositioned by Mr McFarline, a white mine-owner and prospective MP whose native compound 'was full of half-caste children, his own' (*MQ*, p. 58).

The prohibition of inter-racial sex in Southern Rhodesia was enshrined in the Immorality and Indecency Suppression Act (1903), which made sexual intercourse outside marriage between an African man and a European woman illegal. In the 1950s proposals headed by women's groups were made to extend this prohibition to European men and African women, but these amendments were not successful. Indeed, the fact that the then Prime Minister Garfield Todd voted against the amendments was widely unpopular and led to the defeat of his government.[12] The existence of legislation to prevent inter-racial sex between white women and black men but not between black women and white men suggests, like the passage from *Martha Quest,* that the real taboo is the white man's simultaneous fear of and attraction towards a stereotyped black male sexuality that is irresistible to white women (and, by implication, to white men).

It is in her first novel, *The Grass is Singing* (1950), that Lessing most explicitly tackles the elaboration and deconstruction of colonial desire. The novel examines the complex discourses that generate and are generated by the murder of a white woman by her black servant. The novel resembles classic crime fiction, in that it opens with the newspaper announcement of the murder and then unravels what lies behind it, concluding with the murder itself. However, this analeptic narrative structure, where story and plot are at odds, is not merely about playing with suspense. It is designed to encourage an examination of the *discursivity* of the events told in the novel. The newspaper account of the murder is followed by summaries of how it would have been interpreted throughout the country and then, more particularly, by those in 'the district' who knew Mary Turner and her husband.

By virtue of its careful choice of narrative mode, Lessing manages to convey both the pressure of agreed opinion and the pressures that disturb that opinion. Both are clear in the opening chapter because much of it is from the point of view of an outsider, Tony Marston, who, like Jimmy in *A Ripple from the Storm* is just out from England and adjusting to the new environment and its conventions. For Tony, although 'logical enough'[13] the explanation for the murder 'could not be stated straight out, like that, in black and white' (*GS*, p. 21). He repeats this later: 'this case is not something that can be explained straight off like that. You know that. It's not something that can be said in black and white, straight off' (*GS*, p. 27). This apparently casual turn of phrase evokes the distinctness of the black and white races and associates this with logic in order to suggest all the ways in which that racist logic has been questioned by the murder. Mary's dead body is the source of all the apparently illogical (although, to repeat, actually logical enough) blurrings and 'greyings' of the discourse of racial incommensurability. First we see this through the eyes of Charlie Slatter, a neighbour and farmer who has been called in to help deal with the murder:

> Now a curious thing happened. The hate and contempt that one would have expected to show on his face when he looked at the murderer, twisted his features now, as he stared at Mary. His brows knotted, and for a few seconds his lips curled back over his teeth in a vicious grimace. (*GS*, p. 19)

A few pages later we see Tony's shock at an identical expression of hatred and disgust from the local policeman: 'the faces of the two men as they stood over the body, gazing down at it, made him feel uneasy, even afraid ... This profound instinctive horror and fear astonished him' (*GS*, p. 23). Mary's abject body reminds that, as Lessing puts it elsewhere: '"white civilization"...will never, never admit that a white person, and most particularly, a white woman, can have a human relationship, whether for good or for evil, with a black person' (*GS*, p. 30). She continues: 'once it admits that, it crashes, and nothing can save it' (*GS*, p. 30). Mary's dead body represents the crossing and overlapping of racial and gender boundaries. The choice of the word black 'person', which, unlike white 'person' remains unqualified by gender, suggests that the white female desire for the black man must remain implicit.

Indeed, that desire is only ever implicit in the text. The exact nature of the relationship that develops between Mary and Moses is never concrete, although it is suggested in various ways. Lessing describes it in terms of the emergence of the personal (*GS*, p. 178), which makes visible the power relation between the two and unsettles it. Throughout the text, scenes where this power dynamic becomes visible and is then questioned focus on elaborating those connections between race, sexuality and economics that underly it. Mary's sudden marriage to Dick Turner ends her life as a single, independent woman who works in an office and lives with other single women in a 'girls club'. This abrupt change is precipitated by overhearing gossip about her 'old maid' status which focuses on the phrase: 'She just isn't like that, isn't like that at all. Something missing somewhere' (*GS*, p. 48). Mary repeats this phrase, highly suggestive of 'frigidity', to Tony Marston when he asks why she allows Moses to dress and undress her (*GS*, p. 232). The attempt to 'prove' herself a sexual woman attaches to Moses because of his increasingly explicit refusal of the power she has over him as a member of a 'superior' race. As the novel progresses, Moses instead asserts his superiority over her in gender terms. In the first key interaction between them, he flouts her orders by stopping work to drink water. In the second, he stops washing when he notices her watching him. Both instances involve his refusal of her gaze at him and his return of that gaze. After Mary whips him for pausing to drink, we are told that 'for a moment, the man looked at her with an expression that turned her stomach liquid with fear' (*GS*, p. 147); in the second scene Lessing writes:

> A white person may look at a native, who is no better than a dog. Therefore she was annoyed when he stopped and stood upright, waiting for her to go, his body expressing his resentment of her presence there ... She felt the same impulse that had once made her bring down the lash across his face. (*GS*, pp. 176–7)

Unlike her ineffectual husband, whose submissiveness she enjoys, but also despises, Moses is 'a man stronger than herself' (*GS*, p. 156), whom Mary needs, but also fears. As Lessing later writes:

> There was now a new relation between them. For she felt helplessly in his power. Yet there was no reason why she should ... her feeling was one of a strong and irrational fear, a deep uneasiness, and even – though this she did not know, would have died rather than acknowledge – of some dark attraction. (*GS*, p. 190)

Mary's submissiveness is simultaneously arousing and frightening precisely because it plays around with and disturbs her racial 'superiority', suggesting, as Young argues, the covert involvement of inter-racial desire with racial categorisation in the colonial encounter. This is apparent in Charlie Slatter's comment to the Sergeant at the beginning of the novel: 'Needs a man to deal with niggers ... Niggers don't understand a woman giving them orders. They keep their own women in their right place' (*GS*, p. 27). The white man admires the black man for one thing only – his imagined sexual control over black women – and that fantasy underpins the colonialist project. As Lessing writes of Tony Marston: 'he had read enough about psychology to understand the sexual aspect of the colour bar, one of whose foundations is the jealousy of the white man for the superior sexual potency of the native' (*GS*, p. 230). 'The basic problem' is not, as Anton expressed it in the earlier quotation from *A Ripple from the Storm*, 'economic and not social' (or sexual) but, as Young puts it, that we have ignored the fact that interracial sexual desire is inseparable from the economic motive for colonialism.

The point of view that is absent from the text is that belonging to Moses. We are never party to his perspective on events, nor to his motivation for the murder, both of which have to be surmised from how others react to the little that he says. Critics have found this a problematic aspect of the novel. Margaret Moan Rowe notes that he is presented as 'sexual energy rather than as a person'.[14] Lorna Sage relates his 'blankness' to issues of representation: 'how much, that is, can one find others in oneself'.[15] I would argue that this 'erotic silencing' of Moses explicitly suggests the powerlessness of his voice and its overdetermination by discourses of colonial desire. However, one of the things Mary finds in her new personal relation with Moses is that he asks her questions, on one occasion about the progress of the war. This forces Mary to recognise that the war is more than 'a rumour, something taking place in another world' (*GS*, p. 191). It forces her to realise the specificity and impermanence of her own situation, or, as Bhabha might put it, the 'contamination' of the colonial voice by the colonised voice and thus the possibility of its contestation. Thus, *The Grass is Singing* elaborates and deconstructs the workings of colonial desire in order to suggest how the society in which it functions will ultimately be rendered unstable. The disturbances effected in the text by the relationship between Moses and Mary and her murder certainly work towards the 'crash', as it was earlier termed, of 'white civilization'. As Sage later writes: 'Moses "is" the future' (1983, p. 28).

Going Home stages a comparable scene of colonial desire in far less subversive ways. Lessing writes in the essay of meeting two white women on the boat coming to Britain in 1949. Known as 'Durban society girls' (*GH*, p. 26), they are on a trip to Europe, funded by the wealthy family of one of the women, Camellia, who has recently been widowed. Two years later Lessing sees the girls in Trafalgar Square with a black man. The passage continues:

> That was in 1951. In 1953 I was walking along the edge of the sea in the south of France, and there was the young man I had seen in Trafalgar Square with an extremely beautiful black girl ... Then I saw that the beautiful negress was in fact Camellia. (*GH*, p. 27)

A few years later, Lessing sees a photograph in a South African society magazine of Camellia marrying a white South African in a society wedding. Although this is partly a 'passing' narrative,[16] which is structured around the simultaneous denial and attraction of the dynamic of inter-racial sexual desire, this story also suggests the flexibility of racial categorisation. Yet it ends by positioning that mutability as entirely subject to economic imperatives: it is Camellia's uncle who provides the money for the trip and when that runs out she is forced to return home and resume a 'white' identity and marriageable status. The far more negative reading of racial 'hybridity' and colonial desire in *Going Home* resembles the dourly stripped down interpretation of exile and homelessness in the essay. It is striking that Lessing's fiction of the postwar period is far more optimistic about the subversive possibilities contained in such testings of colonial discourses.

Nostalgia and distance

The tone of *Going Home* might appear to be a better 'fit' with the static and depressed mood of the 1950s. During this decade Lessing was, for a time, in the British Communist Party, until she encountered the disillusionment with communism common to many left-wing intellectuals of the period. Lessing left the party in 1957 after the Soviet invasion of Hungary and the revelation of Stalin's atrocities at the Twentieth Party Congress of the Soviet Communist Party in 1956.[17] In addition, she was also aware of the consolidation of colonialist forces in Southern Rhodesia and was analysing what Sage (1983, p. 43) refers to as 'blocked passive British post-war culture'. Lessing's essay emphasises that the latter are interdependent. As Taylor notes, the essay (along with *In Pursuit of the English*) stresses 'the role that colonialism played in the construction of a dominant British national identity' (Taylor, 1982, p. 18). The difference in the tone of the fiction is therefore striking. Although the narrator is often ironic about her characters' beliefs and involvements, there is an important sense of nostalgia for the fluidity and impermanence generated by the war and the inroads this made into colonial identities, discourses and power structures. The narrator of *A Ripple from the Storm* comments of Jimmy and a friend:

> They also felt that after the war things could not possibly go on as they had before. They had jeered at the Atlantic Charter, and greeted the patriot speeches of the high-ups about better times coming after the war with a steady contempt as bait for suckers, the suckers being themselves. But all the same ... [ellipsis original] things could not go on as they had; and the victories of the Red Army in some way proved this. (*RS*, p. 147)

Is this difference in tone between fiction and essay generated by their generic differences, or by the question of distance? Georg Lukács argues, after all, that the novel, more than any other genre, is the form of 'transcendental homelessness'.[18] Elizabeth Maslen, comparing *Going Home* and *A Ripple from the Storm*, suggests that the answer lies elsewhere. She argues that the point of view of *Going Home* (written the year after the visit it describes) is close to the events described in the text, whereas the viewpoint of the novel 'seems to reflect a narrative viewpoint of 1958 rather than of the time in question'.[19] She comments on the ironic detachment that this allows in the novel, but distance also generates a nostalgic relation. Subsequent editions of *Going Home* contain an endnote under the heading 'Eleven Years Later' which uses a more nostalgic tone when discussing the Southern Rhodesian communists in the 1950s: 'it is no accident that the only group of people who knew the Federation ... was dangerous nonsense, that Partnership ... was a bad joke, were Socialists of various kinds' (Maslen, 1994, p. 15).

Admittedly Lessing is often suspicious of nostalgia; Roberta Rubenstein suggests that 'the past ... is entirely equivocal for Lessing'[20] and that she acknowledges 'the impossibility of perceiving an unproblematic perspective in relation to either past times or places' (Rubenstein, 1994, p. 33). In *A Ripple from the Storm* Martha dreams a dream that had 'the peculiar nostalgic quality which she distrusted so much, and yet was so dangerously attractive to her' (*RS*, p. 95). The dream is of a country, which Martha assumes must be England, wondering 'how can I be an exile from England when it has nothing to do with me?' (p. 95). Yet nostalgia for a fictionalised and self-constructed 'home' can, as Rubenstein admits, involve 'emotional resolution' and 'transformative significance' ('Fixing the Past', p. 34), however partial these may be. We may speculate that the absence of this nostalgic distance is part of the reason why Lessing suppressed her 1956 novel *Retreat to Innocence*, which is about the impact of a Czech refugee writer on a conventional upper-class English girl. Clearly nostalgia is important in *The Golden Notebook* (1962), although by the time of writing this novel Lessing had found many additional devices with which to explode conventional notions of home, subjectivity, gender and race. Through the 1950s, however, nostalgia is a key element, which allows Lessing to begin to create an unease in her use of the realist form. Nostalgia for the uncertainties of the war, generated by distance, can therefore provide Lessing with a home, but that 'home' can only ever putatively exist in the act of writing and reading.

Notes

1 Doris Lessing, *A Proper Marriage* (London: Paladin, 1990), p. 159 (henceforward *PM*: subsequent references will be incorporated into the text).
2 Doris Lessing, *A Ripple from the Storm* (London: Grafton, 1966), p. 196 (henceforward *RS*: subsequent references will be incorporated into the text).
3 Until 1923 Rhodesia (now Zimbabwe) was run by Cecil Rhodes's British South Africa Company. The white settler population then chose to become a 'self-governing colony' rather than become part of what was then the Union of South Africa. Ian Smith's government made a unilateral declaration of independence (UDI) from Britain in 1965 in order to avoid making concessions to black advancement. It would not be until the Lancaster House Agreement (1979) after more than a decade of armed struggle that the whites were forced to concede defeat. The Republic of Zimbabwe became independent in 1980 after the victory of ZANU-PF under Robert Mugabe.
4 Christine Sylvester, *Zimbabwe: The Terrain of Contradictory Development* (Boulder: Westview Press, 1991), p. 43.
5 Colin Stoneman (ed.), *Zimbabwe's Inheritance* (New York: St Martin's Press, 1981), p. 4.
6 Doris Lessing, *Going Home* (London: Michael Joseph, 1957), p. 12 (henceforward *GH*: subsequent references will be incorporated into the text).
7 Edward Said, *Reflections on Exile and Other Literary and Cultural Essays* (London: Granta Books, 2000), p. 173.
8 Robert J.C. Young, *Colonial Desire: Hybridity in Theory, Culture and Race* (London: Routledge, 1995), p. xii.
9 Homi K. Bhabha, *The Location of Culture* (London: Routledge, 1994), pp. 112–16.
10 Young, *Colonial Desire*, p. 9
11 Doris Lessing, *Martha Quest* (London: Paladin, 1990), p. 57 (henceforward *MQ*: subsequent references will be incorporated into the text).
12 See Sylvester, *Zimbabwe*, p. 43 and Ruth Weiss, *Zimbabwe and the New Elite* (London: British Academic Press, 1994), p. 29 for accounts of this.
13 Doris Lessing, *The Grass is Singing* (London: Michael Joseph, 1950), pp. 21–2 (henceforward *GS*: subsequent references will be incorporated into the text).
14 Margaret Moan Rowe, *Doris Lessing*, Women Writers (Basingstoke: Macmillan, 1994), p. 17.
15 Lorna Sage, *Doris Lessing*, Contemporary Writers (London: Methuen, 1983), pp. 27, 28.
16 Passing narrative
17 See Jenny Taylor, *Notebooks/Memoirs/Archives: Reading and Rereading Doris Lessing* (London: Routledge, 1982), p. 24.
18 Georg Lukács, *Theory of the Novel: A Historico-Philosophical Essay on the Forms of Great Epic Literature*, trans. Anna Bostock (London: Merlin Press, 1971).
19 Elizabeth Maslen, *Doris Lessing*, Writers and their Work (Plymouth: Northcote House, in association with the British Council, 1994), p. 14.
20 Roberta Rubenstein, 'Fixing the Past: Yearning and Nostalgia in Woolf and Lessing', in Ruth Saxton and Jean Tobin, eds, *Woolf and Lessing: Breaking the Mould* (New York: St Martin's Press, 1994), pp. 15–38, p. 33.

14
'The Raw and the Cooked': Barbara Pym and Claude Levi-Strauss

Clare Hanson

I want to explore, through a discussion of food and other matters, the influence of anthropology on the work of Barbara Pym. Her writing has been subject to surprisingly vehement attack on the grounds of alleged triviality, and like many women writers of the 1950s she has been characterised as a producer of undemanding domestic fiction.[1] Such a view fails to recognise the complexity of Pym's work and the depth of her engagement with the changing modern world. Her fiction is occupied with a conflict central to the postwar era, that between a socio-scientific view of man associated with the rapid development of the social sciences, and older liberal-humanist or religious beliefs. Pym's engagement with the social sciences was sustained and professional. Through most of her career she worked in anthropology: from 1946 to 1974 she worked at the International African Institute as an assistant to the Director, Daryll Forde, and as Assistant Editor for the Institute's journal *Africa* (founded in 1932 and published to the present day). She was responsible for collating and editing material for a series of Ethnographic Surveys of Africa in the 1950s (for example, *The Yoruba-Speaking Peoples of South-Western Nigeria*, 1951) as well as editing articles for *Africa* and making the preliminary selection of books for review. While the general view has been that Pym had little intellectual interest in anthropology and merely regarded her anthropologist colleagues as offering potential comic material for her novels, I want to suggest that her engagement with anthropology had a far more complex and profound (one might say structural) impact on her work.

The discipline of anthropology was at a high point in the 1940s and 1950s, with British anthropology very much driven by the 'structural functionalism' of A.R. Radcliffe-Brown, whose interest was in the pragmatic role of social behaviours in maintaining a network of social relations. In the introduction to a book co-edited with Daryll Forde, Radcliffe-Brown explains his privileging of function in this way:

> When we succeed in discovering the function of a particular custom ... we reach an understanding or explanation of it which is different from and independent of any historical explanation of how it came into existence. This kind of understanding of a kinship system as a working system ... by which particular customs are seen as functioning parts of the social machinery, is what is aimed at in a synchronic analytic study.[2]

Working, like structural anthropologists, with a synchronic rather than a diachronic model of society, Radcliffe-Brown emphasised the specificity of the structures of any given society. By contrast the structuralist Levi-Strauss (by far the most influential of twentieth-century anthropologists) was more interested in the universal structures of the human mind, arguing that the organisational categories through which the mind experiences the world are trans-historical and trans-cultural. In an essay of 1945, Levi-Strauss underlined a further crucial difference between his approach and that of Radcliffe-Brown. While Radcliffe-Brown saw the units of human relationships as having natural and intrinsic qualities, Levi-Strauss argued that no unit in a system of relationships can have any significance in itself. Rather, its significance is determined by its relationship to all the other elements involved. Thus, he concludes, '[a] kinship system does not consist in the objective ties of descent or consanguinity between individuals. It exists only in human consciousness; *it is an arbitrary system of representations*, not the spontaneous development of a real situation'.[3]

While anthropologists such as Radcliffe-Brown and Daryll Forde explored the part played by ritual in oiling the wheels of the social machine (to take up Radcliffe-Brown's mechanical metaphor), structural anthropologists such as Levi-Strauss questioned the objective reality of such a machine, thus going beyond mechanistic determinism to call into question the human ability to know anything other than the relationship between self and world. I would suggest that both schools of anthropological thought contributed to an 'emptying out' of value in the postwar world, and that it is this aspect of anthropology which had such an impact on Pym. As Catherine Oliphant asks in *Less than Angels* (1955), what is the point of anthropology, 'laying bare the structure of society'? And how does it help those in need of a guide to 'the deeper or higher things of life?'[4] This quotation dramatises the tension which structures all Pym's work, between a socio-scientific view of man, and liberal-humanist or religious perspectives.

Less than Angels is Pym's most obviously anthropological novel in terms of its content, focusing on a group of anthropologists linked to a newly-endowed research centre. However, the deep structure of the novel is also derived from anthropological thought. The key categories mobilised by Pym are those of the 'avunculate' and of 'double descent'.[5] The avunculate is the term used to describe the relationship between the mother's brother and her sons in matrilineal societies. This structure was much discussed in articles in *Africa* in which it was noted (with some anxiety) that 'the authority and power of men within a matrilineage depend upon reciprocation of aid and support between men and their sisters' sons'.[6] The avunculate was also of prime importance for Levi-Strauss, who concluded that it was 'the true *atom of kinship* ... the sole building block of more complex systems'.[7] The principle of double descent was also discussed in the pages of *Africa* and more particularly in Daryll Forde's study of the Yako of Nigeria, considered the 'best documented double-descent society in existence'.[8] In societies such as that of the Yako, matrilineal and patrilineal descent systems co-existed, the different structures serving different purposes. It was assumed by Forde and his contemporaries that double-descent systems were transitional, and that they usually appeared in matrilineal societies newly 'invaded' by the patrilineal principle.

Tom Mallow, one of the main characters in *Less than Angels*, is an anthropologist who works on the role of the mother's brother (that is, the avunculate) in a remote African tribe. What he fails to recognise is that his own family structure mirrors that of the African tribe. His father is long dead, and his dominant mother works energetically to manage the family estate. Tom's own position in the family is relatively weak: inevitably so, from a structural functionalist point of view, because of the passivity of his only remaining male relative, an uncle whom he finds hidden away watching daytime television on a visit to the family home:

> Tom found his uncle sitting in semi-darkness, looking at some sporting event on the television set, which had the central position in the room like a kind of altar. Green plush curtains had been dragged across the windows, shutting out all but a chink of sunlight which filtered incongruously through on to the elderly man with his military bearing and white walrus moustache. (p. 177)

The strength of matrilineal ties, by contrast, is stressed throughout the novel. For example, Deirdre, the callow 19-year-old who falls in love with Tom, has no father but lives with her mother and aunt, each of whom is ready to 'fight tenaciously' for Deirdre's rights.

Tom's work has involved the discovery of a double descent system which also feeds into the structure of the novel. However, there is a crucial difference between the anthropologists' understanding of double descent and Pym's use of the motif. While anthropologists studying so-called primitive cultures linked double descent with a transition from matriarchy to patriarchy, Pym foregrounds the way in which in Britain in the 1950s power was passing increasingly from men to women. *Less than Angels* thus traces the co-existence of male and female networks of affiliation, with the underlying implication that this is a society in which patriarchy is being invaded by matriarchy and/or feminism. So, while men continue to control institutions such as the church and the learned societies, extracting service from women who wash, cook and type for them, women have gained more power in personal and in (some) professional relationships. Man's role seems almost to be becoming a ceremonial one, while practical power is devolved to women. As Catherine wryly remarks to Tom, 'That's what seems wrong with so many relationships now, the women feeling that *they* are the strong ones and that men couldn't get on without them' (p. 111). Felix Mainwaring also comments on this cultural shift. Watching the young applicants for the Foresight research grants coming up the drive, he notes that all the young women are carrying their own luggage:

> In my young days it was different, of course; things are so very much changed now. I should hardly have been surprised to see the young ladies carrying the young *men's* luggage. (p. 196)

This sense of men's weakness is intensified by Tom Mallow's death, which also has the effect of calling into question the value of his anthropological work. After his death, his sister and three girlfriends meet at a women's club to try to decide what to do with his papers, sent back from Africa in 'seven or eight large wooden chests'. None of the women want them, and it is decided that they will have to go to Harrods' furniture repository – a mausoleum for the material detritus of life. Rather similarly, the papers of another anthropologist, Alaric Lydgate, are cast onto a bonfire by Catherine at the end of the novel, much to the horror of the neighbours watching what seems to them like a 'strange orgy'. (The name Lydgate recalls, of course, the failed scientific ambitions of Tertius Lydgate in *Middlemarch*.)

Yet Pym does not simply mock anthropological enquiry: she also appropriates its methods, for her own ends. She adopts an anthropological perspective to 'lay bare' a society riven by conflict and power struggles, particularly in relation to gender. It is perhaps no coincidence that in an ethnographic study of the Nupe edited by Pym and published in the same year as *Less than Angels*, Daryll Forde commented on the 'inter-sex hostility' among these people, which was, according to him, accentuated by 'the economic independence and consequent sexual freedom of women'.[9] In a similar fashion, Pym charts a shifting balance of power between the sexes in 1950s Britain, producing her own proto-feminist anthropology. And I would argue that it is her acceptance of anthropology, rather than her rejection of it, which contributes to the tart and pessimistic undertone of her work. The epigraph of *Less than Angels* is telling here:

> What would this Man? Now upward will he soar,
> And little less than angel, would be more;
> Now looking downwards, just as grieved appears
> To want the strength of bulls, the fur of bears.[10]

In *An Essay on Man* Pope attempts to reconcile the restlessness of human life with an abstract conception of an ordered and harmonious universe. The sense of disjunction between an anatomy of pain and an invocation of harmony is strong both in the poem and in Pym's novel, which makes few concessions to a redemptive view of human nature or of its place in the universe. Institutional religion gets short shrift: of the two clerical figures in *Less than Angels*, Father Gemini turns out to have diverted money to his own research in an unethical manner, and Father Tulliver bullies both his wife and a series of female parishioners. Returning to the motif of food, a critique of organised religion opens the novel with Catherine Oliphant's comparison of the men and women shuffling through a self-service restaurant to 'English tourists shuffling round a church in Ravenna, peering at mosaics' (p. 5). This is one of several occasions on which churches are compared to cafeterias, the suggestion being that they offer merely comfort food for the soul. The more crucial point, however, is that the beautiful mosaics of San Vitale in Ravenna were commissioned by the tyrant Justinian, who used religion as a means of social control and regarded all dissent as a form of treason. The implication is that organised religion is more often than not a vehicle for self-advancement.

In the opening paragraph of the novel, as she sits in the café, Catherine invokes food as a metaphor for life itself. Thinking of her work as a writer for women's magazines, she reflects that 'life itself was sometimes too strong and raw and must be made palatable by fancy, as tough meat may be made tender by mincing' (p. 5). Here the term fancy refers specifically to the consoling structures of romantic fiction, but the culinary metaphor also points to the many ways in which culture works on nature, shaping it according to human needs and desires. In this novel culture is understood in strictly anthropological/anthropomorphic terms, and there is no positive endorsement of a religious perspective which would move beyond such a view. It is in Pym's next novel, *A Glass of Blessings* (1958) that she makes her most sustained attempt to integrate anthropological insights and religious belief – with, I would argue, only partial success.

Just as *Less than Angels* is structured around the anthropological concepts of the avunculate and double descent, so *A Glass of Blessings* is structured around the concept of the 'joking relationship', which made an earlier appearance in Pym's novel *Excellent Women* (1952):

> 'What was that about a man being expected to sleep with an unmarried sister-in-law who is visiting the house?' he asked.
> 'That's called a joking relationship,' said Everard precisely.
> 'Not exactly what one would call a joke,' said Rocky ...[11]

Radcliffe-Brown wrote extensively about 'joking relationships', publishing an article in *Africa* in 1948 in which he argued for a comparative study of this phenomenon. He argued that in many societies, joking relationships existed between persons of the same generation brought into proximity through relationships of kinship, or, more commonly, marriage – for example, brothers- and sisters-in-law. Such proximity brought the threat of conflict and/or sexual attraction, a threat which was defused through rituals involving varying degrees of 'sham' conflict or intimacy. As he rather stiffly puts it, 'the joking relationship is a form of familiarity, permitting disrespectful behaviour, and in extreme instances, license'.[12] According to Radcliffe-Brown, joking relationships thus contribute to the smooth running of the social machine, defusing potential conflict and disruption.

Wilmet Forsyth, the central character in *A Glass of Blessings*, enters into such relationships with two men to whom she stands in a quasi 'in-law' relation, the husband and the brother of her closest friend, Rowena. Wilmet is married to a respectable but rather dull civil servant:

she is well-to-do, childless, and bored. When Rowena's husband makes his first approach to her, she compares him rather contemptuously to a badger and later comments on his 'doggy' devotion. When they are lunching together and he suggests further meetings, however, she begins to find the idea of a flirtation rather attractive:

> Then I suddenly thought – why, it's only old Harry Grinners, whom you've known for ten years, no need to treat him with such chilly detachment! 'Endless good lunches with lots of lovely meat?' I said more gaily. 'Is that the idea?'
> 'Darling, you will have *your joke* – that's the surprising and tantalising thing about you.'
> From then on he became more obviously flirtatious in a heavy Edwardian style and we enjoyed ourselves very much.[13]

More or less in parallel with this, Wilmet becomes preoccupied with Rowena's brother Piers. This relationship, too, is cast in terms of a joke: when Wilmet is sent a little antique box for Christmas she is convinced that Piers has sent it to her and comments that '[o]f course *it was all a joke*, really, but it gave me a pleasant feeling of being remembered in a rather special way' (p. 97, my italics).

As the novel progresses, Wilmet becomes aware that the truth behind these relationships is more complex and less flattering than she had thought. Piers is homosexual, and has been flirting with her as a kind of 'cover'; the charming antique box turns out to have been a gift from the bestial Harry rather than the cultivated Piers. Even Wilmet's dull husband has been sufficiently bored by his marriage to have embarked on a flirtation with a colleague. His confession makes them both laugh, but causes Wilmet to reassess her own behaviour:

> But after I had stopped laughing I began to think that perhaps it wasn't so funny after all. I had always regarded Rodney as the kind of man who would never look at another woman. The fact that he could – and had indeed done so – ought to teach me something about myself, even if I was not yet quite sure what it was. (p. 246)

These relationships have fulfilled their function, of allowing the expression of desire without real disruption. However, the revelation of their sham nature forces Wilmet to question the truth of her life and to ask what structure and meaning it has. It is here that Pym moves beyond anthropology to ask not only 'what is this man?', but is there anything beyond 'man' and the structures of the human mind? Characteristically, Pym's emphasis is on questions, not answers. Wilmet herself is a Christian by instinct and training, and towards the end of the novel comes to some kind of accommodation with herself on a visit to a clergy retreat house. However, in the scene when she finds peace in the garden there, multiple interpretations of that peace are offered. As Wilmet stands by a compost heap, Marvell's 'To His Coy Mistress' comes into her mind. However, the fact that she is standing 'in a kind of greenish twilight' calls up too Marvell's 'The Garden' ('Annihilating all that's made / To a green Thought in a green Shade'). 'The Garden' assumes a Christian framework, but also foregrounds the power of the human mind to create structures and worlds ('Yet it creates, transcending these / Far other Worlds, and other Seas') : it plays with the interplay between the human mind and the mind of God. Marvell's poem thus opens up the question of the status and significance of the structures of the human mind in ways which are not so far removed from the questions asked by twentieth-century anthropologists.

We are thus invited to link Wilmet's sense of peace and order with divine *and/or* human powers. This ambivalence – or agnosticism – is further underscored through Wilmet's observation that 'there seemed to be a pagan air about this part of the garden' and her reflections on the beehives: 'I remembered the old saying about telling things to bees. It seemed that they might be regarded as a kind of primitive confessional' (p. 222). By introducing an anthropological perspective (religion seen as a ritual like any other, with no special truth claim), Pym leaves open the question of what, if anything, exists beyond the human mind. This openness and scepticism is further evident in *A Glass of Blessings* through the counterpointing throughout the novel of the figures of Wilmet and her mother-in-law Sybil. Sybil is not a churchgoer, and states her position unequivocally in the opening scene of the novel:

> 'I thought out my position when I was twenty, and have found no reason since to change or modify the conclusions I came to then.'
>
> I could not protest, for there was something about my mother-in-law's bleakly courageous agnosticism that I admired. It seemed to me rather brave for somebody nearing the end of life to hold such views. I wondered if she was ever afraid when she woke up in the small hours of the night and thought of death. (p. 14)

Yet unlike the believer Wilmet, Sybil (whose name has pagan echoes) is active in social work, loyal to her friends and is rewarded at the end of the novel with marriage to her friend Professor Root. It thus remains uncertain whether Sybil's agnosticism or Wilmet's faith brings the character greater happiness or access to truth.

Just as it has been assumed that Pym is a cosy, uncritical chronicler of English middle-class life, so it has been assumed by many critics that she is a straightforwardly religious novelist.[14] My contention is that her fiction offers a far more complex response both to social structures and to the question of religious belief, and that this response is everywhere informed by her knowledge of contemporary anthropological thought. As I have shown, through her work for *Africa* Pym came into close contact with the structural functionalists, and she would also have been aware of the early work of Levi-Strauss. It is to Levi-Strauss's later work, however, that I now want to turn in order to bring together some of the threads of my argument. In his work of the 1960s, Levi-Strauss moved away from an insistence on the primacy of the structures of the human mind, and came to denounce the anthropomorphism of Western society (of which his own earlier work might be considered a prime example). In *The Origin of Table Manners*, the third volume of the tetralogy *Mythologies* which began with *The Raw and the Cooked*, he contrasts the 'ethical system' inherent in the mythology of so-called primitive peoples, and the ethic of the modern Western world. He argues that the ethical system of primitive peoples involves 'deference towards the world', whereas the ethics of the West are predicated on the crude preservation of self. He continues:

> When they assert, on the contrary that 'hell is ourselves', savage peoples give us a lesson in humility which, it is to be hoped, we may still be capable of understanding. In the present century, when man is actively destroying countless living forms, after wiping out so many societies whose wealth and diversity had, from time immemorial, constituted the better part of his inheritance, it has probably never been more necessary to proclaim, as do the myths, that sound humanism does not begin with oneself, but puts the world before life, life before man, and respect for others before self-interest.[15]

Levi-Strauss here returns to humanist (if not religious) values, and goes on to emphasise the ethical significance of even apparently trivial social rituals. He argues that 'such apparently insignificant objects as combs, hats, gloves, forks ... moderate our exchanges with the external world, and superimpose on them a domesticated, peaceful and more sober rhythm' (p. 507). These lines could have been written as a gloss on

Pym's later fiction, which explores the ethical potential of social ritual in terms which would have been immediately recognisable to Levi-Strauss. To take a single example, in Pym's last novel, *A Few Green Leaves*, we see Emma Howick, an anthropologist, devising a menu in order to accommodate the egotisms and anxieties of her two main guests, an Anglican vicar and an ex-Anglican priest who has not only 'gone over' to Rome but also become a 'gourmet food inspector':

> As the party was to be on a Friday, there was the possibility that fish might have to be provided. Were the clergy, or Roman Catholic laymen, still obliged to eat fish on a Friday? Emma wondered.
> 'Fish is now regarded as a luxury,' Beatrix said. 'I'm sure Tom would be the last person to expect fish on a Friday.'
> 'But Adam Prince – a Catholic convert, an Anglican turned Roman,' said Emma uneasily, '*and* an inspector of high-class eating places – he might well look on fish as no more than his due.' ...
> ... 'Still, it might be a graceful compliment to Adam to provide a fish dish of some kind,' said Beatrix.
> But what kind of fish?[16]

What is so deftly captured here is the way in which these 'humble', 'apparently insignificant' things, in Levi-Strauss's words, mediate complex relationships between the world, life, and man. The cooked fish flags up our mediated relationship with other living beings (necessary for our material survival and transformed by us into food). The significance of the fish in relation to Christian ritual is also drawn to our attention, although Pym notes the waning of the custom of eating fish on Fridays – a decline not unrelated, perhaps, to the changing market value of this food. Finally, Pym notes in an understated manner the importance of social ritual in maintaining emotional and spiritual well-being: Beatrix wishes to pay Adam 'a graceful compliment' and thus strengthen social bonds through the offering of fish.

While some strands of anthropology have the effect of demythologising social ritual, Levi-Strauss's *Mythologies* has the opposite effect, of restoring meaning to it. The fundamental question underlying *Mythologies* is this: how is it that men, who are part of nature, can see themselves as other than nature? One answer lies, quite simply, in food: men do not have to cook their food, but do so for symbolic reasons, in order to differentiate themselves from animals. As Edmund Leach puts it, 'Cooking is thus universally a means by which Nature is transformed into Culture, and categories of cooking are always peculiarly appropriate for use as symbols of social differentiation'.[17] Categories of cooking, and rituals for serving and eating food, are also 'appropriate symbols' for different kinds and levels of social affiliation. For Levi-Strauss, the exploration of such categories and rituals can help us to analyse and understand man's place in the world, in the context of a 'world-view' which is not religious but which does not discount our relation and obligation to a wider world. Pym would have found this sympathetic. Throughout her work, she 'lays bare' the structure of society, but while she exposes the rapaciousness which lies beneath so many social encounters, she also, increasingly, foregrounds the humanity which can inform the simplest gesture. Levi-Strauss's final conclusion is that 'the origin of table manners', and more broadly of what he calls 'correct behaviour', is to be found 'in deference towards the world – good manners consisting precisely in respecting its obligations' (p. 507). This is a perspective which Pym would surely have endorsed.

Notes

1 A.S. Byatt, for example, had this to say in an influential 1986 review: 'Why, therefore, in the last few years has there been such a sudden blossoming of attention to Pym's oeuvre? It is easy enough to understand why she has a devoted following of *readers* – she has the ability to create a comfortable little world in which they can relax, locate themselves with ease, confirm their prejudices and enjoy their own superiority. But why the PhD dissertations, the academic conferences ...?'. Review for the *Times Literary Supplement*, reprinted in A.S. Byatt, *Passions of the Mind: Selected Writings* (London: Vintage, 1993).

2 A.R. Radcliffe-Brown and Daryll Forde, eds, *African Systems of Kinship and Marriage* (London: Oxford University Press for the International African Institute, 1950), p. 3.

3 Claude-Levi-Strauss, *Structural Anthropology I* (Harmondsworth: Penguin, 1963), pp. 50–51 (my italics).

4 Barbara Pym, *Less than Angels* (St Albans: Granada Publishing Limited, 1980), p. 191. Subsequent references will be incorporated into the text.

5 Muriel Schulz briefly notes the connection between Tom Mallow's life and work but sees it merely as a comic means of undermining his character. See Muriel Schulz, 'The Novelist as Anthropologist', in Dale Salwak, ed., *The Life and Work of Barbara Pym* (Basingstoke: Macmillan, 1987).

6 See Thomas O. Beidelman, 'Hyena and Rabbit: A Kajuru Representation of Matrilineal Relations', *Africa*, Vol. 31, No. 1 (1961), p. 63.

7 *Structural Anthropology I*, p. 48.

8 See Robin Fox, *Kinship and Marriage* (Harmondsworth: Penguin, 1967), p. 135.

9 Daryll Forde, *Peoples of the Niger-Benue Confluence* (London: Oxford University Press for the International African Institute, 1955), p. 41.

10 From Pope's *An Essay on Man* (1733–34).

11 Barbara Pym, *Excellent Women* (Harmondsworth: Penguin, 1952), p. 92.
12 A.R. Radcliffe-Brown, 'A Further Note on Joking Relationships', *Africa*, Vol. 19, No. 2 (1948), p. 134.
13 Barbara Pym, *A Glass of Blessings* (Harmondsworth: Penguin, 1980), p. 88 (my italics). Subsequent references will be incorporated into the text.
14 See, for example, Joyce Carol Oates, who argues that 'she is, finally, a religious writer' in her essay 'Barbara Pym's Novelistic Genius', in Salwak, p. 44.
15 Claude Levi-Strauss, *The Origin of Table Manners* (London and New York: Jonathan Cape and Harper and Row, 1978), pp. 507–8. Subsequent references will be incorporated into the text.
16 Barbara Pym, *A Few Green Leaves* (St Albans: Granada Publishing Limited, 1981), p. 85.
17 Edmund Leach, *Levi-Strauss* (London: Fontana, 1970), p. 34.

15
'There is a Sweetness in Willing Surrender'? Self-loss and Renewal in the Poetry of Elizabeth Jennings, Kathleen Raine and Stevie Smith

Jane Dowson

Patricia Beer, Frances Cornford, Elizabeth Jennings, Ruth Pitter, Kathleen Raine, Anne Ridler, Stevie Smith and Edith Sitwell successfully published poetry during and after the Second World War. Their dominant preoccupation with spiritual quest has been overlooked, even though it is an identifiable period preoccupation. Spirituality is perhaps still too embarrassing in its implied polarisation from materialist politics. The feminist critic is familiarly positioned between defence and celebration. The demand for defence is compounded by the facts that Elizabeth Jennings and Stevie Smith, along with Edith Sitwell, Patricia Beer and Ruth Pitter, were unmarried. Consequently, the imaginative constructions of mystical union and reciprocal relationship can appear compensatory for a missing human lover. Furthermore, the suicide of Anna Wickham in 1947, Stevie Smith's constant death-wish, Frances Cornford's prolonged depressions, and the mental breakdowns of H.D. in 1946 and Elizabeth Jennings in the early 1960s thwart the attempt to authorise woomen poets' spiritual quests with claims of their strong female autonomy. However, spiritual transcendence can be a gesture of individuality and self-realisation which is independent of cultural ideals: self-loss assumes a sense of self.

Although not obviously gender conscious, the poets implicitly reject contemporary cultural conditions and establish a female identity independent of the social ideals prescribed for women. A distinctly female spiritual quest is marked by the desired psychological fusion with personified nature or a transcendental 'other'. The atemporality of the lyric especially affords a connection of consciousnesses so that these poets sit together in a tradition of women's spiritual poetry as well as their literary moment. In her anthology of women's spiritual and visionary poems, Aliki Barnstone identifies diverse styles but a common advocacy of 'a death of the self in order to unite with the godhead or with the cosmos'.[1] Epistemologically, the work of Kathleen Raine, Elizabeth Jennings and Stevie Smith records an acute loneliness which can be understood as their artistic isolation but also extends to many women's alienation from postwar celebrations of domesticated femininity. It also registers women's felt absence from rational language. Kathleen Raine's publications around this period were *Stone and Flower 1935–1943* (1943), *Ecce Homo* (1945), *Living in Time* (1946), *The Pythoness and Other Poems* (1949), *The Year One and Other Poems* (1952) and *Collected Poems* (1956). Elizabeth Jennings published *Poems* (1953), *A Way of Looking* (1955) and *A Sense of the World* (1958). Like her, Stevie Smith was more productive in the 1950s with *Harold's Leap* (1950), *Not Waving but Drowning* (1957) and *Some are More Human than Others: A Sketch-book* (1958).

One reason for the oversight of this kind of poetry is its confounding of available analytical equipment. In *The Radical Aesthetic* (2000) Isobel Armstrong proposes three new categories for feminist criticism designed to avoid raw identity demarcations: the expressive, the phallic and the ludic. She recommends that 'the great project of this [the expressive] formation is surely the further investigation of affective life'. Spiritual life, an aspect of the 'affective', has, as Armstrong says, been reduced by western criticism to the visual, simply 'seeing into the life of things'.[2] It ignores, for example, the ways that a text calls out the need to 'enter into a relationship with someone'. Furthermore: 'Our culture separates "feeling and thinking from each other in such a way that they are supposedly opposed to each other", Hegel says. Religious feeling is the most protected from thought.'[3] Following Isobel Armstrong, I am arguing for the redemption of the affective as an epistemic source.

A female spiritual aesthetic involves both the intellect and the imagination, liberating the woman poet from the masculine/feminine, intellectuality/sentimentality binaries which have daunted her throughout twentieth-century literary criticism. As Elizabeth Jennings explains in her critical work, *Every Changing Shape: Mystical Experience and the Making of Poems* (1961), mysticism authenticates intuition and dissolves the divide between the rational and non-rational. She is adamant that 'art is not self-expression' and that '"confessional poetry" is almost a contradiction in terms'.[4] However, the poetics of spiritual quest is an assertion of a subjectivity which is yet-to-be and unrepresentable in received rational discourse. These poets validate personal experience while invalidating rational discourse. As Jennings, writes, 'My poems move from feelings not yet known.'[5] The poems draw attention to their processes while pointing beyond themselves to sensations which evade the strictures of language. Stevie Smith's 'Silence', depicts the mystical poet's preoccupation with the contingency of language and vision:

> This is an age when there are too many words,
> Silent, silent the waters lie.
> And the beautiful grass lies silent and this is beautiful.
> Why can men then not withdraw and be silent and happy?
>
> It is better to see the grass than write abut it
> Better to see the water than write a water-song[6]

The language of spirituality both distinguishes and combines sensation and representation.[7] Although not gender-specific, the poem directly expresses women's alienation from symbolic representation – Armstrong, again:

> Affect itself is an ambiguous, alternating force. It moves between the destruction of representation, opening up an abyss in consciousness by violently breaking the barrier of repression, and appropriating, thieving representation. It belongs to a chain of discourse and breaks it: it alternates between being bound and unbound, attached to signification and rupturing it.[8]

Sentiment confronted hard scepticism in the postwar period when modernist ideals of impersonality along with thirties realism were discredited by the extremities of wartime experience. The 1940s saw a neo-Romantic emphasis on personal experience although T.S. Eliot's brand of modernist impersonality was harnessed to his urgency for spiritual renewal. As Blake Morrison concludes with reference to John Wain's contemporary observations:

> Partly because of the growing acceptance of T.S. Eliot's *Four Quartets* [1935–43] as a major work, and partly because of a 'sense of crisis and suffering' caused by the Second World War, Christianity exerted a powerful influence at Oxford in the 1940s: 'Everybody to whom an imaginative and bookish youth naturally looked up, every figure who radiated intellectual glamour of any kind was in the Christian camp'.[9]

In the 1950s, personal experience was not discarded but figured in a more rational discourse by the Movement which has been characterised by the agnosticism emblematised in Philip Larkin's anthology piece 'Churchgoing'. Women poets participated in these postwar crossstreams of democratic individualism and intellectual scepticism towards the personal. When Patricia Beer returned from Italy in 1953, she found the poetic scene 'a death-trap'. Audiences wanted poets to 'go confessional', 'go popular' and 'go American' rather than the 'cold, academic or parochial' which characterised Larkin's lot.[10] Conformity to public demand would, as ever, tar women with the sentimental brush as parodically wielded by Kingsley Amis:

> We men have got love well weighed up; our stuff
> Can get by without it.
> Women don't seem to think that's good enough;
> They write about it.
>
> And the awful way their poems lay them open
> Just doesn't strike them.[11]

'Love' is thus pejoratively relegated to women's confessional verse. However, the diverse spiritual quests of Kathleen Raine, Elizabeth Jennings and Stevie Smith rehabilitate 'love' in the context of mystical union. Their surrender of the immediately knowable in favour of an alternative reality is a rejection of popular ideologies of femininity; it gestures psychological independence and freedom, albeit found through imaginative intimacies with nature, god or death.

Although expressed through dramatisation, dialogue and unidentifiable speakers, the recurring articulation of unpresentably painful loneliness in these poets' work is distinctly personal. Empirically, their yearning for mystical relationship can seem compensatory for the isolation of the unmarried literary woman. According to Betty Friedan, women 'were taught to pity the neurotic unfeminine, unhappy women who wanted to be poets or physicists or presidents'.[12] The loneliness was also the unarticulated condition of women who had conformed to prescribed marriage and motherhood. In Friedan's *The Feminine Mystique* (1963), the 'problem that has no name', was the spiritual atrophy registered by women's inexpressible feelings of emptiness and incompleteness.[13] Friedan argues that self-realisation is a human, not specifically female, necessity:

> Men from varying disciplines have used different words for this mysterious process from which comes the sense of self. The religious

mystics, the philosophers, Marx, Freud – all have different names for it: man finds himself by losing himself.[14]

Although 'losing yourself to find it' is not exclusively female, for women, spirituality, defined as the expansion of consciousness, offers an escape route from their 'deadly dailyness'. The independence of their spiritual quest is validated by the language of self-sacrifice, which had particular resonance as a universal wartime patriotic virtue but was returned to women as a postwar patriarchal ideal; however, *voluntary* surrender gives authority to individual choice and sanctifies the rejection of domestic or any other subservience.

It has to be acknowledged that these poets' ultimate desire is not autonomy but a completeness through mutual interrelationship. In *Every Changing Shape* Jennings defends mystical poetry against charges of a vague flabby collusion with or avoidance of social ideals. For her, it develops consciousness, notably through its access to a transcultural spiritual community. In her essay, 'Too Tired for Words' (1956), Stevie Smith wishes to lose the consciousness of loneliness, ideally through union with a god, but, in its absence, with Death who in several poems is her best friend. Although apparently impersonal, Kathleen Raine's poems exhibit a sense of or need for audience. In 'Message from Home', the hidden dialogic implies the presence of an intimate other: 'Do you remember, when you were first a child / Nothing in the world seemed strange to you?'[15] 'Home' is the other world from where the self came and for which it yearns. In 'Water' the first person plural intimates that the writer's subjectivity is realised in company but if this is not possible then oblivion is preferable:

But still the stream that flows down to stillness
Seeks the end-all of all waters,
Welcomes all solving, dissolving, undoing,
Returns, loses itself, loses self and bounds,
Body, identity, memory, sinks to forgetfulness,
The state of unknowing, unbeing,
The flux that precedes all life, that we reassume, dying,
Ceasing to trouble the flowing of things with the fleeting
Dream and hope and despair of this transient perilous selving.[16]

In an unpublished essay, Raine stated that, '"Writing poetry" changes people, it is a means of self-discovery, we don't create great art but at least we create ourselves'.[17] (The deprecation of her art is matter for another discussion.) In 'Self', the voice asks, 'Who am I?' and vainly searches for the supreme 'other': 'Who out of nothingness has gazed / On the beloved face?' Similarly, there is unfulfilled longing in 'The Unloved': 'I am pure loneliness / I am empty air'.[18]

Kathleen Raine was a respected poet whose mysticism was not out of kilter with her neo-Romantic and apocalyptic contemporaries. As A.T. Tolley states in *The Poetry of the Forties*: 'Kathleen Raine is the most eloquent exponent of her generation of the conception of poetry as a form of knowledge beyond the empirical and rational.'[19] In her words, 'the irrational may not be the spiritual, but it is an opening up of consciousness to a certain degree'.[20] Her poetry is often gender-neutral in its pronouns and seemingly supports a lyric universality rooted in the Romantic tradition which established the genius of the male poet. As Rita Felski concludes, however, 'Frequently the narrative of female self-discovery may take the form of an inward spiritual journey.'[21] She counters the dismissal of women's literature which is concerned with 'subjectivity, spirituality and myth' for being 'repressive' by defining a feminist Romantic vision:

> The Romantic feminist vision is the product of a psychological and aesthetic, rather than political, conception of liberation, less concerned with strategic means for ending the oppression of women than with expressing a paradisal longing for harmony fuelled by a revulsion against the conditions of life under contemporary culture.[22]

For Freud, the 'longing for a lost paradisal harmony', the sensations of loss and desire, constitute nostalgia for the pre-Oedipal mother/child union. However, the processes of these poems evoke imaginative and mental fulfilment of or freedom from these longings. As Felski states, 'Writing, seemingly the most isolated of activities, becomes the means to the creation of an ideal intimacy.'[23] Like Kathleen Raine, for Elizabeth Jennings, the nearest to mystical release from the pains of post-Oedipal alienation is sometimes the memory's construction of a lost paradisal freedom associated with childhood:

We only know a way to love ourselves,
Have lost the power that made us lose ourselves.
O let the wind outside blow in again
And the dust comes and all the children's voices.
Let anything that is not us return.

Myths are the memories we have rejected
And legends need the freedom of our minds.[24]

Again, like Raine, Jennings' first person plural pronouns indicate self-realisation in company. The verse imitates memory's meanderings; this is the space between self-loss and self-discovery. Although mostly unidentified and gender-free, the impulse to alter consciousness, what Jennings calls 'a way to lose a loneliness', is specifically female.[25] In 'Greek Statues' the desired 'stillness' which recurs in Jennings' poems is specifically linked to surrender. Like Eliot in the *Four Quartets*, art – the statue and the poem – constructs, contains and limits the intersection of the timeless with time:

These I have never touched but only looked at.
If you could say that stillness means surrender
These are surrendered,
Yet their large audacious gestures signify surely
Remonstrance, reprisal? What have they left to lose
But the crumbling away by rain or time? Defiance
For them is dignity, a declaration.

Odd how one wants to touch not simply stare,
To run one's finger over the flanks and arms,
Not to possess, rather to be possessed.
Bronze is bright to the eye but under the hands
Is cool and calming. Gods into silent metal:

To stone also, not to the palpable flesh.
Incarnations are elsewhere and more human,
Something concerning us; but these are other.
It is as if something infinite, remote
Permitted intrusion. It is as if these blind eyes
Exposed a landscape precious with grapes and olives:
And our probing hands move not to grasp but praise.[26]

'The hunger to be possessed and to understand'[27] denotes close relationship – here, with the 'something infinite remote'. Expression and language strain at each other and it, implicitly he, must be tangible.

The impersonal pronouns above suggest deeply personal desire to escape from 'the inward agony of self alone'.[28] In 'World I Have not

Made' Jennings stands on the threshold of impersonal verbalisation of personal anguish:

> The trying to love without reciprocity
> All this is here still. It is hard, hard,
> Even with free faith outlooking boundaries,
> To come to terms with obvious suffering.
> I live in a world I have not created
> Inward or outward. There is a sweetness
> In willing surrender: I trail my ideas
> Behind great truths.[29]

The act of writing offers release through the projected loss of consciousness and imagined audience. Writing mediates between this world and an alternative, between the unitary lyric 'I' and the imagined audience. For Jennings, poetry is 'supra-rational'[30] in evoking, not merely describing vision – it is 'not only a medium for the expression of mystical experience but itself an experience of a similar kind'.[31] In 'A Fountain', she perceives and produces 'A stillness there' which echoes the satisfied thirst reached at the edge of some perpetual stream, associated with the loss of self-consciousness:

> Panicked by no perception of ourselves
> But drawing the water down to the deepest water.[32]

For Jennings, 'Imagery is always the arbitrator, even among things almost inexpressible.'[33] In Teresa of Avila she envied the skill 'in finding analogies and selecting metaphors. She is never at a loss for comparison or simile. Her whole approach to the spiritual life is a repudiation of the abstract.'[34] Jennings is less able to avoid abstractions but, as here, succeeds with symbolism.

In *The Second Sex* (1953), Simone De Beauvoir, suggests that although institutional religion may be patriarchal, Christian doctrine can liberate women from the tyranny of male power: 'A sincere faith is a great help to the little girl in avoiding an inferiority complex: she is neither male nor female, but God's creature' and 'Woman is asked in the name of God, not so much to accept her inferiority as to believe that, thanks to Him, she is the equal of the lordly male.'[35] Theology can justify sex equality while spiritual experience provides compensation for the disappointments and inadequacies of relations with men:

> Many women, denied all human love even in their dreams, look to God for help ... Love has been assigned to woman as her supreme vocation, and when she directs it towards a man, she is seeking God in him; but if she is over-particular, she may choose to adore divinity in the person of God Himself.[36]

Jennings tellingly admires the intimate relationship between female saints and God: '[Teresa of Avila] finds her humility in the tenderness of her friendship with God ... she can talk to God intimately.'[37] Likewise, she observes in Julian of Norwich,

> her feminine tenderness, her childlike audacity and her very personal intimate approach to God that constantly remind one of Teresa's autobiography. Both women have a warmth that never degenerates into sentimentality, and a boldness that is too innocent to be mistaken for impertinence.[38]

Unlike Raine's avoidance of gender specificity, for Jennings, the ideal connection or community is sometimes female and many of her portraits are of women. She embraces Julian of Norwich's celebration of the 'motherhood of God': 'To the property of motherhood belongeth kind love, wisdom and knowing ... then he [Christ] is our mother.' Postwar idealisations of woman's fulfilment through marriage and mothering are unsettled in Jennings' portraits of ageing women. The well-known 'My Grandmother' portrays the gulf between the child and the old woman who masks her loneliness with busyness and belongings: 'as if to prove / Polish was all, there was no need of love'.[39] Similarly, in 'Old Woman' age brings isolation:

> When I lie at night
> I gather nothing now into my arms,
> No child or man, and where I live
> Is what remains when men and children go.[40]

'The Visitation' dramatises female intimacy between Mary and Elizabeth, the mothers-to-be of Christ and John the Baptist:

> And those two women in their quick embrace
> Gazed at each other with looks undisturbed
> By men or miracle.[41]

Mary features again in 'The Annunciation' where suffering and spiritual ecstasy are inextricable. Her other female subjects include Teresa of Avila, Mary and Martha and a friend taking holy orders. These biblical and religious women are fulfilled through their direction to a higher purpose but seem remote to the poet.

In 'To a Friend with a Religious Vocation', Jennings most expressly explores the despair of depending upon language for spiritual consolation:

> Thinking of your vocation, I am filled
> With thoughts of my own lack of one. I see
> Within myself no wish to breed or build
> Or take the three vows ringed by poverty.
>   And yet I have a sense,
> Vague and inchoate, with no symmetry,
> Of purpose. Is it merely a pretence,
>
> A kind of scaffolding, which I erect
> Half out of fear, half out of laziness?
> The fitful poems come but can't protect
> The empty areas of loneliness
>   You know what you must do,
> So that mere breathing is a way to bless.
> Dark nights, perhaps, but no grey days for you.
>
> Your vows enfold you. I must make my own;
> Now this, now that, each one empirical.
> My poems move from feelings not yet known,
> And when a poem is written I can feel
>   A flash, a moment's peace.
> The curtain will be drawn across your grille.
> My silences are always enemies.
>
> Yet with the same conviction that you have
> (It is but your vocation that I lack),
> I must, like you, believe in perfect love.
> It is the dark, the dark that draws me back
>   Into a chaos where
> Vocations, visions fail, the will grows slack
> And I am stunned by silence everywhere.[42]

The acute pain of the gulf between herself and the nun, between potentiality and actuality may prelude the psychic fragmentation of her mental breakdown in the early 1960s. This poem resonates with vacillating absence and presence – 'The fitful poems come but can't protect / The empty areas of loneliness'; 'grey days' and 'the dark', 'silences' and 'visions'; 'filled' with 'lack'; 'a sense, / Vague and inchoate'. The ultimate 'silence everywhere' is contradicted by the nine first person pronouns which assert a self, admittedly a being yet-to-become: the 'feelings not yet known'. For Jennings then, self-loss ideally leads to self-realisation through close connection; such connections flash in memory's reconstructions and in a hoped for elusive mystical stillness.

Stevie Smith is not normally associated with spirituality but the quest to lose consciousness dominates her work, particularly in this period. For her, as for Elizabeth Jennings, 'there is a hunger of the heart',[43] which is imaginatively satisfied by union with a male god or Death. Her writing is riddled with human 'loneliness and pain'.[44] A phase of acute depression culminated in a suicide attempt on 1 July 1953. Her essay, 'Too Tired for Words' (1956) is harrowing in its tenuous grasp on hope and includes the tortured verse, 'Love Me!': 'Oh why do they leave me, the beautiful people, and only the rocks remain, / To cry Love me, as I cry Love me, and Love me again'.[45] In 'Too Tired for Words' she characteristically draws attention to the process of manufacturing the dregs of consciousness into her writing:

> The pleasures of tiredness are as exquisite as the pains. Take loneliness for instance, that runs with tiredness. How rich for poetry is this sad emotion. ... And then, of course, if one's lonely, one often feels rather superior too. One *is* different from other people, is one not? ... But this feeling of superiority is a thin cloak. It drops, and one sees loneliness as something to be despised and condemned.[46]

The implicit audience of the rhetorical question may provisionally alleviate the isolation. Prolonged relief from loneliness is imagined in death or abandonment to 'some god or other'.[47] Her *Collected Poems* are threaded with the troubled relationship between spiritual liberty or fulfilment and institutionalised Christianity. As she writes in 'Thoughts about the Christian Doctrine of Eternal Hell', 'the religion of Christianity / Is mixed of sweetness and cruelty'.[48] On the one hand are her satires such as 'The Bishops of the Church of England'[49] and on the other the 'affective' yearnings of 'Ah, will the saviour ... ?'[50] 'The Airy Christ'[51] or 'Oh Christianity, Christianity'[52]. Common to these and the dialectical 'God and Man' or 'An Agnostic (Of His Religious Friend)' and 'A Religious Friend (Of His Agnostic Friend)' is the search for love: 'Is He not wonderful, beautiful? Is He not love?'[53] Notably, her god is consistently male.

Anti-conventional in her cynicism towards organised religion, Stevie Smith is drawn towards a non-institutionalised god who embodies the absolute love and companionship not encountered in human relations:

> There is a god in whom I do not believe
> Yet to this god my love stretches,
> This god whom I do not believe in is
> My whole life, my life and I am his.
>
> Everything that I have of pleasure and pain
> (Of pain, of bitter pain and men's contempt)
> I give this god for him to feed upon
> As he is my whole life and I am his.
>
> When I am dead I hope that he will eat
> Everything I have been and have not been
> And crunch and feed upon and grow fat
> Eating my life all up as it is his.[54]

She included 'God the Eater' in a radio programme broadcast on 12 April 1956. The parenthetical allusion to 'men's contempt' indicates the inexpressibility of the pain, which is most likely the betrayal by her literary contemporaries, especially publishers and by her friends. It may also refer to the unresolved bitterness of her father's betrayal in her childhood. The childlike syntax and repetition typically both minimise and accentuate the desperate desire for reciprocal possession. The poem allows the provisional, and self-consciously textual, reconciliation of warring impulses, between faith and doubt, between life and self-annihilation. 'Mr Over' dramatises the search for a god in and outside human incarnations:

> But who is this beautiful You
> We all of us long for so much
> Is he not our friend and our brother
> Our father and such?[55]

The poem is the place between seeking and finding; the god is imaginatively, but all too temporarily, found in the writing of him. Like Raine and Jennings, Smith hints at prelapsarian or pre-Oedipal bliss in 'A Dream of Comparisons' written '*After reading book ten of Paradise Lost*'. In 'Every lovely limb's a Desolation', the shifts of consciousness connect with T.S. Eliot's timeless moments in the garden. However, for Stevie Smith the immediacy of 'loneliness and pain' clouds the visionary calm. She is also more colloquial than Eliot and anti-poetic in her parodic rhyming:

> But I must wake and wake again in pain
> Crying – to see where sun was once all dust and stain
> As on a window pane –
>
> All, all is isolation
> And every lovely limb's a desolation.[56]

Similarly, in 'The Vision', the timeless moment comes and goes, leaving more resounding emptiness. Unusually, however, communal celebration is evoked as the antidote to desolation.[57]

The obvious has to be stated: the literary construction of an immutable unified absolute Divine Signifier, compensates for the absence of a coherent self achieved through a male partner. In 'The Passing Cloud' the first person singular becomes joyful as it is assimilated into the pluralised 'we'. Language and the ecstatic trance strain at each other to evoke the longed-for experience of being embraced, owned and released by the lover-god:

> I thought as I lay on my bed one night, I am only a passing cloud
> And I wiped the tear from my sorrowful eye and merrily cried aloud
> Oh the love of the Lord is a fearful thing and the love of the Lord is mine
> . . .
> I will laugh and sing, or be dumb if they please, and await at the Lord's discretion
> The day I'll be one, as one I'll be, in an infinite regression
> One, ha ha, with a merry ha ha, skip the fish and amoeba where are we now?
> We are very far out, in a rarefied place, with the thin thin dust in a giddy chase,
> The dust of Continuous Creation, and how is that for identification?

> You'll like it; you must, you know,
> That merry dust does jig so ...[58]

Interestingly, 'far out', for a numbed consciousness, recurs in the later famous poem ('Not Waving But Drowning'). Subheaded, 'Written from the Royal Bethlehem Hospital', 'The Passing Cloud' attributes visionary power to the mad. The verbal playfulness of exaggerated rhyme also deflects any claims to rationality. This is the intelligence of Jennings' 'supra-rational mind' which projects mystical experience onto the reader. As Isobel Armstrong suggests:

> If affect is untranslatable, and cannot be in language, cannot have a content, we might seek for devious evidences of its inscription and consider the way it cheats itself into language or inhibits symbol-making, but in the last analysis the idea of substitution has to be abandoned and replaced by a dynamic understanding of the texts generating new affect patterns and thought structures.[59]

The aesthetics of women's spiritual poetry challenges analytical discourse. It also contradicts the feminine mystique by establishing identity in an alternative space away from social ideals and human relations which stifle women's imaginations. However, this fulfilment of self through surrender, union and release is self-consciously constructed in the processes of the poetry. The god envisioned by Elizabeth Jennings and Stevie Smith, is loving, attentive and gives them freedom of will but is only met in the activity of writing. For writer and reader the poems occupy a place between material and mystical existence, between experience and expression.

Notes

1 Aliki Barnstone, ed., *Voices of Light: Spiritual and Visionary Poems by Women around the World from Ancient Sumeria to Now* (Boston and London: Shambhala, 1999), p. xxii.
2 Isobel Armstrong, *The Radical Aesthetic* (Oxford: Blackwell, 2000), p. 97.
3 Armstrong, 2000, p. 116.
4 Elizabeth Jennings, Preface, *Collected Poems* (Manchester: Carcanet, 1987), p. 13 (henceforth *CP*).
5 Jennings, 'To a Friend with a Religious Vocation: for C', *CP* 1987, p. 64.
6 Stevie Smith, 'Silence', *Me Again: Uncollected Writings of Stevie Smith*, eds Jack Barbara and William McBrien (London: Virago, 1981), p. 236.
7 For more discussion of *the space between*, see Geraldine Finn, 'The Politics of Spirituality: The Spirituality of Politics', in Philippa Berry and Andrew

Wernick, eds, *Shadow of Spirit: Postmodernism and Religion'* (London: Routledge, 1992).
8 Armstrong, 2000, p. 123.
9 Blake Morrison, *The Movement: English Poetry and Fiction of the 1950s* (London and New York: Methuen, 1986), p. 228.
10 Patricia Beer, *Collected Poems* (Manchester: Carcanet, 1990), p. 15.
11 Kingsley Amis, 'A Bookshop Idyll', *Collected Poems 1944–79* (USA: Viking, 1980), pp. 56–7.
12 Betty Friedan, *The Feminine Mystique* (New York: Dell Publishing, 1963), p. 11.
13 Friedan, 1963, p. 16.
14 Friedan, 1963, p. 322.
15 Kathleen Raine, 'Message from Home', *Collected Poems 1935–80* (London: Allen and Unwin, 1981), p. 173.
16 Raine, 'Water', *CP*, 1981, p. 70.
17 Raine, 'Love, Cambridge, Poetry: Extracts from an Unpublished Essay', *PN Review*, Vol. 136, No. 27.2. (November/December 2000), p. 138.
18 Raine, 'Self'; 'The Unloved',(from *The Year One*, 1952) *CP*, 1981, pp. 23, 48.
19 A.T. Tolley, *The Poetry of the Forties* (Manchester: Manchester University Press, 1985), p. 136.
20 Raine, 'Love, Cambridge, Poetry', 2000, p. 136.
21 Rita Felski, *Beyond Feminist Aesthetics: Feminist Literature and Social Change* (Cambridge, Mass.: Harvard University Press, 1989), p. 13. She is actually referring to Margaret Atwood's *Surfacing* and Joan Barfoot's *Gaining Ground*.
22 Felski, 1989, p. 148.
23 Felski, 1989, p. 110.
24 Elizabeth Jennings, 'In this Time', *CP*, 1987, p. 23.
25 Elizabeth Jennings, 'Recapitulation', *CP*, 1987, p. 26.
26 Elizabeth Jennings, 'Greek Statues', *CP*, 1987, p. 63.
27 Elizabeth Jennings, *Every Changing Shape: Mystical Experience and the Making of Poems* (1961) (Manchester: Carcanet 1996), p. 170.
28 Jennings, 'A Fear', *CP*, 1987, p. 39.
29 Jennings, 'World I Have not Made', *CP*, 1987, pp. 51–2.
30 Jennings, *Every Changing Shape* 1996, p. 215.
31 Jennings, 'Articulate Music', *Every Changing Shape*, 1996, p.189.
32 Jennings, 'A Fountain', *CP*, 1987, p. 43.
33 Jennings, *Every Changing Shape*, 1996, p. 57.
34 Jennings, *Every Changing Shape*, 1996, p. 50.
35 Simone De Beauvoir, *The Second Sex* (Jonathan Cape 1988), pp. 633, 592.
36 Simone De Beauvoir, *The Second Sex* (Jonathan Cape 1988), pp. 592, 679.
37 Jennings, *Every Changing Shape*, 1996, p. 51.
38 Jennings, *Every Changing Shape*, 1996, p. 45.
39 Jennings, 'My Grandmother', *CP*, 1987, p. 50.
40 Jennings, 'Old Woman', *CP*, 1987, p. 28.
41 Jennings, 'The Visitation', *CP*, 1987, pp. 46–7.
42 Jennings, 'To a friend with a Religious Vocation: for C', *CP*, 1987, p.64.
43 Smith, 'A Shooting Incident', *Collected Poems* (London: Allen Lane, 1975), p. 242.
44 Smith, 'The Holiday', *Me Again*, 1981, p. 229.
45 Smith, 'Too Tired for Words', *Me Again*, 1981, pp. 111–18.

46 Smith, 'Too Tired for Words', pp. 114–15.
47 Smith, 'Too Tired for Words', p. 116.
48 Smith, 'Thoughts about the Christian Doctrine of Eternal Hell', *CP*, 1975, p. 387.
49 Smith, 'The Bishops of the Church of England', *CP*, 1975, p. 96.
50 Smith, 'Ah, will the saviour ...?, *CP* 1975, p. 177.
51 Smith, 'The Airy Christ', *CP* 1975, p. 345.
52 Smith, 'Oh Christianity, Christianity', *CP*, 1975, pp. 416–17.
53 Smith, 'Why do you rage?', *CP*, 1975, p. 418.
54 Smith, 'God the Eater', *CP*, 1975, p. 339.
55 Smith, 'Mr Over', *CP*, 1975, p. 262.
56 Smith, 'Every lovely limb's a Desolation', *CP* ,1975, pp. 342–3.
57 Smith, 'The Vision', *Me Again*, 1981, p. 38.
58 Smith, 'The Passing Cloud', *CP*, 1975, p. 351.
59 Armstrong, 2000, p. 124.

Index